Published by Moonflower Publishing Ltd.
www.moonflowerbooks.co.uk

3 4 5 6 7 8 9 10

First published in 2025 by Moonflower
Copyright © James Alistair Henry 2026

ISBN: 9781916678019

Cover design by Jack Smyth
Interior design by Jasmine Aurora and Jack Smyth

Cover fonts: Norske, Syncro
Chapter heading font © Takuminokami

Printed and bound in Great Britain by Clays Ltd, Elcograf S.p.A.
Suffolk, UK

James Alistair Henry has asserted his right to be identified as the author of this work. This is a work of fiction. All rights reserved. No part of this publication may be reproduced, stored in any retrieval system, or transmitted, in any form or by any means, electronic, mechanical, photocopying, recording or otherwise, without the prior written permission of the publishers.

Moonflower Publishing Registered Office: 303 The Pillbox,
115 Coventry Road, London E2 6GG, United Kingdom

MOONFLOWER

"High concept brilliance supercharged by low humour, great characters and a gripping plot." - **THE DAILY MAIL**

"Henry's mash-up of fantasy and crime genres is inventive, enjoyably nasty and frequently very funny." - **THE FINANCIAL TIMES**

"Works beautifully… More than good enough to give the likes of Ben Aaronovitch and Adam Simcox a run for their money." - **SFX**

"Visceral, twisty and tension-filled... sublime world-building, luscious detail and snappy dialogue." - **WRITING.IE**

"Lots of delightful touches… a fun and well-worked out, engaging read." - **FORTEAN TIMES**

"It's fast-paced, intricately plotted, and packed with richly drawn characters. It's downright astonishing. Easily my book of the year." - **M.W. CRAVEN, AUTHOR OF FEARLESS AND THE WASHINGTON POE SERIES**

"Bark-out-loud funny in places, with a sardonic, slightly satirical tone." - **RADIO TIMES**

"Will ensnare crime lovers, fantasy fans and history nuts alike." - **MATTHEW GRAHAM, CREATOR OF LIFE ON MARS**

"Funny and original… a debut to brighten winter's dark nights." - **COUNTRY AND TOWNHOUSE**

"Pagans is an incredible combination of lovingly-crafted worldbuilding and pacy crime plotting. Alternative history at its finest!" - **LOUIE STOWELL, AUTHOR OF THE AWARD-WINNING LOKI: A BAD GOD'S GUIDE SERIES**

"A debut author to keep a close eye on." - **THE DAILY MIRROR**

"The concept is pure genius… It manages to be both a great alt-history and a really good mystery thriller… Enormously enjoyable." - **KJ CHARLES, AUTHOR OF THE DOOMSDAY BOOKS**

For Richard and Julia
– and my family, for being patient.

JAMES ALISTAIR HENRY

PAGANS

TWO COPS. ONE KILLER.
HUNDREDS OF GODS.

MOONFLOWER

CAST OF CHARACTERS

SAXONS

Aedith Mercia: *Detective Captain, London Police Force Homicide Division, Woden's Cross Station. Daughter of senior politician Lod Mercia, sister of Edric, adoptive mother of Coram.*

Earl-Elector Lod Mercia: *Politician and clan chieftain from Mercian region (see glossary), father to Aedith and Edric, husband of Sweterun.*

Coram Mercia: *Adopted son of Aedith Mercia, student.*

Edric Mercia: *Brother of Aedith, son of Lod and Sweterun.*

Sweterun Mercia: *Wife of Lod, mother of Aedith.*

Cheol Agapos: *Sergeant in London Police Force, Woden's Cross Station, reporting to Aedith Mercia.*

Ava Naeku: *Constable in London Police Force, Woden's Cross Station.*

Beocca Tancred: *Major in London Police Force, Special Branch.*

Odda Hengist: *London Police Force Commander, Woden's Cross Station.*

Dæglaf Adamu: *Lieutenant Colonel in London Police Force, Woden's Cross Station.*

'Father' Oswin: *Teacher, Rowan Berry House.*

Wigmund: *Caretaker, Rowan Berry House.*

Hildred Emor: *Business owner.*

Stithulf Hatt: *Security guard.*

Eawynn Wettin: *Administrative assistant to Unification Summit.*

Gif Denby: *Tattoo artist.*

Not-An-Uncle Dryer: *Freelance consultant and fixer.*

CELTS

Drustan of Dumnonia: *Detective Inspector with Dumnonian Tribal Police Agency.*

Deedra Kesair: *Tribal leader, chieftain, media influencer.*

Gorsedd Angwin: *Tribal diplomat, ex-member of proscribed terrorist organisation.*

Andraste Maol Nuadat: *Independent business owner.*

Fairgus Blaenu: *Low-level criminal.*

Conwenna Pennpras: *Pharmaceutical therapist, independent consultant.*

PICTS

Banba Godwin: *Independent IT consultant, Woden's Cross Station.*

MAP OF THE LANDS

DEMOCRATIC REPUBLIC OF SCOTLAND

→ ALIGNED TO NORDIC ECONOMIC UNION

- DUN DÈAGH
- STRIVELIN
- GRØNN HUL
- EIDENHAUGR

KINGDOM OF IRELAND

- NORTHERN U:NEILL
- CONNACHT
- SOUTHERN U:NEILL
- LEIRSTE
- MUNSTER

THE WALL

NORTHUMBRIA
- YORK
- LEEDS
- MANCHESTER

NORTH WESTERN TRIBAL LANDS →

- GWYNEON POWYS

GREATER MERCIA
- BIRMINGHAM

EAST ANGLIA

ESSEX

UNALIGNED

DYFED
- CARDIFF

WESSEX
- BRISTOL

LONDON — CITY OF LONDON

KENT

SUSSEX

- DUROTRIGEA
- GLASTONBURY
- EXETER

DUMNONIA

↑ SOUTH WESTERN TRIBAL LANDS

ISLAMIC CALIPHATE OF SOUTHERN EUROPE ↓

KINGDOM OF ENGLAND

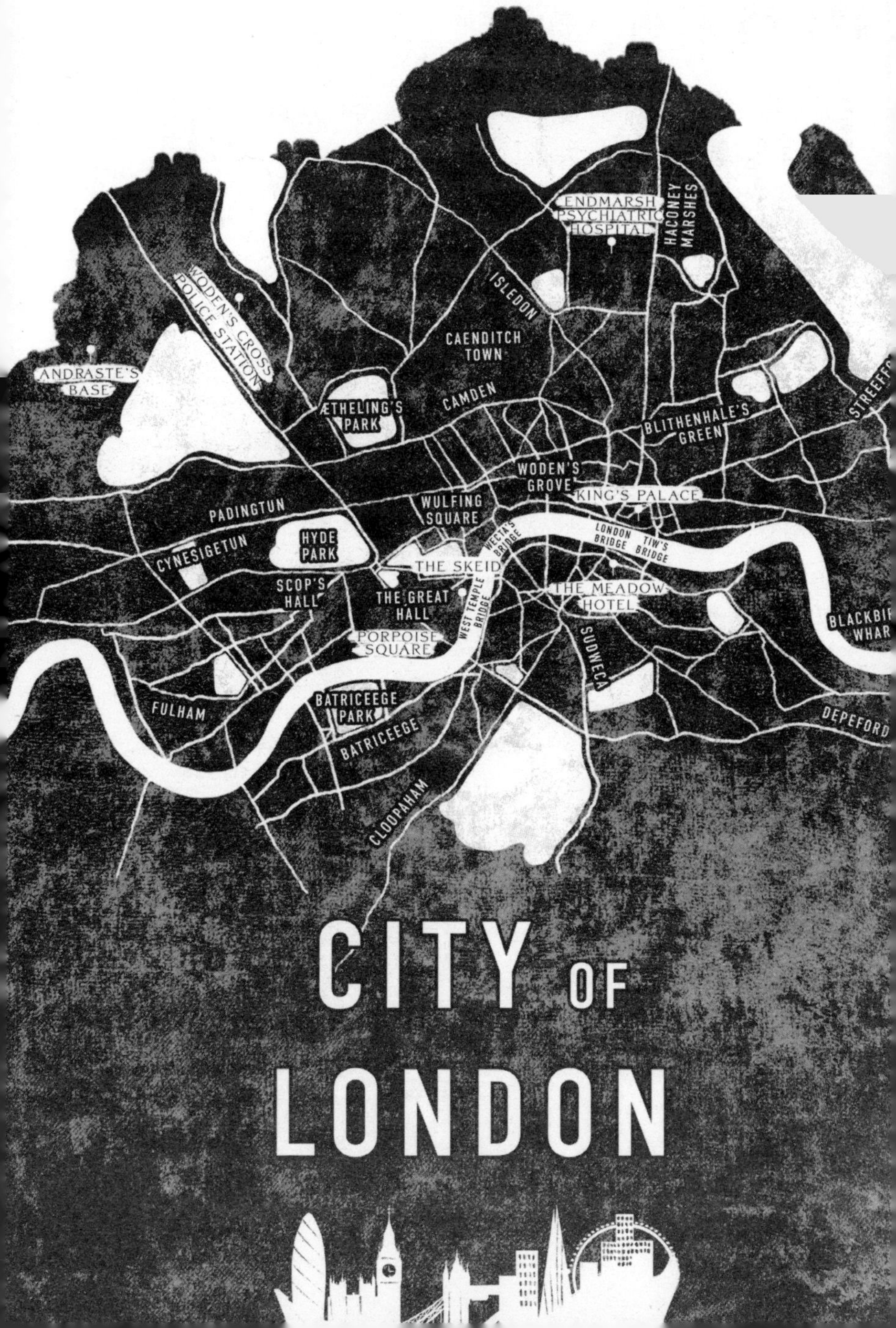
ANDRASTE'S BASE
WODEN'S CROSS POLICE STATION
ENDMARSH PSYCHIATRIC HOSPITAL
HACONEY MARSHES
ISLEDON
CAENDITCH TOWN
ÆTHELING'S PARK
CAMDEN
BLITHENHALE'S GREEN
WODEN'S GROVE
KING'S PALACE
PADINGTUN
WULFING SQUARE
HYDE PARK
CYNESIGETUN
WECTA'S BRIDGE
LONDON BRIDGE
TIW'S BRIDGE
THE SKEID
SCOP'S HALL
THE GREAT HALL
THE MEADOW HOTEL
WEST TEMPLE BRIDGE
PORPOISE SQUARE
SUDWECA
FULHAM
BATRICEEGE PARK
BATRICEEGE
DEPEFORD
CLOOPAHAM
CITY OF LONDON

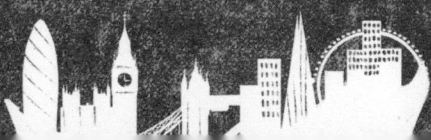

Extracted from Pan-African Collective Intelligence Services, Country Profiles, Factsheet: Britain

This developing nation just off the coast of the Islamic Caliphate of Southern Europe is populated by an uneasy alliance of three nation states divided by religion, culture and language: the Celts of the Tribal Lands of the West Country and Wales, the English Saxons of the East, and the Norse of the Democratic Republic of Scotland to the North, behind a heavily militarised border known as the Wall.

Of the three nations, the Norse are the most prosperous, with Eidenhaugr (Edinburgh) as the financial capital of the broader Nordic Economic Union, with Saxon England struggling to keep up, and the Tribal Lands in the West suffering from years of repression and plundering of their national resources by their neighbours.

Extracted from *Lagos Economist: Yearly Global Index,* current edition

As it has for the last two centuries, the Pan-African Unified States remains the world's dominant superpower, with the Mughal Empire of India and the European Islamic Caliphate nipping at its heels.

Meanwhile the Nordic Economic Union (comprising the Democratic Republic of Scotland, Islenska, the Danelands, the Sápmi/Nynorsk/Suomi Protectorate and the Kingdom of Sverrland) prefers to focus on financial matters, while acting as a bulwark should the various squabbling nations that make up the Tsarist Conglomerate ever pull themselves together and try to expand westward.

Further east, the Han remain ahead of their rival dynasties, but are quietly forging links with a number of weak North European countries in an attempt to establish footholds outside their traditional borders. Their desire for control over a number of cold-water ports has not gone unnoticed by the Pan-Africans.

Various superpowers have stakes in the vast natural resources of the plains, prairies and mineral wealth of the North Americas, but a series of treaties with the indigenous First Nation people there have kept a fragile balance with no one faction being allowed to take overall control.

ONE

Oladele had long dreamed of seeing one of the great English forests in the autumn. Tayo, her fiancé – no, husband, she had to get used to saying that – had been less convinced. Days before the honeymoon was booked, he was still showing her photos of sun-kissed beaches, palm trees, sailing holidays even, but she stayed firm and now here they were, half a world away, hiking under grey skies through primeval woodland. The summer had overstayed its welcome this year and though technically the season had moved on, hardly any of the leaves had begun to fall, let alone turn the brilliant reds and oranges they had been told to expect.

Tayo had begged Oladele to at least hire a local guide. Two of the guys from his office had taken a cheap flight to England for a stag week a few years ago, and the local they'd found had been amazing, apparently. He'd introduced them to the local brews, taken them on a druidic vision quest, even found them a replacement hire car when their 4x4 had broken an axle on a dirt track. But Oladele had refused.

'We can explore the country ourselves,' she said. 'I don't want some local in fancy dress who shows us all the tourist sites then goes back to his mobile home and wifi at the end of the day. Let's get out there, have an adventure. This isn't Lagos. This is *wild!*'

So they had hired a lodge deep in the woods, with a porter who cooked an evening meal for them and kept the fridge stocked with local food, every item replaced at the end of the day whether they ate it or not – although thankfully the first day's boiled leeks never made a reappearance.

'I can't believe we're only ten miles from London,' marvelled Oladele as they strode through yet another woodland glade. Tayo mumbled something in reply, though seemed more focused on casting nervous looks around the trees. Oladele sighed. She knew he was worrying about wolves. She had tried to convince him there were no wolves left in England, but Tayo had said weren't there plans to reintroduce them? Or maybe that was bears.

'Also, I should have brought a thicker fleece,' he said.

Oladele rolled her eyes – uncomfortably aware she had been doing this a lot during their honeymoon – but pushed on womanfully through brambles (she'd brought some thick gloves with her for this exact purpose) and into the next glade (or was it a dell?), a wide saucer-like depression in the forest floor with a single mighty oak at its centre.

Someone had got there before them. A man, a white man with a drooping moustache – and he *was* white, positively anaemic – was leaning back against the tree's wide trunk. He wore only a tattered pair of trousers, his chest covered in tattoos, mainly black but with an interwoven design in maroon. His arms were outstretched, his head on one side, feet together. It was a curious pose. Like many locals, the man had a metal band around his neck, made from carefully twisted wire. The British didn't have much, but they were great craftspeople.

'I think it's a religious thing,' said Tayo, shading his eyes with a cautious hand. 'We shouldn't disturb him.'

But Oladele was already striding forward with her mobile phone held out. She would ask him first if she could take his photo, of course; it was important to be respectful of other cultures. If he said no, she would put the phone away, but maybe they could talk a little. She could do with some ancient wisdom at this point, and this local looked like he might know a thing or two.

'Hello?' she tried, but the man didn't look up. As she drew closer, she realised the glints of silver at his wrists and ankles weren't jewellery, as she'd first thought, but nails, driven into the tree through flesh and bone. His throat had been slit. What Oladele had taken to be a snaking red tattoo were rivulets of dried blood.

Oladele lowered her phone just as Tayo caught up with her and came to an abrupt halt. 'Oh,' he eventually said, after a long silence. 'Will they give us some money back on the trip, do you think?'

Oladele started searching for a spot where her mobile could conceivably connect with the local police department, trying to ignore her growing suspicion that this marriage wasn't going to last.

TWO

The black sedan jerked to a halt as the ambulance sped past, sirens wailing. It was gone in a second, a green and white blur, the familiar sign of the green apple lost in the London traffic, allowing the car to be on its way once again, the electric motor starting back up with a minimal whine.

Aedith hated the sedan, but her father had insisted, so in a petty act of defiance she had given the driver the night off so she could drive herself. Coram would have made the finger runes for 'unimpressed' if he'd known about it, but she'd left him at home doing maths revision under Hilde's supervision. Right now, she was beginning to envy him. The streets were busy, and the liminal boundary between pavement and road, barely respected at the best of times, was now entirely theoretical.

Normally, Aedith would have put the blues and twos on and slid through in the wake of the now-departed ambulance, under the guise of escorting it, but the town car was unaccountably siren-free. It did have bullet-proof windows, but that only meant you couldn't wind them down and yell at pedestrians. Or shoot them.

She stopped at a traffic light. As if on cue, a man slammed a hand against the car's side window. The hand was grimy; the owner's mismatched clothing more so. A tattooed face peered in at Aedith with drunken indignation. An abstract Wayland the

Smith design, made up of interlinking circuit-board patterns, reached up the man's face to his hairline; Wayland having been the patron spirit of choice at most IT departments a decade or so ago, although he was out of fashion these days. Probably the man had lost his job some years ago, when the Mughal Empire had swept in and bought up most of the native telecommunications industry, such as it was.

For his part, the man seemed taken aback to see not, as he must have expected, a foreign dignitary or some social-media celebrity, but a Saxon woman in her mid-thirties, blonde hair in twin braids, wearing silver rings on both arms and an expensive contemporary take on a classic shift dress. He recovered quickly and began mouthing obscenities; at least until Aedith pulled Lungpiercer out from the glove compartment and tapped the barrel against the glass, making him back up swiftly into a crowd of his contemporaries.

The light turned green. Aedith steered the sedan round a moustachioed Celtic elder in traditional robes leading his ox across the street, pointed the car's nose towards the West End, and floored the accelerator. The sooner she got there, the sooner she could leave. Aedith hated parties.

The Meadow was a stone's throw from London Bridge, a short walk from the King's Palace and widely regarded as the capital's finest hotel. For Aedith, it had been the site of family get-togethers ever since she was a child. Consequently, she hated it. Replacing Lungpiercer in the glove compartment before handing the sedan over to a valet went against every instinct she had. She soothed her grumbling spirit beast (her therapist had suggested it was a falcon, but Aedith was pretty sure he was trying to flatter her, to get in with her father, and had fired him shortly afterwards) with the notion that she was about to enter combat in the social rather than physical realm, requiring different tools entirely, but it was still huffing to itself as she showed her ID at the entrance, took a deep breath and walked into the party.

'What idiot did your hair?' said Deedra Kesair. 'You should have them killed.'

Deedra wore an elegant black dress; Lombardian, possibly – the signifiers of high fashion weren't far up Aedith's list of priorities. Her auburn hair was pinned up high, the torc around her neck so finely wrought it was more of a ghost-like suggestion of identity than an object in its own right. The entire left side of her face was covered in swirling black tattoos, stretching down the neck and as far as one could see, which was quite far (elegant didn't mean practical), around one of her breasts.

'You've put on weight!' said Aedith, embracing her with every evidence of delight. 'It suits you. I like you fatter.'

Deedra pushed her away and smiled. The crooked canines Aedith remembered from school were long gone, straightened by Moorish dentistry, but somehow this made her look more, rather than less, feral.

'Be honest,' she said. 'If you had to arrest three people in this room, who would you pick?'

'That reminds me,' said Aedith. 'Smile as if I'm going to take your picture. Obviously, I'm not, because your freaky Indij tats would give my phone malware, but I need the cover.'

Aedith pulled the phone out of the concealed pocket of her dress and pointed it towards, if not actually *at*, Deedra, who gleefully pulled a variety of celebrity faces while Aedith scanned every attendee she could without making it too obvious.

'Your father's in the corner with some Scotch,' said Deedra, making a 'just seen someone I know' face, and quite probably she had. 'Drink *and* delegates.'

Aedith's phone was going to town, harvesting faces, flashing up names and job titles faster than she had any chance of processing them. Didn't matter, just good policy to lock down as many identities to a particular time and place as you could, when the opportunity arose. Obviously, the only people who let their phones announce their identities to all and sundry were those who had no intention of committing a crime or were powerful enough to get away with it if they did, but you never knew when the data might come in handy.

The Meadow's thing was fusing Nordic chic with an earthier English interpretation of the afterlife: pale stone floors with elaborately carved wooden pillars, as much greenery interwoven with fairy lights as could be hung from one ceiling, and constant harp music. The hotel's rooms were more of the same, with authentic grave urns daringly placed in every north-east alcove. Young Aedith had been convinced the urns were filled with burned dead people. Edric had tipped one out once, ignoring his sister's screams, to see what was really inside: an empty cigarette wrapper, the crumpled receipt for room service (jollof rice and chicken), and a dead moth.

Aedith had never told Edric, but she credited his action that evening for two significant shifts in her belief system: religion was almost certainly bullshit, and trying to piece together someone's life from scraps they'd left behind was all she ever wanted to do from that point on. She didn't join the police for another twelve years, but mentally she was down the recruiting station there and then.

'EARL-ELECTOR LOD (MERCIA)' noted Aedith's phone above the bearded head of a barrel-chested man in his fifties, crammed into a black suit, handing an empty tumbler to a passing waiter and bearing down on Aedith before she could pretend she hadn't been cataloguing the attendees of a social gathering instigated primarily for his benefit.

'It's been reasonable, darling,' said Deedra, blowing an air kiss and practically skipping to the other side of the room.

'You can't just mingle with school friends,' rumbled Lod, kissing Aedith's cheek with his always-surprising delicacy. 'Or it's not proper mingling. You need to meet new people.'

The suit aside, Lod could have been any one of the Mercia family's patriarchs from the past couple of thousand years. Aedith had seen the carvings: glowering eyes under a heavy brow, tangled beard and flowing hair, tattoos climbing up the neck, fingers covered with silver rings. The women were traditionally embroidered into tapestries instead, although Acdith had made her feelings very clear on that score. When Lod's time came, however, Aedith would make sure that whichever artisanal woodworker was honoured with the commission put in a mobile phone and a data tablet loaded up with spreadsheets: two weapons that Lod had used to keep the Mercians at, or near, the top of the Saxon pecking order long after spears and axes had faded from fashion.

'I meet new people all the time, Dad. They're usually standing over a corpse, denying everything, but it still counts.'

Lod grinned. Half his teeth were silver, from the same source as the rings. When he died, *if* he ever died, they'd have to be pulled out and melted back into the family hoard. 'How's the boy?'

'If he ever comes out of his room, I'll let you know.'

'Pffff,' said Lod with a sly glance. 'Teenagers.'

Aedith opened her mouth, closed it again. 'Fine. Parade me round to show people your daughter has a real job. I know how much that means to you.'

'Nonsense, I just want to make some introductions. Try not to arrest anyone with more than three bodyguards, it might get messy.'

'I'm not—' Aedith tried, but Lod was already steering her towards a robed Pan-African woman in her fifties sipping a cocktail, an equally distinguished man standing next to her with one arm around her waist.

'Senator Legat of the Congolese Delegation,' said Lod. Legat nodded, flashing Aedith what was to all intents and purposes a genuinely warm smile. 'And her husband Fabrice. My daughter, Aedith.'

'I think we've met, actually,' said Aedith. 'Your husband and I.' She smiled brightly. Fabrice looked blank.

'My husband comes to your beautiful country a few times every year,' said Legat. 'To attend to various charities.' Fabrice's face remained impassive.

'That will be it,' said Aedith.

'And what is it your daughter does?' asked Legat.

'She works for the civil service,' said Lod quickly, bowing his head and leading Aedith away.

'Pulled him out of a brothel on Porpoise Square last year,' said Aedith in a low voice, as they approached a table spread with witty references to the host nation's culinary tradition: spiced barley cakes, fried apple slices, honeycomb with gods-knew-what sprinkled on it. Most of it was untouched. 'Some poor kid beaten to death in the next room. Don't think Mister Legat knew anything about it, but he was spirited away by Special Branch before I got a chance to ask any difficult questions.'

'Interesting,' said Lod. 'Was he into boys or girls?'

'As far as I remember,' said Aedith, helping herself to a barley cake, 'he didn't discriminate. Is that why you wanted me here? I'm sure you already know the dirty laundry of most of the attendees.'

'The Pan-Africans value open displays of family bonds,' said Lod. 'Couldn't very well bring Edric along, could I?'

'Of course not. That would require you to let him out.'

Lod shrugged. 'He needs to pay his dues, he knows that. He'll be free at the proper time. Although yes, fine, I did have another motive, I need you to give me a read.'

He gestured expansively out at the crowds. There had to be at least a hundred and fifty people in the room, counting waiting staff and harpists.

'A *read*?' said Aedith. 'You'd be better off with a drone.'

'I have technology. I value your intuition.'

'Eugh,' said Aedith, '*flattery*.' But she looked out at the party anyway.

Lod bit into a barley cake. 'These are really very good,' he said to a waitress, who blushed and retreated backwards, looking at the ground. He grinned. 'Still got it.'

'Dad, shut up,' said Aedith.

Lod swallowed the rest of the cake obediently and waited.

'Right,' said Aedith. 'Two of the waiting staff work for the Mughals, that guy over there looks Saxon but has a wrist mic and is actually very, very, very light-skinned mixed race, so I'm going to take a racist leap and assume he's with the Pan-Africans. The rest are probably working for you. The Norse aren't big on human intel, so I'm guessing they have microphones in the pillars, or maybe even someone in the building opposite with one of those fancy long-distance ones outside that picks up vibrations from the windowpanes. The Celts, I assume, have no human intel or technology and are weirding out about something, but keeping their distance from Deedra, which is mildly interesting. What's this party even for?'

Lod tugged on his beard, a sign Aedith had realised years ago meant he was at least mildly amused. 'There's a theory that if England, the various Tribal Grounds of the West and our Nordic neighbour up beyond the Wall joined forces to become one nation state, we might finally make something of ourselves. You may have heard me mention it once or twice. Anyway, the new Summit negotiations begin in three days.'

'Oh,' said Aedith. 'That. I knew there was a reason my squad were pulled off murders to clean up shanty towns while the hookers jack up their prices.'

A new Unification Summit took place roughly every five years, or possibly it was one Summit that rumbled on more or less permanently and just stuck its head above the surface every now and then. It had been going on since before Aedith was born and she had every expectation it would still be going on long after she was dead. It had become an industry in its own right, not all of which, as Aedith could attest, was entirely legal.

'You don't feel any involvement in the future of your country?' asked Lod.

Aedith rolled her eyes, aware even as she did so of how every encounter with her father seemed to pull her back into her teenage years, a period in her life she thought of mainly as 'that time I didn't have a gun'.

'Dad, we're three kingdoms that happen to be stuck on one island,' she said finally. 'It's like one those "a Tribal, a Saxon and a Nord go into a bar" jokes. As soon as one faction decides there's something to be gained from unifying with a second, the third opposes on principle. The Tribals have land but no money, the Norse have money but not as much land as they'd like, and we've got just enough of both we're not going to risk giving any of it up. Never mind that whole other island over the water.'

The Irish Tribes had been invited to the first Summit, some thirty years ago. It had gone badly, and they seemed to have thrown in their lot with one of the bigger Chinese dynasties since, which meant they got a lot of new roads and airports as long as they kept away from their squabbling neighbours to the east, which seemed to suit them just fine.

Aedith's phone trilled.

'Work calls. Good to see you again. I'll tell Coram you asked after him. Give my love to Mum.'

Lod grunted, raising a second barley cake in salute, but Aedith had already stopped, phone pressed to her ear.

'Wait a second. Dad, do you know what the Tribals are stressing about over there?'

Aedith nodded over at the small knot of delegates turned inwards in a worried huddle in one corner, well-dressed for the most part, torcs glowing dully in the reflected lights of the phones into which they were all suddenly staring. The older men had the long moustaches falling out of favour with the young, who preferred to keep clean-shaven in the Pan-African style, presumably while listening to Speed Beat at dangerously high volumes. The women had taken their style cues from Deedra, pinning their hair up high, the better to reveal whichever side of their face had the tattoos on. Was there any significance to which side was adorned, which was free? Probably the phase of the moon you were born in, or something. She should probably look it up at some point.

'If I *had* intel on our trusted neighbours and allies from the Celtic Nations,' said Lod, somehow without heavy irony, 'it might suggest they have grown concerned at the failure to arrive of their senior negotiator, the absence of which leaves them rolling with considerably less than a full set of dice.'

'And do you know anything about this missing negotiator?'

'I do not,' said Lod. He wasn't pulling at his beard any more. 'Why do you ask?'

'Because,' said Aedith, 'he's just turned up. Dead. Nailed to a tree in Epping Forest.'

THREE

At first, Drustan thought he'd dodged the Saxon checkpoints going East into London, the big blond reeve with the machine pistol and the knife strapped to his hip waving the coach straight through. Three buses were already being searched, lines of track-suited Celts shivering on the side of the road while sniffer dogs went through their meagre possessions. Drustan stared straight ahead as the ancient vehicle shuddered round the queue, worked back up through its gears and ploughed onwards up the motorway, belching black fumes, Pan-African-built electric cars overtaking it with insouciant ease.

But now they'd been sitting in the bus station for over half an hour and the doors had remained firmly shut. It wouldn't have been any different if he'd left from the Tribal Grounds above the Bristol Channel either, tried to pass himself off as one of the hillfolk. The border was softer than it used to be, under the latest High King, but there was too much emotional and corporate investment in security theatre for it to be abandoned. At least for now.

The old Saxon woman sitting next to Drustan had a chicken on her lap. Drustan and the chicken met each other's gaze with equanimity. Both knew their destiny lay in other hands. Meanwhile the other Saxons on the bus chatted away happily. Now they were over the border, of course, they had little to fear.

'*Swa þonne se ealda cyning cwilþ.*'

'*Gehyrest ðu þæt unwyrþan sweg hie forþiað on þæm drylican soncræfte-boxe?*'

'*Heo suþe gesoden bleat leac agen.*'

Drustan closed his eyes, touched a fingertip to his torc. It helped him think, divert his mind to a new course, think in Saxon, or a version of it that would keep him alive in the city.

'The old King's dying then.'

'You hear that rubbish they're playing on the radio these days?'

'She's only done boiled bloody leeks again.'

'You want to buy my chicken?'

The Saxon woman held out the bird to him. It clucked hopelessly.

'No thank you,' said Drustan.

'Tight-arse bloody Celts,' said the woman, scowling, but now two cops, one broad, one tall and gangling, were climbing aboard the coach. They wore plain clothes – literally, their suits were cheap and grey – but held out badges of office on silver chains.

'We'd like to take this opportunity to welcome you to London, Capital of the East, Seat of the High King,' said the tall one.

'Although we don't let just anyone in,' said the stocky one. 'So, get your papers ready.'

The woman next to Drustan fumbled in her handbag. 'Not you, love,' said the lanky one. 'You're all right.'

The woman nodded and carried her chicken off the bus, followed one at a time by the other Saxons. None of the Celts moved.

The stocky one surveyed the remaining passengers with a baleful gaze. 'What a shower.'

*

Eventually, once papers had been checked and tutted at, cursory body searches made, and a series of wholly unnecessary radio calls made back to base, the other Celts were allowed off the bus. Drustan knew full well what was going on. The police quotas for the day had been met and it was unlikely a creaking system could cope with any more undesirables pushed through it. This whole bureaucratic filter was a performance, a show of force to remind visitors from the West whose turf they were on. Drustan had experienced it many times and knew how best to deal with it, holding back to let the others off first. If there was going to be an incident, best it not be in front of witnesses.

'Finally, the bottom of the barrel,' said the lanky cop, acknowledging Drustan's existence for the first time. 'Papers, if you'd be so kind.'

Drustan took his overcoat and battered kitbag down from the overhead locker and made his way towards the door. The cops were waiting. Drustan's travel papers were in his hand, but the lanky cop ignored them, eyeing his suit instead.

'Well-dressed for an Indij, isn't he, Flad?'

Flad, the stocky one, leaned over and brushed a little imaginary dust off Drustan's shoulder.

'Very nice, Eadwulf.'

To be fair, it was a good suit, the only one Drustan owned, made from black, closely woven cloth. A little crumpled, but hard-wearing, easy to keep clean. A tailor, back West, had tried to pay him for a thing. The tailor's daughter had gone missing and Drustan had brought her back, once he was sure she wanted to come back. Drustan couldn't take the man's money, but his suit had got torn in the course of events, and when the tailor had offered to replace it, 'like for like,' Drustan couldn't find a reason to turn him down. He wore the suit with an open-necked white shirt, the torc just visible beneath the collar. No Celt ever wore a tie.

Drustan looked straight ahead while Eadwulf went through his documents. 'First time off the reservation?'

Drustan couldn't remember what his travel history said. It was unlikely to be accurate, and he was tired from the journey.

'Just look at the godsdamn papers,' he said.

The cops shared a look which ended with the point of Eadwulf's seax against Drustan's throat. Drustan was impressed. He hadn't even noticed the lanky cop reaching for the knife. Maybe a quick release catch on a back holster. Saxons loved their gadgets.

'You need to show the law a little respect, my friend.' Eadwulf's voice was low, calm. He could have been giving traffic instructions. Flad yawned extravagantly.

'I think I'm going to need to see some more identification,' said Eadwulf. 'Not sure this is entirely in order.'

'Of course, officer,' said Drustan. Slowly, deliberately, he reached into an inside coat pocket, pulled out a plastic wallet, held it open, smiled politely. Eadwulf didn't look at it, just kept eyeballing him.

'I hope you're not having a little joke with me here.'

'Eadwulf,' warned the other cop, but it wasn't getting through.

'Because,' Eadwulf continued, 'although we in the East are justly renowned for our sense of humour, it can, from time to time, desert us.'

'*Mate*,' coughed Flad.

Drustan angled the wallet towards the taller man, so there could be no misunderstandings. Above a shiny silver sigil was the word 'Detective'. Below was 'Inspector'.

'Oh shit,' said Eadwulf, hurriedly putting the knife away.

'Sorry about that, sir. Lot of troublemakers around at the moment. Tribals *and* Saxons.'

Drustan walked past him off the bus, hefted the bag on his shoulder. He turned back, watching as they tensed.

'Which way to Epping Forest?'

FOUR

It was past midnight by the time Sergeant Agapos had driven Aedith as far into the forest as the rough track would allow. He parked up next to the other official vehicles. A bored Saxon paramedic sat on a tree stump in the glare of the arc lights, puffing on an electronic cigarette. Cherry vapour drifted into the woods, becoming one with the mist forming in the cool night air.

Banks of lights placed around the clearing's single oak pointed at the body, which glowed white as if it was providing the light rather than being illuminated by it. The forensics team in white overalls were pushing numbered sticks into the ground, conferring in low voices, snapping off photographs with a bright flash: spirits summoned from the woods performing their strange rites.

Aedith changed into her rubber boots. Agapos handed her a heavy overcoat he kept rolled up in the boot.

'I like your dress,' he said. He was probably being sincere.

Like a full quarter of the Metropolitan force, Agapos was dark-skinned and broad-featured. Descendants of African sailors who had ended up on the banks of the Thames a few hundred years ago, Agapos's ancestors had been embraced by a local warlord and found employment first as mercenaries and then, when foreign notions of a civilian peacekeeper force made their way across the Channel, as local constables. Most were more Saxon than the Saxons now. Aedith had caught sight of the blessed coin Agapos wore on a chain beneath his stab vest, given to him as an engagement present by his now-husband, a customs officer the exact size and build of Agapos but from the opposite side of the colour chart, being a Norse who'd moved South for the warmer winters. The face on the coin had one eye. The nose was wider than standard depictions, but the name 'Woden' was engraved on the other side.

'Gorsedd Angwin,' said Agapos. 'Celt, single, late thirties, well-liked by all accounts, or at least respected. Last seen yesterday evening, drinking with the other delegates, although apparently not to excess. He got a call around ten p.m., left the bar, and that was the last time anyone saw him until the tourist couple found him this afternoon. On their honeymoon. Got a statement from them, the woman was very helpful. Husband seemed kind of a limp dick.'

'They still around?'

Agapos shook his head. 'Cut it short, heading home already. Would have detained them, but... Pan-Africans.'

Aedith said nothing. English law had almost nothing to compel foreign visitors to help out with an enquiry. Even if they did, a decent bribe higher up the chain would have them on their way by the next shift.

'Should get most of the squad back by the weekend,' said Agapos. 'Those homeless camps aren't clearing themselves.'

Aedith couldn't complain. You had to work with what you'd got. And what she had right here was a victim who'd been dead for at least four hours. Probably more. Almost certainly killed at this spot: the tree bark was black with blood, the earth under his crossed feet stained with it. There had been no rain for a month;

the ground was cracked and thirsty. Unlikely there'd be any tracks. Aedith bent down, studying the metal spikes at the man's ankles.

'Masonry nails,' said Agapos. 'In his wrists, too. Available from any DIY store. Probably fired from a nail gun. You can rent them for the weekend. I got one for the decking last summer.'

Aedith nodded, brushed away some of the clotted leaf mould at the man's feet. You never knew when you might find a dropped train ticket, crumpled receipt, maybe an ID card. She hadn't found one yet, but you always looked. Nothing, of course. She got to her feet, stood back.

'You're a big guy, you work out. Could you do this by yourself?'

Agapos scratched his jaw thoughtfully. 'Maybe? If I drugged him first.' He looked back into the woods, considering. 'Carry him into the woods, lean him against the tree, nail up one wrist, then the other, then the ankles, then slit the throat. Yeah, could be done.'

'Wow,' said Aedith, impressed. 'Remind me never to be late with your pension paperwork. We'll see what the tox screen gives us for drugs. But why so public?'

'Punishment beating and someone lost their cool? Debts, maybe?' Agapos was studying the man's tattoos. 'I know a few of the Tribal marks, can't see any of the big gang tats. You said he was a diplomat?'

'A senior one, apparently. The Tash may not have the biggest talent pool for high-ranking staff, but unlikely you'd get past the interview stage covered in the Sons of Lugh or whatever. You've ruled out religion, I couldn't help but notice.'

'Religion?' Agapos sounded confused. 'Like a hate crime?'

Aedith nodded. 'Remember those Woden's Heirs nutjobs a few years back? Hung their vics from mobile masts with barbed wire and recorded the whole thing, hoping for the wisdom of the gods to come pouring out.'

The recordings had come in pretty handy as evidence, Aedith remembered. The tabloids had loved it, and as most of the victims had been addicts or criminals, had cast the whole thing with a 'divine justice' angle that hadn't been entirely condemnatory.

'Hung them up by the ankles,' Agapos pointed out. He was scowling now. Aedith was never sure how religious her sergeant was. He wasn't one of those who was always waiting for you to hit a low point so they could invite you to their temple or got upset if you celebrated Yule without an actual boar's head hanging above your fireplace, but you never could tell. 'At least they knew basic observance. Technically, this guy's upside-down.'

Aedith nodded absently. It was the outstretched arms that were irritating her for some reason.

'Is it supposed to be a T-shape? Is this a Tash thing?' Aedith couldn't picture a Tribal large enough to haul another man out into the woods and nail him to a tree single-handedly. They were usually on the skinny side, even before poverty and/or malnutrition had done their work, but she supposed big Celts must exist.

'Um,' said Agapos, sounding uncharacteristically nonplussed. 'I suppose you could ask that guy?'

A slim bearded Celt in a dark suit and overcoat was walking out of the trees towards them.

A couple of uniforms were running towards him even as he lifted his warrant card. They backed away. The forensics guys looked at each other, confused, as he drew closer, but the Celt obviously knew procedure, turning aside from the tape between the trees and working his way round to Aedith and Agapos, holding a hand up against the lights now shining right into his face. His facial hair was close-cropped, his hair long and partly braided, swept back over the collar of his coat. His torc was a dull gunmetal grey.

'DI Drustan,' he said. 'I was told Detective Captain Mercia is running this case?'

Agapos was gaping at him, slack-jawed. 'Where the hells did you come from?'

'Are you Captain Mercia?'

Aedith raised a hand.

'Ah,' said the man. 'My apologies.'

They shook hands briefly. Agapos was still staring.

'My sergeant thinks you maybe cast the runes, walked the ley lines, that sort of thing,' said Aedith.

'They gave me the GPS coordinates,' said Drustan, holding up his phone. 'I got a taxi down the track as far as I could, walked until I saw the light through the trees. Could we talk?'

'You want the case?' said Aedith, ten minutes later, handing Drustan a coffee. 'Go right ahead. I could do with my stats lowered.'

Drustan grinned at her. 'I apologise for raising your hopes. I'm here in an advisory capacity only.' He took a sip from the paper cup, raised an eyebrow. 'This is good. Moorish?'

'The forensics team run on the stuff,' said Aedith. 'My family have a few connections with Iberia, so I imported one of the better machines to keep them sweet.'

'We're still using ground acorns where I come from,' said Drustan. 'Your family being Earl Lod?' He wasn't even looking at her.

'And you pretended you didn't even know which of us was Detective Captain Mercia,' chided Aedith gently. 'No, the Iberian links are on my mother's side.'

Drustan flicked his gaze back to Aedith. A sideways half-smile, part contrition, part something else. His eyes were very dark. Perhaps, like many Celtic men, he wore a little kohl.

'The Tribal elders are concerned this death may have been politically motivated,' said Drustan.

'Death?' said Aedith. 'Polite word for it. We're working on it being a murder. I don't know much about Tribal culture, but it doesn't feel like a sexual adventure gone wrong. Unless it went *really* wrong quite a long time before it got to the forest.'

'I concur,' said Drustan, mildly.

Aedith drained her coffee. 'Your elders think this diplomat being killed might in some way benefit my father and I was put on the case to cover it up,' she said. 'They pulled some strings to get you up to London as quickly as possible to shadow me and make sure I don't get away with it.'

'The famed bluntness of the Saxons,' said Drustan, with a happy sip. 'You'll have to excuse me. My people like ambiguities, shades of grey. It always takes me a little while to adjust. In fact, there is no suggestion your father was involved, but I've been asked to get in on the ground level, offer my knowledge and contacts within the Celtic community to help the investigation along. And perhaps, yes, so there can be no perception it's in any way compromised. Your Commander Hengist was surprisingly helpful. He has offered me lodgings and the support of the Saxon police service until such time as this case is closed.'

'Great,' said Aedith. 'Do you want a look at the body before we pull it off the tree?'

'I'd be very grateful,' said Drustan, and he sounded like he meant it.

*

'You know him?' asked Aedith. Drustan had been looking at the body for a long time. He shook his head.

'What about the tattoos? We know the big Tash crime family sigils' – Aedith hadn't been able to catch the slur in time and winced – 'sorry... But we didn't recognise any of these.'

Drustan seemed to have already moved on. 'Mostly religious and academic, a few sporting. The man must have liked his hurling. Standard working- to middle-class stuff. Although I can't make out...'

Drustan pointed to the start of a tattoo on the left side of the man's chest, above his heart, disappearing under dried blood. Aedith peered closer. Were those fingers? Forensics were packing up, starting to pull off masks, strip out of their overalls, becoming earthly humans again. She always found it a disappointing sight, somehow.

'Can we get can something to clean up here?'

One of them passed Aedith a cloth and a bottle of purplish liquid. She dampened the cloth, moved it toward the man's chest, hesitated at Drustan's intake of breath.

'There's a religious thing?'

He pulled a face. 'Would be best if the first person to touch the body is of the same tribe. Or close enough.'

Aedith shrugged, handed him the cloth, watched as Drustan sponged the dried blood off the centre of the man's chest with slow, deliberate moves, murmuring something as he did it, although she didn't catch the words. Wouldn't have understood them if she had, anyway.

The tattoo Drustan had revealed was the outline of a hand. Plain, simply done, as though someone had tried to push the victim away and left an imprint.

'I've seen this before,' said Aedith.

The Celt pulled the sponge back as if contaminated. Aedith had seen a similar look on a man's face once. On one of her first call outs, she'd gone to the aftermath of a religious hate crime: a sacred yew burned down in Cheapside. She'd found the local priest sitting on the pavement amongst the ashes, eyes empty, rocking backwards and forwards, thumbing through a necklace of cowrie shells as the phone in his pocket rang unchecked. It was the expression of a man who had come face to face with blasphemy.

'He was in the Fomóir,' said Drustan quietly.

'Well, shit,' said Aedith.

FIVE

Agapos drove Aedith home. She could pick the sedan up from the station in the morning. Later in the morning. Unlikely anyone would try and move it; they all knew what the diplomatic plates meant.

'Terrorism then, ma'am?' asked Agapos. He only called her 'ma'am' when he was worried. 'Does that mean politics?'

'The Fomóir haven't been active for twenty years,' said Aedith. A memory came then, unbidden, of Tribal community leaders on the news, their voices replaced by actors, her father's bodyguards checking the underside of the car every morning before the school run. And then, one day, the Tribals got their voices back and the checks stopped. 'But yes, if it wasn't politics before, it is now. Which is irritating. What do you think of DI Drustan?'

A uniform had agreed to take him to the training academy Hengist had offered as temporary accommodation. A few hundred trainees would wake up in the morning to find a Tribal DI in their midst. It would be good for them. Diversity training.

Agapos shrugged. 'Hard to read, Celts. He's quieter than most I've met, which suits me. You know what they say: you can't fill your mouth with flour then blow into the fireplace.'

'Sure,' said Aedith, digesting that. 'Well. See you in the office.'

She took pleasure in slamming the patrol car door as noisily as possible. Even at two in the morning you could feel the neighbours' outrage. They seemed convinced the house prices dropped every time a police vehicle drove through the street, and perhaps they were right. There were apps that could tell you this sort of thing now.

It took Aedith another four minutes to get through the door security, eventually having to fish the crumpled bit of paper with the code on it from the depths of her coat pockets. Her father had insisted on installing the new system last spring, over Aedith's protests. Deep down, she knew he was right, but only gave in when her mother joined in the assault.

'It's not just for you,' she had said. It was one of Sweterun's better days, the kind where she could get out of her chair and into the garden, sit under the apple trees. The blossom hadn't fallen yet. 'It's for the boy too. He can't protect himself yet.'

'He's thirteen,' said Lod. He rarely sat with them in the garden, preferring to stand with his back to them to observe as much as possible; see if the compost heaps were plotting with the stacked firewood, planning a pincer movement on the leaf bin. 'Nearly a man now. He'll have to fend for himself soon.'

'Do you actually believe that?' asked Aedith, sipping cautiously from her cup of mint tea. 'Or is it something you feel you have to say?'

Sweterun pursed her lips in disapproval, but Lod turned back, gave her a grin.

'Different generation,' he said, almost but not quite apologetically. 'You bring him up however you think best. We won't interfere. Apart from in matters of security, obviously.'

Hilde was going through some paperwork on the kitchen table when Aedith came in. Her duties as childcarer, housekeeper and bodyguard had started to include accountant as well. She was almost certainly due a raise. Aedith gave her a nod as Hilde tidied up and went to her room without a word. They barely needed to talk these days. If anything important needed saying, one of them would say it.

Coram was asleep when Aedith checked on him, half under the covers, his tablet screen full of maths diagrams. She put it away, plugging it in so it would be charged for school the next day, and pulled the duvet up over his shoulders. For a moment she felt a near-overwhelming desire to kiss him on the forehead but retreated to the doorway instead, watching him, one hand on the light switch. He looked less like his father when he was asleep, the black wing of hair over one eye instead of swept directly back. She had once suggested cropping it short, but Coram had scowled at her and she had never mentioned it again.

He stirred a little in his sleep, face twitching.

'It's not,' he mumbled. 'It isn't.'

Aedith switched off the light and closed the door.

Drustan's room was small, with the minimal amount of furniture a cadet police officer in the High King's Police Force might need: single bed, sink, battered chair, wardrobe set into the wall, a cheap desk. Someone had scratched 'Osmund is a Wanker' into the wall with the point of a compass.

Hanging his coat up in the wardrobe, Drustan removed his shoes and placed his socks in a carrier bag he had brought with him to use for laundry. He removed the carved jet statue of the Morrigun from his kitbag and placed her on the desk. The incense he usually burned when setting up a temporary shrine would have to wait; no sense setting off the smoke alarms and getting the cadets all riled up about some Indij waking them up in the early morning with his mumbo-jumbo. A treacherous voice whispered that none of this mattered anyway, but he ignored it and lit a candle instead, laid the crow feather in front of it and assumed the Fifth Position of the Resting Bear: sitting back on his heels, eyes closed, arms out flat, palms up.

The Goddess didn't come to him, of course. It had been so long since she had, Drustan had almost forgotten what it was like; the sudden metallic taste in his mouth, the feeling of someone brushing past him, so close sometimes he could feel her hair across his face, her breath against his cheek. And then she would speak to him, in the borrowed voices of women he had known: relatives, lovers; once, through a distant crackling landline, a Mughal bank worker who had been kind enough to talk a lonely young man through his first attempt to send money home from a foreign country.

She didn't speak to him that night, or perhaps his mind was too tired and befuddled to receive her; a possibility he found himself clinging to like a child. In the end, Drustan hung up his suit, blew out the candle and slept as best he could.

Six

Woden's Cross police station was in an area of London comprised mainly of grey office blocks and greyer hotels, clustered around a disused train station that had been the main transport link to the East until twenty years ago, when a bomb had shattered every window in a one-mile radius. The office blocks had been repaired but the station had stayed closed. No one had ever found out which side the terrorists had been on, although a number of young London-based Celts had been arrested and never seen again.

The youthful officer at the gate let Drustan through with a perfunctory wave of her hand once he held his ID up to be read by the scanner set into the wall. She wore one of the new carbon-fibre automatics at her hip. Those would be turning up in the Tribal lands within a year – just had to hope the Tribal cops got more of them than the wolfheads or the mead smugglers.

Aedith was waiting for Drustan in the central foyer, holding a coffee, her shift dress gone, replaced by a grey felt shirt, black trousers and a military-style greatcoat. The processing area was filling up with bare-chested Saxons, faces daubed with cheap supermarket warpaint, hands cuffed behind their backs. The small group of prostitutes waiting to be bailed out – male, female and friends of the aelves – displayed their delight at the entertainment laid on for them by making a truly impressive series of catcalls, until their arresting officers started threatening to add more charges, at which point the noise only got worse. The fact that fully two-thirds of the officers in attendance were Afro-Saxons wasn't going unremarked by the prisoners either.

'Summit protesters starting early,' said Aedith, sipping her coffee. '"Keep England Saxon" and all that. Get themselves all riled up by the social media, but really it's any excuse to ale up, display the ab-hoard and break some windows… Grab yourself a coffee from the machine if you want one. We're tracking our victim's phone.'

Drustan walked into the incident room just as the ghosts of the last investigation were being taken down, overly saturated photos of well-dressed bodies minus their heads being stuffed into cardboard boxes by a succession of support staff, watched over by an older officer in an expensive, if ill-fitting, suit.

'Tabloids called him the Fengyr,' said Aedith. 'Saxon bogeyman, loosely translates to "The Hunter."'

She held up a crude, verging on fevered, sketch of a figure straight out of the Pan-African comic books Drustan had devoured as a youth. It depicted a broad-chested male in black military trousers and boots, his chest adorned only with bloody runes, wearing a blank-faced burial mask of worked iron. In his right hand a large seax dripped unrealistic amounts of gore. In his left was a head, gripped tightly by its hair.

'Saxon on Saxon, we think – I imagine a win-win as far as you're concerned. That's if you even think he's human. Never appeared on CCTV or left any prints, leading to one theory he was the true Fengyr of legend, an aspect of Woden himself. Either way, Captain Ceolbert never did track him down, but he did get a plum promotion to Border Control out of it. It's going to be bottles of Frankish brandy and all the strip searches you can arrange, eh, Ceolbert?'

The older officer glared at Aedith, yanking the sketch out of her hand and stuffing it into another box of photos. These were all of the heads.

'Better luck next time,' said Aedith, clicking a sympathetic tongue at Ceolbert as he stalked out, the last of his staff trailing behind him.

'They never found him?' asked Drustan, intrigued. 'The Fengyr?'

Aedith shook her head. 'From what I heard, Ceolbert never got a single lead, beyond all the vics being well-connected and having a hand in the treasure chest to some extent. Or links to child porn – our lad in the mask didn't seem very keen on that, either. Killing spree suddenly ended and the high-ups didn't seem inclined to push it. None of the families kicked up a fuss. All kept out of the press and most of the deaths were marked down as suicides – which seems statistically unlikely, what with the decapitations.'

'And Ceolbert got a promotion, you say?'

'Fate works in mysterious ways, Inspector, I'm sure you know that's true whatever badge you're wearing. Help me pull these tables together, will you?'

Drustan was impressed to see Woden's Cross Homicide Department had its own tech guy. Although 'guy' wasn't entirely accurate; under the green hoodie covered in the repeating oak-leaf pattern popular amongst fans of a certain strand of Dumnonian turbo-folk, and an explosion of plaits, dreads and tattooed cheekbones, Drustan could just make out a young woman, sitting in front of the bank of monitors that had blinked into life one by one, sipping from a recycled bamboo cup with one hand, scrolling through lines of code with the other.

'Banba's our tech support,' said Aedith. 'Got her in on work experience a few years ago and she upgraded our entire database. We gave in and handed over the keys some time ago. Banba, meet DI Drustan.'

Banba nodded, but her attention was on the map laid out on the computer screen in front of her, a pulsing blue dot moving slowly along London streets.

Drustan leaned forward. 'That's his phone?'

'It's been moving since yesterday evening,' she said. 'Barely stops for more than a few minutes.'

The accent hit Drustan like a cold sea wave. He stared at her. 'You're a Pict?'

'Mum's a Pict, Dad was a London reeve. Took a posting North a couple of years ago, we never saw him again.'

'Mixed race,' said Aedith. 'Diversity hire. You should see the grants we got for the canteen.'

Banba was ignoring her, looking at the screen. 'It's stopped,' she said. 'No, wait, it's off again.'

The blue dot had reversed course.

'We're just waiting for the okay to move in before the battery runs out. Stroke of luck the location was left on,' said Aedith. 'Unless it wasn't.'

'Someone's playing you lot,' said Banba. 'Either way, it's a Haakonarson. Battery life isn't great on those things.'

'Why do think someone's playing them?' asked Drustan.

Banba shrugged. 'Location was switched on at eleven, an hour after the victim was last seen. If I wanted to distract the cops, I'd turn the phone into a beacon, send it all over town.'

'Or the victim wanted you to know where his killer had gone.'

Banba didn't look as though she cared all that much. Tech guys had the luxury of focusing on the problem in front of them. The big-picture stuff was above their pay grade.

Agapos appeared. Somehow, someone had found a bullet-proof vest big enough to go all the way around his chest. The sergeant had his own phone in his hand, the case decorated with a panoply of kitsch Mughal animated creatures: snakes and birds in primary colours with exaggerated cartoon eyes.

'My sergeant's a big fan of the game where you walk around collecting sacred creatures,' said Aedith. 'Don't judge him.'

'We're cleared to go,' said Agapos, ignoring her. 'Two longships waiting outside.'

Drustan picked up his overcoat from where he'd laid it across a chair, but Aedith put out a hand.

'No room in the vans,' she said sympathetically. 'And you've some paper hurdles to clear before you get to play with us locals.'

Drustan felt a sudden flush of anger. 'I've been cleared with your commander. The elders were promised full cooperation.'

'Needs to work on both sides,' said Aedith. She opened a drawer, took out a handgun, something old and heavy, checked the sights and clip and holstered it. 'So have a little think about when you feel like changing "them" and "you" to "us" and "we".'

The annoying thing was, Drustan thought as he watched Aedith and Agapos head out of the incident room, she made a perfectly good point.

Agapos took the lead van, holding back while Aedith took point in the ex-pursuit car she'd bought at auction – a blunt-nosed walnut-brown beast, small for a four-wheel drive – growling through the West London traffic. A cyclist – androgynous despite head-to-toe lycra, head shaved, goggles and cycle mask 3D-printed in the style of a Dogon ceremonial mask – drew alongside Aedith. They moved to put their hand on the wing mirror, then saw the expression on her face and hastily pulled it back again.

'Two hundred yards ahead,' said Banba in her earpiece. 'Hasn't moved for three minutes.'

Aedith pulled up in front of a small supermarket and scanned the street ahead, ignoring the angry beeps of a delivery van behind her.

'Any pattern yet?'

'Random stops, as far as I can tell,' said the earpiece. 'Outside a school, launderette, doubled back to the other side, hotel, couple of offices.'

Surely a taxi, but all the London cabs Aedith could see were on the move, their distinctive blue curves sliding through the traffic, for-hire lights blinking, tireless in their hunt for passengers. One of the rideshare apps? RoadWay insisted on black cars putting out at least eighty kilowatts; nothing that big here.

A vehicle pulled away from the supermarket. Bland grey town car, man in a suit sitting in the back. A private car? She couldn't see the plates without getting out.

'Shit,' said Banba in her ear.

'What's going on?'

'Battery's starting to go. Signal's fading.'

Godsdammit. Aedith drummed her fingers on the steering wheel. Follow the town car or wait? She could leave the vans here for Agapos to keep watch, but they were hardly subtle. Count of five and she'd take off after the car. Five, four, three, two—

'Signal's back!'

The town car pulled away into the traffic. Aedith released the handbrake, keeping her foot right on the biting point. If she followed it in the next few seconds, she could probably keep up with it.

'Has it gone? Has the signal moved?'

'Negative! Still outside the supermarket.'

The town car moved away, forgotten immediately. Had the phone been dumped? Aedith couldn't see a bin close to hand. It could have been dropped down a drain; maybe just left on the street.

'It's going! South, towards the traffic lights.'

Not a single vehicle was moving.

Drustan peered over Banba's shoulder. One of her screens showed a view of Aedith's car but, frustratingly, didn't reach quite as far as the pavement. A street camera was just visible, however; a black globe nestled under the eaves of an off-licence.

Drustan pointed. 'Do you have access to that?'

Banba flicked her gaze over to it for the shortest amount of time imaginable before returning to the blue dot. 'Private system. I can get to it, but the feed's password-protected.'

He pulled up a chair. 'Bring it up.'

Banba's hands flickered briefly over a second keyboard. 'Knock yourself out, for all the good it'll – hey!'

Drustan typed something into the keyboard, a new screen opening up. Aedith's car was in the background, the nose of the first police van just about visible four cars back, if you knew where to look, and just disappearing off-screen, a moped, pushed along the pavement by its helmeted rider.

'DI Drustan says to follow the moped.'

Aedith put a finger to her ear. 'Confirm? It's definitely moving?'

The blue dot on the screen blinked twice, then vanished.

'Shit,' said Banba.

'Could you pass me the mic?' asked Drustan.

'Drustan here,' said the earpiece. 'The battery's gone, signal's down, but it's the moped. Follow the moped with the black panniers. Looks like a courier.'

Aedith was really going to do the clutch plate some damage at this point, but she wasn't ready to go just yet.

'How the hells do you know he has black panniers?'

'I travelled to the spirit realm and asked the Goddess,' said Drustan. 'Through the eyes of the birds she saw the truth and via the spirits of the air she was able to communicate the truth and could you just take down the guy on the moped before he gets away, please.'

'Your guy hacked the CCTV feed somehow,' came Banba's voice.

'Well, shit,' said Aedith, impressed. She released the car into the traffic. 'Agapos, I'm taking him. Get up here.'

SEVEN

'Courier,' announced Aedith, dropping a brown padded envelope onto the table and pulling off her plastic gloves before looking around. 'Woden's balls, you lot got here fast.'

The investigation room was full of reeves now, most of whom were giving Drustan the shield-eye. It could have been confusion. The small dark Celt couldn't have looked more out of place among the well-fed and broad-shouldered Saxon reeves; a cat who'd wandered into a hall full of hounds who weren't sure why they couldn't just eat it.

'Camps are all empty,' said an older officer through a triumphant moustache. 'Summit's spooked them, we reckon, too many boots on the ground. Flown south for the summer.'

Aedith nodded and gestured vaguely towards Drustan. 'DI Drustan, Tribal police,' she said, ripping open the envelope and sliding a sleek black phone into her gloved hand. 'He's here to help with the investigation, give us inside information on the community. He's the one who spotted the moped, by the way.'

'I would *really*,' murmured Banba, 'like to know how you did that.'

Drustan said nothing. Aedith's team had reacted more stoically to his presence than he had expected: a few nods, no obvious mutterings. It was probably a bit early to find wicker curse totems in his locker. Although no one had yet offered him a locker.

'Can I talk to the courier?' asked Drustan, then saw Aedith's eyes narrowing and checked himself. 'Can *we* talk to the courier?'

Aedith smiled. 'You're in luck. He's claiming Native rights. Says he'll only speak with a Celtic officer.'

'Fairgus Blaenu,' said Aedith outside the interrogation room, one hand paused on the door handle. 'Am I pronouncing that right?'

Drustan shrugged. 'Sure.'

Aedith checked a printed form. 'Just finished serving five years at the High King's pleasure for armed robbery, been out for a week, straight into the gig economy, claims to have an alibi for the previous evening, says the package just appeared in the office and no one knows who brought it in. Agapos is checking.'

'He said he'd only talk to a Celt? How many Tribal officers are there in London?'

'A handful, maybe? None senior, to my knowledge. But he has the right, under the regulations. My guess is he's playing for time.'

She opened the door. Blaenu was a slight hunched figure in cheap sportswear, already-sharp features twisted by a poorly healed scar running from the corner of his left eye down to his mouth. He didn't look delighted to see Drustan.

'Morning, Fairgus,' said Aedith. 'In response to your request, I'm pleased to say I've found a colleague of the correct ethnicity to allow you to tell us everything you can about how your morning's gone thus far.'

Drustan gave him a bland smile. Fairgus said nothing.

'Well,' said Aedith. 'I'll leave you two to get along. Drustan, let me know if you want me to pop back in to play good cop, Saxon cop.'

*

Agapos was waiting outside the door.

'Recording?' asked Aedith quietly.

The sergeant nodded, ushering her into a small side room, plastic chairs facing an ancient monitor and speakers wired into a desk that was ninety percent ancient disc recorder. 'Video and two audio feeds. Mildritha from Custody speaks Tribal, we can get her in to translate. She's on her way now.'

He shut the door behind them, Aedith sitting down just as the monitor went black, the soft hiss from the speakers replaced by a popping, then silence.

'Annoying,' said Aedith, mildly. 'Maybe someone should tell Mildritha there's no immediate rush.'

Drustan placed the device on the table. It was small, black and heavy, making a pleasing clunk as he put it down.

'They'll get the video back up soon,' he said. 'Ten minutes or so, I'd guess.'

Blaenu shrugged, unimpressed. Drustan took a photo from his pocket, unfolded it, slid it across the table. 'Ever seen this man before?'

It wasn't a great picture. A gust of wind had blown Gorsedd Angwin's fair hair across his moustachioed face while he squinted proudly into the camera, resplendent in fleece and cagoule, a range of tall hills or low mountains behind him. A hiking holiday in the Independent Scottish Republic apparently, just a month or so ago. He didn't look like he'd once belonged to a banned terrorist organisation; more like a middle-class civil servant enjoying the outdoors. He certainly didn't resemble the bloody ruin on the tree.

Blaenu didn't look down. 'Where's my lawyer?'

Drustan winced with regret, putting the device back in his pocket. 'Going to take a while, I'm afraid. Invoking Native rights brings a whole new set of procedures. They need to find a qualified brief. Until then, it's just me. Does this man look in any way familiar?'

Blaenu shrugged.

'Maybe take a longer look,' suggested Drustan. 'I'm sorry to say there's every chance you're about to be pulled into a murder enquiry, so any help you can give us at this early juncture would be greatly appreciated.'

Blaenu leaned forward, the chain connecting his cuffs to the table rattling through the loop'. He studied the picture, brow furrowed in a pantomime of deep thought, before tutting to himself and shaking his head sadly.

'Sorry mate, never seen him before in my life.'

Irritatingly, it was probably true. Blaenu seemed the type to drag this out as long as possible; make even an honest answer sound like a lie in the hope he'd eventually be released out of sheer irritation. To be fair, it was a policy that usually paid off.

'And what about your client? The one who wanted you to pick up the package as soon as possible, but not deliver it until the following morning. That didn't strike you as odd?'

This time, Blaenu met Drustan's gaze and didn't look away.

'Someone in the office took the call. Nothing to do with me. I just go where dispatch sends me. What was it, drugs? Can't pin that on me.'

Blaenu was lying now. But Drustan was running out of time. He took off his overcoat and jacket, hung them from the back of the chair, and started unbuttoning his shirt sleeve.

'We haven't got long.'

Blaenu pulled his hands back towards himself, the chain rattling.

'Smack me around all you like, reeve. I've said everything I'm going to say.'

Drustan frowned. 'Nobody's hitting anybody, Fairgus. But we need to talk.'

Drustan pulled back his sleeve, held his wrist up to Blaenu, showed him what was marked there.

Aedith rattled the door.

'He's locked it from the inside. How did he even get a key?'

Agapos put his hand to his pocket. It came back empty. It was all Aedith could do not to laugh at the sour look on his face.

'Sneaky sod, isn't he? The duty sergeant has copies, get over there—' but the door had opened.

Blaenu's cuffs had been removed, but his demeanour was anything but that of a free man. The Celt was sagging in his chair, eyes fixed on the floor, arms slack by his sides.

Drustan held out the key to Agapos, who snatched it up with a scowl.

'My apologies, sergeant. I felt time was of the essence.' He looked at Aedith. A brief nod of contrition. 'Mister Blaenu has agreed to sign a written statement to the effect that he doesn't recognise the victim as depicted in the photograph and has minimal knowledge of the client who requested his services, although he's prepared to share with us what he does know. As regards the death of Gorsedd Angwin, I made a couple of calls. Three witnesses will testify to having spent the previous night with Mister Blaenu in a popular sports bar in the West of the city, which should be backed up by CCTV.'

'Funny,' said Aedith. She didn't sound in the least amused. 'I thought his lawyer hadn't got here yet; yet here you are.'

'Not at all,' said Drustan. 'Mister Blaenu has waived all rights to a lawyer, although I have tried to persuade him legal representation would be in his best interests, particularly given the nature of a separate piece of intelligence he has decided he would like to pass on to Detective Captain Mercia in the spirit of cooperation with the authorities, in what is a politically sensitive time.'

Aedith and Agapos exchanged a look.

'Good of him,' said Aedith finally.

Drustan nodded earnestly. 'Mister Blaenu has asked if his name could be kept out of further proceedings, as he feels any lack of discretion could put his physical wellbeing in serious doubt.'

'We'll certainly take that into consideration,' said Aedith. 'What's he got for us?'

'Four tonnes of fertiliser smuggled East two weeks ago in three separate goods vehicles, destined for London,' said Drustan. 'Along with a number of illegal firearms and electronic devices that could be assembled into a timer. The buyer was very specific that the goods should arrive at least two days before the start of the Unification Summit.'

'Godsdamn,' breathed Aedith. 'Any idea who made the order?'

'The chain of command appears to run through a number of proxies,' said Drustan. 'But it looks very likely the head of operations is a figure high up in a Tribal family, based here in London. Do you know a Deedra Kesair?'

EIGHT

The man leaving Hengist's glass-walled office was dark-skinned and shaven-headed with a straightforward kind of handsomeness that could put him at any age from mid-thirties to late fifties. He had a close-cropped beard and wore an aggressively bland grey suit. He gave Aedith a faint smile, smirked at Drustan and was gone.

Aedith made a hissing noise. 'Tancred.'

Drustan held the door before it completely swung shut.

'I know the name. Special Branch?'

'He is now. Beocca Tancred was my tutor at the academy, asked my father for my hand in marriage. I'd only been in about a month, barely out of my teens. He thought I'd be impressed. My father pulled some strings to get him out of the way, got him reassigned, promoted even, and he did very well for himself. He's a major now. I should have shot him on the range.'

If Commander Odda Hengist heard anything of this, he didn't react. 'Take a seat,' he said.

'You could have warned me before you called the fingernail pluckers. Given me a chance to check it out.'

Aedith's arms were folded, her shoulders hunched, sullen. Something of the teenage girl in her when facing authority, noted Drustan.

'I could have,' said Hengist mildly. 'But I don't need you wasting three days we haven't got chasing missing fertiliser. And if the victim really was Fomóir, there's a certain procedure. Unwise to delay. As it was, Special Branch wanted to take over the Angwin investigation too. They weren't happy about the involvement of our Tribal colleague here, I can tell you that much. I persuaded them we could deal with the boring murder crimes, call them in if we heard about anything that sounded like it might blow up.'

Station Commander Hengist was a large man and, even with short hair and a neat beard, perhaps the hairiest Drustan had ever seen. A bear crammed into a police uniform. Behind him, a framed ram's head hung from the wall. Drustan had seen them before, a toy, or a joke. If you connected them to your phone remotely, they'd *baa* notifications for you. People usually took the batteries out after a couple of days.

Hengist followed Drustan's gaze over his shoulder.

'Present from my kids. Good to meet you, DI Drustan. We spoke on the phone earlier.' They shook hands formally; Hengist's grip was light, careful. A man who knew his own strength. 'Captain Mercia will have to tread lightly with the Kesair,' he continued. 'Her personal connection with Deedra complicates matters. Any hint of intelligence being passed on and Tancred's men will shut this whole department down and salt the earth. And they'd be right to do so.'

Drustan turned to Aedith. 'How exactly do you know Deedra Kesair?' He tried not to sound intrigued.

Aedith sighed. 'We went to the same school and were… best of enemies, let's say. She was the only Tribal and took a lot of shit for sitting out religious assemblies, bringing her own food in on feast days, all that stuff. I pulled her out of a few fights, really to stop her killing any Saxon kid stupid enough to try and bully her, but she took to me after that. We kept bumping into each other afterwards and our relationship's never changed. I like her. I just don't know why.'

Hengist rubbed the back of one hand with another. Drustan stared, fascinated. The hair projecting from the cuff of his shirt ran uninterrupted right down to his black-inked knuckles.

'Inspector, what do you know of the Kesair in the West?'

Drustan pulled his gaze away reluctantly. 'Nothing you couldn't find online. Financially, socially, they're closer to the Saxons than the homeland. A lot of our people think the tattoos, the determination to be more Celtic than the Celts, it's all an act. They've found a niche in the East and they're good at exploiting it.'

Aedith shook her head. 'It's not an act. She punched the teeth out of another kid once for messing with an icon hanging on her wall. Triple spiral thing.'

'A triskele,' said Drustan.

Aedith shrugged. 'Sure. All I'm saying is, she believed in it then. Who knows what she believes now?'

Hengist drummed his fingers on the desk.

'Where are we with the phone? Or the last place anyone saw the vic: the bar.'

'Angwin was drinking with his colleagues until he got a call and went off on his own. Didn't appear distressed or worried, just said he'd see his colleagues the next day and walked out. Phone was wiped clean before it was given to the courier. His fingerprints are the only ones forensics found on the envelope. Banba's trying to unlock it, but it's a long shot without the password and the phone company tend to push back pretty strongly against state demands, so we need to tread lightly. I've got plain clothes checking out the bar's CCTV, any cameras outside. Nothing yet.'

'Press?'

'We got lucky there, someone leaked to one of the big news sites but gave the wrong coordinates. By the time the photographer got to the scene we'd taken it all down. Without the juicy images the story's not worth much. Just another—' She paused.

'Just another Celt got himself killed in the East,' said Drustan, without rancour.

'I'm sorry, but yes,' said Aedith. 'We may find it useful to push the story later, go public and see if we get any useful intel amongst the usual torrent of bollocks that will come flooding in. Might be able to use the fact Angwin was a diplomat as a hook, most people don't even know the Tribals have diplomats. Although if it turns out he did have Fomóir links, that's going to complicate things.'

Hengist nodded. 'Do we know where he stayed while he was up here?'

'Official buildings just south of the river, but there's no sign Angwin ever slept in the room he was designated. Possibly he was just a neat freak, but we're considering the possibility he had other accommodation in London he didn't tell anyone about.'

Hengist nodded and pushed himself back in his chair. It creaked in protest. 'Take a moment then.'

Aedith blinked. 'Take a moment?'

Hengist waved a thick, short-fingered hand at Drustan.

'Show our colleague round the station then take him out for lunch; we've got a community liaison budget we never use. The coroner's doing her work over at Saxnot's. I'll call you as soon as the results come in.'

Hengist hauled himself to his feet, picked up an empty coffee mug and blinked at it, disappointed, before putting it down again.

'Yes, sir,' said Aedith, standing up. Drustan followed, just as the eyes in the ram's head blinked open and swivelled in different directions. The mouth opened and shut mechanically a couple of times before it spoke.

'On way home, pls pick up milk,' it said in a bleating, tinny voice, which didn't match up with the mouth's movements at all. 'Get dinner if you want it. I'll be out.'

Drustan let Aedith out first, closing the door quietly behind them.

NINE

'Gym,' said Aedith, pointing at a door as she walked past without stopping, Drustan pulled in her wake. 'Armoury, canteen that way, showers up there.'

Aedith pushed through two sets of double doors, down some stairs and held her laminate up to a large set of steel doors. They rolled back halfway, stopped with a grinding noise while they solved some internal mechanical problem, then completed the process more quietly, revealing the pitted concrete and worn yellow health and safety sigils of a sizeable underground car park.

'Let's get some lunch, then,' she said. 'See how far I can stretch that liaison budget.'

She led Drustan down a spiral staircase, reminding him of a documentary about Moorish fortresses: how the stairs spiralled upwards clockwise, forcing attackers to use their off-hand, assuming they were right-handed. Were left-handers reserved for the front line of castle attack?

'What did you make of our Commander Hengist?'

Drustan shook himself out of his historical reverie. 'I think he needs a larger office,' he said.

'A sophisticated reply,' said Aedith, without approval, leading Drustan past a row of battered patrol cars. 'He's good police. Keeps a shieldwall between us and the pricks at the High Table.'

They were at the unmarked cars now, all either four-wheel-drive or sporty or both. Each one glowed like a jewel. Saxons drove their work cars like they hated them but kept their private vehicles pristine.

Aedith stopped in front of a mid-brown, snub-nosed vehicle Drustan recognised from the CCTV.

'Here,' said Aedith. She pressed a button on her key fob. The doors opened themselves, slowly, with a low mechanical hum.

Drustan nodded. 'Does it have a name?'

Aedith looked him, eyes narrowed.

'I heard Saxons like to name things,' he said. 'Just out of curiosity, I wondered if you kept to the tradition.'

'Yes,' said Aedith. 'It's called "Roadfucker".'

Aedith's mood changed the moment she turned the engine on, captain and machine humming happily as the car powered around the underground maze of the car park, up the off-ramp and onto the street with no discernible drop in speed.

'You've been to the capital before, then?'

Drustan subtly tugged on his seatbelt to make sure he wasn't about to end up in the cramped rear seats at the next corner. 'A few times, tracking fugitives mostly. No one notices another Tribal on the building sites or cleaning up in a coffee shop.'

Aedith shot him a look. Drustan was thankful she didn't hold it too long before turning her attention back to the road. They were moving south-east, as far as he could tell, towards the river, the flyover taking them up and over the very centre of Hyde Park. Vast and dark, Hyde Park was, according to a series of popular films, filled with the twisted cannibal descendants of a tribe of Celts who had come East to assassinate a High King centuries ago but got lost on the way. Drustan had visited the Park on his last visit, killing time rather than royalty while he waited for a suspect's flight to come in from Addis Ababa. He hadn't spotted any cannibals but had enjoyed an ice cream from a park vendor. The suspect had never got on the plane in the end, having got wind the Tribal police were hoping to intercept him, and was eventually indicted by Pan-African police on charges of tax evasion. The Goddess worked in her own way.

'I'm sorry about the Tash thing,' said Aedith suddenly. 'Unprofessional. It won't happen again.'

'It's fine,' said Drustan, peering at the road signs warning of upcoming roadworks, structural works on the bridge that on the current trajectory would take them across the river and into Southwark, where the accents turned more thickly Southeast Saxon and the buildings constantly threatened to sink into the marshland. But Aedith veered off the main road before the bridgeworks began, nosing the car down a side street.

'Give me five minutes. Something Leofstan said earlier.'

'Leofstan?'

'Old guy with the moustache. Went undercover a few years ago and we could never make him get rid of it.'

The car stopped next to a high chain-link fence, closing off an area where three or four workshops backed onto one another. Or would, if they'd still been going concerns. Instead, Drustan could see piles of pallets and rusting, half-stripped vehicles, interspersed with tarpaulins slung over ropes, smoke-blackened steel drums, cheap sleeping bags on rain-darkened cardboard.

Aedith stepped out of the car, pushed back a loose section of fence and looked around. Drustan joined her. Nothing moved.

'No one's even supposed to have got here yet.'

'By no one you mean…'

'I mean until your man Angwin was discovered on his tree, my squad had been reassigned to clear up, making the city look nice for the Pan-Africans here for the Summit, along with media who bother to turn up. This place is normally full of meadheads, drifters; keep themselves to themselves for the most part, not high up the list for relocation, but they've gone anyway.'

Drustan nudged an empty mead bottle with his foot. 'Unbroken.'

Aedith shot him a look. 'We should recycle it?'

'I've been in camps when the reeves have come through. There's panic, things get dropped, smashed, broken glass everywhere.' And blood too, but Drustan wasn't going to press the point right now.

'Huh. You're saying this was more in the nature of an orderly retreat?'

'I'm saying something spooked these people, but they didn't flee in panic, they took what they could and went back to the shadows.'

'Well,' said Aedith finally, 'they'll have to stay in the shadows for now. Let's get some lunch.'

Aedith eventually found a parking space in sight of a large low building, put together from huge blocks of white stone seemingly dropped from above at haphazard angles.

'Some Pan-African architect,' she said. 'Used to be all light industrial stuff round here, call centres, everything the Caliphate didn't want to do themselves. Then the Paris and Berlin imams gave the nod to automation, chatbots and the like and that was the end of that. International Development gave the city a grant to redevelop some of the land into a conference centre on condition one of theirs designed the building.'

Drustan squinted out of the car window. If you looked carefully, the blocks became less randomly arranged, resolved themselves into the shape of—

'Is it supposed to be a longship?' It was rather clever.

'They called it the Skeid. Said they were being "culturally sensitive". Patronising bastards. It's where they'll be holding the Unification Summit.'

Drustan got out of the car. The pavements were wider here than around the station, the signs in a more formal font, pedestrians more smartly dressed, beech trees planted at regular intervals. The two dark-suited Saxons in front of the Skeid's foyer hadn't taken their eyes off him since they'd arrived. Both had thin wires trailing from their ears down into their collars and tell-tale bulges under their left arms. He sensed rather than heard the thin whine of a drone as something small and black dodged high up from one white block to another and was lost behind an air-conditioning unit the size of a car. Further along the top of the building, something glinted behind a low breeze-block barrier: a sniper's scope.

'Is there always this level of security?'

'Hasn't been before,' said Aedith, chewing her lip thoughtfully. 'And it doesn't even start until tomorrow. A reaction to the ghosts of the Fomóir rising, possibly.'

She waved at an invisible figure three storeys up, grinning at the disapproval emanating from the suits opposite. 'There's a café inside but it was never the most relaxing place to eat anyway, so I thought we'd go there.' She pointed across the road to a narrow-fronted restaurant between two boutique clothes shops, one displaying Mughal wedding dresses so covered in feathers and roses that the clothing itself seemed like an afterthought.

They had to wait for a limo with blacked-out windows and diplomatic plates to pass before they could cross the road. Drustan didn't recognise the flag flying from the bonnet.

'One of the minor Tsars,' said Aedith. 'Like flies around shit in this place.'

Drustan stopped in front of the window of the second shop, a baroque display of sportswear and special forces armour. Mannequins, their triangular heads fitted with sensors to track passers-by, moved articulated limbs in a glacial but vaguely threatening dance as they walked past. Drustan waved his hand in front of the nearest figure, but the programming had been well done and it refused to be distracted, the point of its lopsided pyramid continuing to somehow stare at him.

'It's no dummy,' said Aedith. The mannequin turned to face her, tetrahedral head tilting to one side. Clearly it, like Drustan, was unsure of Saxon humour. 'Shall we eat?'

TEN

The restaurant was called The Pavilion and apparently as Mughal-owned as the rest of the street. A waiter in a traditional long tunic took their coats and led them to a rear table. Plucked strings and a warbling female voice were piped in from speakers hidden somewhere amongst the ornately carved columns and arches, gold lamps hung on chains over every table, but the main sensory overload was the smell: warm bread, hot spices, a soapy-smelling herb.

'The only Mughal restaurant in London,' said Aedith, gesturing expansively to Drustan to take a seat. 'Or the only one worth coming to, anyway.'

The waiter laid the menus down with grave reverence, placed two bottles of light ale on the table, and withdrew.

'I brought Agapos here once. Poor guy managed one course before he ran outside. Said his teeth were sweating, so my advice is to take it easy.'

Drustan nodded cautiously. By chance, or maybe out of thoughtfulness, Aedith had given him the seat against the wall. Discreetly, he checked out the other diners: diplomatic staff for the most part, a few Pan-Africans – probably journalists, going by their shabby clothing, notebooks, and the number of empty beer glasses on their tables. Oddly, the notebooks were just that: actual paper notebooks. Not a phone or tablet to be seen.

'Every intelligence service in the East wants to listen in at this place,' said Aedith, sliding the menu to one side without looking at it. 'But they spent more time trying to take out each other's bugs than putting in their own. Also, the guy that owns it is part of a big Kashmiri tech clan so he put jammers in all the walls.'

Drustan checked his mobile. No wifi or phone signal. He slid it back in his pocket.

'Means we can speak freely. As freely as we want to, anyway.'

The waiter was back, hovering politely by their table.

'Shall I order for you?' asked Aedith.

'If it's not too much trouble,' said Drustan, humbly.

Aedith ran through the menu at speed. When they were alone again, she picked up her ale, waiting for Drustan to do the same.

'Will you drink with me?' It was the most formal she had been since they had met. Not for the first time, Drustan wondered if beer was the only thing Saxons took seriously. And sport, obviously.

'Of course.' He clinked his bottle with hers self-consciously. They sipped together.

'Watered-down horse piss,' said Aedith with a cheerful belch, 'but kills you slower than the tap water. So, tell me, what's your priority with this case?'

Drustan raised an eyebrow. 'My priority? I've been sent here to catch the killer of Gorsedd Angwin.'

Aedith tutted impatiently, caught the waiter's eye, and pointed to their table. After numerous small dishes containing crispy things and brightly coloured sauces had appeared, she took another swig of ale.

'Celts get killed in the East every day. Not usually nailed to trees, I'll admit, but Angwin's not the first to be murdered far from home. But we've never been sent a Tribal DI before. Are you even murder police?'

Drustan dug the edge of a crispy thing into some orange sauce and bit it off.

'Back home, we make do with what we have,' he said finally.

'Which means?'

'It means we have fewer specialised departments. I've dealt with homicides in the past, but my remit is probably broader than your Saxon system would allow. In so far as I have a formalised role, I'm tasked with enforcing any *geas* issued by our elders.'

Aedith blinked. 'The hells is a *geas*?'

Drustan helped himself to some more sauce.

'If a crime is deemed to have been committed,' he said, trying to cover his mouth while he ate, 'our elders will issue a *geas*, a command. That a fugitive return to the community to answer questions, for example, or an important person travel through contested territory without harm coming to them.'

'I don't understand,' said Aedith. 'Issue a command to who?'

'Reality,' said Drustan gravely.

'And does reality normally obey commands from Celtic elders?'

'Not these days,' said Drustan, wincing. 'My apologies, that sauce was unexpectedly sour. No, sadly, with the waning of the power of our priestly caste in the last thousand years or so, it was deemed such commands needed enforcing in the material world. In this case, said *geas* has been laid upon the killer of Gorsedd Angwin, whoever that might be, that they turn themselves in for questioning, or, failing that, answer to the Goddess. I have been tasked with… helping fate along, let's say.'

'Answer to the Goddess,' said Aedith, when the waiter had finished depositing platters of rice, meat and wedges of flatbread on their table. 'That sounds final.'

'Yes. It means once I've identified the perpetrator and made every attempt to bring them to justice, I am empowered to execute them if I have reasonable grounds to do so, such as an attempted violent escape, defending the life of an innocent and so on. I'd have to take into account I was operating under Saxon jurisdiction, of course.'

'Glad to hear it,' said Aedith, then casually: 'And you had no idea the victim had been a member of the Fomóir before you wiped the blood off his chest?'

Drustan met her gaze across the table. 'Am I being interrogated?' he asked. 'I was led to expect more in the way of rubber walls and drains in the floor.'

Aedith didn't rise to the bait. There was no point. They both knew what Drustan was saying was true.

Aedith shook her head. 'We've shared beer,' she said. 'We sit across a feasting table. You are beholden to answer as much or as little as you wish, I won't take offence. Would you believe me if I said I'd never beaten a confession out of anyone?'

Drustan thought about it for a moment. 'Oddly enough, I think I would. Could you say the same for the rest of your department?'

'Could you say no Tribal cop you've worked with has ever been in the pay of organised crime? Some of the older ones never looked the other way when the Fomóir were moving guns across the border, knee-capping farmers who didn't cough up for the cause or want barrels of mead buried on their land?'

Neither of them had so much as raised their voice. In the end it was Drustan who smiled and held up his hands in conciliation.

'I had no idea Angwin had been a member of a barred terrorist organisation. The elders don't tend to send us off with folders stuffed full of information, I'm afraid; we're mostly left alone to discover information on our own cognisance.'

'Helpful of them.'

'More them trying to influence the investigation as little as possible. I have my own contacts in London. They'll get back to me in their own time. Possibly a more holistic approach than you're used to.'

Aedith opened her mouth then shut it again, clearly deciding to let that one go. 'No reason to think the Fomóir are back on the streets of London?'

Drustan shook his head. 'We don't want those days back any more than you do.'

'Glad to hear it.' She looked down at the table. 'Now, the mistake Agapos made was going straight into the spicy stuff. I recommend you get plenty of rice and that potato and spinach stuff, try a bit of the sauce at a time. You'll build up tolerance in no time.'

Drustan nodded, his face solemn. 'This is actually very good.' Mixing a forkful of rice with a dab of chicken in red sauce, he regarded it with a worried eye for a moment before plunging it into his mouth and chewing. 'My understanding of Saxon initiation rites is limited, but at least this one appears to be nutritious.'

'I'm not hazing you!' Aedith put down a sizeable piece of flatbread, wounded. 'I thought you might enjoy eating away from the canteen, that's all— you're taking the piss, aren't you?'

Drustan grinned at her as the waiter appeared by Aedith's elbow and bowed. 'How is your meal?'

'*Khana bahut accha hai!*' said Drustan cheerfully. '*Mujhe* mineral water *chahiye?*'

The waiter bowed low, flashing a sideways smirk at Aedith's startled expression and left.

He returned to his food, eating for some time before apparently becoming aware that Aedith was staring across the table at him, arms folded.

'You absolute arsehole,' said Aedith.

Drustan blinked at her, startled. 'You don't want the water?'

She leaned back. 'Explain.'

'Ah. Yes. In my early years, before joining the Tribal police, I was forced to leave my own lands, over... let's say, a misunderstanding. I was lucky enough to have an uncle who did some security for the Mughal empire. He brought me over, found me employment there for a few years. I picked up a few phrases, got used to the food. For the record, the chicken jalfrezi is delicious, but perhaps a little hot for my palate.'

The silence was long enough to bring worried glances from a neighbouring table, until Aedith finally gave in and laughed. Leaning across the table, clinking her nearly empty beer bottle against his.

'Sorry for being a patronising Saxon bitch.'

He grinned at her. 'Apologies for not telling you earlier. You know, this food really is very good.'

Aedith pushed back her empty plate, belching discreetly into a napkin. 'You never answered my question about priorities.'

Drustan was still eating. 'I didn't?'

'You told me your orders, the reason you came here. What I'm wondering about is the meaning behind the orders.' She lifted a conciliatory hand at Drustan's frown. 'I'm not saying you're on a secret mission from the elders, I'm just wondering how strongly the Summit figures in all this.'

'Would the elders have sent me if Angwin had been a construction worker rather than a senior diplomat about to engage in a political process that will affect the path of the Celtic nations for the foreseeable future? No, I think not. My task here is to bring a Celt's killer to justice or assist the Saxon authorities – you – to bring them to justice to the best of my abilities, but the political context can't be overlooked. If there's something else going on here, I want to know about it.'

'So how does Deedra Kesair potentially plotting to lob a truck's worth of explosive into the proceedings figure in your investigation?'

'Ah,' said Drustan, putting his fork down. 'I have to admit, it concerns me. Although, as a plan, it doesn't strike me as a sensible one.'

'I know Deedra,' said Aedith. '"Sensible" doesn't come into it. She's a lunatic.'

'You misunderstand. The Kesair clan stand to do extremely well out of the Summit, if it proceeds as expected.'

'They do?' She sounded genuinely taken aback.

'Very much so. Revived claims to ancient lands now thought to have considerable mineral resources; the loosening of some financial restrictions on various investments. I see no reason for them to throw all that away with a crude terrorist attempt.'

'Not that it's any of our business,' said Aedith. 'What with Hengist handing it straight over to Special Branch.'

'As was right and proper.'

'Of course. And if we were to come across any further information relating to the Kesair, we'd be duty bound to pass that to Special Branch too. Once we knew it was relevant.'

'I assume any further intelligence would have to be thoroughly checked before being handed further up the chain.'

'Of course. No point wasting their valuable time.'

'Tell me though, Captain, what's *your* priority?'

'Solve the crime, keep the peace. If I'd wanted anything more complex than that, I'd have done what my father wanted and gone into politics.'

Drustan nodded. 'So, let us agree our fates are entwined until such time as Angwin's murder is solved.'

'They'll be entwined for a while then,' said Aedith, her tone gloomy. She made the gesture to the waiter that they were done, a simple finger-rune Drustan had never been able to master, for some reason. 'No witnesses, no real evidence, no fingerprints other than the courier's, no CCTV from the bar the night the victim went missing, work colleagues never talked with him about personal matters and no friends or family in a hundred-mile radius.'

'Ah,' said Drustan. 'Now that might not be *entirely* true.'

She stared at him. The waiter materialised but was ignored.

'How would you feel,' asked Drustan, 'about making one more stop before we return to the station?'

ELEVEN

Aedith's phone chirruped as she closed the car door.

'Orva's finished the post-mortem. She's ready when we are… Is this really the best place to park?'

She looked back at Roadfucker, sitting uneasily between a battered flatbed truck loaded with cabbages and something that had once been a family estate until it had been propped up on bricks and had its tyres removed. Along with its doors, bonnet, and engine.

Drustan whistled at a thin child in oversized sportswear watching them interestedly from a nearby doorstep, tossed them a coin and nodded at the car.

'Another if it's untouched when we get back.'

The young Celt gave him a grin – gappy through malnutrition, violence or maybe even the natural processes of childhood – sauntered across the pavement and leaned against Roadfucker's flank, before pulling a slim blade out of nowhere and cleaning their nails.

'Entrepreneurial spirit alive and well on the streets,' said Aedith stoutly. 'Gives me hope for the future.'

'What I'm going to need you to do,' said Drustan, rapping on a chipboard door that someone had started to paint a cheap battleship grey for approximately a third of the way up before getting bored and wandering off, 'is try and come across a little less like a high-ranking Saxon police officer for the next twenty minutes or so.'

'Done,' said Aedith.

These streets had once been full of small hotels run by family groups of Celts catering for the nearby train station, but with that shuttered and closed for two decades, the purpose of the area had gone with it. Travellers from the West would take the overnight coach to save money on accommodation now, stumble bleary-eyed through the checkpoints a mile southwest, and disperse into the city before their cash could fall into the grateful wallets of their relocated countrymen. Now the buildings were either waiting for demolition, crammed full of Tribal families still hoping for a better life while scraping whatever meagre benefits they could from the Saxon purse, or put to purposes optimistically described by the local borough council as belonging to the 'grey economy'.

Before joining Homicide, a younger Aedith had taken part in a raid on an illegal brewery in the basement of a building a few hundred yards down the road. The pipework she'd helped smash up had drip-fed lab-engineered hallucinogens into mead that was at least fifty percent sugar beet, poured into bottles stolen from a local recycling centre and sold on the streets at an enormous mark-up. Those desperate enough to drink it hadn't cared about going blind as a result, as long as what was going on inside their eyelids was more interesting than the outside world. Many of them ran out into traffic. Most of them had been underage. None of it felt very grey to Aedith.

Still, the graffiti on these streets was impressive: abstract spirals that made your head hurt if you looked at them for too long, stylised depictions of urban animals pursued across buildings by hunters that bore some resemblance, if you put your head on one side, to Saxon cops. Or were the animals cops and the hunters Celts? Half the street art here would probably qualify for some kind of bleeding-heart Pan-African development grant if you tried hard enough.

A chain rattled behind the door. It opened a crack. Drustan said something Tribal in a low voice and was answered in kind. A hand pushed itself out, palm upwards.

'They need our phones,' said Drustan, handing his over. 'We'll get them back, untouched, you have my word.'

'Do I have theirs?' asked Aedith but took her phone out anyway. Her spirit beast didn't approve of her handing it over, although it was mollified a little by the weight of Lungpiercer, holstered on her hip under her greatcoat.

The hand withdrew. The chain rattled again then slid free and the door opened, releasing a smoky scent, something lighter underneath. Whoever had opened the door had already walked away, down a short flight of stairs leading to another door, this one much sturdier. Their underworld guide, a slight figure in a black hoodie and army surplus combat trousers, rapped hard on the metal surface and waited.

Aedith sniffed, confused. 'Lemon?'

'Verbena,' said Drustan. 'Crushed and burned as a protection against evil magics.'

'Fair enough,' said Aedith.

The inner sanctum of whichever criminal group owned this safe house (no civilian, not even the most paranoid, needed that many metal doors between them and the street) was disappointingly dull; suburban, even. Pan-African-themed wall hangings, Mughal knockoff lanterns hanging from the ceiling, cheap

Moorish bookcases. Aedith wasn't being a snob, she had those bookcases at home, much to Sweterun's disgust. Although hers were crammed with police textbooks and the occasional unused celebrity chef's offering; the volumes here were thicker, more sober: histories, political biographies, translations of great bardic works. Out of nowhere, Aedith remembered she still had three boxes of Edric's university books in her study, waiting for him to get out. It would be some time yet.

These books' current owner, Aedith guessed, was sitting in a chair in the centre of the room. The chair looked more expensive than any of the furniture around it, but due to function rather than form: steel wheels fitted with thin rubber tyres, two handles projecting from its back.

The hoodie lurked at the back of the room. Aedith couldn't get a good look at his shadowed face or see any obvious Tribal markings, just a neatly trimmed beard, a gunmetal torc barely visible around his neck. He could have been Drustan's twin. For the first time, Aedith found herself wondering what tribe her new colleague belonged to. She suspected one of those all the way down the tip of the West Country, although she probably wouldn't know it even if he told her.

'I'm sorry we couldn't meet at my office,' said the middle-aged woman. She looked familiar. A mugshot? One of those 'just in case' photos that got flashed up at morning briefings? 'I'm making do with temporary accommodation due to a reshuffle at one of my rivals, bringing about a more aggressive bid for expansion. The last time this happened I ended up in this chair, so you'll have to forgive me if I don't rise for the presence of the *gwithyas*.'

'Andraste is a respected member of the Tribal community in London,' said Drustan. 'She heads a number of charitable endeavours looking out for those who others would let fall through the cracks, finds them employment. She also owns a number of properties across the cities.'

'I think I know some of them,' said Aedith. 'Would these cater for those with, let's say, "specialised" interests?'

Andraste smiled at her. She didn't look dangerous at all, or even particularly Celtic. Her hair was a bland mid-brown, cut in a conservative style. No facial markings and those that could be seen under the sleeve of her plain blouse were delicate, tasteful. She could have been one of the mums Aedith would run into on the rare occasions her schedule allowed her to pick up Coram from school.

'Nothing as sinister as you make it sound, Captain.' She did sound Tribal at least, a wry flowing cadence with something of the valleys to it, perhaps. Aedith didn't have much of an ear for dialect. It had been one of Lod's great disappointments. 'We're very discreet, stay as close to the boundaries of the law as we can, especially bearing in mind how many of our clients are lawyers. Or judges. We're also very conscientious about paying our taxes.'

An operation such as Andraste's wasn't about making money anyway. Or at least not primarily. She collected and bartered information, and you didn't have to bug the rooms of her establishments, or even put the punters under the influence, to get it. High-ranking Saxons with stressful jobs went to girls (and young men) run by people like Andraste as much to be listened to afterwards as for the act itself. And those chosen by Andraste would be good listeners. They wouldn't have been run off for the Summit either, unlike the street-level hookers being moved on before the foreign press arrived, such as it was. If anything, Andraste's takings, in cash and information, would see a considerable boom over the next few weeks. The foreign press would contribute on both counts.

'You're here about Gorsedd Angwin,' said Andraste.

'I don't know,' said Aedith. 'You tell me.' She wasn't doing much to keep the irritation out of her voice.

Andraste gestured to two mismatched chairs opposite. 'Please.'

They sat. The black hoodie brought in cups of herbal tea, distributed them and left again, although Aedith couldn't help noticing he didn't move far outside the door.

'Until a few years ago, Gorsedd was a regular client,' said Andraste. 'Work often brought him to London, and he had a regular relationship with Eimear, one of my girls.'

Aedith stared doubtfully at her tea, dark leaves floating about the bottom of the plastic cup, smelling faintly of liquorice. She took a sip. It wasn't that bad. 'When you say "relationship"…'

'Paid,' said Andraste. 'Although I think it went beyond that. Men often think it does, but in this case I think there really was something there beyond the sex. And there wasn't as much of that as you'd expect. Angwin needed an outlet, somewhere he could let his guard down, as much as such a thing was possible with the line of work he was in. I suspect you already know this, but he was a foot soldier for the Fomóir.'

'We saw the tattoo,' said Aedith.

Andraste nodded. 'We had a few of the higher-ups in the Fo' as regular customers. We liked to get advance warning if we could, avoid them running into judges, senior politicians, but even when they did it never seemed to matter that much. More in common with each other than those below, I suppose. Gorsedd was never a high-ranking member, but he was respected by those that were. Picked up by the *gwithyas* a few times but never gave them anything. Never drank too much, never shot his mouth off. He talked with Eimear, but about literature, philosophy, verse even.'

'One of those sensitive, thoughtful members of a banned paramilitary organisation,' said Aedith. Drustan shot her a warning glance but she ignored it.

'He made an impression,' said Andraste, shrugging. 'And in this line of work, you have to remember details about clients, provide them with what they want with a minimum of interaction. You can't write it all down, so it has to go... here.'

She tapped the side of her head.

'I'd like a chat with Eimear myself,' said Aedith. 'Could that be arranged?'

'Not by traditional means,' said Andraste. 'She died in a road accident while Gorsedd was back West, six years ago now. No one thought to tell him. He was destroyed when he arrived and found out from another client. Big-name journalist, writes for the *Saga* now, nasty piece of work, took some delight in telling the man from the Fo' his special girl had been hit by a car. You could see by his face he realised he'd done the wrong thing the second he'd said it. Took four of my boys to pull Gorsedd off him. We put Gorsedd in a spare room, thought he was going to drink himself to death after a week. But when he walked out, he was a new man.'

'Sober?'

'That was the least of it. He held himself differently. Straighter, less bowed by the weight of the world. There were a couple of high-ups in the Fo' still in the house when he came out of his room. He walked straight up to them, said he was out. Didn't ask them, told them.'

Aedith took this in. 'They just let him leave? That doesn't sound like them.'

'It was the way he said it. I was in the room when he told them. He didn't threaten them, and he could have, he knew where many, many bodies were buried, in every sense. He told them he'd had enough, that he was out, wasn't even the same man. He was...' – Andraste hesitated – 'he used an odd phrase. He said he was shape-shifted.'

Drustan frowned. 'He used those exact words?'

'No, of course not. I'm using the language of the oppressor for the assistance of your friend here.'

'Appreciate it,' said Aedith. Drustan gave her a look.

Andraste thought for a moment. 'He used the word *"athshaolaithe"*.'

Drustan's expression didn't change, but it was the closest to puzzled Aedith had seen him.

'I don't get it,' said Aedith.

Drustan turned to her. 'Angwin was talking in mythic terms. As though he'd become a new creature, like the myths, turned into a salmon or a swan.'

Aedith looked from Drustan to Andraste. 'With all due respect,' she said carefully, 'no one in the room actually believed that was the case, did they?'

'We are a spiritual people,' said Andraste, finishing her tea and then placing her plastic cup down on an upturned wooden crate as carefully as if it was the finest china, 'but I don't think anyone there was inclined to, let's say, a literal take on the more mystical elements of our belief structure. I believe he meant a more internal change, that his spirit was somehow replenished while his outward form remained the same.'

'Don't take this the wrong way,' said Aedith, because she couldn't help herself, 'but I'm glad I won't be writing this meeting up in an official report, because that bit specifically might give me problems.'

She sensed Drustan wince next to her, but Andraste couldn't entirely conceal a smile.

'I didn't see him again for a few years,' she went on. 'Not on our premises anyway, although our paths crossed at a few social events. He'd become something of a specialist in hostage negotiations, oddly enough. Trusted by both sides. I'd say he saw the freedom of as many Saxons as his own people. Defused an embassy siege a few years ago. The one with the Tsarist rebels. Special Branch hanging off the side of the building with gas masks on, grenades good to go, and Angwin walked in with his hands up. Rebels, all the staff and two reeves who'd got caught up in it walked out half an hour later.'

Aedith stared at her. 'Frozen hells, that was him?'

'His presence was kept out of the papers, happy to let the High King's men get all the credit, but yes, that was Angwin's doing. No surprise to anyone who knew him he became one of the Tribes' main diplomats a year later.'

'You say you met him at social events sometimes,' said Aedith. 'Here? In London?'

Andraste nodded.

'But he wasn't taking advantage of your facilities any more?'

'Not in the sense you mean. He had his own place in London after a while anyway.'

'He did?' Aedith and Drustan exchanged a glance.

'The official accommodation was never slept in,' explained Drustan. 'Makes sense if he had somewhere else to stay.'

'One of the first hostages he released owned property all over London. Valuable land. He tried to gift some to Angwin. He wouldn't accept it, but there was a flat kept laid out for him; he'd stay there whenever he was up in the city.'

'Do you remember where it was?' asked Aedith.

Andraste reached into a handbag slung from the side of the chair, tore a page from a diary, wrote something on it and handed it to Aedith. 'It sounds a strange thing to say – about an ex-terrorist who became a hostage negotiator who became a diplomat – but I honestly can't think of anyone who'd want Angwin dead, not in that manner, at least. The ghosts in his past were just that: ghosts.'

Aedith looked at the address. A quiet part of the city. She'd get Agapos to check it out.

'No sons or daughters,' asked Drustan. 'Revenge passed down a generation?'

Aedith felt herself start. Her spirit animal was whispering to her, feathers ruffling, although she couldn't make out it what it was trying to tell her.

'It happens. But it's a bullet in the back of the head on the walk back from the pub, or a knife in an alley, not a ritual in the woods.'

The black hoodie returned, bent next to Andraste, murmured something into her ear.

'Ah,' said Andraste. 'I'm afraid we have to cut this meeting short. It appears this location isn't quite as secure as I'd hoped. Apparently, another party are on their way to try and restart the takeover bid they had to abandon on a previous occasion.'

Two more men in combats appeared, both of them carrying machine pistols slung over their shoulders, neither paying Aedith or Drustan the slightest attention.

Aedith got to her feet. As she did, she realised what her spirit animal had been trying to tell her ever since Drustan had introduced the woman in front of them.

'Andraste Maol Nuadat?' she asked.

The men stopped moving.

'Captain Mercia,' warned Drustan in a low voice. Aedith barely heard him, conscious only of the woman in front of her and Lungpiecer, heavy in its holster.

'Ah,' said Andraste. Her voice was as calm as it had been since she had entered the room. 'I thought you knew. I don't go by that name any more.'

'I bet you don't,' said Aedith. Without the men moving, their weapons seemed suddenly very much closer to hand.

Andraste's gaze didn't leave Aedith's. 'I believe we can escape our past, to an extent,' she said. 'For what it's worth, my father kept me away from his work as much as he could. I'm glad his attempt to kill Earl Lod failed, and I bear no grudge for what happened after. It was a quicker death than any of my father's rivals would have given him.'

The black hoodie took the handles of Andraste's wheelchair, began backing it out of the room.

'We don't have to be our fathers' creatures,' continued Andraste. She was holding a small pistol in her lap, pointed at the floor, almost demurely. Had it been in her bag? Aedith hadn't even seen her hand move. 'Or if we are, we can choose not to follow in their footsteps. Not too closely, at least.'

'We should go,' said Drustan.

The Tribal child caught the coin Drustan tossed them, peeled themselves off Roadfucker and walked briskly away. Their phones had been placed on the driver's seat, with the windows still closed and no sign of the vehicle having been touched. A neat trick.

'You should have told me,' said Aedith, sitting down. She picked up her phone, turned it over in her hand. Like the car, it seemed as she left it, although she should probably get Banba to give it the once-over when they got back.

'On balance, yes,' said Drustan, closing his door with a quiet clunk. Aedith tried to buy Saxon where she could but wouldn't compromise on Nordic engineering. 'I apologise for the lack of forewarning. I hoped your desire to progress the case would outweigh any personal feelings you might have when you realised the identity of my contact.'

'The way you talk annoys me,' said Aedith. She turned the engine on, but kept her foot off the clutch, drumming her fingers on the steering wheel.

'Voice or syntax?' asked Drustan, interested. 'Our Saxon textbooks were always rather out of date, I'm afraid. Those of us who picked it up as a second language often sound overly formal. The younger generations don't seem to have the same problem, due to social media, I imagine. Should we be driving to the morgue now?'

Aedith said nothing. She picked up her phone, put it down again. Drustan glanced at the safe house, back to Aedith.

'I'd let it play out,' he said in a quiet voice. 'It'll be over by the time any backup gets here. No one's going to rush to get between two groups of armed Tribals anyway.'

Aedith said nothing.

'Andraste can look after herself,' said Drustan.

'It's everything,' said Aedith, engaging the clutch and releasing the handbrake, letting Roadfucker roll out onto the street. 'Voice, the way you speak, all of it. Maybe a bit of quiet on the way back, eh?'

Drustan nodded solemnly. As the safe house fell away from her rear-view mirror, Aedith thought she could hear a faint popping sound. It might have been a car engine backfiring. Or it might not.

TWELVE

A female officer stood politely at the hospital entrance, staring fixedly straight ahead until Aedith had finished giving Agapos Angwin's last known address. Drustan waited for a sideways glance from her but got nothing. Good discipline or a lack of imagination? Finally, Aedith put her phone away.

'He's going straight there,' she said. 'Without a warrant, so we may have to rely on his creativity, which doesn't *not* worry me. Constable Naeku.'

The woman nodded her head. 'Ma'am. Sir.'

Naeku couldn't have been older than her mid-twenties, dressed much like Aedith in black trousers and a white shirt, her hair arranged in a traditional Saxon manner: shaved close at the sides, the rest braided, held back with leather ties. Unlike Aedith, Masai ritual scarring was dusted across her face, raised dots across the backs of her hands. The more recent generation of Afro-Saxons were reviving interest in their history, keen to carve out a new identity separate from the pale-skinned warrior nation they'd washed up with centuries ago. One of the most popular television series across the Pan-African States for years had featured a Lagos police officer mistakenly sent on a cultural exchange to a street patrol in London. Learning the mysterious ways of the Saxons, the officer ultimately became better at Saxoning than those around him while still promoting Pan-African values, then forging his team of mixed creeds and colours into an effective crime-fighting unit in the process. Drustan had watched a few episodes while growing up on the reservations, cheaply dubbed into his own Tribal dialect. He'd enjoyed it at the time.

'I put Naeku in to attend the post-mortem as punishment for something,' said Aedith. 'Can't remember what.'

'Failure to return from shopping excursion with the correct biscuits, ma'am,' said Naeku.

'Ah yes,' said Aedith. 'Seems a bit harsh now.'

'Not a problem, ma'am.'

'Orva got anything interesting for us?'

'She wasn't sure, wanted to show you herself.'

Naeku led them through the warren of hospital corridors, signs carefully labelled in both Saxon and standardised Tribal, although Drustan couldn't help noticing a few attempts had been made to scratch off the latter. The place smelled like every other hospital he'd ever been in: cleaning products and something that always reminded him of, but probably wasn't, burned flesh.

'Mind where you step,' warned the tall, crop-haired woman in the lab coat as Naeku ushered them into the path lab before taking guard outside. 'Bit of a spillage.'

Aedith pulled a face.

'Coffee,' Orva added quickly.

The lab was larger, better-appointed than any Drustan had been in, with its own mini-morgue, drawers (presumably) stacked with those whose time in London had come to an unspecified end. Photos of Orva and her family tacked up on the walls and a

'World's Greatest Mum' mug almost but didn't quite manage to take the edge off the shiny blankness of it all.

Aedith followed Drustan's gaze to the back of the room, where a sheet-covered body lay on a trolley. 'Is that our boy?'

Orva mopped up the last of the spill with brisk efficiency and nodded.

'May I?' asked Drustan, taking the edge of the cloth.

'Detective Inspector Drustan, I presume,' said Orva. 'Please, go ahead.'

It wasn't Gorsedd Angwin lying on the trolley before Drustan. It may have been the same body he had last seen up on a tree, but where something of the man had lingered on their first encounter, it was gone now, just meat left. Drustan had seen bodies before, of course, laid out on slabs or in other, less dignified positions, and had grown used to their lesser, often shrunken, nature. But this one looked more at peace than others Drustan had seen, even considering the ragged slash across the throat, holes in wrists and ankles, and Orva's long, clean, Y-shaped cut down the centre of the chest.

'Traces of sedatives in the blood,' said Orva. 'Not enough to completely knock him out, I'd say, but make him compliant, certainly. Stomach contents consistent with what I'd been told was his last meal: salad, bread, fish.'

'Nothing else in the blood?' asked Aedith. 'No drug use? Heavy boozer?'

Orva shook her head. 'Healthy lad. A little wine in his stomach, no other alcohol.'

Aedith frowned. 'Wine? It was a Saxon bar he went to last thing, wasn't it?'

'It was,' said Drustan. 'I checked the notes.'

Saxon bars rarely sold wine. Those in the East drank beer or spirits, nothing in between.

'He didn't drink it long before he died,' said Orva. 'No puncture wounds anywhere, he wasn't injected with the sedative, so the wine was probably the delivery system.'

'So, he left the bar after taking a call on his phone,' said Aedith. 'He went to a second location, drank some wine, almost certainly drugged, after which he was taken into the forest where he… let's say, "met his end".'

'What's this?' Drustan pointed at Angwin's left side. A narrow horizontal wound, neater than the others.

'Stabbed,' said Orva. 'Between the second and third ribs. Didn't see it until I'd washed all the dried blood off. Probably the same weapon used to cut the throat.'

'A seax?' asked Drustan. Aedith said nothing. Long knives were a touchy subject for Saxons. Attempts had been made to cut down on the casual carrying of the national weapon, but nationalists had gleefully thrown their weight behind a culture war over the matter. Regular knife murders on a Friday night and the occasional school stabbing were a price most Saxons seemed willing to pay to distinguish themselves from effeminate Tribals or the boringly sensible Norse.

Orva nodded. 'Looks like that was the last injury, maybe to check the victim was really dead? Although I'd have thought cutting the throat would have done it, myself.'

Aedith held up a clipboard, examining a careful documentation of every one of Angwin's tattoos, ready to add to the database. The system was designed for Saxon ornamentation, but Celts had been fed into it along with the few Norse who'd ended their days South of the Wall. Drustan had heard talk of putting scarification in as well, but as most of those who went in for that were Afro-Saxon reeves, it had gone down quite badly with the police unions. Orva had copied out the symbol of the Fomóir onto the form along with the other hundred or so tattoos covering the body from calf to neck, in a neat hand, but only one, the smallest, was outlined in red.

'What's this?' Aedith held out the clipboard to Drustan. He glanced at the design, checked it against Angwin's body. There it was, just under the left collarbone where it would have been obscured by the blood from the wound at Gorsedd's throat: two intersecting horizonal arcs, extending a little beyond the meeting point at one end.

'That's what I wanted to talk to you about,' said Orva.

Drustan stared at the design until the two arcs suddenly resolved themselves into a rounded body, the lines twisting over and becoming a tail.

'It's a fish,' he said.

Orva nodded. 'I thought so too.'

Aedith cocked her head, confused. 'What style is that?'

Drustan shook his head. 'It's not Tribal.'

'Excellent. I'm so glad you're here.'

Drustan was still looking at the design. Too simple to be Tribal but not angular enough to be Saxon. He'd never seen anything quite like it.

'There's nothing like this on the database,' said Orva. 'Not on any database I've been able to access, anyway. Sometimes artists go off the reserv—' Aedith coughed discreetly – 'sorry, "get a bit creative". It's frowned on, but even then, they have to keep a record, or they lose their licence. This was either done abroad, it was unlicensed, or he did it himself. I'd rule out the last one, it's too neat.'

Drustan was still looking at the design. Unlike the elegant Tribal swirls that flowed across Anwin's body, branching out and linking back, the fish was separate, apart.

'The first one I saw I thought might be Caliphate,' said Orva. Her own tattoos were classic Saxon: harsh, angular depictions of Hel, goddess of death, mixed with scientific sigils, reaching up the sides of her face and disappearing into her hairline. Like all medical students, she would have shaved her head during her training, inscribed each year as it came. 'Something about the lines, the proportions. The hospital has a subscription for the database in Damascus, but when I tried to search for it – nothing'.

'Wait,' said Aedith. 'What do you mean, "the first one you saw?"'

Orva was already across the floor, pulling a handle of a drawer, sliding out the body of a woman in her mid-fifties. She was short, stocky, had lived harder than Angwin, broken capillaries across a lined face and bumpy, swollen nose, her skin tinged with yellow, her hair lank and grey.

'Ethel Noakes. Pulled out of Mother Thames two weeks ago,' said Orva. 'Hadn't been in there long, and nothing in the lungs so it wasn't the water that killed her.'

'Alcoholic, I assume,' said Aedith. The woman was Saxon, her tattoos indicating manual labour: runes for low-grade forklift skills, minor electronics assembly.

'Almost certainly,' said Orva, 'Although oddly enough, no alcohol in her system. Looked like she'd been sober for at least a month.' She pointed to ugly purple marks around the woman's neck, either side of a neat surgical cut going up to the chin. 'No, she was strangled. I went in, checked. Hyoid bone in her neck was broken, indicative of considerable force, then she was thrown in the river to cover it up. This is just a theory, mind. No one reported her missing, there's no budget to investigate. But look.'

Orva pointed to a tattoo on the woman's thigh. Cruder than Angwin's, resembling a balloon more than a fish, but when Drustan squinted, he could see it.

'That's when I checked the database the first time,' said Orva. 'No match. Didn't think much of it at the time.'

'Huh,' said Aedith.

Drustan looked up. 'Excuse me. No one reported this woman missing, but you still know her name?'

Orva laughed politely, then realised he was serious. 'Oh, I'm sorry. "Ethel Noakes" is slang for an unidentified corpse. "Edgar" for a male. Speaking of which…'

She pulled on a third handle, sliding out a younger male.

'Norse?' asked Drustan. Northerners did a more discreet line in tattoos, keen to distinguish themselves from their less sophisticated neighbours, but clan bloodlines were still important. This man – if you could call him a man, he looked barely in his twenties – had elaborate runic tracings running down his arms and across his thighs. He was neatly groomed, hair undercut and faded on the left side, with a drooping fringe on the right that looked as though it still had product in it.

'Prostitute. We do have a name for him: Ulf Haldorson, came from a reputable family above the Wall, but they wanted nothing to do with him. Homeless, died of a drugs overdose, marks of recent drug injection. He's been here a month while the city's lawyers try to get them to pay for his return. No sense spending money on a cremation here if they don't have to.'

Orva took the youth's right hand, held it up. On the white skin of the underarm...

'The fish again,' said Aedith.

'You said "drugs overdose",' said Drustan. 'Nothing here to suggest foul play?'

'People can be drugged against their will,' said Orva. 'Also, after I remembered the fish, I took a second look at the puncture marks. Tox screen suggested he'd been a long-term drug addict, although there were no other needle wounds. Going by damage to his nasal cavities, erosion of his septum, he snorted, he didn't inject.'

'This is all conjecture, of course,' said Aedith, thoughtfully tapping the clipboard against her chin.

Orva held up her hands. 'Absolutely. And you know the last thing I'd want to do is throw more cases at you if I wasn't sure. But there are others.'

'Others?' said Drustan. 'How many others?'

'Thor's cock,' said Aedith, eyes wide, 'You're not going to open the rest of those drawers, are you?'

'Too late for that,' said Orva, pulling a cardboard file from her desk. 'They've all been sent to the warm halls by the city. But this morning I went through recent, supposedly accidental deaths looking for the same foreign mark. There's another four in the records. One Norse, another Tribal, two Saxons, all on the edge of society, none apparently missed, all seemed to have made an attempt to clean up their lives a month or so before they died. All their deaths were concluded to be accidental.'

'The same killer?' asked Drustan. 'Or one group taking on another?'

Orva hesitated.

'Gut feelings are fine,' Aedith told her. 'Nothing's being written up yet.'

'The timeline, the manner of the killings – assuming these *are* all killings – suggest one individual. Patient, careful, maybe even charming.'

Aedith blinked. 'An odd word to use.'

'No,' said Drustan. 'I agree. There's something intimate about each of these – if the other two were murders. A killer who could persuade Angwin to drink drugged wine could talk Haldorson into taking an overdose, maybe even administer an injection. Your Ethel Noakes. She was strangled – was it from behind?'

Orva shook her head. 'Bruises consistent with someone's thumbs being pushed deep into her throat. Someone looked her in the eyes while they killed her.'

'Add "physical strength" to the list then,' said Aedith. 'Great, now I have to break it to Hengist we have a spree killer.'

'Perhaps,' said Drustan. 'Or perhaps not. Spree killers rarely change their M.O. This one was, what, cautious to the point we'd have difficulty confirming all these deaths as murders, then meets Gorsedd Angwin and decides to get creative?'

'Or more confident,' said Orva.

'Did I say how much I always enjoy our meetings?' asked Aedith sourly. Her phone rang. She retreated to the corner of the room, speaking in a low voice.

Drustan turned back to Angwin. 'What happens to him now?'

Orva pulled the sheet back over the body. 'No family. Severed ties with his tribe years ago. Normally that would mean a quick municipal cremation, same as with the other poor sods, but there's an unusual number of well-wishers offering to pay for his return when we're done. Anyway, I'll put everything back. I know your people like to go into the afterlife as intact as possible.'

Drustan nodded. 'He'll be taken West for a pyre, I imagine. Cedar wood and fine oils.' He'd attended a few of those, officiated at more than one. But Orva shook her head.

'I had a call earlier. Body to be taken to a private location here in London.' She smiled at Drustan's expression. 'He'd left instructions. People can surprise you as much in death in as life.'

'Hold that thought,' called Aedith from the other side of the room. She was putting her phone away. 'Agapos got to Angwin's lodgings.'

Her face looked grim, thought Drustan. 'Trouble getting in?'

'Not exactly. The door was already hanging off its hinges and armed cops posted outside. Special Branch. They wouldn't let Agapos in, which shows a certain confidence on their part. Our friend Tancred got an anonymous call an hour before our brothel madam coughed up, spotted a piss-obvious false wall and put his lads to work with sledgehammers.'

Orva was tidying up, closing the drawers. The movements of the living held little for her. Her interest had returned to the dead.

'You want me to ask what they found,' said Drustan.

'In the flat of our friend who'd had a breakdown after the death of his favourite sex worker, changed his ways, renounced violence and got the same tattoo as a load of people who've turned up dead? They found explosives, Detective Inspector. Enough to level an entire London borough. And guns. Crates of guns.'

THIRTEEN

'Think we might owe your guy a favour,' said Major Tancred.

Aedith had driven north to a long, quiet, leafy avenue. The houses were all at least four storeys high with immaculate gardens populated by Tribal nannies looking after blond-haired children. Drustan had also noted an abnormally high density of statues of a smug-looking woman whom he was eventually able to identify as Urd, the crone goddess of fate generally and wealth management specifically. Aedith had seemed to take great pleasure in parking Roadfucker across two private parking bays.

When he exited the car, Drustan could only think he had never seen so many police vans in one place, and those were just the marked vehicles. A small crowd had gathered, their camera phones pointed towards the steady stream of grey-suited Special Branch officers still filing down the stairs, each carrying a squat black plastic case. One of the police vans, the one with noticeably more antennae and aerials on its roof, had its own camera, semi-discreetly housed inside a smoked glass ball, just above the rear doors. It slowly panned back and forth, recording the crowd as they recorded its masters in turn.

Aedith and Drustan passed quietly through the crowd, Agapos holding up the tape barrier for them. The uniformed officer next to him made no effort to help. Special Branch had their own crowd control plods who looked like standard uniforms but with no badge numbers on their lapel. The seaxes slung from their stab-proof vests wouldn't follow regulation either. Most would have engravings that would get a standard beat cop six months' desk duty to quietly reflect on the consequences of their actions.

Agapos remained on the street, the only Afro-Saxon reeve in view. To give Tancred his due, Drustan thought, he must have worked hard to get above Special Branch's notorious alabaster ceiling.

Tancred had been all smiles as he greeted Aedith at the front door of the converted flats. He dutifully led her up the stairs, one member of the service helping another. He hadn't appeared to have noticed Drustan at all.

"'Our guy?'" Aedith asked Tancred, as they stood aside to let another crate go past.

'Whoever nailed our Tribal friend to a tree,' said Tancred, 'it seems he might have averted a terrorist spectacular that would have made us look like a right bunch of nobs. You ever catch him, I'm tempted to put him up for a commendation.'

The front door was hanging off its hinges. By Drustan's estimation, the lock had been blown out by a shotgun, a breaching ram doing the rest of the work.

'Made a bit of a mess, I'm afraid,' apologised Tancred, as they stepped into the ruin that had once been a smart, understated flat with good access to the only Underground station this far north. The false wall had been smashed through no more carefully than the front door.

Tancred heaved up the final plastic case, snapping the catch and pulling up the lid to reveal half a dozen gleaming black handguns, snug in their foam packaging.

'Imagine this lot out on the streets,' he tutted. 'Going toe-to-toe with our brave men and women in uniform. Doesn't bear thinking about.'

He snapped the lid shut and handed it over to be taken away.

Aedith was refusing to be drawn. 'I was told there were explosives?'

Tancred smiled broadly. 'Bomb squad took those first. Don't trust the Specials with that sort of thing, but we're allowed to play with the guns.' The smile fell away. 'Commercially available stuff, although you need a licence, obviously. Probably from construction projects. Detonators were from a mining company, over the border. They'll have some questions to answer.'

Drustan walked up to the remains of the false wall, covering a door leading to the large spare room where the cache had been found. He pushed his thumbnail into the line where the new plaster met the existing architecture. It sank into the white surface easily.

'Don't worry about that, we've already swept for fingerprints,' called Tancred. It almost sounded friendly. 'Wouldn't want our Tribal colleague getting caught up in our sweep,' he said to Aedith. 'There'll be a lot of torcs pulled out of their beds tonight. Speaking of which – your friend Deedra.'

'You have evidence she's implicated in this?'

'Only circumstantial.' That the Kesair owned construction companies across London and mining companies out West was public knowledge. 'But we're going to have some serious questions for her, and the last thing I need is her or any other of our Tribal countrymen getting advance notice, assembling the lawsmiths before we're quite ready.'

'I think you misunderstand the nature of my relationship with Deedra,' said Aedith mildly. 'Also, apparently, whether I'm a professional police officer or not.'

Tancred backed away; his hands raised in mock-contrition. 'Merely a word to the wise,' he said, then glanced at Drustan. 'Consider it a tasty berry thrown to the birds. They can choose to pick it up or ignore it, such are the freedoms we have here in the East. My commiserations on the passing of your contact, by the way.'

Drustan frowned. 'Gorsedd Angwin wasn't known to me before his death.'

Tancred clapped his hands to his head, a pantomime gesture of contrition. 'Apologies, never meant to confuse you. I'm talking about Fairgus Blaenu. The courier.'

Drustan didn't respond.

'We took him into our custody a couple of hours ago. Your Commander Hengist only just found out about the transfer. I've been filling him in on the details, although I'd have to describe his attitude as unenthusiastic.' Tancred made a sad clicking noise with his tongue.

'If you don't mind,' said Drustan evenly, 'I guaranteed Blaenu his safety while he continued to cooperate, so I'd very much like to hear the details as well.'

Drustan knew Aedith was looking at him but kept his attention solely on Tancred. He also kept his hands in full view and was careful to make no sudden movements. In fact, he made no movements at all.

'He did cooperate,' said Tancred. 'Gave us lots of useful information, in fact, although sadly his cooperation ended very suddenly, at the point when he removed the sidearm from one of my officers and shot himself in the head.'

'I see,' said Drustan. Aedith said nothing. 'I trust you reprimanded the officer concerned for being so careless as to make a loaded weapon so easily accessible to a prisoner.'

'It was Sergeant Godric here,' said Tancred, waving expansively at a squat scarred officer in an expensive suit, the value of which seemed inversely proportional to the investment put into the teeth revealed when he grinned at them, being mostly black. The tattoos that crawled around his right eye and up across his bald pate reminded Drustan of Saxon contractors he had run into across the Mughal Empire from time to time, who wore necklaces made from dried human ears and made jokes about chasing civilians into minefields.

'I did ask the Sergeant if he needed time away from work, therapy to deal with post-traumatic stress and so on,' continued Tancred, 'but he insisted he carry on with his duties.'

Godric picked up the last crate and walked out of the flat.

'That man's a godsdamn hero,' said Tancred.

'Did you see those weapons?' Aedith asked.

She hadn't said a word on the way back to the station. Sensing her mood, the squad were keeping their heads down. Banba had her earphones in, hood down so low over her face it was a wonder she could see the columns of data scrolling down her monitor.

Drustan nodded.

'Since when,' Aedith continued, 'did the Fomóir have access to brand-new gear? Correct me if I'm wrong, but the last time the Fo' were able to get themselves some shooters, they did well to get a crate of hunting rifles from some minor Pan-African arms corporation who wanted to get shot of their factory seconds. Half the time they didn't even have the right ammunition.'

'It was overkill, agreed,' said Drustan, 'but are you saying Special Branch managed to plant all that in such a short space of time?'

Aedith folded her arms, leaned against a filing cabinet. 'Oh, it was planted all right. Gorsedd's being fitted up, but not by Special Branch. You're right, they're not that quick. And Tancred's happy enough with such a big score he's not going to ask too many questions.'

Drustan looked down at his thumb, still whitened from the plaster. 'That false wall was put in after Gorsedd was killed. Maybe the same evening.'

'Seems likely,' said Aedith. 'Although I have enough trouble believing a lone man could drag our vic into the forest and nail him to a tree – I *really* can't believe he popped back to Angwin's secret flat to plaster over twenty-odd crates of special-ops level weapons and ammunition. You're absolutely sure Deedra doesn't stand to gain from the Summit being subverted?'

'I can believe she's playing different sides against each other,' said Drustan. 'That's how her tribe have survived for centuries in hostile territory. But she's smarter than this, by reputation, at least. And if the Kesair want someone dead, they don't leave bodies for the Saxons to find. Or anyone else.'

'I'm also wondering,' said Aedith slowly, 'why she'd be bothering to source enough fertiliser for a bomb if she also had access to mining explosives and detonators. This whole thing stinks. Godsdammit, a couple of days ago I'd have cut through the crap, just phoned her up and asked her. Not an option now.'

She jerked her head over to Constable Naeku, who'd just set a pile of paper printouts down on her desk. 'Got anywhere with the tattooists?'

'None of the registered Tribal artists know anything about a fish design. Not in this style, anyway. When I've worked through the list I'll get onto the unlicensed and officially retired, but it'll take a while.'

'This might speed the process.' Commander Hengist had entered a room full of police officers without any of them noticing, which meant either they were quite poor at their jobs, or their commanding officer was that rare thing: a big man who really was light on his feet. Looking less genial than earlier, he thrust a sheet of paper at Aedith. She frowned. 'What's this?'

'Appeared on my desk an hour ago. Apparently, there's an artist near the Bridge who specialises in fish tattoos. Or at least is prepared to do them no questions asked.'

'You don't know where it came from?'

'You're asking if I took it to Forensics for fingerprint analysis before I brought it down to you? No, Captain Mercia, I did not. I assume someone at the front desk took a message and it found its way up to me instead of the big room full of reeves milling about asking questions about fertiliser when they're supposed to be tracking a spree killer. Maybe I could leave this with you and get back to my internal politicking?'

'Sir, yes sir.'

Hengist crashed out of the room, making a lot more noise on the way out than he had on the way in. Drustan moved closer to Aedith. 'Does he often spin on a penny like that?'

'I wouldn't say he was placid, exactly, but I've never seen him worked up about a misplaced tip-off like that before. We could go and chase it up now, I guess.'

Drustan nodded, but something about Hengist's demeanour had rung false. Underneath the bluster, he had seemed worried, even anxious. Or he was reading too much into the behaviour of someone he barely knew.

'You coming?'

Drustan nodded.

*

'I practically lived here when I was a student,' said Aedith as they walked down the road, following the instructions on her phone. She'd thought the address felt familiar. The street where the tattooist had his parlour wasn't close enough to the bars to count as officially vibrant, but with enough music shops and art supply stores to pull the students away from their booze for long enough to waste a decent percentage of their student loans. She'd certainly converted enough of hers into vinyl before she discovered drinking.

'It's not going to be easy to get a statement out of them. If they're even open.'

Drustan nodded. Aedith suspected it was the same across the Kingdoms. Tattooists liked to keep their own hours, often working from early afternoon through to the evening. They were artists as much as medical staff, trusted by clients to engrave their darkest stories upon their skin, transcribing tragedies, victories, lost loves and hard-won triumphs. Saxon artists were under no obligation to reveal to the reeves any stories told in the parlour: entire court cases had established this as an absolute right.

'Could always threaten to take away their licence,' she said. 'That's worked before.'

When Aedith's phone finally beeped, indicating it had led them to the right address, the tattoo parlour was closed and clearly had been for a few days, going by the small pile of free papers and takeaway menus building up on the other side of the glass door.

She wiped the glass with her sleeve, peered in. No lights inside but everything was orderly, a cloth over the chair, all the tools put away neatly. She took a few steps back, looked up. A flat above the shop, but with a 'For Rent' sign, so the neighbours weren't going to be any help. Any other part of the city, she might have been embarrassed by a 'No Unemployed, No Tribals' sign, but that wouldn't have gone down well here. A stout man in an ill-fitting sports jacket walked past them, steadfastly refusing to acknowledge a Saxon female and a Tribal male looking as if they were seconds away from breaking into a building. Only when he got past them, noticeably quickening his pace, did Aedith spot the keys dangling from his hand being quietly slipped back into his pocket.

'What do you think?'

Drustan watched the man go. He wasn't speeding up, but he wasn't slowing down either. 'I think that's someone who was about to let himself into his tattoo parlour and changed his mind at the last minute.'

Aedith nodded. 'Hey!' The man broke into a lumbering run. She sighed. 'I honestly don't know what I expected.'

At a different time of day enough people might have been around for the man to have slipped into a crowd or found enough anti-establishment types to slow Aedith and Drustan's progress with an outstretched foot or shove in the back. As it was, they passed only an elderly and bemused woman who clutched her shopping more tightly to her at the sight of Drustan but otherwise seemed determined to ignore what was playing out in front of her.

She probably made the right call, Aedith thought, catching up with the man a second before Drustan, elbowing him into a shop front and letting him sprawl to the ground, yelling in pain.

'Police!'

'I am police, you prick,' said Aedith, pulling out her warrant card. 'Detective Captain Mercia, this is my colleague from across the border, Detective Inspector Drustan.' She paused, frowning. 'First name or surname?'

'It's complicated,' said Drustan.

'Of course it bloody is. Come on you, up you get. We're going to have ourselves a chat in your shop.'

FOURTEEN

The tattooist's name was Gif Denby, he told them, once he'd let them into his shop and locked the door behind them. Aedith put on a brew as a means of apology for shoving him into a window.

Denby came as a powerful disappointment to Drustan. The skin artists he'd encountered, here and in the West, were a mystical elite, as imposing as priests, ready to face death rather than betray their secrets and those of their clients. Apart from being physically unimpressive, Denby barely shut up the moment he'd hung up his coat. He didn't even have many visible marks of his own, just a few on his arms and hands denoting a childhood spent on the south coast, an interest in fishing, and allegiance to a few traditionally unlucky and unloved sports clubs.

'It was my wife's business, truth be told, the studio,' he said, sipping gratefully from the chipped mug Aedith had handed him.

Denby's studio, like all Saxon studios – and they were almost always Saxon, Tribal artists tending towards the peripatetic and often working out of vans or even boats – was plastered with pictures of clients' artwork. It was all very straightforward: sporting achievements, significant work milestones, important birthdays. There was a strong municipal vibe. He probably made a small but steady income from local schools sending trophy winners and valedictorians. Drustan didn't see any fish anywhere or recognise any of the faces.

'I only got trained so I could help her out when it was busy. And then she left, and my taxi business collapsed with the whole gig-economy nonsense, so this was all I had. The Fishers started coming to me a few years ago because I could be... discreet, if you know what I mean. They told their mates and things grew from there. But they went quiet a few weeks ago. Then stuff about them starts popping up on the socials, gets me looking over my shoulder. I've hardly been to work since; started taking delivery jobs instead. Bit worried I've got myself in amongst a bunch of maniacs, to be honest. Is it true what they're saying? That they're behind the whole Summit, trying to take over all the Kingdoms?'

Drustan tried to look as though this wasn't the first he'd ever heard of 'Fishers'.

'No evidence for that,' managed Aedith, who was presumably doing the same. 'At all.' She scrolled through the pictures on her phone until she found Angwin's morgue shots; pointed at the fish mark. 'This yours?'

Denby nodded. One of the few things he had in common with the other artists Drustan had encountered: he wasn't squeamish. 'One of the first guys who came to me. Friend of a friend, sort of thing, five years ago maybe?'

'And let me guess, you were slipped a little extra cash on condition you never got round to registering it on the database?'

Denby squirmed. "They said their whole thing was starting fresh, turning over a new leaf. So, I didn't... write things down as much as I should have, maybe.'

Aedith kept her face unchanged. Drustan only just managed not to curse out loud. What they'd gained by Denby being more than happy to spill the beans to the first person he encountered, they were going to lose because everything he'd done had, by the sound of it, been under the counter. That meant no records, no paper trail.

'All right, Denby. At least tell us how many Fishers you marked over the years.'

'Maybe... thirty? Could have been more.'

'All in secret?'

Denby nodded, downcast. He was going to lose his licence now and he knew it. Something told Drustan this was just the latest of Denby's businesses that was about to go under. He'd pop back up again with something new, until that collapsed as well.

'All right,' said Drustan. He had a special soothing voice he liked to use on members of the public who weren't used to being asked questions by someone wearing a torc, and he used it now. 'Can you remember the first Fisher who came to you? How long ago was that?'

Denby furrowed his brow, a parody of someone being asked a difficult question.

'That depends,' he said. 'The first person who wanted a Fisher mark, you mean? Because that was about six years ago.'

'That's... very helpful,' said Drustan, and left it to Aedith to follow up.

'Wait,' she said. 'Let me phrase this carefully. Did you ever meet a Fisher before that? One who *didn't* want the mark added?'

'About two years before that,' said Denby, promptly. 'A big guy came in, asking to get his mark covered up. That was the first time I ever saw one.'

'He wanted a mark *covered up?*' Aedith's tone was of utter disbelief. To get a mark altered was one thing. You could do that, with special dispensation. Trans people did it all the time – it was no longer considered rewriting history but revealing the story that had been there, hidden, all along. But getting a mark completely covered up was considered beyond the pale, the move of a psychopath, or someone beyond all hope. Even when undercover officers and intelligence agents were allowed to change marks, or add fake ones, they had to use special inks, given under licence, that would fade in a few years. And they were offered generous counselling packages afterwards, help to reconstruct a psyche that might otherwise become fractured, open to infection from dark spirits, psychological predators drawn to a rend in a person's identity.

'That was the start of problems between the wife and me,' said Denby gloomily. 'She was against it. I thought if it's bringing him unhappiness, if we could cover it up with a fake birthmark or something, what's the harm?'

He was definitely going to lose his licence now, thought Drustan. There was nothing either of them could do.

'Can you describe him?' Aedith's voice was calm, focused.

'Um,' said Denby. 'Blond. Big guy, at least six feet. Early thirties, maybe? Had the Fisher mark on his neck.'

'His neck?' asked Drustan. 'Not his chest?'

Denby shook his head. 'Side and back of his neck. It was faded too; he must have had it from years back. Stretched as well, like he'd had it as a kid, maybe and then got a lot bigger. Worked out a lot, I reckon, from the look of him.'

'"Physical strength",' said Aedith quietly.

'What else can you tell us about him?' asked Drustan, trying to keep the eagerness out of his voice. Sound too invested and witnesses either clammed up or started exaggerating, trying to please you. 'Did he have an accent?'

'Kentish way, maybe? I said we couldn't help, but then, when my wife had gone, I told him to come back the next day when she'd be out. I did it then, covered it up to look like a skin condition, sort of thing.'

'Did you talk while he was having the work done? Anything at all could help us here. Did he mention a workplace, perhaps? Did he pay by card?'

'Can't say he was the chatty type, exactly. He paid in cash, left as soon as I was done.'

Of course. Too much to hope a quick phone call to a bank might find their killer.

'No indication of his job, where he worked?'

Denby shook his head.

'All right,' said Aedith. 'What about other marks? School, workplace? Sports, maybe?'

'He was wearing overalls, long sleeves. Didn't have any other marks on his face that I remember.'

Drustan perked up. 'Overalls? Like a decorator?'

'They were dark. Could have been army surplus. Although when he paid, I did see something on his wrist. A bird. A sparrow, maybe? I could draw that for you?'

He quickly sketched out a small woodland bird on a scrap of paper. Surprisingly, Denby had talent.

Drustan was struck by a thought. 'Could you draw his face?'

'Um.' Denby looked more ashamed of himself than at any time since they'd met him. 'The thing is, I don't really do faces. My wife was very good at them, but I really did animals and circuit diagrams. I'm really good at those though, if I could interest you, maybe?'

The hope that suddenly appeared on his face was pitiful.

'I'm all right, thanks,' said Aedith.

*

'Do you think he's in danger?' asked Drustan when they were back outside the studio.

'I think if the killer wanted to eliminate him, he'd have done it a while back. I'll ask a local uniform to keep an eye on the place, but as long as he only swings by to pick up the post, I suspect he'll be fine.'

Drustan was unconvinced. 'And if it becomes known our friendly tattooist had a rep for helping out the Fishers?'

'Then maybe he won't be fine. I left him my phone number anyway. Our friend Denby might seem inept, but I wouldn't underestimate his survival instincts.'

FIFTEEN

'Closest thing we've got to a lead so far,' said Aedith, standing in front of a whiteboard on which she'd written 'SAXON', 'SOUTH-EAST', 'FISH MARK (COVERED) ON NECK', 'SPARROW ON WRIST' 'SIX FOOT' and 'OVERALLS (DARK)'. 'Someone we should be looking to eliminate from our enquiries, anyway.'

The squad filled the room, some sitting quietly, others leaning, arms folded. Agapos stood on the other side of the whiteboard, glaring at them indiscriminately.

'You lot on foot patrol, get interviewing anyone near the bar on the night of Angwin's death, see if they remember anyone fitting this description. Naeku, you've been on the database, any clue where that sparrow comes from?'

Naeku, perched demurely on a chair at the front of the room, nodded her head. 'Yes, Captain. It was a care-home thing. Children's homes specifically. Turns out they used to mark kids in care with the home's totem animal on the wrist back in the day, but they banned it around twenty years ago. There isn't a database exactly, but I'm going through the records.'

'All right. Focus on the South-East specifically and let me know as soon as you find anything. The rest of you, look into these fish marks. Ask around. You get a decent lead or spot anyone who's got one, quietly make a note and we'll come back, don't want to spook them.'

A reeve in a crumpled suit pointed to the older cop with the moustache. 'What about Leofstan, Captain? Reckon we should put him in a cell for the time being, just to be on the safe side?'

Leofstan grinned, holding up his arm, shirtsleeves rolled back. A salmon, or possibly an eel, stretched from his upper arm down to his hand, the thumb making its lower jaw, the next two fingers the top of its head. He opened and closed his hand, making the beast snap fearsome teeth together.

Aedith nodded thoughtfully. 'Worth considering, Constable, but you're not looking at the bigger picture. Then where would the city go for entertainment at children's parties?'

A laugh ran through the room at that. Drustan scratched his jaw, mentally taking notes. Few Tribal investigations involved more than four or five officers. Holding the attention and respect of a room this size required a particular skillset. It wasn't one Drustan could see himself acquiring any time soon.

Aedith continued. 'We're not looking for any old fish mark, otherwise we'd be hauling in every angling club between here and the Wall. It has to be in this style.' She pointed to a copy on the whiteboard. Again, Drustan couldn't help thinking how alien it looked, with its single looping line, the straight edge on the tail. Nothing like Saxon or Tribal styles at all. If the Caliphate didn't consider tattoos haram, it surely would have belonged there.

But the reeve in the suit wasn't finished yet.

'No offence, Captain, but are we sure it's not a Tribal-on-Tribal thing? Seems like we could save a lot of time by focusing on that particular community.' He avoided looking at Drustan as he said it.

'Good of you to consider the logistics of the operation,' said Aedith in a voice dry as dust, 'but information as yet only divulged on a need-to-know basis suggests those carrying the mark come from a variety of ethnic groups, although no Afro-Saxons reported so far.'

Agapos nodded solemnly at that one, making a play of lifting the sacred coin that hung around his neck and kissing it. They had a practised double act going, the princess captain and her Afro-Saxon sergeant. So much of the Saxon world had a performative aspect to it, Drustan thought, loath though any of them would be to admit it. Any theatre, outside seasonal rituals or mystery plays devoted to whichever deity was in ascendance at the moment, was held in great suspicion, regarded as a foreign intrusion or a cheap attempt to manipulate emotions that would come to no good. But get a group of Saxons together and one of them would always start playing the fool in one way or another.

'So,' concluded Aedith, 'let's spread the net wide and try and leave our prejudices at home, shall we?'

The room didn't like that one as much, but they seemed to accept it. The reeve in the suit opened his mouth for one more dig, but the officer next to him dug an elbow into his ribs to shut him up. If they didn't agree with their captain, they weren't prepared to make a stand over it. The performance worked. Breaking apart into clumps of threes and fours, the reeves set out to carry the word of Detective Captain Mercia throughout the land. Or London, anyway.

SIXTEEN

The next morning, under the guise of trying to figure out the coffee machine, Drustan stood for a while watching information flow into the open-plan office. Nothing got past Agapos's desk, which suggested every piece of information that had been phoned in, texted, emailed or gleaned from confidential informants had been a total bust.

'You're in the way of the biscuits,' said Banba.

'My apologies,' said Drustan, and stepped to one side, but Banba didn't move.

'I've got a problem,' she said, in a low voice. 'Sort of a dilemma.'

'I see.'

'I've been digging into the order placed with the courier, trying to work out where it came from?'

'Diligent work, it sounds like.'

'Mmm,' said Banba, who still hadn't looked him in the eye. 'Except I've run into an issue.'

'Let me guess,' said Drustan. 'You've come up with a useful piece of information in a way that was quite creative but wouldn't allow you to share it with your actual serving police colleagues.'

Banba looked at him now, alarmed.

'You have a noisy typing style which noticeably ramped up an hour ago, then suddenly stopped,' said Drustan. 'Also, you keep sighing.'

The Pict seemed to come to some sort of decision. 'Okay, fine. The courier firm bought a cheap off-the-peg website. Didn't bother changing the password from "password". Doesn't allow you to make edits, but if you were, you know, curious, you could go back in the timeline, see old drafts, revision, orders that have been cancelled. Except that's technically counter to the "preserving evidence" laws, so if you did find something interesting you couldn't put it in a report and having done it in the first place could get someone in quite a lot of trouble. If she *had* done it, which she definitely didn't. If it even is a "she".'

'I understand,' said Drustan.

'So, *possibly*, I have a bit of information that might be really useful to the case, but no way of handing it over without incriminating myself.'

'Show me.'

'I'm ashamed to tell you I fell asleep for a moment just now and went on a brief dreamquest,' said Drustan, letting himself into Aedith's office. 'As my people are known to do every now and then. It's one of the reasons we're rarely employed as long-distance lorry drivers.'

He nodded at Banba, standing anxiously outside the door. She scuttled back to her desk. Aedith watched her go, then turned her attention back to Drustan.

'Uh huh.'

Drustan closed the door behind him.

'Obviously you can't alter the direction of a police investigation on the basis of one man's wild imaginings, even if he is a fellow officer, but I feel it would be remiss of me not to bring it up.'

Aedith opened her mouth to say something, then shut it again and pondered for a moment before nodding thoughtfully. 'Certainly, it would be culturally insensitive to ignore any information a colleague might bring me, just because I don't personally believe in all that hocus pocus, smoke and bones bullshit.'

'Glad to hear it,' said Drustan. 'My vision concerns the order the courier company took, to move that phone around for a few hours.'

'Agapos checked with them,' said Aedith, looking suddenly disheartened. She was a bear, sitting on the riverside, waiting for a big, tasty trout, and all Drustan had brought her was an old stick. 'The order was made anonymously, paid online. Untraceable.'

'Indeed,' said Drustan. 'But that was the *second* order.'

Aedith now looked more interested.

'There'd been an earlier request, just a few minutes before, which was then deleted. Quite hastily. Same request, but this one was from an existing account.'

'Well, hello,' said Aedith.

'A small firm named, rather blandly, Ash and Stone. Registered as office supplies, or at least they were. They shut down yesterday, scrubbed all traces of themselves off the internet, disappeared from our view as best they could. Remarkable. Unless you were to look very closely indeed, they may as well never have existed.'

'Almost as if,' said Aedith, tapping a pen thoughtfully on her desk, 'someone cocked up and made a link they were never supposed to make, fessed up and then they had to burn the whole place to be on the safe side. Intern given a job above their pay grade, you think?'

'Or someone rushing a job.'

'Office supplies,' mused Aedith. 'Why did you say, "as best they could"?'

'I'm afraid what the raven gives with his left claw, he often takes back with his right.'

Aedith's expression was unreadable.

'I found one connection to the case from Ash and Stone,' Drustan continued. 'The company had used Blaenu as a courier before, specifically requested him for a PR event a couple of months ago. Launch of a new fashion website. Officially, Blaenu was contracted to take a few grands' worth of flowers, although the vagueness of the order would suggest his delivery was less botanical and more…'

'Pharmaceutical,' Aedith finished for him. 'And I think I know where the raven's going with this one. The fashion launch was for Deedra, wasn't it? Who we can't even cough near without Special Branch closing us all down.'

Drustan nodded.

'Well, shit,' said Aedith. 'Still, tell Banba, excellent work.'

'I'm sure I don't know what you're talking about,' said Drustan smoothly.

Agapos tapped on the door, opened it a crack. 'It's Naeku. Says she's got somewhere with the children's home.'

Naeku had unrolled a map of the South-East and spread it across the biggest table in the investigation room. 'I made a list of every care home in the area, open or closed, over the last twenty years. Some of the bigger ones did mark their kids back in the day, before it was banned, but those are on the tattoo database and none of them are sparrows, so we can count them out. That left eight, six of which are still open, and happy to confirm they never marked their kids. Two remaining, both closed down years ago. The first I can't find anything about, but the second was under investigation for a while. They never found anything officially untoward, or put it in the report if they did, but there was a copy of one of the home's financial statements.'

Naeku laid a slim pile of documents on top of the map, the uppermost a photocopied cover of an institutional crest: a stylised boar made up of intersecting runes, facing right, with 'Rowan Berry House' written underneath in stern letters.

Aedith looked at Drustan. He shrugged.

'I'm not seeing it,' said Aedith.

Naeku suppressed the faintest possible hint of a sigh, pointed to a long curving line along the beast's back, traced it to a sharp angle back along its underside where it reached back once more then formed a loop connecting up with a straight line.

'A fish,' said Drustan in wonderment.

'*The* fish,' said Naeku. She moved across to the map, circled a small town with a red pen. 'It's here. Or should be. The home itself closed down eight years ago, but the building was never sold. So the owners are still around, even if they're not answering their phones.'

'All right then,' said Aedith. 'Good work, Constable. DI Drustan and I will check it out.'

SEVENTEEN

Drustan had never been further East in the Three Kingdoms than London. He'd always found descriptions of the city as 'cosmopolitan' over-egged: seeing a Moorish tourist every now and then or a bunch of Mughal students spending their gap year building playgrounds for disadvantaged Saxon youths didn't make you the next Paris or Damascus. But once Roadfucker had left the confines of the city and got out into what could charitably be called the 'countryside', if you ignored the data centres and Pan-African corporate farms, he could feel the bloodlines narrowing. He'd be surprised if there was a single Tribal within a hundred miles.

Aedith seemed to sense his unease. 'If you think this is rough,' she said, not taking her eyes from the potholed road, 'you should try the island of Sheppey some time. It's like the arse-end of the Saxon gene pool, webbed feet and monobrows, the lot. We used to get sent there for riot training sometimes. Just had to turn up in the vans and it would kick off before we even opened the doors, it was terrifying. We found out later one of our instructors had family there. They made a nice living kicking the shit out of cadets twice a week.'

Drustan nodded politely. He had zero intention of ever visiting Sheppey. 'What's Mercia like?'

'You ever likely to go there?'

'Who knows?'

'You should, one day, if you get the chance. It's prettier than this. Rolling hills, forests, flowing rivers. My family are from the northern end before you're into the real hill clans and then the Wall. My father still thinks I should talk like a Mercian.'

The last in exaggeratedly flat vowels. The Mercian accent was legendarily associated with power. A good third of the Saxon High Kings since the Norse had been pushed north of the Wall had been Mercian, and Lod's clan had almost always been at their side. In the rare event that a Mughal film or a Pan-African mini-series featured a Saxon, they liked to use one with as close an approximation of a Mercian accent as they could get.

'By the way,' said Aedith, slowing the car to ease it round a particularly spectacular pothole. 'What do you make of Constable Naeku?'

He looked at her, surprised. 'She seems like good police? And smart. The only one of us to spot the fish hidden in the boar, apart from anything else.'

'Oh, sure,' said Aedith. 'Absolutely.' She shot Drustan a look that could only be described as *sly*. 'But you know, on a personal level.'

Drustan frowned. Was Aedith pushing him for dirt on her junior officer? He hadn't thought she was the type. 'I can't say I've had much time to get to know your team outside the office,' he said carefully. 'If you're trying to tell me Constable Naeku's personal opinions regarding working alongside a Tribal officer are in any way negative, I have to say she's kept things very professional in the workplace.'

'I'm trying to tell you Naeku fancies you,' said Aedith. 'You fucking plum.'

'Oh,' said Drustan.

After a prolonged silence, Aedith handed Drustan her phone and told him to navigate.

'Nice-looking place,' said Aedith. Roadfucker's passenger door had closed behind Drustan with a whisper, but Aedith's comment was enough to make a crow detach itself noisily from a nearby tree in protest. It didn't go far, just landed on the roof of Rowan Berry House, eyeing them first with one eye, the other.

The building was large: three storeys high, with extensions on the side that reached back into overgrown woodland that had once been a large garden; rusting play equipment just visible, slowly being swallowed up by brambles and climbing vines. The whole place looked long-abandoned, most of the ground-floor windows boarded up, the perimeter's six-foot chain-link fence cut through in multiple places; probably intruders looking to strip the valuable copper from roof or walls.

Drustan had been startled by the familiarity of the small towns they had driven through on the way to Rowan Berry House. He had grown up in settlements just like them. The architecture was different, the graffiti in another language, but the people huddled in doorways in hand-me-down clothes had the same lined and weary faces, the same dull expressions. Here was another place on the edge of the map, where no tourists would visit in search of spiritual enlightenment or for the incredible views.

At least on the way, Drustan had spotted signs of life. It was clear that no one had been to Rowan Berry House for some time. The front door hung open on one hinge, revealing broken glass and more graffiti inside.

'Do you think it looked much better when it was open?' asked Aedith.

'Maybe,' said Drustan. 'I grew up in places like this.'

Aedith eyed him curiously. 'How was it?' Idly, she picked up a loose piece of wood, banged it against the doorframe. 'Might be vagrants inside. Give them a little warning so we don't take them by surprise, stop someone with hepatitis lunging at us with a broken bottle.'

The sound echoed around them, dying without consequence.

Drustan shrugged. 'Some were fine. Others less so. Shall we go in?'

Aedith nodded, took a torch from her coat pocket and clicked it on. She seemed unaffected by the blank melancholy of the place, although Drustan noticed she kept her other hand near her holstered weapon as she stepped over the threshold. He followed her, glancing behind him as he did so. The air was stale and cold. It felt like they were walking into a trap.

Someone had been in the home before them. Perhaps many people. A room that had once been a dining hall had wooden chairs and long tables overturned, some piled up and broken in one corner, blackened where someone had seemingly tried and failed to start a fire.

Aedith pointed her torch at the wall. Someone had carved 'Fuck You Father Oswin' into the plaster. 'Is that a name or a title? Where you grew up, anyone ever called "Father" like that?'

'No,' said Drustan.

Aedith grunted. 'Hold this, would you?'

He held the torch steady for Aedith while she pulled her phone out, took a photograph.

*

The second level was less disturbed, which wasn't to say untouched. Someone had made a half-hearted attempt at ransacking the place: tearing open cartons of cardboard boxes, strewing the contents aside, but seemingly giving up when they'd realised they contained only small red books. Drustan picked one up, opened the covers. The pages inside were thin, dense with text, the occasional woodcut.

Aedith appeared at his shoulder. 'What is that?'

'The Fishers' sacred book, looks like. Every cult has an operations manual these days.'

'Anything good?'

He flipped through it. 'Desert tribes, monsters, fathers begetting sons…'

'I look forward to it appearing on a streaming service soon. Come on.'

Drustan slipped the book into his pocket and followed her. The door across the hall opened up into a big room filled with chairs and desks, facing a larger table at the far end. A classroom?

'I have a feeling,' said Aedith, taking out her phone and pointing it at each wall in turn, 'this is where our killer found his inspiration.'

The walls were covered with paintings of a man – presumably the same man – bearded, hung up on two crossed wooden beams, arms outstretched, wrists and ankles pierced with nails, blood dripping from a wound in his side. If he'd worn a torc, it could easily have been Angwin.

Drustan turned around slowly. The pictures were across all four walls. 'I can't imagine it was easy to get your schoolwork done, surrounded by all this.'

He picked up a pile of untouched pictures from a table, black and white line drawings, waiting to be coloured in: a trumpet, a burning tree, a naked couple against a jungle background, a serpent wrapped around them, its tongue flickering inches from the woman's face. It was the stuff of nightmares. The red books were everywhere in this room too, piled up on desks, some swept to the floor, covers broken, pages torn.

Aedith made a dismissive sound. 'My school had pictures of Woden hanging from the world ash, stabbing himself in the side with a spear, all over the library. Blood everywhere. You got used to it. Some of the girls were quite taken with it, never knew if that was the plan or not. This guy here must be out of their book. The Fishers'. It seems our killer took it to heart.'

Drustan looked at the serpent, back up at the walls.

'You think he was raised a Fisher?'

Aedith took more photos. 'Must have been, if he grew up here,' she said. 'And if I spend any more time in this building, I'm going to start feeling sorry for the prick. But we need to find the records room. If there is one.'

A soft creaking sound from below, as though someone was trying to move quietly through the building and had moved a piece of furniture. Aedith and Drustan froze. All Drustan could think was that there was almost certainly someone downstairs doing exactly the same thing.

As Drustan moved to the doorway, Aedith eased her handgun from its holster and nodded to him, giving him cover.

Drustan peered round the doorway, ducked back again. 'Someone coming up the stairs. Moving slowly. Doesn't look like they're holding a weapon.'

*

The man was in his late fifties, wore a padded coat and had a face like one of those dogs rich Moorish women liked, the ones whose faces were all squashed in. When Drustan released his arm from round his neck and Aedith had holstered her weapon and held out her warrant card, he collapsed gratefully onto a small wooden chair, wheezing until he got his breath back.

'Caretaker,' he managed eventually. 'Had some break-ins lately, so I'm keeping an eye on the place.'

Aedith looked around the room. 'Lately?' It wasn't in as bad a state as those on the ground floor, but half the windows were broken and it looked like someone had made a nest out of some old cushions in one corner some time ago.

'Started up again a couple of weeks ago,' he said. 'Reckon they were looking for something specific, turned the whole place over. Didn't find what they were after, anyroad. I tidied up, best as I could. I'd moved the important stuff out months ago.'

Aedith and Drustan shared a look. The man was recovering from his shock now, giving Drustan a suspicious look, lingering on his torc. 'Don't get many of your lot out this way,' he said. 'Used to get travellers, coming through, but some of the local lads put a stop to that.'

Drustan could imagine how. Petrol bombs thrown in the middle of the night was the traditional method.

Aedith snapped her fingers, pulling the caretaker's attention back to her.

'When you say "important stuff", what exactly do you mean?'

EIGHTEEN

The caretaker, who introduced himself as Wigmund, lived in a mobile home overlooking the sea. Looking out of the trailer's window, Drustan realised he hadn't seen the ocean for a long time. The beaches East weren't right anyway, all earth and pebbles, sucked by the tide then abandoned, leaving behind a greasy foam studded with plastic bottles and burned driftwood.

Wigmund heaved a carton of folders out from under a camp bed, another from on top of the oldest washing machine Drustan had ever seen. There were reservations in Dumnonia with more recent technology than this.

'I kept them close,' said Wigmund, with a sly look to Drustan. 'Never know when something might come in handy.'

At first, Drustan took this without rancour as some sort of slur against Tribals. Then he realised Wigmund had absorbed the fact he was a cop and completely recategorised him in his mind, Drustan's ethnic derivation instantly forgotten. He was like one of those old ladies who kept a note of every registration plate of every car that visited the house opposite at all times during the night, in the hopes they might help the nice reeves who came over to crack the case. Quite often, they did.

'We're lucky you've been so thorough, sir,' Drustan said with all due solemnity. 'There's a real chance that break-in the other night was by someone looking for exactly this information.'

Which was unproven, but Wigmund was wriggling with glee at the thought of outwitting the unknown intruder. Drustan wondered if he might be so pleased if it turned out to be, as he suspected, the killer. Maybe so. Saxons were a funny lot.

Aedith had already pulled out the first folder of records. Boys' names. School reports.

'How far back do these go?' she asked. 'We're looking for someone who may have come through the home twenty, twenty-five years ago.'

Wigmund's face darkened. He reached to the back of the box, took out a smaller sheaf of papers. 'Back in Oswin's day, that would be. Not sure the place ever recovered from that.'

'Oswin?' prompted Aedith, and Drustan knew she'd remembered the letters carved into the wall too. 'I think I've heard of him. Wasn't there a scandal of some sort?'

Which Drustan knew was a leap, but Wigmund was already nodding. He pushed the papers into Aedith's hands. 'I've got nothing against religion, even whatever fringe stuff it was they had going on here. Each to their own, I say. I've made my offerings to Beowa every morning,' – he gestured to a small carving of a bearded warrior, set above the doorway – 'and it's never done me any harm.'

Drustan met Aedith's gaze and suspected she was thinking *doesn't seem to have done you much good either*, the same as him, but said nothing.

'He was a brutal man, Oswin. Called himself "Father", by the way, demanded the boys call him that too. Used to beat them in the name of that god of his, the one they put pictures of all over that classroom. Said they were born of sin, whatever that meant, and saw it as his job to keep them pure.'

'Did he mark them?' asked Drustan. He nearly pointed at his neck but didn't want to lead the man.

'Oh, he marked them all right,' said Wigmund darkly. 'Whenever a new boy arrived, he'd take them straight down the town to get that fish put on the side of their necks, so they could see it every time they looked in the mirror and think of all the sins they had stored up inside them, fit to burst, he liked to say. The artist in the town, he refused to do any more after a while, after the rumours started to get around.'

'Rumours?' said Aedith, helpfully.

'Been rumours for years, that Oswin took a special interest in some of the lads. Cared about more than their souls, if you see what I mean. Then, one of the older lads, he snapped, beat Oswin half to death one day, right in the middle of that classroom. The reeves came to take the boy away, but when they looked in Oswin's private study, they found photographs.'

'Ah,' said Drustan. A piece of the puzzle had just slotted into place.

'I don't suppose,' asked Aedith, 'you remember the name of the boy who attacked Oswin?'

'Wulfstan,' said the caretaker. 'He didn't have a surname. Orphan, I think, like a lot of them. Quiet lad. Kept himself to himself. I ran a little shop down in the town in those days, selling sweets, odds and ends and the like. He'd come in from time to time, buy trinkets. He really believed in everything the school told him, you could tell. He'd tell me there was a better place after death. I'd tell him I know, full of mead and good women. He never liked that very much.'

'What happened to Oswin?' asked Aedith.

Wigmund rifled through the second carton. 'Ended up in a wheelchair in a low-category prison. The sort where you're allowed out at weekends, if you have anywhere to go. Oswin didn't. He died there about five years ago. Got off easy, if you ask me. Here we go.'

Wigmund held up a photograph. Drustan winced, thinking of the pictures Oswin had taken. But of course it was a class portrait, taken some twenty-five years ago. A small group of boys, ages ranging from nine to perhaps fifteen, stared blankly at the camera. Their hair was cut short, sides shaved with clippers, perhaps even a cut-throat razor in those days. Drustan imagined Oswin taking care of that personally, holding the boy's head with one hand, pulling the blade up with the other. He would have enjoyed that moment of casual power. Each of the boys had the fish mark on their necks, the youngest's still covered with a dressing.

Wigmund pointed to one of the boys, the tallest, his expression as blank and detached as the others, hair so blond as to be almost white. 'That's him,' he said. 'That's Wulfstan.'

NINETEEN

Aedith secured the cartons on Roadfucker's back seats, pulling the seat belt across them as though they were passengers rather than cargo. They certainly fitted into the tiny space better than humans would have done.

'Agapos,' she said into her phone. 'Try a search for a lad named Wulfstan, attended Rowan Berry House some twenty years back. Orphan, most likely.'

She put her phone away, waited until Drustan had put on his seat belt, tugging on it a couple of times to be on the safe side.

'That's enough to go on?' he asked. 'Not even a surname?'

Aedith turned the key, Roadfucker's engine turning over with a low growl. 'If he was in the system enough to be passed onto a children's home, he'll have a reference number. We can at least see where he is now. Or if he died in a road traffic collision a couple years back, we can cross him off the list.'

'Is it really a list, with just one name on it?'

'The sort of questions I encourage from my squad,' mused Aedith, turned the car around and pointing its nose back towards London, 'or anyone who was maybe looking into tips on Saxon investigation techniques, are those that actively open up the direction of enquiry rather than poking holes in it. Questions like "Do I know anyone who could age that photo up so we can get an idea of what Wulfstan looks like now?" or, "If I don't have anything helpful to say, should I perhaps shut up and let the Detective Captain get back to the station without killing her car's suspension on these shitty roads?"'

'Noted,' said Drustan. 'I must say, I find these moments of cross-cultural collaboration really throw up some gems from time to time.'

After ten minutes of Aedith trying to navigate between potholes, they were on a better road and Roadfucker was finally able to move up into a higher gear. Drustan took the Fishers' book from his pocket, opening it at random. A dense page of text, broken up by an illustration of a giant, being faced down by a young boy with a sling.

'Don't give much to his chances,' said Aedith, glancing down. 'Can you read in the car? Not something I ever managed without losing my lunch.'

'We haven't had any lunch.'

'Good point.'

Half an hour later, Aedith had pulled in between two roadside food vans. She handed Drustan a bottle of water and cardboard tray of something impaled with a cheap wooden fork.

'It's on me,' said Aedith. Drustan nodded, accepted the peace offering. They stood for a while, watching the traffic whip past. For the first time, Drustan saw an autonomous vehicle, a big Pan-African-made electric lorry, driving seat ripped out and replaced with sensors, flashing orange lights on every corner of the vehicle to warn other drivers. How long until it was the non-automated vehicles that had to apologise for their presence, he wondered?

'All that stuff back at the home,' said Aedith, through a mouthful of minced venison. 'Kids born with sin, punishment beatings, that mad shit with salt and snakes. Is that what the Fishers are all about, do you reckon? Doesn't really square with what we were told about Angwin getting into it and going from low-level terrorist henchman to risking his life as a hostage negotiator, does it?'

Drustan was still working through the Fishers' book. The pages were so thin that the grease from his own culinary choice, battered salmon, was turning large sections completely transparent.

'So far, it's more Oswin than Angwin, all monsters and vengeance and retribution. As far as I've got, anyway,' he said. 'If Wulfstan bought into this, he must have been living in fear every day of his life. Until something snapped.'

'What I'm wondering,' said Aedith, 'is if he is the killer, does he believe? Beating the shit out of Oswin doesn't mean he abandoned the gods he'd been told to worship.'

'God, singular,' said Drustan absently. 'Seems they believe in one god above all. The individual up on the boards is closer to a demigod, as far as I can tell. But yes, it's plausible. Wulfstan as the true keeper of the flame, declaring war on the other Fishers, making this some kind of... internecine struggle?'

'Except you don't believe that, do you? You think when he snapped, attacked Oswin, he stopped believing entirely.'

Drustan nodded slowly. 'I think he lost everything on that day. He'd been given something he could hold on to, after whatever events had brought him to that terrible place, and managed to convince himself that the things Oswin was doing were right and proper, and when one day he realised he was being lied to, he had some sort of psychotic break. From which he has probably never recovered.'

Aedith eyed him sideways, over the remains of her burger. 'You're reading a lot into one photo and a brief description from a caretaker.'

Drustan abandoned his fish, wiping his fingers with a napkin.

'I don't speak to my deity any more,' he said. 'Or rather, she doesn't speak to me.'

Aedith said nothing.

'We Tribals have a more personal relationship with our deities than you Saxons,' Drustan continued. 'We talk to them; they talk back to us.'

'You mean she talked to you…' Aedith was trying to find a polite way of framing it. Drustan found it rather touching. '…when you were chemically relaxed, let's say?'

Drustan shook his head. 'Not necessarily. It can help, of course, but there are other ways to commune. I came across some when I was working for the Mughals. Incense and certain techniques to relax the brain. Chanting, repeating the same phrase over and over until it loses all meaning, that sort of thing.' He could tell Aedith wanted to say, *I've been to meetings like that*, or something similar, but was repressing the impulse. 'The Goddess used to appear to me. Literally so, I would hear her, sometimes see her, and we would converse. She would help me make sense of recent events, put things together in ways I hadn't considered.'

Aedith said nothing. She didn't believe him, he knew. Or perhaps she believed that *he* believed what he was saying, but that wasn't the same thing at all. He continued regardless. 'And then, a few years ago, she stopped coming. I continue the rituals, they help settle my mind, but the deeper purpose is gone. I lost something. If that Wulfstan boy became the killer, and it's a big "if", I suspect he lost something too.'

'I see,' said Aedith, although clearly she didn't.

'You don't follow any of the gods, do you, Captain Mercia?'

She shrugged. 'Never saw the point. Our gods never seemed to care if you believed in them or not, so I made a decision early on in life that if they didn't bother me, I wouldn't bother them. It seems to have worked out so far.'

Drustan gave her a curious glance. 'And that's acceptable? Socially, amongst your people?'

She laughed, a short barking noise. 'I would say my people don't care who or what you believe in as long as you don't go all Father Oswin about it. A viewpoint that suits me down to the ground. But my next question is: if you're correct, and young Wulfstan stops following the faith Father Oswin had so carefully beaten into him over the years, why does he not move on? Why start hunting Fishers and taking them like trophies?'

'An excellent question,' said Drustan.

The drive back to the office was silent. It was possible, Drustan thought, that he had created some awkwardness, bringing up religious matters like that. If the case had been straightforward murder, or smuggling, perhaps, he would never have mentioned it and the cultural differences between them would have been along the lines of comparative arguments of torcs versus armrings. But the killer had brought religion into this, heedless of how uncomfortable it would make any investigating Saxons. Best not to pretend they were one country divided only by a language. The differences between them were deep and wide. It didn't make him hold out much hope for the Summit, that was certain.

TWENTY

Agapos put a thick sheaf of printouts down on Aedith's desk. 'Every lad who passed through Rowan Berry House in that time period and would have had the fish and sparrow tattoo. Cross-referenced with the local artist. He's retired now but kept good records. Wasn't a fan of Oswin's, so he was keen to help.'

Aedith raised an eyebrow. 'You're not going to make me read them, are you?'

'No, boss. Every one of them accounted for. A lot of them dead from drink-related causes, most of them in and out of work. A few moved away, made something of themselves. And every single one that remains has an alibi for the time of Gorsedd Angwin's death. Apart from Wulfstan.'

Agapos placed two more printouts on Aedith's desk. She picked up the first piece of paper. To Drustan's eyes, it had disconcertingly large areas of white.

'Why do I feel, Sergeant, you're setting me up for disappointment?'

'I'm sorry, Captain, this is all there was on him.'

Aedith skimmed the first sheet, passed it to Drustan. The word 'scant' existed for exactly the amount of information before him. The child Wulfstan was definitely an orphan, that was something, but who his parents had been, no one in the kingdom seemed to know. He had been taken to the home at the age of nine, had lived there until he was fifteen, had received moderately good grades until the point at which he had initiated a violent physical assault on Father Oswin, described in what could laughably be called a report as 'the boy's primary educator, later discovered to have large quantities of illegal material and a history of abusing those in his care'.

It seemed nobody had known what to do with Wulfstan. To Saxons, beating half to death someone who had not only abused you but taken photographic evidence of doing so was considered a justifiable reaction rather than an outright crime, which meant Wulfstan's fingerprints weren't in the system. If Wulfstan had been a Celt, he would have been able to present a defence of his action, the level of punishment depending on the poetic quality of his statement. It was a set-up that, in Drustan's view, weighed the scales too heavily in favour of the practised bullshitter. Neither system had started taking DNA samples from those charged until a decade or so ago.

'It says here he was allowed a fresh start, whatever that means,' said Aedith, reading from the second sheet. 'Too old to go to a new home. If he'd signed on, there would have been some record, but there isn't. So maybe he took a job somewhere under a new name perhaps. Either way, no trace of him from that point on.'

It was understandable, perhaps even laudable. But it didn't help the case. Whoever Wulfstan had become, he had vanished utterly from the system.

'Okay,' said Aedith finally. 'There are things we can do. There's someone in Missing Persons with the up-aging software, so let's at least have a guess at what he looks like now, show it around the station, see if it jogs anyone's memory. If this kid did grow to be a spree killer, chances are he's slipped up a few times between then and now. Maybe we can track down some of the other kids, see if they remember anything that could help us.'

Agapos nodded. 'I can get on that.'

'And if this Wulfstan is nothing to do with the murders?' asked Drustan.

Aedith looked at him sourly. 'Then he might at least be able to tell us more about the Fishers so our time isn't entirely wasted. I still don't see how the worlds of Father Oswin and Gorsedd Angwin connect. This is one obscure cult with two very different world-views, as far as I can tell.'

'There are those who kill in the name of Woden, others who heal,' said Drustan mildly.

To his surprise, Agapos nodded in support. 'Feels like you're overthinking it, boss. That you might be overthinking it, I mean,' he corrected hastily. 'I'm just saying, the Fishers haven't exactly thrived here. From what I can see, their whole thing feels like bits cut and pasted from more successful religions. It's not surprising the worshippers they've picked up have been weirdos and oddballs.'

Agapos was saved from whatever cutting riposte Aedith was about to give him by the ping of an incoming email.

'It's from Tancred,' she said, picking up her phone. She frowned. 'He's never used my private email before.'

She flicked the link over to her work screen, which immediately filled with a video of a large private house behind high cast-iron railings which were being cut through, even as they watched, by a Special Branch officer with an oxyacetylene torch. Next to him, dozens of officers in body armour were pulling masks over their faces. The camera moved round to show officers lying on top of vans peering through the scopes of sniper rifles, then finally back for a close-up of Tancred giving Aedith a cheery thumbs-up before pulling his own mask down.

Aedith scowled. 'He's live-streaming the raid just for me, the rotten bastard.'

Drustan stared at the house. It looked Saxon but the high, chained gates the cops were studiously ignoring were decorated with Tribal icons: triskeles, leaping deer, entwined branches forming the face of the Goddess. Or at least 'a' Goddess.

'Deedra's official residence,' Aedith confirmed.

Tancred must have strapped the camera to his tac vest, because now everything went first-person shooter: yelling officers, tear gas thrown in through windows, shots fired, Kesair bodyguards beaten with truncheons and thrown to the floor and finally a shrieking woman dragged out of a side door, expensive dress torn, mascara visibly running down the side of her face that wasn't covered in tattoos, flailing at the cops manhandling her until one of them punched her in the stomach and she folded in half.

Tancred took the camera out, pulled down the mask, posed for a grinning selfie with the collapsed woman and winked at Aedith.

'One for the album,' he said, and the stream went blank.

Aedith put down the phone and exhaled heavily.

'Did you see that?' asked Aedith.

'I did,' said Drustan. 'Assuming you mean what I think you mean.'

Aedith nodded. 'Yep. That wasn't Deedra'.

Agapos blinked, confused. 'It wasn't?'

'Come on, Agapos,' she said impatiently. 'Deedra snorts tear gas for breakfast, would have taken ten of those arseholes to bring her in.'

'Tattoos were perfect,' said Drustan. 'Correct hair, build. But I agree. No Kesair chieftain would go down that easily.'

'She *knew* Tancred was coming for her,' said Aedith. 'Got a double in so she could bugger off out of it and carry on with whatever mad shit she's got planned.'

'What do we do now?' asked Agapos. 'If that's not her, they'll realise eventually. Doesn't give us much time.'

'Time to what?' asked Aedith sourly. 'We don't know where she is, and Special Branch have almost certainly tapped our phones, so if I try to contact her in any way that'll just alert them of their cock-up all the sooner.' She looked up at the large clock on her office wall and pulled a face. 'Don't have time to do anything anyway, overtime budget being what it is. Let's meet back here tomorrow.'

Agapos nodded and took the news out to the rest of the office, to muted, only semi-sarcastic, cheers. Aedith tapped the phone on her desk a couple of times before putting it in her coat pocket.

'Coming for a drink, Detective Inspector?'

Drustan shook his head. 'A kind offer, but I plan to avail myself of the delights of the academy canteen.'

Aedith snorted. 'Dear gods, the memories. Enjoy your boiled beef and turnips.'

TWENTY ONE

It was honeycakes that had first caused Eawynn Wettin to wonder if there was more to life. Or rather, the countless hours she and the other lower-level Saxon administrative assistants spent every Unification Summit at the Skeid arranging tables of pastries so they could be thrown out at the end of the day after being summarily ignored by the delegates of the three kingdoms. Of course, sustenance had to be provided, but tipping endless plates of food into the bins always seemed such a *waste*. There were starving Tribal children on the streets of London, and starving Saxon adults too, who would have appreciated them, but there seemed no way to get the food to them without completing endless amounts of paperwork, by which time the food had all gone stale anyway.

Eawynn's husband had died unexpectedly earlier in the year. He had been a decent man, if not an outstanding one, and his loss had found Eawynn asking all sorts of questions about her existence she'd never been expecting to contemplate at this point in her life. Somehow, the simple matter of wasted food, just one irk among a whole irk-catalogue built up over the four Summits she had been a part of during her administrative career, took on a great significance. It began to seem to Eawynn that if she couldn't solve this issue regarding the movement of calories from the uninterested to the desperate, her whole life could somehow be weighed as having no meaning whatsoever. She tried just taking the food on her own cognisance, but security concerns had been raised and she'd very nearly been arrested, not to mention shot.

The next day, Eawynn mentioned her concerns to a higher-ranking administrator, who promised to look into the matter but seemed to instantly forget it. Fortunately, the conversation was overheard by another administrator, this one higher-ranking, but off to one side of the org chart. Somehow, *this* administrator had levels of connection that cut across not just the normal bureaucratic strata, but societal lines too, hinting at a network that included Saxons, Tribals, Norse and even a couple of Pan-Africans among their number. Very quickly, a system was devised whereby unwanted food could be moved out of the building to people who needed it.

A stray mention of a similar event involving loaves and fishes was caught by Eawynn, much to the apparent embarrassment of the mentioner, a fellow Saxon and IT worker named Ceolweard, who tried to deny everything, but Eawynn persisted, which led, a year later, to a water-based ceremony where she joined the ranks of the Fishers.

That had been the previous Summit, five years ago. This Summit felt very different, and not just because the Unification bit was being spoken aloud a lot more often this time round. It wouldn't have been obvious from outside, but the build-up had been imbued with a momentum Eawynn had never felt before. There was a buzz, and it was felt most keenly by Eawynn and the other Fishers, thanks to their web of cross-cultural connections. From whispers at the last Fisher meeting Eawynn had attended – held in a draughty building that had once been a bank, something that those who were deeper into Fisher lore found particularly amusing – it seemed that the High King had started using words like 'legacy' and 'historical'. The Tribal elders had picked up on this and murmured interesting things into backchannels that went through the Wall to the ears of the Norse hedge-fund traders and tech bros who actually ran things and, for the first time in Eawynn's memory, people started using the term Unification without little finger quotes around it, instead talking about how one might, you know, theoretically at least, turn three countries into one.

If there was one thing the Summit-adjacent Fishers were for, they decided, it was bringing people together in a positive cause without bloodshed. So, they began to coordinate their efforts, quietly making sure the right people got the important messages, smoothing the processes of cattle-wrangling and game-playing that had to happen before the Summit even officially got under way. And because they had no axe to grind in the process of bringing three kingdoms together as one, other than wanting it to happen peacefully, Eawynn and the other Fishers were becoming integral to its chance of success.

This wasn't attention they'd planned for, or even welcomed, particularly after the sudden loss of Gorsedd Angwin. Shocking, but, as the whispers went – and Fishers were just as inclined to whisper as anyone else – not entirely surprising, bearing in mind Angwin's background. Eawynn and the other Fishers working the Summit weren't scheduled to meet in the old bank building for another week, so had to make do with hushed conversations and quick tearful embraces behind the scenes, but there was too much work to do for anyone to deal with it right now, especially when it looked like this could be the year when the Summit was really going to amount to something.

Eawynn looked around the foyer of the Skeid, unsatisfied. The banners for the main lobbying groups were set up, tables laid out with delegates' nametags, seating arrangements and itineraries printed out. Then she realised: she'd left the catering purchase orders in her car. You could do it all via email, of course, but Eawynn knew from experience how much harder it was to get the leftover pastries out of the door and to the people who could use them without pieces of actual old-fashioned paper to flourish at the security people who stood at the boundaries of each political zone, like gatekeepers of the underworld.

Eawynn was asked to show her laminate no fewer than four times before she was out of the Skeid and back in the car park to the rear of the building. Passing the long rows of dark limousines, press vans and poorly parked medical vehicles, she clicked her key fob to unlock her car. She was thinking, not for the first time, that the four-wheel drive was really far too large for just her, now that her husband had passed – surely time to trade down – when a large hand pressed over her mouth and a needle slid into her neck, sending her into darkness and ice.

TWENTY TWO

By the time Drustan's bus had dropped him around the corner from the academy, all that was left in the canteen were a few barley cakes and a vat of rapidly cooling leek soup. Seeing his lack of enthusiasm, one of the remaining catering staff, a Tribal woman in an ill-fitting tabard, held out a plate of fried potatoes topped with a chicken thigh covered in yellow sauce.

'Big *gwithyas* in for a seminar earlier,' she told him. 'No one told me he had a peanut allergy. I'll reheat if for you if you're not a sufferer.'

Drustan assured her that he wasn't. When she brought it over for him a few minutes later it smelled astonishing.

'Watch yourself,' said the woman quietly, under the guise of passing him some cutlery, then walked out of the canteen. A couple of cadets started a loud conversation the moment she was gone, as if they hadn't been staring at Drustan from the moment he walked in. Drustan finished his meal. It was delicious.

The handle on the door to Drustan's room was angled noticeably lower than when he had left it that morning. There was a gap of a few millimetres at the base of the door where the carpet runner had come loose and as Drustan walked past, careful not to slow his pace, he saw a shadow shift briefly inside. He estimated at least two people were waiting for him inside, possibly three. Luckily the fuse box that controlled this whole block was only a couple more doors down the corridor, and it was the work of a moment to flip up the plastic cover and pull down the main control fuse, sinking the entire block into darkness.

Complaining groans rose up from the rooms around him as he walked back, although the sounds from behind Drustan's door were more confused, even worried. He pushed the door open, ducking low under the first swing, and shoved the first cadet into the second, catching the third in the stomach with an elbow that made him drop the pillowcase he had presumably been planning to use as a hood, and collapse, moaning, to the floor.

The first two cadets made a valiant attempt to untangle themselves and rush Drustan – all credit to their combat instructors – but it wasn't too difficult to dodge to one side, so they collided with the wall instead. After that, the fight had gone out of them. They crawled towards the door, Drustan considerately stepping aside to let them pass.

The third cadet was made of sterner stuff, however, morally and physically. Presuming all the rooms in the block were of the same proportions, it seemed unlikely he could fit in his bed without folding himself in half. Hauling himself off the floor, he growled at Drustan, forming his great hands into fists and hurling himself across the small room – at least until his target unaccountably moved around him, letting him crash into the desk, skull connecting with the wall with an audible thump.

The cadet stopped, shaking his great bull-like head and looking down at his fists as if trying to remember where he'd last seen them.

'You're all right,' sympathised Drustan, sitting on the table, palms flat on the surface. The cadet made another angry noise and would certainly have charged again if someone hadn't used that moment to locate the fuse box and flip the main switch back on. The lad stopped in his tracks, blinking stupidly as, in the cheap electric light, the meanness of the room became apparent: the grey pillowcase on the floor, statue, candle and crow feather thrown off the desk, a heavy object in a plastic carrier bag next to Drustan on a chair.

Drustan reached into the bag and pulled out a sheep's head, eyes wide and idiotic, blood staining the wool at the truncated neck.

A crowd of cadets had gathered in the open doorway, drawn by the noise and the sight of two of their number crawling painfully down the corridor in the general direction of away. An instructor, all tight t-shirt and gelled hair, shoved his way through his charges, causing them to evaporate *en masse*. He opened his mouth to yell at the large recruit, saw Drustan and closed it again.

'Good evening, Sergeant,' said Drustan. 'I'm sorry about the noise. Some of your charges wanted to demonstrate recent advances in exercise techniques. Until the lights went out, causing some confusion, and I'm afraid the whole experiment had to be abandoned.'

The instructor hadn't taken his eyes off the sheep's head.

'Found this on the stairs,' said Drustan, putting the head back in the bag. 'Didn't want anyone to trip over it. I wonder if you could take it away for me?'

The man took the bag and left without a word.

'What's your name, son?' asked Drustan.

'Ord,' mumbled the cadet, shaking his head, either overcome by events or just generally slow on the uptake. Drustan supposed both could be true.

'A good name,' he said, giving the lad a reassuring pat on the back. 'Ord, I'm going to need your help with a situation.'

TWENTY THREE

'You're home early,' said Hilde, not looking up from unloading the dishwasher. 'Criminals all done for the day?'

Aedith grunted, locking Lungpiercer in the miniature safe built into the wall next to the house shrine: a small alcove dedicated to the Cofgod, without whom milk would spoil, packages would be delivered to the wrong house and heating bills, Hilde assured her, would be considerably higher. The current offerings were an expensive, if stale, chocolate truffle, a broken memory stick Hilde had found on the pavement outside and a tarnished silver ring of Aedith's that she hadn't worn since she was a teenager. Its setting was broken, the amber bead that was supposed to fit it having fallen out long ago. The Cofgod liked broken things and so, Aedith suspected, did Hilde.

'Coram done his homework?' asked Aedith. Hilde put away the last of the plates and turned her large blue eyes on her. She was Northumbrian, where the Norse had officially been driven out a thousand years ago but their blood still ran strong. It was being constantly teased for it that had led Hilde to move to the relatively cosmopolitan London, although Aedith didn't know how much she got to see of it.

'I think you need to talk to him'.

Hilde slid a phone across the table. It was a cheap Mughal model: Coram had wanted the latest Moorish device, but Aedith hadn't seen the need when it would mostly be broken within a twelvemonth anyway. Coram had pushed back with his choice of case: black plastic hand-engraved by a street vendor with images of skulls, swords and angry impish creatures making profane gestures. Aedith had chosen to let that one slide: you had to pick your battles.

'Porn?' she asked. Hilde shook her head, but Aedith knew before she even hit the play button what she was going to see: a large, bearded man, a white flag intersected by two red lines: one vertical, one horizontal on the breezeblock wall behind him. The logo – and no one was clear exactly where it had first appeared – was becoming increasingly popular in online culture, along with Svart, a cartoonish dark elf frozen in a posture of feigned innocence and superimposed over images of beaten or injured criminals of any ethnic source other than 'pure' Eastern Saxon.

The bearded man began his latest rant, concerning the false claims of the Tribal people (referred to here in more colourful terms), the weakness of the Saxon government, such as it was, in standing up to their dubious claims, and the necessity of firm action on the part of the honest and downtrodden Saxon homelander to take matters into their own hands.

'It's not just that,' said Hilde. 'He's building up to something. I can tell.'

Aedith hit pause with a weary finger. 'I'll go and see him now'.

'We only watch them to take the piss.'

Coram had been doing his homework when Aedith went into his room. Or was at his desk, anyway. Knocking first of course, because you never knew what you might encounter with teenage boys. Obviously, as a police officer, Aedith would only be able to state in court that Coram had his homework laid out before him as she entered: whether he was actually *doing* it or not was a very different question. But not one for now.

Aedith took a seat on the edge of his bed. Coram's gaze stayed fixed on the floor, black fringe hanging over his eyes. Aedith couldn't remember the last time he had actually looked her in the face.

'How do you take the piss?'

'This one streamer, Sandon, does a thing where he auto-tunes the vocals, turns them into folk songs. They sound ridiculous, but kind of funny. He gets a ton of views for them.'

Aedith frowned. 'So they get spread more widely?'

Coram screwed his eyes shut, as though in real physical pain. 'Not among people who actually *believe* them! You don't have to worry, it's only old people that get brainwashed by that stuff. Although…'

'Although what?'

'I mean, not everything he says is completely mad. The Indij do cause trouble. There's a couple of Tash kids in my school and you can't talk to them, they hate everyone. And they talk in their own language amongst themselves, so you don't know what they're saying. Osric, in the other class? He says they could be planning to kill us all and we'd never know it. Everyone shouted him down, but technically it's true.'

'Don't say Tash.'

Coram blinked, confused. 'That's what they call themselves. It's just short for "moustache".'

'I know what it's short for, but it's disrespectful'.

Coram flushed, crossing his arms. Dammit, she was losing him. If she ever had him in the first place.

'You know I'm working with a Tribal officer right now?'

Incredibly, Coram looked right at her, if only for a moment. 'What's he like?' He waved his hands vaguely. 'Does he try and curse people and stuff?'

'No more than I do.'

Coram looked disappointed. There was still a lot of small boy there, the nine-year-old Aedith had brought home, white-faced and shocked into silence by the death of his parents. There were glimpses of the man he might become, too. Aedith saw more of the latter these days. He didn't seem much like his father, although she had only met him briefly. It had ended badly.

'Are you worried?' she asked. 'About those Tribal kids?' She could pull up their records if she had to, but they were unlikely to be any real trouble. Far more likely to be the victims of crime than the Saxon kids around them, but you never knew.

Coram shook his head. 'No. Osric's full of it. He brought his seax into school the other day, trying to look cool, but the girls just laughed at him.'

Aedith made a mental note to check out Osric instead.

'You know your seax is never to leave that wall, right?'

Coram had been presented with his blade last year, aged thirteen, by Earl Lod himself. Watered Damascus steel, engraved with runes for prosperity and courage, just like the one he had presented to Edric – and look how that had turned out. Coram's was in a case of toughened safety glass, attached firmly to the wall. Aedith had screwed it there herself.

A flash of annoyance moved across Coram's face. '*I know.* Gods, you're not my *mother!*'

Aedith nodded. It was true, she wasn't.

'Well then,' she said briskly. 'I'll see you in the morning.'

'Wait,' said Coram. 'Can I ask you something?'

This was new. Aedith waited, then eventually realised she ought to nod or something. Coram tried not to fall over his words, which had apparently been brewing for a while.'

'I was wondering if I could visit Uncle Edric?'

One thing Aedith had learned from years of interrogations was never to let her surprise show. Most criminals weren't the brightest, often assuming you knew far more about what they'd been up to than you did, so when they said something like 'and then I tried Ælfwig, you know, the guy who sells virtual gold,' you had to pretend you'd known Ælfwig was the virtual-gold guy all along. So, even though Coram had never referred to a single member of Aedith's family by any sort of honorific before, she was going to pretend this was the sort of thing Coram said all the time.

'Any particular reason you'd like to see your Uncle Edric?'

'He writes to me, at Yule and on my birthday. I thought it would be good to go and see him. If that was all right with you. We're doing a thing at school, talking about our family history, that sort of thing.'

Now Aedith was definitely going to have a word with Coram's tutor. Probably he hadn't meant to inspire Coram to get chatty with the one member of his adoptive family locked in a high-security psychiatric hospital, but it was best to nip this kind of thing in the bud where possible. Maybe take Lungpiercer with her, for dramatic effect.

'I'll think about it,' she said.

Aedith closed Coram's door quietly and stood on the landing for a moment, trying not to remember what had happened four years ago. She still didn't know if she should have done anything different. If she'd have been capable of doing anything different.

Hilde was waiting for her on the landing. She gestured down the stairs. Aedith nodded.

'He wants to see Edric,' said Aedith at the kitchen table. Hilde had made them both coffee. In many ways, their set-up was a perfect domestic arrangement. It certainly put less pressure on Aedith to have a relationship when she essentially already had a wife at home.

Hilde drew her breath in sharply. 'That came from nowhere.'

'Apparently there's some school project. Family history or something.'

'He talked about that. Didn't even bring up his birth family. I thought it was a sign of progress. But if he wants to see Edric… I don't know.'

'I don't like the idea. But I also don't believe in treating my brother like a shameful secret, even if my father does.'

'Maybe it would be good for him.'

'Edric, or Coram?'

'Perhaps both.'

Aedith held her surprise in for the second time that evening. Hilde had never previously stated her opinion on matters Mercian. A sudden buzzing sound interrupted the thought; Aedith's phone vibrating across the marble worktop even before it began playing the theme tune of a popular pre-school animation show about a large hound who solved woodland crimes.

'Agapos?'

'The Detective Inspector's on the move. I can pick you up in ten.'

Hilde silently removed Aedith's still half-full mug, tipped out the coffee and began rinsing it in the sink. There was no disapproval in the act, but Aedith felt guilty anyway.

She hung up the phone. 'All right then. Tell Coram I'll take him to see his uncle when the next visitor slot's available.'

TWENTY FOUR

'Our Tribal colleague's made a friend,' said Agapos. Aedith didn't respond, keeping her binoculars trained on Drustan as he walked the cadet across the car park to an electric sports utility vehicle that could only have belonged to one of the Academy's physical trainers, parked on the edge of the circle of yellow light cast by a nearby streetlamp. Aedith had enormous respect for those officers who had chosen to make a career out of educating the next generation of cops in how to survive out on the streets but, aesthetically, their taste in cars was indistinguishable from that of a hairdresser.

Agapos had picked Aedith up in his husband's vehicle, a sensible four-door saloon with plenty of room in the boot for hiking gear, or weightlifting equipment or whatever revoltingly wholesome activities they did in their own time.

The cadet, who had a dazed look about him, stood by as Drustan knelt by the car, doing something fiddly with the lock.

'Ambitious,' said Aedith. 'We had a presentation from the manufacturers last year, wanted an official endorsement from the Huscarl to use in their big ad campaign, show off how un-stealable they are.'

Agapos looked at her, interested. 'Any good?'

'Impressive. Triple lock, immobiliser, private security on the scene within twenty minutes in any urban area. We told them to do one, obviously.'

The lights on the vehicle flashed green twice and the door opened. The cadet got into the driver's seat, looking even less happy than before. Drustan walked round to the passenger side, vaulted over a low wall and disappeared.

Aedith lowered the binoculars. 'Huh.'

'Do we go after him, Guv?'

She shook her head. 'He's setting up a decoy. Maybe. Let's sit tight for a minute, and—'

A hand tapped lightly on Aedith's window. Agapos reached for his sidearm.

'Leave it,' said Aedith tiredly. She pressed a button, the window slowly sliding down.

'Good evening,' said Drustan. 'If you're here about the power cut earlier, I must confess it was entirely my fault, but thankfully easily resolved with no harm done.'

'Got yourself a partner?' asked Aedith, nodding at the cadet, who was staring into space, gripping the steering wheel so tightly Aedith could see the whiteness of his knuckles even without the binoculars.

'That'll be young Cadet Ord. We had a bit of a misunderstanding earlier, to make up for which he's agreed to act as my driver for the evening. I had a hunch as to where that fertiliser might have hidden itself away.'

'Did you?' said Aedith. 'And did you consider sharing that with any of your Saxon colleagues before kidnapping a trainee reeve and stealing a car?'

'I did, but your suggestion that Special Branch are tracking our mobile devices gave me pause, and to be fair, it is only a hunch.'

'What I think the Sergeant and I might do,' said Aedith, after a pause, 'is follow in your wake. In a purely observational capacity, of course.'

'I would be delighted to have your company,' said Drustan and he sounded like he meant it.

'How's your boy?' asked Agapos, as the instructor's car slid out into the streets. Agapos moved after it, keeping two car-lengths' distance.

'Some lad in his class showing off, brought his seax into school,' said Aedith, scrolling through Deedra's social-media feeds to see if she'd updated in the last six hours (unlikely, but you never knew). They were heading east, buildings slowly darkening not just from the setting sun behind them, but from the soot of hundreds of years of household and ceremonial fires, blown by the prevailing winds into areas too poor to clean them up. 'How do you suggest we deal with that?'

'Scare the hells out of him,' said Agapos. 'Smoke bombs, get those laser pointer things coming out of the darkness, red dots on the forehead, I love that. Just say the word. Wait.'

He stamped on the brakes, jerking the car to a halt. Aedith looked up, displeased. 'I'm regretting ever sending you on that advanced driving course.'

Agapos pointed straight ahead. A group of young Tribals, thirty or so, male and female, were swaggering across the road, cans of beer in one hand, mobiles in the other. Most were stripped to the waist with their hair spiked, skin daubed in spirals, some in paint, others freshly carved, blood trickling down onto tracksuit bottoms or combat trousers. All stared into the car windscreen as they crossed, daring Agapos to do something, a couple making finger runes for 'disdain', another for something Aedith didn't even recognise. She'd have to check with Coram when she got home.

Saxons would have chanted, roared at them with arms outstretched, but Tribals were quieter, even when pissed up and ready for a fight. The last of them, a moustachioed male, a foot taller than the rest, was so decorated with clan markings and warpaint his original skin colour could only be seen on the palms of his hands. His gaze shifted slowly from Agapos to Aedith, and he spat, loudly and with considerable accuracy, at the windscreen.

Silently, Agapos activated the screenwash. By the time the wipers had done their work, the Tribals had passed, moving down an alley between a betting shop and a cheap venison takeaway. Drustan's vehicle had been waiting patiently for them ahead. Seeing Agapos on the move again, the instructor's car slid forward, and their journey resumed, residential areas giving way to semi-abandoned shopping centres and a succession of decreasingly impressive temples.

Aedith was the first to break, still thinking of the Tribals. 'Special Branch kicking all this off, you think? Turned over one too many rocks maybe?'

Agapos shrugged broad shoulders. 'Or the Summit. Half my Tribal informants are getting cocky, think we won't be able to push them around much longer. The other half think it's an excuse for another landgrab, turn more of their ancestral grazing fields into data centres.'

'What do you think?'

Agapos laughed, flicked the headlights onto full beam. The streetlights were running out now, the road narrowing as they passed through industrial areas abandoned and overgrown enough to count as light woodland. In another ten minutes they'd be out of the city altogether and into farmland.

'I think whatever happens, we'll end up with less budget to shovel more shit.'

Apparently Drustan wasn't planning on abandoning London entirely. Just as the industrial zone seemed to be fading out altogether, the instructor's car pulled up on the side of the road, next to a group of shipping containers that may as well have been dropped from a Pan-Pacific cargo airship, going by the carelessness with which they had been positioned.

Or, considered Aedith, as Agapos pulled in behind Drustan and killed the lights, they'd been positioned very carefully, to stop anyone driving past getting a good look at the concrete buildings with the tall chimney just visible down an overgrown country road.

Agapos opened the boot, passing out tactical vests and shotguns. Aedith buckled on her vest, chambered a round into Lungpiercer, then took a shotgun and weighed it appreciatively.

'Got a shooter?' she asked Drustan.

'I'm afraid,' said Drustan, buckling on his own vest, 'current operational parameters don't permit me to be armed on official investigations without the permission of my superior officer.'

'Good job this isn't official, then,' said Aedith, tossing him a shotgun and bandolier of cartridges. Behind her, Agapos, who'd just pulled on a bright red 'Police' armband, sighed and took it off again. 'What about your little friend there?'

Ord was still in the car, staring at Aedith and Agapos with the wide-eyed reverence of a tween girl finding herself on public transport with all her favourite social-media stars at once.

'He's just a cadet. I thought we'd let him keep an eye on the vehicles.'

'He wants to learn how the bee makes the honey, doesn't he?' said Aedith. 'Come on, son, let's get you kitted out.'

'All right then,' announced Aedith.

Technically, they were good to go. Sure, Drustan and Ord's tactical vests were considerably more vintage than was ideal, and Aedith was fairly sure Ord was only carrying his shotgun the right way around by chance rather than training, but she'd been in more unlikely units. It was a straight line down the road to what she had realised was a past-its-best foundry. The peeling sign reading 'Edwin Lamb & Sons, Foundry and Machine Shop' was a clue. 'Before we go, let's at least pretend we're going in with a bare minimum of intel. What makes you think the fertiliser's ended up here?'

'I had occasion earlier this evening to consider the noble Saxon sheep,' said Drustan. 'Best,' he continued, off Aedith's puzzled expression, 'not to enquire further on that particular issue. But I did recently stumble across a list of businesses the Kesair have bought over the years through various shell companies, and was reminded that one of them was a foundry owned, until few years ago, by a Mister Lamb and his various offspring.'

Aedith squinted critically into the chamber of her shotgun, turned it upside down and pushed five cartridges into the magazine tube.

'Don't suppose you "stumbled" across this list on the Woden Cross database?' she asked, sourly racking a cartridge into the chamber. 'Just out of professional interest, you understand?'

Drustan shrugged vaguely. 'The exact details elude me. I'm afraid I was distracted by a growing suspicion that we'd been sent down the wrong path regarding the fertiliser. Certainly it's what you might want for an explosion, but it's just as useful if you have something equally flammable but less... theatrical in mind. And where better to keep that under the radar than out here in the countryside?'

Aedith frowned. 'You think they're melting something down? Turning gold torcs into ingots?'

Drustan did one of his annoyingly vague shrugs. For a moment, Aedith considered using the pepper spray clipped to her vest, but it passed.

'And when you say the Kesair,' she said, 'you mean Deedra.'

Drustan nodded.

'You think she's there now?'

'It's possible,' replied Drustan. 'I hope she isn't. I hope this ridiculous hunch of mine is nothing more than that and you followed me all the way out here for nothing.'

'Detective Inspector Drustan,' said Aedith quietly. 'Might I ask exactly what you think a bunch of Tribal fanatics might be doing with two truckloads of incendiary material, if it's not to make a bomb or smelt gold? Because if it's not that, what exactly about an old foundry raised your suspicions?'

Drustan looked at her. His expression was unreadable. The moon emerged briefly from the cover of the clouds above them. Aedith realised for the first time his eyes were darker than usual. He had even drawn lines in kohl extending out into his hairline, dots above his eyebrows. Warpaint?

It was Drustan's turn to load his shotgun, rack a cartridge into the chamber. 'Hopefully, we don't find out.' He moved to take a step forward, but Aedith put a restraining hand on his arm.

'Wait,' she said. 'Let's send Huginn in first.'

*

Agapos lifted the drone from the foam case on the back seat and placed it on Aedith's outstretched palm. Norse tech, barely bigger than her hand and, despite having four rotors and a camera attachment pointing straight down, it didn't appear to weigh anything at all.

'Technically, they belong to the city planning department,' said Aedith. 'They've been after one of our parking spaces for years, so we came to a deal. Supposed to be a matching pair, but Muninn took a dip into the Thames six months ago and he's never been the same since.'

'I can't keep apologising for that,' muttered Agapos.

The rotors began to spin with a barely perceptible whine, the drone abruptly lifting off Aedith's hand and vanishing into the night sky. The sergeant held out his phone, the screen a muddy blur.

'Not as impressive as I would have hoped,' said Drustan. Agapos made some adjustment, screen shifting to dark green, black rectangles seen from above, lighter green blobs moving around of their own accord.

'Night vision,' said Aedith.

Agapos scowled. 'Lot of security for an abandoned foundry.'

They were clustered round the screen now. Even Ord had been pulled in.

'Move it back there, youth,' said Aedith, not unkindly. 'I don't want your cadet nits all over me, thanks.'

Drustan pointed at the screen. 'There.' A cluster of blobs, close-packed. 'Those aren't moving. How low can you get the thing without anyone seeing it?'

'Much lower and we lose line of sight. Agapos, try the forward camera.'

Agapos nodded, traced another symbol across the screen. The picture blurred for a second, the drone tilting down, the night vision clearing. No need for it now, lanterns hanging on the walls casting a glow over at least two dozen bodies held in a wire cage, hands clasped behind their backs. One of the people, a woman perhaps, long grey hair over a white face, looked up through the roof of the cage, straight into the camera.

'Pull it back,' said Aedith urgently. The woman's mouth opened wide as she shouted wordlessly, her face shrinking as the drone raised up into the sky. Agapos switched back to night vision, green blobs congregating on the cage.

'That's blown it,' said Drustan. 'Guards coming to check out the disruption.'

Aedith nodded. 'Human slavery? That one shouting might be the distraction we need, as long it's just the captives that know we're coming.'

They moved down the lane, hugging one side. Aedith nudged Drustan and pointed upwards, the drone hovering almost silently above the foundry.

'Battery's not great on those things, but we'll keep our eye in the sky as long as possible.'

Agapos, eyes fixed on his phone screen, made a complicated gesture. Fortunately, Aedith was able to interpret, ushering them silently down a side turning in the lane as two figures approached: Kesair tribesmen, heavily tattooed, wearing tracksuits and flipflops, cheap machine pistols slung over their shoulders.

'Hey,' said Aedith once they'd passed. She hit the first in the face with the butt of her shotgun as he turned. The second was wise enough to raise his hands. Agapos stripped both weapons of their magazines, tucking them into his tac vest, shoving the pistols into the hedge.

'First lesson for you, cadet: always carry plenty of zip ties,' said Aedith to Ord, binding both tribesmen's hands behind their backs and leaving them face-down in a ditch. 'I usually bring a dozen, minimum.'

But Ord was staring hungrily after the machine pistols. Drustan could practically see the Saxploitation movies running in his head. 'Forget it,' he said quietly. 'Hard to control, too wide a spray. We don't want civilian casualties.'

Ord looked back at him, nodded tightly. Saxons were an odd breed, spent half their time piling in on anyone with one foot outside their ethnic group, but would take orders from the Mughal Empress herself if their backs were against a wall.

'We haven't got long before they wonder where their patrol went,' said Agapos. He checked his phone. 'They're clustering up at the far end right now. Whatever's going down with those captives, it's happening soon.'

'Any sign of Deedra?' asked Aedith.

'Hard to tell at this range, ma'am,' said Agapos. 'None of these green blobs look thinner or more expensive.'

Aedith grinned. 'I suppose this isn't one where we send you in first pretending to be Hired Gun Number Four or the like.'

Drustan looked at Agapos. 'Do you do much undercover work, Sergeant?'

'You would be surprised,' replied Agapos in a perfect upper-class East Coast Pan-African accent.

'The Sergeant here has been the head of a corrupt Yoruban NGO with London financial interests,' said Aedith, 'an Ashanti arms dealer looking to smuggle explosives to a bunch of

Cumbrians who wanted to put a big hole in the Wall and, on one memorable occasion, an Ivory Coast gambler with a milk of the poppy addiction. Now, how about we stop braiding each other's hair and see what the cold hells is going on with that cage?'

TWENTY FIVE

It took eight minutes for the four of them to work their way silently to the centre of the foundry complex, Agapos checking his phone's screen to keep them out of the way of any patrolling green blobs. There weren't many. The Kesair were congregating towards the rear of the site, a patch of open ground where a glossy black four-wheel drive was parked, the interior illuminated by the firefly glow of a mobile phone.

Drustan was the last to duck behind the corner of a static caravan which hadn't been used as an office for fifteen years, if the calendar just visible through the grilled window was any evidence. May of that year had been the river goddess Melusine. Traditionally, Melusine's breasts were covered by river weed, although clearly there hadn't been much to hand at the time this particular photograph was taken.

'In the car, was that Deedra?' Drustan guessed Aedith would have little interest in Tribal mythology and now didn't seem the time to educate her. He nodded. The Kesair princess in the back seat was smaller in real life, wearing a drug-dealer's puffa jacket instead of catwalk high fashion, but otherwise looked just like her social-media photos.

'What about the guy next to her, looked like a priest?'

Drustan risked a quick peek around the corner. An older man, face concealed by a hooded robe. Deedra shifted her mobile for an instant and Drustan saw a torc around the man's neck: heavy, silver, a repeating leaf pattern in the silver instead of the usual twisted wire. Mistletoe.

'We have to get those captives out of there,' he said, his voice tight.

Aedith scowled at him. 'We came here for Deedra. We can still take her. Wait until she's away from the rest of her pack, take her down.'

Drustan shook his head. 'Deedra's not going anywhere, I promise you. But if we don't get those people out of that cage in the next few minutes, things will get very bad.'

Aedith cursed under her breath, but something in his tone had convinced her. 'Agapos, take the youth, go and cause a distraction. Run back to the cars if you have to. There's a walkie-talkie in the back seat, see if you can raise someone. We'll double back to the cage. Don't get yourself killed.'

Agapos nodded and made a hunched run to the far side of the caravan, Ord at his heels. Drustan was strangely proud of the lad. If he survived the night, he'd go far.

Drustan and Aedith silently retraced their steps. Without Agapos's phone, they could only hope they wouldn't run into a patrol. Their luck held out until they reached the foundry entrance. Aedith took a peek over the low wall.

'Two tribesmen. Both armed. Maybe we sneak round the other side?'

But Drustan was already buttoning his coat over his vest, slinging his shotgun over his shoulder and behind his back, out of sight.

'Give me a moment.'

Before Aedith could respond, Drustan vaulted casually over the wall, pushing up the sleeves of his coat and holding his hands up in placation to the guards. Their gun barrels dropped uncertainly as they spotted the marking on his wrist. He was within arm's reach of the first guard now. But then a radio crackled on the second's belt.

Aedith was already halfway there by the time Drustan had punched the first guard in the throat and unslung the shotgun to swing its butt into the side of the second's head, both men collapsing where they stood.

The radio asked something in a plaintive tone. Drustan picked it up, rapped out an order in what he hoped was a Kesair accent and turned it off.

'I told them we had to switch to a new channel. Should confuse them for a while.'

Aedith was already dragging the unconscious tribesmen, now cable-tied, out of sight. She paused, glaring back out into the complex. 'Where's our diversion?'

On cue, a car alarm a few buildings away starting shrieking, followed by shouts, a brief rattle of gunfire. Drustan met her gaze, pointed into the cavernous foundry exterior.

'Agapos knows what he's doing. We should go inside.'

The captives had gone quiet. Aedith joined Drustan, looking through a wire-meshed window against the back wall. The cage fenced off an outside yard. The people inside sat quietly, most gazing down at the floor, a few squatting on their haunches, still staring up at the night sky, perhaps hoping to glimpse the drone again. Their clothing was as bright as their faces were grey, Pan-African castoffs: t-shirts of Ghanaian metal bands, Ethiopian cartoon characters, wide-legged vibrantly coloured trousers a good couple of years out of fashion. Charitable donations, sent North by big-hearted Pan-Africans to help starving whites through the long cold winters. Going by the facial markings, or lack thereof, there were all sorts in there: Tribals, Saxons, even a couple of mixed-race Norse who must have fallen on hard times.

Aedith frowned. 'I know them. Some of them.'

Drustan was looking at a dark open passage. It would lead to the building the cage was attached to, a round red-bricked structure with a high chimney. 'Socially?'

'No, from the homeless camps. When they started emptying out, I assumed they'd sniffed trouble in the air, run for the woods.'

Drustan thought of the unbroken bottle, the lack of the usual signs of reeves moving through in force.

'They were taken,' said Drustan. 'Or lured here, at least. Promises of hot meals and a bed for the night, perhaps.'

'And what are they getting instead?'

But Drustan was already moving. 'We need to get in there.'

'We need to call backup. Fuck Deedra, this is bigger than us or her now.'

Drustan paused at the entrance, looked back at her, holding up a confiscated radio. 'I'll call it in now. But you know we don't have time to wait.'

Aedith stifled a curse and followed him into the darkness.

Drustan followed Aedith's torchlight as it moved around the interior of a sizeable chamber. It was round, big enough to park four cars in, if they could have somehow got through the doorway.

Brick walls narrowed above them to a chimney a hundred feet high. Pallets covered most of the floor, piled high with oversized white plastic sacks.

He reached over to Aedith's shotgun, quietly clicked the safety on. She scowled at him. 'What's this now?'

'We shouldn't even have torches.' He moved Aedith's hand down, illuminating a grey haze, still swirling low to the ground around from their entrance. An acrid taste in the back of Drustan's throat. From her expression, Drustan knew Aedith could taste it too.

'That's the fertiliser.'

He nodded. 'One spark, the whole place will go up.'

'They're hiding it here? What was this place, a kiln?'

'For bricks, I imagine. Bottles, maybe. But they're not hiding it.'

Drustan crouched by the nearest sack. It had been slit open, they all had; thin grey dust piled all over the floor. 'This is where it's supposed to be.'

Aedith moved her hand across the floor, brushed the dust off a ring bolted into the concrete floor. The metal was shiny, a rich orange colour. She stared at it, puzzled.

'Gold?'

'Bronze,' said Drustan. There must have been thirty of the rings at least, spread across the floor.

'What are they for?' Her voice was quiet, cold.

Drustan nodded across the chamber. 'For them.' The cage would be on the other side of that wall. It would take just a few minutes to bring the captives here, chain each one to a ring and then...

'Human sacrifice,' said Aedith finally.

Drustan opened his mouth, shut it again at a noise from outside the kiln, the shadow of a tall, hooded figure moving towards them cast by a plastic lantern. LED bulb, Drustan noted absently. Like the bronze rings, no danger of sparks. Aedith pulled Drustan behind a pallet piled high with sacks. They ducked low. Their footprints were obvious in the dust, but they weren't the only ones. It would have taken many trips to bring that much fertiliser in.

Drustan gripped his shotgun tightly, knowing it was worse than useless. It wouldn't even have to misfire, the hot vapour from the barrel with the first shot would be enough.

The priest was just visible around the corner of the pallet, dark hooded robe, trailing tattoos down the side of his bearded face, re-emerging onto the backs of his hands from under the cuffs of a crisp white shirt. Smart suit trousers too, black dress shoes barely touched by the fertiliser dust. He was chanting, drops of water falling all around, brushed from a silver bowl by a sprig of herbs, sanctifying the building before sending the captives to whichever Tribal gods he followed.

Get to the captives, Aedith mouthed. *I'll deal with the priest.*

Drustan blinked at her, but Aedith was already stepping out from the pallet, shotgun held in both hands like a club. The priest met her gaze but continued chanting while he finished flicking the last of the water onto the floor. There was another tattoo on the underside of his wrist, dark wings curling out from the white shirt cuffs. Then his hands fell to his sides. He nodded once at Aedith, a faint smile crossing his lips. Unnerving, but at least she had his attention. Drustan slipped away.

A guard had turned up to check on the captives by the time Drustan got to the cage. No time for finesse, Drustan sprayed him full in the face with pepper then shoved his head against the wall. He went down without a word. The captives made no noise throughout, just stared at him through the wire. Even when he'd smashed the padlock off the cage door, they made no attempt to escape.

Drustan pulled his warrant card out, held it up in the lantern light.

'Police', he said. He yanked the door open, pointed back down towards the track. 'Quick as you can. Don't look back.'

The grey-haired woman was the first to break and run past him and then they all did. A couple slowed to give the guard on the ground a kick. Seconds after the last had fled, Aedith appeared, moving at a full run. She had grey dust across her face and had ditched her weapon. The front of her tactical vest had a horizontal slash, revealing one of the Kevlar plates.

'He's got a lighter,' she said briefly, and kept running, Drustan already at her heels. Either there was far more fertiliser than necessary, or the walls of the kiln were weaker than anticipated, or perhaps both, because they were barely a hundred yards away when the building exploded.

TWENTY SIX

Drustan clambered to his feet and put his hand out, staring at the flakes of snow settling on his palm, and wondered idly why they felt so warm. Something had happened, he could remember that much. A force like a huge hand smacking him in the back, followed by a wave of sound so loud it hadn't so much jolted his brain as forced every single neuron apart from its neighbour. They were only now beginning to knit themselves back together.

He heard voices shouting and for a moment thought he was back in the Mughal hills, but the shouts were in Saxon. Figures surged around him, cops and paramedics wearing hi-vis vests only lightly covered in the grey-white flakes, which Drustan was starting to realise was ash that was falling from the sky for some reason. He could see Kesair tribesmen, but they were sullen and silent, squatting on the ground, the fight gone out of them. Evaporated, Drustan was starting to remember now, along with their priest. They'd dropped their weapons, surrendering to the armed response team who were already cuffing them and loading them into the back of a large van with wire mesh across the windows.

An armed cop loomed out of the ash, barking something at Drustan from behind a compact rifle with so many devices attached it resembled some arcane recording device rather than a weapon. Fortunately, Drustan had lost his shotgun, although he was still holding his warrant card, which he waved vaguely in front of him. The cop nodded and moved on.

Drustan walked past a paramedic attending to a group of dazed captives, another armed reeve doing his best to make sure no Tribesmen were trying to sneak out pretending to be prisoners.

A big cop in plain clothes and a tactical vest put his hand on Drustan's chest, shouted something at him about someone still missing. Something about his broad features was familiar, as was the name 'Aedith' he shouted over and over again. Drustan shook his head dreamily and kept walking. He passed a young reeve, barely more than a teenager, sitting on the floor, tears and snot making tracks down his face, staring at a hand sticking out from under a collapsed wall. Drustan kept walking.

As ruins turned into young saplings, he saw in the distance a figure, barely visible through the ash, a young woman, wearing a faded grey denim jacket, covered in patches, over a long skirt. Her feet were bare. She looked back over her shoulder, half her face covered with swirling black markings, then disappeared into the darkness. Drustan could have sworn she had looked right at him, yet somehow hadn't seen him at all.

Was that Deedra? Changed her clothing, tricked her way past the *gwithyas* once again? No, Drustan had passed her earlier, hands cuffed behind her back, a senior cop holding a mobile up to her ear so she could talk to her lawyer.

Drustan stumbled after the young woman.

The foundry was far behind him now, the ground under his feet shifting from concrete to close-packed earth, but the ash was still falling. Drustan tried his torch. It went out almost immediately, so he banged it with the heel of his hand until it came back on, illuminating broken ground, air hazy with ash, but no sign of the woman. He leaned against a broken wall for a moment, tried to spit the acrid taste out of his mouth.

Behind him, he heard shouted commands, captives coming to their senses, fleeing into the woods rather than be picked up by the cops – and who could blame them? Had the girl been one of those in the cage? She was undoubtedly Tribal, her skin beneath the facial tattoos as pale as his own, yet she had seemed calm, languorous even, her jacket and hair untouched by the falling ash.

Something moved ahead of him, flitting between trees and vanishing again. He spat out more ash and picked up the pace, pushing between thin branches that whipped back at his face and body, his torch beam falling on what must have been a workshop or a garage before nature and neglect had taken their toll. He could hear faint sounds on the other side of an ivy-covered wall but there was no door to open. Drustan scrambled over the half-collapsed stone and found himself staring up at a figure a foot off the ground, nailed onto the only wooden support beam still standing.

This woman was older, perhaps in her fifties, wearing what had once been a smart business suit, although her sleeveless white blouse was stained with dirt and blood now. The hair covering her face was greying ash-blonde. The discreet arm-rings on her bare outstretched limbs, glinting in the torchlight, suggested upper-middle-class Saxon. The nails that had been driven through wrists and ankles were the same that had been used on Gorsedd: dull grey, utilitarian.

He reached up, gently pulling down the neck of the woman's blouse. Below the collarbone: the design of a fish, about the width of his hand.

Jerking her chin up, the woman stared into Drustan's face and screamed.

TWENTY SEVEN

'They put Deedra in the cells downstairs,' said Aedith. 'Won't even tell her lawyers where, they're falling over each other in the foyer right now. But what I want to know,' she continued in a level tone, 'is at what point you realised human sacrifice was on the cards?'

They were in Aedith's office. Drustan had stumbled into the station with the morning shift once the paramedics had given him a once-over and declared him sufficiently mentally stable to give a statement to an independent officer. He'd decided against mentioning the woman he'd followed in the woods because in the cold light of day, he was no longer sure she had been real.

Aedith had appeared an hour or so after Drustan, limping, bruised and with bandages on her bare arms where she'd been nicked by flying debris. Their eyes had met across the incident room, but Aedith's gaze had moved down to his wrist then flicked away and she'd gone to check on Agapos. Since then, Drustan had managed to get a couple of hours' sleep on a cot bed set up in a spare interrogation room and showered in the cramped station gym. His clothes stank. Constable Naeku had taken them away, brought him tracksuit bottoms and a t-shirt a size too big, with the unofficial police crest: a severed Norse head on a shield above two crossed seaxes. Management had been trying to persuade the rank and file to abandon it for years now, to no avail.

The door to Aedith's office was firmly shut behind them. Aedith had made herself a coffee but not offered Drustan one, a brutal move by police standards.

Drustan sighed, rubbed his eyes with his hands, looking blearily at the kohl smearing his fingers. Always embarrassing having to ask Saxons for make-up remover.

'We've suspected the Kesair of clinging to the old ways for some time now. Never had any proof. We always thought they exaggerated to give themselves an edge, maybe just a few fanatics here and there getting carried away.'

'Who's "we"?'

When Drustan didn't answer, Aedith reached forward, took hold of his wrist and turned it over. The mark of a black bird against the clean pale skin, its wings bent round to form an almost perfect circle.

'Those two guards – you pushed up your sleeves deliberately so they would see it.' Of course she had noticed. He had suspected she might. 'And I saw the same thing on the priest, before he blew himself to the heavens along with gods know how many other people. So, tell me Detective Inspector Drustan, of whatever tribe you belong to, what are you exactly?'

Drustan looked down at his wrist, twisting it a little so the office light reflected off the tattoo. Twenty years since he had accepted the mark and it was as black and fresh as the day he had put on the blindfold and been led by the elder into the stone temple, deep in the forest.

'I'm not a priest,' he said finally. 'Although the role is hard to tell apart from the outside, and I'll admit we encourage a certain… solemnity to the position. Makes it easier to get answers from those in the West more inclined to superstition. Respect for tradition, is another way of putting it. I doubt it would work on Deedra, or anyone with a more sophisticated grasp of modern realities, but it has its uses.'

Aedith gave him a look over her coffee before taking a long swig and wincing. 'You're windbagging, Celt. Tell me something or tell me nothing.'

Drustan looked at her. 'I'm not trying to obfuscate or confuse. I actually find the straightforwardness of the Saxon manner enormously refreshing, but it's not easy to emulate.'

Aedith made an exasperated sound. Drustan threw his hands up in supplication. 'I'm a member of what you could call a secret society. Somewhere between a poet and a lawyer. We don't have a name. Many of us are in the police, others operate at different levels of society. Tribal society has a lot of what you'd call shieldwalls, barriers with dialects, beliefs, subcultures. Those of us with the mark can move with greater freedom, get things done. The priest's mark means he was a member of the same society. I didn't know him. I doubt we'd ever met.'

'If you'd seen the mark, would it have made any difference? To anything?'

'Knowing he was going to shackle thirty people to the floor and burn them alive? Not a great deal, no.'

Aedith opened her mouth to say something, but Naeku was knocking at the door. She entered, pressed a piece of paper into Aedith's hand, withdrew again.

Aedith looked down and cursed.

'The victim's dead. Heart attack in the ambulance on the way to the hospital.'

'Blessings be upon her soul,' said Drustan, absently.

Aedith looked at him. 'I'm assuming she was marked with the fish.'

'She was,' said Drustan. 'Has the hospital released the body yet?'

Aedith shook her head. 'Not yet. Although Forensics are on the scene at the foundry.'

'They'll find the same pattern. She was nailed up just like Gorsedd, almost certainly drugged first. Possibly the explosion at the foundry panicked the killer before he could finish the job and slit her throat.'

The desk phone trilled. Aedith picked up, nodded. 'Hengist wants to see us. Our little escapade must have landed him in the shit with the top brass.'

'Does Tancred know we have Deedra yet?'

'Well,' said Aedith, 'that's the question, isn't it? Hengist booked her under a false name, trying to throw Special Branch off the scent, although Deedra's lawyers will break through eventually.'

Something was happening in the office outside, officers rising from their desks, moving as one to gaze at something just out of sight. She scratched her bandaged arm absently.

'You just gave the victim a blessing.'

Drustan nodded.

'I thought you weren't a priest?'

'We have a different relationship with the gods. Any of us can commune with the higher powers, ask them questions, challenge them, go against them if need be. We *have* priests, but they're not pillars of the community. We're free to disagree with them, violently if necessary.'

Aedith was still keeping half an eye on the office. The officers all stared straight ahead.

'How violently does a poet-slash-lawyer get to disagree with a priest, in your experience?'

'Well,' said Drustan carefully, 'I once composed a satire that made a senior druid kill himself, if that answers your question. It wasn't long after that the Goddess stopped speaking to me.'

Aedith stared at him.

Another knock at the door, which immediately opened a crack to reveal dreadlocks under a hoodie.

'No, no, it's fine,' said Aedith. 'I might just take the thing off its hinges, let people come straight in.'

But Banba's face was screwed up with worry. 'Sorry to bother you, ma'am, but you need to see this.'

The Pict had paused the image, expanded it across her wall of monitors, a glitched trembling mosaic.

'Show me,' said Aedith.

Banba hit the space bar. The head and shoulders of a figure in a black hood. A plastic mask covered their face and eyes, semi-military in nature, the sort of thing middle managers wore when they went into the woods with tacticool gear to paintball. The figure had been badly superimposed onto stock library footage of white clouds moving slowly against a blue sky, the edge of the hood blurring and fading.

'Hail, true Britons,' said the voice behind the mask. It had been made artificially harsh and deep by electronic means, but the speaker was almost certainly a man.

'Oh good,' said Aedith. 'The conspiracy videos have begun.'

'I'm not sure, ma'am,' said Banba. 'Keep watching.'

The view behind the speaker had changed to a woodland scene: early morning light filtering through the branches of oak and ash. Northern temperate woodland, filmed from a depression, and Drustan was already starting to think the view looked familiar when the camera completed the full three hundred and sixty degrees and centred on a man, seemingly resting against a tree, although it was obvious that if the camera shifted a little to either side, the nails that held Gorsedd Angwin to the trunk of the oak would be plainly visible.

Aedith stared. 'Oh shit.'

'Yes,' said Banba. 'It's the real thing.'

The picture wobbled for a moment, then stabilised on Angwin. Agapos leaned forward, squinted. 'Is that camera mounted on a helmet?'

'On his chest, I'd guess,' said Aedith from somewhere behind Drustan. 'Wearing it like a bodycam.'

Angwin's eyes were closed but he was mumbling something in Tribal dialect.

'What's he saying?' asked Aedith, but Drustan was watching a latex-gloved hand hold up a long-bladed knife, a classic seax, using the point to lift Angwin's chin up. The Celt opened his eyes and smiled into his killer's face, repeating the same words louder now until the edge flashed across his throat. Blood gushed out and down to the forest floor as the light went out of Angwin's eyes, his head dropping to his chest.

The point of the seax pushed into Angwin's side, to no response, and withdrew. A gloved hand wiped blood from his chest, revealing the fish tattoo for a moment before it was covered up once more by the last of the blood running from the ruin of what had been a throat.

'Pause it,' said Aedith. 'Check his wrist for a sparrow.'

It was no use. The killer's latex gloves disappeared into dark sleeves.

'Godsdammit. It could be anyone.'

'Look upon the Fish,' said the voice, with no more emotion than if it had been reading out a shopping list. No real accent either, that Drustan could make out. He was speaking Saxon English, but it was flat, uninflected. 'They try to turn our countries into a mongrel nation, to bring us all down so their twisted religion might rise up, delivering our children to them not from fear, but willingly. But know this, they would be nothing without the elites, the pampered rich who would sell us to the Blackamoors, the Mongols, the Franks across the water who have grown fat upon the poisoned milk of the desert tribes.'

Angwin's body, now looking as Drustan had first seen it, made a slow dissolve into a second body, a woman's, nailed up at the same angles, but here on the beams of an abandoned building. Darkness crowded the edges of the frame, an LED lantern hung on a length of broken rebar by the woman's side casting a pitiless illumination. Unlike Angwin's gentle expression, the woman's face was tight, drawn, tendons standing out on her neck as she fought against the pain, her breathing harsh, ragged. Yet, as Drustan watched, she threw no curses against her attacker, no threats to find him in the afterlife. Her effort seemed to be all internal, as if the killer in front of her, dressed again in overalls and plastic mask, was merely a part of the scenery.

Again, the point of a blade pulled down the neck of a sleeveless blouse to reveal the symbol of the fish, then the seax lifted to her throat – and the camera juddered at the explosion from somewhere behind the killer. Banba's collection of screens returned to the masked figure against the blue sky – the library footage now tilting to reveal flat grasslands suddenly cut across by chalk cliffs. Was that Dover?

'Rise up, Peoples of Britain, of all three Kingdoms,' said the figure. 'Protect your nations and end this Summit.'

The screens went black.

'It's all over social media,' said Banba. 'He's released some sort of manifesto too. I'm printing it off now.' Her printer was already chattering. The first page was coming through: a mess of runes at the top, a headline reading 'FOR THE TRUE BRITONS' in an unimpressive font, then paragraph after paragraph of closely-typed rant. There were many exclamation marks.

'He was saying "I forgive you",' said Drustan.

Aedith was distracted. 'What?'

'Gorsedd Angwin. Before his throat was cut. He looked his killer in the eyes and said, "I forgive you".'

'Why the hells would he say that?' Aedith looked genuinely bewildered. Drustan shrugged. There was probably something about it in the Fishers' book.

'I've read about spree killers who want to be caught,' said Aedith, back in her office. 'Sending little messages to the reeves, taunting them. But this is a step beyond that. I don't think Wulfstan – if that was Wulfstan – cares if he's caught or not, as long as he takes out as many Fishers as he can before we get him. But "Briton" is a Tribal term. Who's he talking to? And what have Fishers got to do with the Summit?'

'I think he's trying to talk to everyone,' said Drustan. 'Both kingdoms: Celt and Saxon. Maybe Norse too, some of the runes in the manifesto look pretty familiar. He seems to think the Fishers are mixed up with the Summit somehow, which seems a stretch.'

Aedith sipped her coffee. She'd handed Drustan a cup without a word. 'So, he wants to unify the country against… a summit that wants to unify the country? I'd called that mixed messaging at the very least.'

'"Separate but equal", isn't that what the radio tricksters like to say?' Drustan picked up the manifesto. Four pages so far and the printer was still whirring. He flicked through it. 'None of this adds up. There are dozens of conspiracy theories here, all stirred up together. And I don't mean "The Pan-Africans never went to the moon" stuff, there's mad stuff: wifi summoning dark elves, the Wall being a big hologram put up by the Norse, the High Table tracking agitators by putting microchips in their honeycakes—'

'I happen to believe in that one,' said Aedith, her face solemn.

'I authorised the raid on the foundry,' said Hengist.

Drustan hadn't seen the station commander on his feet before. His head nearly reached the ceiling tiles. Hengist stood by his internal window, looking down at the wide central stairway that punched through the building as if left in the wake of a giant fist. Civilian workers and officers moved through the levels carrying clipboards, internal memos, on their way to meetings. If you didn't know this was a police station it could easily have been mistaken for a largish corporation, perhaps some sort of planning department. In a sense, it was.

'I'm not following you, Commander,' said Aedith.

'The paperwork got delayed, unfortunately, but I've signed it now. This sort of thing happens from time to time.'

Hengist had an empty cardboard box on his desk, rarely a good omen. Perhaps there was still time to salvage the situation.

'Detective Captain Mercia was just following a colleague who had the luxury of being able to make an impulse decision,' said Drustan. 'By which I mean myself, obviously. By the time she caught up with me, we realised a number of captives were being held at the facility, leaving us with really no choice but to act. I take full responsibility—'

Hengist waved a large hand at him, and Drustan fell silent.

'We've got information back on the victim.' Hengist sounded detached, tired. 'Eawynn Wettin. Civil servant, administrative assistant, been working the Summits for twenty years, on and off. Hard worker, well-liked by her colleagues by all accounts.'

'Was she working with Angwin?' Aedith was studying Hengist's face, trying to get a read on him, it looked like to Drustan. Something about her manner was wary, concerned. Drustan didn't know Hengist well enough to be able to tell if he was acting out of character, but something was worrying Aedith.

'Nothing concrete. Unlikely but not impossible they might have met in some official capacity but nothing in her email history.'

Hengist put his large finger on a single sheet of paper, pushed it silently across the desk to Aedith, then pointed to a small speaker mounted high in the corner and tapped his ear. Drustan was impressed. Few officers knew how easily speakers could be rewired to double as microphones. Maybe Hengist had a few surveillance courses in his background.

'Anyway,' Hengist continued, perhaps just a little louder than necessary. 'I'm sorry to tell you I need to step away from control of this investigation.'

Hengist turned his gaze back to the window. It was the first time Drustan had seen Aedith lost for words. She opened her mouth, shut it again, took the paper, folded it, slid it into a pocket.

'May I ask why, sir?'

'I've been very tired lately. Difficulty with the work/life balance. I've got plenty of leave accrued, so I'll be taking a few weeks off and seeing how things go. Lieutenant Colonel Adamu will be taking over as Station Commander. He's of the old school, something of a traditionalist but fair-minded, I've always thought. Treat him with respect and he'll do the same with you.'

Aedith opened her mouth to protest but Hengist shook his head. Drustan watched Aedith compose herself into the personification of a junior officer receiving unwelcome but dealable-with news.

'I'm sorry to hear that, sir. That you'll be away for a while, I mean.' Her voice was brisk. She stood more formally now, hands clasped behind her back. Hengist caught Drustan's gaze and nodded. Slowly, Drustan nodded back.

'Major Tancred will deal with the political and terrorist implications of the case,' he continued, as though it was a minor formality. 'I'm sure you'll show Special Branch nothing but the high levels of professionalism I've come to expect from you, Captain.'

Drustan honestly couldn't tell if Hengist had brought any irony to that last bit or not, but Aedith remained impassive.

'Of course, sir. May I ask if Special Branch are likely to find a role for our Tribal liaison, Detective Inspector Drustan? I've found his specialist knowledge of the Celtic immigrant community invaluable, along with his impressive list of contacts.'

Drustan said nothing.

'I imagine, Captain Mercia,' said Hengist, 'that Special Branch will want to operate by their standard procedure of keeping information on an in-house basis, although Major Tancred wanted me to pass on DI Drustan his grateful thanks for the work he's done so far. Any contacts he has that he thinks might be useful could be passed on to Special Branch in list form.'

Drustan's face didn't move with that one, although Aedith was unable to keep the faintest of smirks from crossing her lips.

'I will give Major Tancred's request all due consideration,' Drustan assured Hengist.

'Marvellous,' said Hengist, scratching his wide jaw distractedly. 'I'm afraid Major Tancred had the sad duty of informing me that the academy has unexpectedly accepted a fresh intake of cadets and will no longer be able to provide the DI with accommodation, so if he could return and pick up his belongings at his earliest convenience, that would be much appreciated.'

Drustan nodded. 'Of course.'

'Well,' said Hengist. 'I'm sure I'll see you again in due course, Captain Mercia. DI Drustan, it's been a pleasure.'

Hengist enclosed Drustan's hand in his and shook it. He barely had to reach up to take the ram's head down from the wall. Placing it reverently in the box, he followed it with a few cardboard-bound files, cheap plastic pens and a coffee mug that had once proudly sported the crest of some sports team, made ghostly by too many trips through the dishwasher.

'Couple of street reeves finally got that shoplifter you were after, Captain,' he added, apparently as an afterthought. 'All that high-fashion stuff. Interview room fifteen. I know it's not a priority right now, but you may want to throw some questions at her before her family turn up and make a fuss, see where it leads you.'

Aedith nodded. Hengist put a hand on her shoulder as he passed her on the way to the door. He stopped, looked around. 'At least I'll have time for reading.' And then he left.

TWENTY EIGHT

Drustan followed Aedith through the maze of corridors to the back of the building. This whole side was a relic of the upgrade the station had gone through thirty years before, in the time of bombs on the streets, whole communities of Tribals brought in for questioning in a single night, although apparently the rubber floors with the drains in the middle had been tiled over some years ago. Modern police didn't use the rooms any more if they could help it, what with them being so far from the cells, suspects having to be brought up and down numerous flights of stairs. Of course, many of the older hands on the force still regarded that as a feature rather than a bug.

The name written in whiteboard marker on the door's plastic sheet was 'Alder Gough'. Standing to attention outside the door was an older uniformed officer who'd put one hand on his sidearm the moment he'd heard footsteps approaching. The moment he saw Aedith, he nodded, smoothly turning a key and letting the door swing open. His expression didn't change when he saw Drustan, but he didn't take his hand off the weapon either.

'Any recording devices inside?' asked Aedith.

'No ma'am. Power's been erratic for some time on this level. Lighting only.'

Aedith stepped past him, Drustan close behind.

*

'Aedith, my darling!' Deedra looked genuinely pleased to see her. 'You haven't brought any vapes, I suppose; I'm absolutely gasping.'

Deedra should have looked diminished in the starkly lit utilitarian room, with its sturdy laminate table and metal-framed chairs, all bolted securely to the floor. Instead, in her gleaming puffa jacket over a black dress, her smoky eye make-up apparently untouched by explosion and arrest, she merely looked as though she was hanging out in some backstage area, waiting for the real show to begin. Which, thought Drustan, to a certain point of view was correct.

Aedith took a seat opposite her. A large and ancient tape recorder squatted in a niche in the wall. Aedith pulled it out, yanking the wires until they slithered free. They'd been severed years, maybe decades ago. She grunted, pulled a plastic bottle of water from her greatcoat pocket and placed it before Deedra, who daintily removed the lid and sipped.

'You know,' said Deedra finally, 'your commander's been very naughty keeping me from my lawyers. I imagine they're having absolute conniptions, wherever they are.'

'He's also keeping you from Special Branch,' said Aedith. 'Who are only slightly less likely to put a bullet through your Indij head than I am. I should have let those kids have you at school, saved us all a lot of bother.'

Deedra's eyes sparkled. She grinned slyly at Drustan.

'Hello, Inspector. We haven't met, but my people made me aware you were in town. Are they treating you well, my countryman? I know the constabulary here can be terribly rough on those of us from the West. Let me know if you need some new clothes, that t-shirt's terribly ill-fitting.'

Drustan's expression didn't change.

'You've never even lived in the West,' said Aedith. 'My family spend more time there than yours ever did.'

'Ah yes,' reflected Deedra wistfully. 'Your lovely little summer house on the edge of the moors. It's quite beautiful, you know.' She was addressing Drustan now. 'Wild ponies, her and her charming brother endlessly swimming in limpid waters. Did your father buy the property outright, do you know, Aeds, or did he just sort of take it after the original owners were found dead?'

'Killed by your tribe, if I remember correctly,' said Aedith. 'And don't mention my brother again, or I'll push your face into that table and you'll have to get your teeth done all over again.'

'Of course, sweetheart,' said Deedra, contritely putting her hands flat on the table, palms down. 'Now do ask your questions, I'm only too happy to have an excuse to catch up.'

'The woman,' said Aedith. 'The one nailed up in an outhouse five minutes from where you were getting ready to have your little banefire.'

For the first time since entering the room, Drustan saw uncertainty in Deedra Kesair's face. Not guilt, or even evasion, but the slightest flicker of puzzlement before the perfectly groomed brows moved back to a state of amused innocence.

'I'm afraid I quite genuinely don't know what you're talking about, Aeds. I've never nailed anyone up in my life. Not my level of kink. Now, if we're talking about lightly suspended from silk ropes, that's an area in which I will admit to a certain amount of experience.'

'But you will consider burning alive a couple of dozen homeless people. I'm just wondering to what end?'

'Oh darling.' Deedra flicked something infinitesimal off the sleeve of her coat with a disappointed finger. She looked bored now, sulky even. Aedith leaned back in her chair, arms folded, daring the other women to shock, perhaps even impress her. Drustan wondered if their relationship had changed at all since their schooldays. Then the smell that had been lingering faintly in the room ever since they had entered registered properly with him: smoke and ash, the smell of the foundry.

'Human sacrifice to bring good fortune,' said Drustan. 'On the eve of a great battle, or an important ritual. The Saxons did it too, although they stamped it out years ago, under pressure from various trading partners over the years.'

The Mughals had been the most fastidious about it, if his desultory history lessons had been correct, being appalled a couple of hundred years ago when one particularly enthusiastic High Queen had shown her guests, a group of Mughal merchants making an early and tentative trade expedition, the severed heads of a thousand prisoners, murdered in hopes of sealing a particularly tedious deal to do with fishing rights. The Mughals had instantly withdrawn, the High Queen removed a few years later.

Deedra took a long draught from the water bottle, fastidiously screwing the top back on once she was finished.

'We couldn't take any chances with the Summit,' said Deedra. 'You have no idea the political pressure my clan is under, apparently siding with the Strawheads – yes, we have little names for you too, darling – in order to get this thing over the line. We've worked too hard and too long for a seat at the High Table to let it slip away. I was simply doing due diligence, and if that requires a few rather sad and tired people to move into the afterlife on our behalf... well, it was, not to put too fine a point on it, a sacrifice I was prepared to make.'

'I don't care *why* you were doing it,' said Aedith. 'The woman, did you know anything about the fish tattoo? The video, is it anything to do with you?'

Deedra pulled an 'awkward' face, looked sideways at Drustan. 'I honestly have no idea what she's talking about.'

Aedith rubbed her face tiredly. 'All right,' she said finally. 'Let's get her back in the system. Not long until Special Branch find out we have her and putting the wrong name on the door won't stall them for long.'

Deedra gave her a look filled with, as far as Drustan could tell, genuine sympathy.

'Oh sweetie,' she said. 'You're doing this completely wrong. 'This isn't how you deal with a hostage at all.' She turned to Drustan. 'Tell her, *Filí*.'

Aedith frowned at Drustan. 'It means poet,' he said. 'In a way. And she has a point. Tancred must have realised they have a decoy by now. You can use her to bargain with them.'

'Bargain for what?'

'To stay on the case. Tancred wants the glory, wants his name on all the headlines when the killer goes down. He doesn't want to do the work; he wants the promotion at the end of it. We get her out of here, contact Special Branch, hand her over when certain promises are made.'

'Look at the two of you,' said Aedith quietly. 'All Tribals together.'

Deedra polished her cuffs on her sleeve, held them up before her to check her make-up as best she could. 'It's either that, my love, or you make the call you've been putting off your whole life and get your father to pull some strings on your behalf.'

Aedith ignored that. 'I hand you over to Special Branch now, you won't get access to your fancy lawyers. You'll likely disappear into the system, turn up one day with a bullet in the back of your head if you turn up at all. You sure you don't want to buy yourself a little time with any information you might have on what the hells else was going on at that foundry besides burning a load of people alive?'

Deedra examined her nails for a long time. 'Your secret police won't hold me,' she said finally. She was matter of fact now, nothing boastful about it. 'And it may astonish you to hear I don't tell my friend from school turned *gwithyas* everything, but I've never lied to you. I don't know anything about a woman being nailed to a wall or whatever has you so riled up. Entirely possible one of my boys had a little side project going on, but if so, that's the first I've heard of it.'

'What about Ash and Stone?' asked Aedith.

Deedra was silent for a moment. Drustan could see her reaching back, finding the information, hefting it, wondering how it had value.

'Party supplies?' she asked. 'I'd offer to hook you up, darling, but I'm sure you have your own contacts. Anyway, they're not answering their phone, I called them a couple of nights ago.'

'About what?'

'About an actual party, trying to mend some fences when the Summit starts. They're a legitimate events organiser, you know, the naughty potions are just a little extra. Or were. I was even considering acquiring them for my own purposes actually, but there were rumours about some other group hovering with their own offer and I had no intention of being pulled into some sort of horrid bidding war.' Deedra yawned, bored now. 'Could we move out of this ghastly little room, please? There's a very real chance some of my family were beaten to death in here and it's making me maudlin.'

*

'What do you think?' asked Aedith. The armed officer was looking straight at the wall. Saxon cops in this part of the station knew how to blend into their surroundings, hear nothing and say less.

'I think she's telling the truth,' said Drustan. 'About the second victim, about Ash and Stone, and about making a deal with Special Branch. She's willing to help you out, oddly enough. How are you going to play it?'

Aedith thought for a moment. 'I hate this cattle-trading,' she said finally. 'Making deals, owing favours; but it might be only way to stay on the case. Here's what I'm going to do: tell Deedra's lawyers we have their client, booked under a false name for her own safety. Then pass the good news to Tancred. That way we're not *not* co-operating.'

'That won't be enough to keep the case.'

'We'll see,' said Aedith. 'Hengist's a good man, but his talents lie in paperwork and keeping meetings short. That's not even a dig, that's a useful skillset in a senior officer. I still don't understand why he's taking leave. Perhaps Tancred put pressure on him somehow?'

'I suspect if our friend the Major had that level of power, he wouldn't have stopped at getting Hengist to take leave, he'd have forced him out. Perhaps Hengist is unofficially recusing himself? Taking himself out of the case without being able to say so?'

She stared at him. 'Why the hells would he do that?'

'Because he's involved in some way he can't tell you about without putting the entire investigation in jeopardy.'

'A relative, perhaps?' Aedith shook her head. 'No, his wife's family live up by the Wall. His wife and kids might have been threatened, I can see that making him step aside for a while. Either way, he left us a gift, but he's a dead end now.'

'What are you going to do?'

'I'm going to make a call.'

TWENTY NINE

Tancred's press conference the next day, streamed by Banba through to the office wall screens, was brief and professional, at least at first. The actions of the killer were deplorable and clearly aimed at destabilising the Unification Summit, although there were no plans to stop its formal opening on the Friday. Captain Mercia and her team would continue their fine work on the murder investigations while Special Branch would focus on the possibility of a terrorist threat. There had been an incident at a Kesair-owned foundry on the outskirts of the city, near the location of the second killing, which was thought to be the result of a gas explosion, although terrorism hadn't been ruled out as a cause. Deedra Kesair was helping police with their enquiries, although her lawyers were stressing this was purely voluntary and she was free to leave any time she chose.

Journalists were barking questions, which were going ignored, but a sterner voice at the back of the crowd wasn't taking no for an answer. The camera zoomed in on an older Tribal woman, facial marks denoting her as a second-generation immigrant, smart business suit and lanyard putting her with one of the new streaming news services.

'Major Tancred, I'm getting reports that both victims were members of the same minor cult, apparently with pre-Caliphate origins. Any comments on these so-called "Fishers"?'

Aedith cursed but couldn't help enjoying how tense and unhappy Tancred had suddenly become, shuffling his notes for a moment before being able to bring himself to look the journalist in the eye. 'I'm afraid operational security doesn't allow me to comment at this particular time,' he said. The photographers went to work, their flashes highlighting his clenched jaw and pursed lips. He nodded briefly, to no one in particular, and stalked from the stage.

'Someone's put pressure on him to get this wrapped up as soon as possible,' said Aedith.

'Agreed,' said Drustan. 'But who?'

Her phone trilled once. A text message.

'Trouble?' asked Drustan, rather irritatingly, since Aedith was sure she hadn't let her expression change. On the screens, Tancred was ignoring questions and striding away from the cameras, ignoring shouts from journalists and a few carefully selected influencers.

'It's my father,' she said. 'He wants to talk.'

Lod was waiting for her in a small café round the corner from the station, which catered mainly for contracted civilian workers and those uniforms who found the in-station catering too sophisticated. The air was hazy with the aroma and air-borne grease of deep-fried root vegetables and burned venison. The cheap radio behind the counter blared out popular Saxon hits: discordant horns and rhythmic chanting backed by what sounded like a series of car crashes.

'I like this place,' said Lod, both hands around a burger almost the size of his head. 'I think I'd like to be buried here.'

Aedith rolled her eyes. There were a lot of places where Lod apparently wanted to be buried. In reality, Aedith knew her father had no intention of dying, and no interest in what happened to his remains when he did: he just wanted to remind her the Mercians had a legacy and they were all just links in a mighty chain that ideally would go on for ever into the future: mining asteroids and living in hab domes on Mars, probably.

'I'll update the spreadsheet accordingly,' said Aedith. 'Did you tell Tancred to keep me on the case?'

'Didn't have to,' said Lod, and took a mighty bite of his burger. Aedith waited impatiently while he chewed and swallowed, juice running down into his beard. Finally, he said in a low voice: 'The Summit might actually come to something this time.'

Aedith took an unimpressed sip of her tea, said nothing.

'The High King wants his legacy. Bringing the Three Kingdoms together would get him sung into the eternal halls, drinking mead with his ancestors until the end of time.'

'He's really on his death bed?'

'Not there yet but close enough. I've spoken with the other Earl-Electors. We're sticking to our routines, no one needs to see the crows gathering, but plans are being drawn. But as much as he wants this, others are dead set against.'

'Other Electors?'

Lod shook his head. 'Greater powers, over the whale roads. The kind with thinktanks, legal departments, expense accounts that would keep your department running for decades.'

'The kind who could plant crates of expensive weapons and explosives in a Tribal diplomat's grace-and-favour flat?'

'All in a morning's work.'

'And Special Branch? Where do they stand in this?'

'Counter-terrorism became their own faction decades ago. Trusted with too many secrets, they went from servants to masters.

Of some, at least. They couldn't care less about the Summit or legacies; they just don't want to see their power reduced. For now, they're content to follow the paths they're given, and for that, they need you. They threaten and cover up, they don't investigate. For as long as they want the truth, your interests and theirs are aligned.'

'Dad, have you ever heard of a company called Ash and Stone? Party supplies, technically, but they were going well outside their remit before suddenly packing up their tents and disappearing into the night.'

Lod shook his head and belched delicately, wiping his chin with a paper napkin.

'Doesn't ring a bell. And I didn't interfere with your case because I didn't need to. Not to say I couldn't pull some strings if asked.'

'Then why are we talking?'

'I can't talk to my own daughter?'

'In the middle of a workday? There are better times. I assume you had something important to discuss.'

Lod gestured for the bill, went silent for a moment. The music had stopped now, replaced by an Aunt Nancy, ranting across the airwaves about Saxon sovereignty, Tribal freeloaders, arrogant Norse bankers. Aedith followed Lod's gaze, taking in the other patrons of the café: attentive, absorbing every word, most of them nodding along.

'There's more of this stuff lately,' continued Lod in a low voice. 'Different sources but all chanting from the same saga. Planted weapons and explosives are the things that come up on your radar, this is what comes up on mine. The sluice gates opened a couple of months ago and now every arsehole with an opinion has a slot on a breakfast show, a book that's come out a bit too quickly, a comfy seat in front of some nodding-dog committee on the High King's table that's got journalists all over it, for obvious reasons.'

'Greater powers.' Aedith sounded more doubtful than she felt. Lod wasn't one for conspiracy theories.

'A lot of factions benefit from keeping the Kingdoms divided, constantly playing us off against each other. Corporations, billionaires, anyone who enjoys free access to our resources, natural or public, or just wants to hide away cash Pan-African tax collectors would like to get their hands on. They want to keep things that way and a Unification Summit that's about more than pretty words threatens them. You're chasing a small fish into deep water. I feel duty-bound to warn you about the sharks.'

Aedith could feel her cheeks flushing. Lod always had this effect on her. She remembered a game of Hnefatafl one Yule, trying to box in her father's king piece, him expertly pulling her into trap after trap, picking off her guard pieces one at a time while all the time running a commentary on the weaknesses of her strategies; how she needed to look at the board as a whole, not just her small corner of it. She'd been eight years old. Edric had refused to play with him any more two Yules before that.

'Dad, this small fish has already killed at least two people. I need to stop him before he kills any more. The Summit's his excuse. If I have to chase him into the foyer of the Skeid and put a bullet in his brain in front of the assembled delegates of the three nations and the entire Pan-African media, don't think I'd hesitate for a moment.'

The café owner, a short Northerner who Aedith had once overheard making approving noises at a report about Saxon car-bombers taking out a Norse patrol at the Wall, approached them, clearly pretending he hadn't heard that last bit. His hands shook a little as he offered to take care of the bill himself. Lod, of course, wouldn't hear of it, but made great play of appreciating the man's gesture, something that would be noted in the great ledgers of the Mercians and one day repaid in full when the glorious End Times came. Aedith didn't know how Lod could cope with this sort of nonsense on a daily basis; it must be *exhausting*.

Lod grinned at her when they were alone again. 'You get used to it.'

'I didn't say anything.'

'You never have to.'

Aedith pushed her empty cup aside. 'Thanks for telling me there's a political dimension to this case, Dad, I'd never have guessed otherwise. Now I have to return to the office, because now that video's gone out, my squad will be fielding eighteen phone calls a minute from random nutters claiming to be the killer. Some of whom will genuinely believe it.'

Lod toyed with one of his rings, easing it over his knuckle then pushing it back again. It wasn't his wedding band. He never played with that one. 'You know they're calling him the Hook now?'

'Who?'

'The killer. He catches fish, so they're calling him the Hook. Pleasingly straightforward.'

Aedith tried not to purse her lips, doubly annoyed that she now knew how Tancred felt.

'That got out there fast.'

'I told you, greater powers. Although, word to the Witan, they're not the only players in the game. Some of them might even be willing to help you, if you tread carefully.'

Aedith grimaced, suddenly tired of being just another player on one of her father's gameboards. She pulled on her coat. 'I have to go.' She didn't say where. She just wanted to get out, and telling Lod she was about to take her ward to the psychiatric hospital where Lod had imprisoned his own son for the past ten years wasn't likely to lead to a smooth exit.

Lod put a hand over hers as she reached out to leave some coins on the table. At first, she thought they were going to go through the 'I'll pay/No it's my turn' routine, but instead he looked up at her. Eyes that were usually creased with amusement and mischief were calm and still.

'Daughter,' said Lod. 'Be careful.'

THIRTY

The turning to Endmarsh wasn't marked on the roundabout, but Aedith knew to take the third exit anyway. Or Roadfucker did, at least – Aedith was barely conscious of driving. Coram was sitting very still in the passenger seat, wrapped up in the parka she'd brought back from a trip across the Wall last year. It had been far too big for him at the time. Now she could see at least an inch of wrist beyond the sleeve.

They passed a sign reading 'Endmarsh Psychiatric Hospital', Coram flinching.

'You sure you want to do this?' Aedith tried to keep her tone light. Hilde had subscribed her to a parenting podcast she listened to on her phone sometimes, down at the station gym. The last one had been about teenage rebellion: how telling your child you were proud of them, or worried for them, could backfire, that they went through a stage when the last thing they wanted was their parents' approval and that they'd go out of their way to elicit disfavour. Aedith had to admit, if Lod had taken her aside in her teens, told her how much he wanted her to join the police, perhaps one day rising to the rank of captain, she'd probably be a diplomat by now. Or a criminal.

'It's for credits at school, I told you.'

Aedith remained unconvinced the Cynwald Academy for Academic Excellence had specifically requested Coram visit an insane asylum for a cosy chat with his adoptive uncle, but she'd said he could do it, so here they were.

'You know why he's in here, right?'

Coram nodded. They'd never really talked about it, but you could get the nuts and bolts of it online: Edric, prodigal son of the powerful and influential Earl-Elector Lod, attends one of the Kingdom's few prestigious universities, is subjected to a campaign of cruelty and bullying by Cenhelm, son of, well, no one really. On paper, the balance of power tips firmly towards Edric; in reality, Cenhelm, a well-liked and charming young psychopath, launches a psychological assault against Edric for no obvious reason, turning the entire faculty against him by falsely claiming victimhood, accusing the Earl's son of using powerful connections to besmirch his name, etc.

Aedith remembered Lod confronting Edric about it on a half-term break, telling him to man up, confront his opponent, deal with it the Saxon way. Instead, on his return to university, Edric purchased some wolfsbane from the dark net, baked it into some iced biscuits which he boxed up prettily and left on Cenhelm's pillow with a forged note claiming to be from an admirer. Cenhelm, who really should have known better, staggered back from a drinking-society night out, saw the biscuits and was found dead the next morning.

It took the local police almost no time at all to determine Edric as the poisoner: the lowest form of killer in the Saxon hierarchy of murder. He would have been much more respected if he'd walked up to Cenhelm in the refectory, pulled out a seax and beheaded him there and then. He might not even have gone to prison for more than a few years, once details of Cenhelm's multiple campaigns of bullying and intimidation had come out; even a couple of lecturers came forward to claim they were being blackmailed over real or imagined slights to Cenhelm's honour. But no one could forgive the underhand, un-Saxon nature of the murder.

Lod pulled strings to have Edric committed to an institute on the grounds of criminal insanity; an act seen as borderline malfeasance, but understandable under the circumstances. Aedith, studying for her police exams at the time (and didn't the news sites love *that* irony), often wondered if it wasn't the poisoning in particular that had offended Lod so much as Edric getting himself caught.

'Good,' said Aedith. 'Then you'll know why I'm not bringing biscuits.' She nosed Roadfucker up to the sentry box, held up her phone with the code rune the hospital had sent.

The security guard's scanner buzzed angrily.

'I'm sorry,' said the guard. 'It's been playing up all morning. Who are you here to see?'

'Edric Mercia.'

The guard frowned. Of course, if you were unfamiliar with the name, it sounded ridiculous, like calling yourself 'Harold Northumbria' or 'Cuthbert East Anglia'.

Aedith tried again. 'Edric *of* Mercia'. She could sense Coram next to her, folding himself in with embarrassment. Tough tits, he was the one who wanted to come here.

The guard's face cleared. 'Ah. Here you go.' She punched a button, the metal arm across the driveway slowly dragging itself up into a salute. 'You know the way?'

Aedith nodded curtly, driving through the second Roadfucker had enough clearance.

Coram pushed one of the plastic chairs in the visitors' room, scraping it an inch or so across the floor, a confused expression on his face. 'I thought they'd be fixed to the floor.'

'I don't believe the patients who are likely to use chairs as weapons are allowed visitors. Now stop embarrassing me and sit down until Edric gets here.'

Coram took a seat, casting a worried look around him. In fact, everyone here looked disappointingly normal: three or four patients in beige tracksuits in conversation with their families, a few orderlies in scrubs hanging back, talking amongst themselves in quiet voices. You could have mistaken it for the foyer of some weekend retreat if you ignored the reinforced windows, the soft foam cups, the fact that every clipboard held by an orderly had a pen firmly attached by a chain so no one could get hold of anything pointed.

'Having second thoughts?' asked Aedith.

'No,' said Coram, then, 'Yes.'

'Too late.'

Her brother approached them, walking casually, no orderly in attendance. His hair was longer than Aedith remembered, and he had a bruise on the side of his face. He nodded at Aedith, gave Coram a curious look, then pulled out a chair, placing himself across the table from the pair of them.

'So,' he said. 'Aedith said you wanted to talk to me about a school project.'

Coram nodded, looked hesitantly at Aedith.

She took the hint. 'I'll give the two of you a chance to talk,' she said. She walked to the furthest corner of the room and found an empty chair, two down from a patient who was sitting alone, looking out of the window. He was dark-skinned, in his fifties at least. Aedith wondered if he'd been a reeve. He had the face, somehow. His hands were gnarled, wrapped around each other, twisted like roots. He looked over at her and scowled. 'Someone's sitting there,' he said sharply.

Aedith nodded, moved one chair along. 'Better?'
The patient nodded.
'Excellent,' she said.

THIRTY ONE

Naeku must have been somehow able to sense Drustan approaching her desk because she turned around before he got there, her expression exuding brisk professionalism and a controlled poise. Drustan wondered if she was one of those who threw the whole thing off at the end of the working day, became a lighter, happier person who got the first round of mead in and chewed dried mushrooms to commune with the elves all weekend. If so, he should ask her how she managed it: ever since he had become a detective inspector, he had felt the role harden around him like armour, holding in everything else he had ever been, could ever be.

He knew most Saxon cops regarded Tribal police as political appointees at best, savages mocking the uniform at worst. Since Drustan's brief time in uniform all those years ago, being sent to work with his Saxon counterparts to track persons of interest who'd crossed the border (in either direction), he'd realised you had to become all that you could be, just to raise their expectations from somewhere below the basement.

'Constable, would you be kind enough to drive me over to where I found Eawynn Wettin? I could take a RoadWay, but I'm not sure the department would cover the extravagance.'

'To the foundry, sir? I think Forensics have already finished up, if you wanted to ask them anything?'

Drustan shook his head. 'I want to follow up on the crime scene. I was a little dazed after the explosion; it's possible I missed something. It's for my own peace of mind, really.'

Naeku nodded, picked up her coat. It was cut along the same semi-military lines as Aedith's greatcoat, although that could have been coincidence. There were times when Drustan wondered if spotting patterns everywhere made him a better cop or merely a more suspicious human being. Of course, it was entirely possible one naturally led to the other.

The ash had settled across the ground for hundreds of metres around the foundry in every direction. No sign of Drustan's own tracks leading out from the kiln, let alone the smaller tracks of a young woman. Or those of the killer and his victim.

Drustan held back a tree branch so Naeku could follow him into the woods. He hadn't noticed she was taller than him until now. He was getting a sense of someone carefully containing herself to pass unnoticed, or at least unremarked upon, within Saxon society. Of course, she *was* Saxon, he reminded himself, or at least a variety of it. She had a clearer place in Eastern society than he did, anyway.

'May I ask what you're looking for, sir? I know Forensics have finished up here, but if you're expecting to find something else…'

Perhaps she was expecting him to drop to the ground, pinch some earth between his fingers, cautiously taste some moss before spitting it out and declaring that no fewer than a dozen hikers had passed this way, just a fortnight hence. It was tempting to put on a show, but Drustan couldn't help feeling that in reality Naeku would see straight through it, leaving them both embarrassed.

'You read the reports, Constable. Did you see any mention of a young Tribal woman? Denim jacket with patches, long skirt?'

Naeku shook her head. 'Not that I remember, sir.'

'You don't need the "sir",' said Drustan. 'Not out here, anyway.' Too late, he remembered what Aedith had told him. Fortunately, either she'd misread the room or Naeku was just that professional.

'I didn't see any mention of a woman, DI Drustan. Other than Deedra Kesair, of course. And the victim.'

'Me neither.'

'Who do you think she was?'

Drustan shrugged. It was a good question. The kiln explosion had rattled his brain pretty thoroughly. It wasn't beyond possibility that it had shaken something loose, and whatever it was had lasted just long enough to show him just what he needed to see. Did it even matter now? The woman was a loose end, to join all the others. If the killer had no connection with the foundry, it was the most enormous of coincidences that the second victim was being nailed up at the same time Deedra was about to commit a human sacrifice on a scale unheard-of in the mainland in thirty years. And there was another loose end somewhere, something Drustan knew he had forgotten, put to one side, then become distracted. It itched at him.

'Constable Naeku, what are your thoughts?'

She looked startled. 'My thoughts?'

Drustan tried out his reassuring smile, painfully aware it often came across to Saxon eyes as a sinister leer. 'I was the one who found Ms Wettin. Emotionally, that's going to disrupt my thinking, affect how I see the case. I could use an independent eye here.'

'Well, it seems unlikely the killer just happened to be here just as it was all going off at the foundry. That the events were unconnected, I mean.'

Drustan nodded. 'Go on.'

'So.... he knew the sacrifice was going to happen? Carried out his crime knowing we'd get here eventually, find Wettin's body and connect it to the Kesair? Except he didn't plan for you and Captain Mercia already being at the site, so he didn't get to finish the job.'

Drustan kept walking, peering through the trees. They were getting closer to the scene now, but the constable was right. It was unlikely he'd find anything on the ground Forensics had overlooked.

'Constable Naeku, what you are proposing is an unusually well-informed murderer.'

'Yes sir. Also... a professional.'

He turned back to her. 'Professional?'

'Overalls, gloves, shoe protectors. He knew how to go about his business without leaving any evidence.'

Drustan tried not to look disappointed. Anyone who watched more than a few episodes of Pan-African police procedurals knew all the tricks for evading the *omokunrin* in the labs. It was causing real problems in the courts these days, juries refusing to convict without the eight layers of DNA evidence they'd been taught to expect but the justice departments didn't have the funds to provide.

But Naeku hadn't finished. Or at least, she wanted to say something else, Drustan could feel it, but the Saxon chain of command made it tricky to volunteer one's opinions to a senior officer if you didn't want to be ridiculed for talking out of turn.

'Speak up, Constable. I asked for your opinion. Failing to give me it in its entirety would be tantamount to disobeying an order from a superior officer.'

The dots of scarring above Naeku's brows twitched as she tried to work out if Drustan was joking or not. He kept his face steady. No satisfaction in making it too easy for them.

'His body language, sir, from the video. He's done this before.'

'Undoubtedly.'

'You misunderstand, sir. I mean DI Drustan. I mean, he reminded me of Orva. In a way.'

'The pathologist?' Interesting.

'And my father. He's a dentist.' Drustan tried not to react but Naeku caught it anyway. 'Not every Afro-Saxon goes into the force, you know. I'm saying there's something similar in the body language. Practical. Like… he's used to wearing gloves. Even the way he used his seax, like it was a tool, not something to be shown off at a march or a knife show.'

'You think he's a surgeon?'

'Or a butcher.'

Drustan took this in. 'Do you have a seax, Constable?'

'I was given mine on my fourteenth birthday. It's at my parents', in the garage somewhere.'

A middle-class view, although Drustan didn't say it. The more comfortable you were in Saxon society, the less likely you were to wave your seax around like a badge of honour. That said, it wasn't only basement-dwellers who covered their walls with replicas of historical weapons. Plenty of accountants and headmasters had collections of long knives that numbered into the hundreds and were all too quick to turn to them in a domestic dispute, or when things turned nasty with the neighbours. Grisly details of the aftermaths filled true-crime podcasts on half the earphones in the Kingdom.

Drustan ducked under the boundary tape strung up between the trees. Oddly, it made him think of Yuletide. His family had never bothered with it much, but he'd once spent the season in a seaside hotel on the Saxon east coast, looking for an embezzler who, it turned out, had been long dead. The owners had gone all in, great boughs of pine hung over the fireplace, tiny, wrapped gifts among the pine needles. They'd made him welcome, hadn't cared at all he was Tribal. It was about tradition, the way they'd explained it, not religion. Everyone was welcome. Gifts on tree branches. Why was he thinking of this now?

Naeku was standing beside him.

'This is where you found the second victim?'

Drustan nodded.

The wooden beams were bare now, small dark holes in the wood where the nails that had been driven through Eawynn Wettin's wrists and ankles had been pulled out with pliers. Drustan had held her up while the paramedics had done the best they could. He could still feel her heart pounding against his shoulder as he had held her, the sudden weight as the last nail was removed, a uniformed reeve carefully gathering them up in a plastic evidence bag even as Wettin was stretchered back through the trees. There wasn't as much blood as Drustan had expected. To the left, a bare nail where the lantern had hung.

Plastic gloves didn't always provide as much safety from the law as a criminal might hope. Drustan had caught a rapist once, a Saxon working for one of the big logging companies who'd been helping himself to girls from the local reservation. He wore disposable latex gloves, just as the killer had, and had finally become careless, peeling off his gloves and dropping them in a garage bin. It had never occurred to him that you could leave your fingerprints on the inside of a glove. The rapist had been swiftly removed by the logging company, sent to another site, although Drustan had caught up with him a year or so later.

Sadly, the killer here had been smarter, even when he'd been unable to finish the job due to an unexpected explosion. Or an earlier-than-expected explosion, anyway. There was a professionalism here, as Naeku had said, and Drustan was starting to think it was contrasting poorly with his own. Loose ends, loose ends…

'Do you mind if I ask what you're looking for, DI Drustan? I know you said you wanted another pair of eyes, but…'

That wasn't quite what he'd said, but there was something there. Looking. Eyes? Forensics, of course, had only been looking *down*. And then it clicked into place.

'Look up in the branches, Constable,' he said. 'Small, plastic. You'll know it if you see it.'

Ridiculous to think it could have survived, of course. It had probably been blown to smithereens by the kiln blast if it hadn't already crashed due to battery failure. He'd led Naeku out into the woods on nothing more than a fantasy and all she'd return with was more stories about weirdo Tribals calling out to the spirits of the forest and getting nothing in return.

Naeku was squinting above his head. 'That?'

And there it was. The drone.

Gifts in tree branches.

THIRTY TWO

Coram talked to Edric for nearly an hour. At regular intervals, Aedith felt a buzzing at her thigh and reached for her phone, only to remind herself each time she had handed it over at reception along with her keys. Phantom vibrations, the body's folk memory. How long did you have to give up social media for before your body stopped craving it? Looking out of the window provided little diversion beyond seeing some of the more far-gone patients being given physical therapy by their orderlies: walked round the lawn for an indeterminate period before it was judged time to get back inside. The ex-reeve (Aedith had decided) two seats down, who she had hoped would perhaps beckon her over, whisper to her some gnomic wisdom, had very slowly fallen asleep.

Finally, Coram appeared to be done. No sense that the conversation had been particularly traumatic, or even that interesting: every time she'd taken a discreet glance, Edric had looked mildly uncomfortable or distracted, only looking his adopted nephew in the eyes for one moment at the end in response to some mumbled question. Whatever his reply was, it was brief, and after absorbing it, Coram seemed to have run out of things to say. He got up, thanking Edric politely.

Aedith walked over to them. 'All finished?'

'Yes,' said Edric. 'Always a treat to have visitors. My last was a very pleasant lady from the Wectan Temple.'

Aedith grunted. The Wectanites were a notoriously flaky sect, reliant on visions and prophecies published verbatim in pamphlets or cheaply animated on discs sold outside railway stations and bought by those who liked to scour them for hidden insights or predictions on where to invest their meagre pensions. The Temple elders lived in penthouse apartments; the more vulnerable members who actually had the visions housed in substandard dormitories. Wectanites were drawn to institutions for the mentally challenged like wasps to spilled mead.

'She offer you a contract?'

Edric smiled without a trace of humour. 'They can't touch you until you're officially released. I had to break it to her I'm not mad enough to create the product they want and the chances of me walking out of these sacred halls and into one of their cardboard flophouses are slim to none. I don't think she'll be coming back.'

Aedith nodded. 'Go and get my keys from the reception and wait in the car,' she said to Coram. 'I'll be out in a minute.'

When he had left the room, Aedith took a seat.

'He'll let you out eventually,' she said. 'He'll find a way to clear your name or blacken Cenhelm's further. And then he'll introduce you to the right people, get a team to build you a social media profile, start pushing you up the political ladder.'

A strained silence. Aedith drummed on the table for a moment. She never knew what to say to him. 'At least you won't have to make any more of those bloody awful baskets.'

Edric laughed then, despite himself. 'It's good to see you, sister.'

He held a hand up to get a short, stocky orderly's attention. 'Is there any chance you could get my sister and me a cup of tea?'

'I could get you water,' said the orderly. 'Nothing hot.'

'Of course,' said Edric humbly, nodding at the orderly's retreating back. 'That's Wynnstan,' he said. 'One of the better ones. He plays a good game of nine-dice when he can be sweet-talked into it. Been known to give me a second helping of leeks on Sundays too, although I don't actually like leeks, so maybe that one could go either way.'

'What happened to your face?' asked Aedith.

He raised a hand to his cheek as though he'd forgotten about it. Perhaps he had. There had always been a gentleness to Edric. It was still there, but it had grown noticeably fainter the last few times Aedith had seen him. Or there was something more centred about him; it was getting harder to get a read on him these days.

Aedith occasionally visited cons in prison, to get information out of them, sometimes even take messages to them, if it suited both sides. It wasn't just the older prisoners who became institutionalised; some of the younger ones, those who were already broken, took hold of the harsh certainties of prison life and found themselves unable to let go when the time came. It wasn't that they didn't want to leave, they just weren't able to cope when they were out. Others thrived. Aedith had always worried about Edric turning out like the former. Perhaps she should also consider the latter. Although this place wasn't a prison, of course. Behind bars at the High King's pleasure, most inmates would be able to count down to their release, however far away. Here, your stay was in the hands of Wyrd, Goddess of Fate, and she delighted in never showing the full length of her blade.

'One of the other clients took issue with me being given kitchen work,' said Edric. 'For reasons that are perhaps obvious.' Then, without a break, 'Does our father know you're here?'

'I don't inform him of my every move,' said Aedith, then realised that wasn't a no. 'I have no reason to think he's aware I'm visiting you. Or would have any problems if I was.'

'He's down for the Summit I imagine. I suppose staff are looking after Mum.'

Aedith shrugged, uncomfortably aware that in a few years they might, under other circumstances, have been having the 'which of us has to go and look after the aged parents' conversation. 'How was your chat with Coram?' she asked, mostly to change the subject.

'Awkward and stilted.'

'Pretty sure that describes your entire teenage years.'

'Can't disagree with you there. I think he may have had me on some sort of pedestal, oddly enough.'

Aedith frowned. 'What makes you say that?'

'He seemed worryingly close to reverent. Don't worry, I soon convinced him there's nothing cool about being locked up in an insane asylum. Last thing I want is to start a craze among the kids. Although I think he really wanted me to answer questions he's too embarrassed to ask you.'

'Not boy stuff, surely. They cover it at school and Hilde's always happy to get the diagrams out and explain the technical stuff.'

'It wasn't that. Right at the end, when we were running out of time, he wanted to know what it's like to kill someone.'

'Oh,' said Aedith.

Aedith dropped Coram back home before she went back to the office. They didn't talk much on the way.

She parked outside the house, nearly drove off the second the boy had got out, but something stopped her. She turned the engine off, moved to lower her window, stopped. All she wanted to do was call out, to tell Coram if there was anything he wanted to know, he just had to ask; but she couldn't bring herself to say it.

Coram paused for a moment, his back to her, then he walked into the house and closed the door behind him.

Aedith realised a delivery van was waiting patiently behind her. She lifted a hand in apology and started the car. As she left the avenue, she wondered once again if there was anything else she could have done that day she'd met Coram's father. There wasn't, but it didn't make it any easier.

THIRTY THREE

Huginn lay on a table in the investigation room, never to fly again. Drustan and Aedith gathered over it with the reverence of priests. Only minor supplicants, mind: Banba – pulled away from her phone records and CCTV and now bearing cables, card-readers and a pair of tweezers – was the true initiate, the haruspex. Naeku had gone back to trying to contact the tattooist. Agapos and the rest of the squad were over in Command, where a senior uniform was trying to explain to them how the new org charts would work now that most of the arrows flowed through the box labelled 'Special Branch'.

Banba picked up the drone, squinting at it with a critical eye. Only one rotor was left of its original four and the belly camera was hanging by a single wire. The smaller, forward-facing lens was untouched, however, and the central body had held up remarkably well, barring a few scratches.

'I might be able to do something with this. All depends if it was pointing in the right direction when it ended up in the tree.'

She plucked some moss from the jack in Huginn's side, plugged in a cable. A stylised depiction of a treasure chest blinked undramatically into being on the wallscreen.

'Let's see what we have,' said Banba.

One moment the drone was looking down at Deedra's car from some two hundred feet up in the air – heads and shoulders of green-filtered Tribesmen flowing around the vehicle and between buildings, trying to locate Agapos and Ord who were putting up a respectable insurgency operation from somewhere off-screen – then the screen showed only a burst of static as the kiln blew.

A disappointed sigh from Aedith, then the picture returned, horizon spinning over and over, microsecond glimpses of the foundry, images of Tribesmen knocked to the ground by the blast, captives running everywhere, getting further and further away as the drone crashed through branches, coming to rest upside down about six feet from the ground. The picture wobbled, then stabilised on a figure, head down, hanging from wooden beams, illuminated by a lantern hung up next to her. Another figure with its back to them had fallen to the ground, shaking its head, dazed. It wore overalls, held a seax in one hand.

'Frige's tits,' said Aedith reverently. 'There he is.'

The picture froze. Drustan heard himself swear.

'Relax,' said Banba, amused. 'I'm turning it the right way up.'

The figures on the central wall screen in front of them flipped suddenly, resumed movement, the killer getting to his feet, brushing himself down, recovering from the blast.

'You're a big one,' said Aedith. 'Over six foot. Maybe as much as six four. Be a good lad and turn your face to the camera, would you?'

Instead, they watched as the killer held Wettin's chin up, apparently examining it for life signs, then something must have alerted him. He sheathed his seax, pulled the lantern off the beam, fled to the right. The picture held for a while on Wettin, then froze.

'That's it,' said Banba. 'That's all there is.'

Aedith frowned. 'Go back to when he lifts her head up. He looks to the side, just a little. There. Hold it.'

Banba gave the space bar an obliging tap.

'Do you see it? On his neck?'

The night vision bleached out the killer's features, apart from a standard Saxon haircut: shaved undersides, the rest of it worn a little longer, held back with product. The sort of haircut possessed by a good ninety percent of Saxon males. No tattoos at the sides of the scalp, which wasn't unusual, but at the right side of the neck, disappearing into the overalls, a dark blotch.

'That's what Denby was talking about,' said Aedith. 'Concealing the fish tattoo, making it look like a birthmark.'

'Circumstantial,' said Drustan, uneasily. 'Banba, can you get in any closer?'

The killer expanded into the frame, but at the cost of clarity, individual pixels almost visible now. Banba tutted. 'Best I can do, I'm afraid.'

'Go back to him taking down the lantern,' said Aedith. 'There. Stop.'

The killer stretched his arm out, a gap widening between sleeve and glove. There, on the wrist, visible even in the green tones of night vision: the mark of the sparrow, just as Denby had drawn them.

'It's him,' said Aedith. 'It's Wulfstan. Print that out, would you Banba? And... What exactly are you doing there, DI Drustan?'

Drustan had one hand pointed at the screen, the other arm pointed at ninety degrees to the right.

'Taking my bearings,' he said. 'Captain Mercia. Would you stand in front of me for a moment?'

Aedith obliged.

'You're Eawynn Wettin.'

'Sure.'

Drustan mimed sliding a seax into a sheath on his hip, picking up a lantern, turning to the right. 'I'm going in this direction,' he announced.

'Into the stationery cupboard?'

'Here, yes. But there….'

After a moment, she got it, gave a low whistle. 'I missed that.'

Banba looked over from the printer. 'Missed what?'

'He's not running away,' said Aedith. 'The explosion came from the right. He's surprised – or at least he's concerned enough not to check properly that Wettin's actually dead – but he runs *towards* the foundry, not away from it. He's a six-foot Saxon carrying a bag of something, pretty sure he's got a nailgun in there along with his seax. He's not exactly going to blend in with Deedra's crew, is he?'

'Added to which,' said Drustan, 'he has to know the whole place will be swarming with police within twenty minutes. Unless…'

The silence hung in the air for far too long until Aedith finally broke it.

'Unless he *is* police,' she said. 'That theory goes no further than this room. For now.'

Agapos arrived some twenty minutes later, clutching a handful of printouts. Aedith and Drustan were in Aedith's office, Banba at her desk, going through lines of code, but even through the interior window, Drustan could see her heart wasn't in it. Civilian staff sometimes had these moments: considering themselves almost on a level with the cops they worked with, until something murky stirred in the deep waters and they started to wonder if a quiet office where their clients weren't murderers and their co-workers didn't carry guns was maybe a more attractive prospect than it had seemed a few months ago.

Agapos realised something was up with impressive speed. 'What is it?'

'I'll fill you in later,' said Aedith. 'But somehow we're going to have to pull down the collar of every reeve that passes through this building without them noticing.'

The sergeant didn't react to that. Perhaps this could be the sort of thing Aedith said on a regular basis.

Aedith looked at the papers in Agapos's hand. 'What have you got there? I thought Special Branch got to go around paperwork, not create more of it.'

'Transcripts of all the calls so far from people claiming to be the Hook.'

'They're going with that then,' said Aedith, taking the papers. 'How many so far?'

'Thirty-seven. Most of them using the same voice disguiser app.'

'May I?' asked Drustan politely.

'Be my guest. Agapos, I'd better run you through what we have so far.'

Aedith led Agapos out to the incident room, while Drustan fanned the transcripts out on Aedith's desk. '*I am the Hook,*' read the first. '*Those who mark themselves with the fish worship the god who hangs from the tree and they are cruel in the name of mercy. They hide their true face under a mask of kindness and love but underneath they are all the same. Angwin was a terrorist. Wettin would sell this country from underneath her people. They must be stopped and the people must know who all the fish are who walk among us.*'

Drustan knew that it didn't mean anything that the writer had used the victims' real names – the information was already out there. But it felt unpleasantly personal nonetheless.

The next call was shorter and more to the point. '*Death to all the traitors I killed them I am the Hook and I will kill again.*' Many of the callers – this one included – had made no attempt to block their numbers, so it would be a simple matter to call them back if anyone wanted clarification on any of the matters they had brought up. Many of them seemed convinced the borders between the three nations should only work in one direction. '*Let more of the stinking Celts come East and why would not the Moors follow them and the Norse come South and take our lands too, we should take their lands first and kill them every one and make all this land ours.*'

One individual had made three separate calls, such was his determination to identify himself as the most-wanted individual in the East of England. '*I am the one they call the Hook I am the instrument of Woden on this earth and he will reward me in the afterlife for what I have done. I killed the Tash and the whore woman too and I will gut all the Fish traitors who want to let the races mix and turn the East into a nothing nation.*'

The second was more of the same, perhaps with increased emphasis on the perfidy of the Fishers and their plans to undermine the Saxon nation. The third, and most recent, had a more pleading quality: '*I will tell you why I did this, I am not working against the reeves even though the fish hide amongst them, I have important information but I cannot talk to just anybody.*'

The transcript noted that the caller, who identified themselves (of course) as 'The Hook', had demanded to talk to a senior officer, but when given an excuse as to why that wasn't possible right now, had hung up.

Only when Drustan flipped back to the first of these three calls did he note the time, stamped blandly in the top right-hand corner of the sheet. Then he checked it again, and rifled through the other transcripts.

'Banba, what time this morning was the Hook video uploaded? Exactly?'

'Exactly?' She brought up the video, checked the timestamp. 'Ten-fourteen and nineteen seconds.' She caught herself. 'Well, that's the time it appeared on the site. Depending on how busy things were at the time, the actual uploading would have happened, what, four or five seconds before that? Beyond that, we're into milliseconds.'

'It was uploaded to just that one site, correct?'

She nodded. 'It's appeared on hundreds since, obviously. Maybe thousands. The sharing services have been trying to take it down ever since but it's out there now.'

'And the account it was uploaded from?'

'A burner. Created just for that one upload, deleted since. No way of tracking where it came from, I'm afraid.'

'Can I watch it again?'

'Sure.' She hit a button. The silhouetted head and shoulders appeared.

Aedith joined them. 'You won't get anything from the host service. The Pan-African Security Agency can't do it with international warrants and tac teams stationed outside the CEO's house, imagine how little sway we have.'

Drustan let the video run for a while, then paused it, holding out two transcripts. 'That doesn't matter for now, it's the timing that's important. These two calls – look at the times.'

Aedith frowned. 'Ten-sixteen or thereabouts. Doesn't mean anything. These nutters started calling the second they clicked play. These two weren't even the first to call, there was one before that at ten-fifteen. Claims the dark elves took the video from inside his head and wants to know what the High King plans to do about it. Although that guy left his real name and he's been calling in as long as we've had a landline, so we're giving him the benefit of the doubt on that one.'

'Except the ten-sixteen callers both refer to the fish tattoo. Look.' He passed Aedith the two transcripts. '"Those who mark themselves with the fish" on the first call, and "the Fish traitors" on the other, the one from the guy who called three times. The tattoo isn't revealed on the video until three minutes in, I've checked. Nobody could have known about the fish until ten-seventeen at the earliest, unless…'

Aedith took the paper from him, checked it.

'Unless they were the killer.'

'Yes. Or had prior knowledge of the video somehow. Banba, how easy would it be to take that video, do all that editing, upload it? Could one person do it on their own?'

'Of course. But…' Banba stopped, hesitant. 'This is just my opinion, right?'

Aedith glanced at Drustan, looked back at Banba. 'Everyone's just queuing up to take a big shit on my lone-wolf theory today but go ahead.'

Under the dreads, tattoos and hoodie, Banba looked genuinely uncomfortable.

'I've watched the video three times now. It's crude. It's… *gránna*.'

'Low quality,' Drustan translated.

'The stock footage with the clouds, the cheap filter on the voiceover, it's all low-quality stuff. But the editing's good. The message gets through. I've seen music companies do the same thing, trying to get some turbofolk collective to go viral like they've just been found on the rez, when really it's some CEO's daughter's room-mate with a record contract. This is a professional package trying to look amateur.'

Aedith's face was grim. 'This is just a theory. Any way to prove it?'

'Maybe. If I can get hold of the original file, the one they deleted, I'm pretty sure I can prove the recording quality is way higher that you can buy off the shelf. I'm tracing it back as far as I can.'

'You find something, you let me know. Before you do that, our repeat caller – he didn't block his number. See if you can get a trace off it. Might be time we paid him a visit.'

Banba reapplied herself to her keyboard. Aedith glanced at Drustan and nodded towards her office. When they were both inside, the door firmly closed, she tore open a padded envelope, let two mobile phones clatter onto the desk. 'Black-market burners. Standard charger. I've already put our contacts in, some basic apps, maps and the like. Won't be able to connect to the department database, not over wifi anyway, but better than nothing.'

'You think Tancred's still listening in?'

'No reason for him not to. That's no longer who I'm worrying about. Something my father said. There are factions behind this, connected to the Summit in ways I don't understand yet.'

For the first time since Drustan had met her, Aedith looked unsure of herself. Then she laughed briefly, without humour. 'I should do my own video, warning about microchips in every can of mead, Grendel's children coming to get us through the wifi.'

Drustan took a phone, slipped it into his pocket. There was more security he could load in his own time, apps no one in the

East even knew existed, or if they did, would be keen to punish with time inside at the very least. Might be giving Special Branch more rope to hang him with, but he'd have to take the chance.

'Speaking of Special Branch, where are you going to stay, now they've taken away the academy? I could find you a safe house, got a couple that aren't even on the system any more.'

'Thank you, but that won't be necessary. It's a good opportunity to reconnect with some old contacts. I'll let you know as soon as I have somewhere confirmed.'

'All right then.' Aedith took a slug of hour-old coffee and grimaced. 'Wonder if our Pictish enchanter has located the repeat caller's mobile yet.'

'You're not convinced? That it's him, I mean.'

'The Hook goes to all this effort then calls us from his own phone? Even if I believed in the gods, they wouldn't make it this easy for us.'

A murmur from outside. Aedith peered out into the main office. 'The hells is going on there?'

Agapos had wrenched open the door of a solid grey metal cabinet and was passing out firearms to every officer within reach. No one was even holstering them. Officers were clustering round Banba's monitor, pointing and arguing.

Aedith stepped out of her office, her own weapon somehow already in her hand. 'What is it?'

Naeku was checking the slide on her weapon, chambering a round even as she nodded back towards the monitor. Banba made an arcane gesture on a trackpad, flicking the image onto the wallscreens: the plan of a building, filled with light blue dots, most of which seemed to be congregating on a large square at the north side, where the building opened up to the street. It was, Drustan realised, a schematic of Woden's Cross police station. A green dot was positioned in the centre of the square, blinking on and off but not moving, even as the blue dots flowed towards it.

Banba turned to Aedith. 'I tracked the phone, ma'am.'

'And?'

'He's in the foyer. He just walked in.'

THIRTY FOUR

The killer had parked his stolen vehicle – not the one he used for work; that was usefully invisible in the city, but the people he was supposed to meet would have spotted it a mile away – in the alley behind the building where he had been told to wait. He had arrived early, so had drawn out his seax and begun sharpening it, running the whetstone down the edge over and over again, the soft sound of mineral against metal a balm to his soul. He wasn't one of those who saw their blade as part of their identity: it was just a tool. But a careful man kept his weapons and his wits sharp. And the killer was a careful man indeed. That was why he had arrived two hours earlier than instructed, and a good thing too, as he had seen many interesting things. The workers in the small but expensively decorated building where he had been told to arrive being ushered out and a man in overalls carrying a long roll of plastic sheeting in. Two men clambering up the fire escape of the opposite building with long packages slung over their shoulders. A woman dressed in the hi-vis vest of a traffic warden walking up and down the road, apparently inputting the same details of the same vehicles into her phone over and over again, yet never looking at them, her eyes never leaving the street corner from where she would have been expecting the killer to arrive.

The killer didn't begrudge any of them their roles in his betrayal. He had known for some time his path would have to diverge with that of those who had up to that point been so helpful. He was by nature a loner. The focus groups, brand meetings and that one brief consultation with the woman described as a senior fashion consultant who had spent approximately twenty minutes in his company before leaving in tears, had been wearying, but at least they had all been focused on the same task: alerting people to the existence of the Fishers.

He had been doing great work in the shadows, they told him; really great work, but now it was time to move to the next level. They explained to him about the Unification Summit, and he couldn't honestly say he followed the entire slide presentation, but the Fishers seemed to be involved at a critical level and that was enough for him. 'I'm in,' he'd told them, and there had been a great deal of whooping and high-fiving, followed by forms to sign – swiftly withdrawn after he picked up the pen he'd been offered and pushed it through the hand of the form-holder. The whooping had stopped abruptly and someone the killer took to be nominally in charge spoke for the first time, apologising profusely while putting on the record (not that there'd be a record) that of course no paper trail was necessary, even going as far as to harangue the man trying to remove the pen from his hand for his presumptuousness as he stumbled out of the door leaving a trail of bloody paper towels.

Later he was asked, very hesitantly, by another member of the team (he didn't see the form-holder again) if he was happy to take a personality test. He had stared at them.

'Nothing complicated,' they said hastily, 'it's really just an introspective self-report questionnaire indicating differing psychological preferences in how people perceive the world and make decisions?'

A lot of the people the agency used ended sentences like this, as though they'd just asked a question. To their evident surprise, he volunteered to take the test. He'd thought about becoming a psychologist at one point after all, to see what made people tick. He knew what made himself tick, of course, but most people he met didn't seem to share the same outlook, and it would ease his passage through the world much more smoothly if he could set off as few red flags as possible.

An hour and five sheets of multiple-choice questions later, they'd declared the process finished, but seemed unwilling to give him the results, beyond telling him he was a 'Salmon', rarest of the personality types, able to stay below the surface for considerable amounts of time, only surfacing when driven by deep underlying need. The killer thought that sounded about right, but probably hadn't required him taking an afternoon off work to formalise something he already knew: he had been made unlike other people, but could get along with them for most of the time as long as he didn't do anything too reckless.

After that test though, and by the time of the third or fourth meeting, talk had slowly moved away from the dangers the Fishers posed to the natural order of things and the crimes they had got away with over the decades, and back towards the Summit. They thought they had the measure of him, the killer had realised, and though they didn't usually work with individuals possessed of his particular skillset – at least not directly – they saw him as one of the team now and felt freer to relax around him, once they'd made sure he didn't have anything pointy within arm's reach.

The killer had seen this sort of thing happen before. People were intimidated by him at first: he was a big man, he kept himself in shape, he had little interest in social niceties and that discomfited most people. Some, like the fashion woman, could tell who he really was on an instinctive level almost straight away, and became so unsettled they had to leave his presence as soon as they could. The killer didn't take it personally, it was a sensible reaction. But most, once they got used to his shell, the outside person who quietly got on with his job and didn't make a fuss, mentally put him to the back of their minds and in doing so, could too easily reveal their authentic selves.

A true maniac – the sort of person the agency wanted him to be, were certainly happy for the news sites to describe him as, had planted descriptions of him as such all over social media for the receptive to find, in fact – would have taken his revenge in a white-hot fury, storming the building, seax in hand, leaving a few minutes later covered in the glory of battles. But he wasn't a maniac, in the sense he was expected to be, anyway; and the snipers on the roof would have taken him out in seconds. Instead, he kept to the plan, quietly turned the car away and left.

One of the first Fishers he had ever caught had been a scrawny, elderly, Tribal bomb-maker who had only got the tattoo because no one else would take him. The man had spent an afternoon teaching the killer how to make the most basic explosive device: how to attach a timer to some black-market mining explosive without blowing yourself up in the process. It wasn't how the killer liked to do things, but he never turned down an opportunity for self-improvement. The killer could tell the man had genuine enthusiasm for his work, even though he was strapped to a table at the time, most of his fingers broken. He had been a good teacher, regardless, and as a reward, he had been granted the mercy of a swift death. The Indij didn't even seem to begrudge the moment when it finally came, the seax cutting his throat with such force the head practically came away: the killer had learned more finesse since those days.

The killer suspected the bomb-maker felt he was overdue his moment with the gods by some decades. He hadn't even cried out for the Fisher god as the seax approached, but the old Tribal deities instead. The killer had felt a little conflicted about that: was the bomb-maker really a Fisher at all if he didn't truly believe? But he had taken the mark, and you had to draw the line somewhere. Kill them all and let their god sort them out.

The killer checked his watch, then glanced briefly at his rearview mirror. Behind him the office rose up and out as if punched from beneath by an unseen giant fist. Red flame turned into black smoke even before the soundwave caught up with him, setting off the car alarm of every vehicle on the street.

The elderly Tribal had known his stuff after all. The whole process had been efficient, even spectacular, but not really how the killer liked to do things. He'd go back to the old ways after this.

THIRTY FIVE

Four miles away, as the crow flies, Aedith was pushing through a thick cordon of armed cops, her warrant card held high, as though every reeve here didn't already possess their own. Drustan flowed quietly in her wake.

The man in the foyer was over six foot tall, with short blond hair, undercut around the sides and with a grey dressing visible on the back of his neck above the collar of an unseasonably bulky coat. Like Aedith, he held a totem high above his head: a battered mobile phone, the same one (presumably) that Banba was still tracking in the office, which was abandoned now that all the staff had rushed down three flights of stairs, only to be held back by some invisible barrier. The man had thirty clear feet all around him.

'You see his wrist?' asked Aedith. Drustan nodded. The mark of the sparrow, but cruder than Denby's work, facing in the wrong direction. Drustan looked around until he found the desk sergeant, bald, grey-bearded and staring, still holding a landline phone making an audible dialling tone. Taking the phone from the man's hand, Drustan quietly placed it back in the receiver.

'What's the situation, sergeant?'

The man blinked at him, seemingly unsure of what kind of terrorist situation he was in. Drustan sighed, took out his own warrant card. The sergeant nodded, whatever spell he was under broken.

'He claimed he was the Hook, sir. Said he was turning himself in. We've had three of them so far, so I told him to take a seat. That was when he said he had a bomb.'

The Hook, if that was who he was, was unzipping his coat now with one hand, staring wild-eyed at something far beyond the ranks of armed reeves surrounding him. Drustan followed his gaze to a security camera high up on the first flight of stairs.

Aedith had worked her way through to Drustan's side.

'Bomb squad are in traffic, but on their way. Top brass are all at an awards ceremony on the other side of town. Tancred's in the building, but no one knows where, which means currently we're the highest-ranking officers on scene.'

'Lucky us.'

'Now *technically*,' she continued, 'Tribal detective inspector is a parallel rank to Saxon captain, so he's all yours if you want. Home turf gives me moral advantage, but I'm willing to let it go if you are.'

Drustan watched as the man held his coat open. The bomb vest looked as one would expect: a loose webbing of straps and wires supporting half a dozen flat grey bars of what could have been putty, but almost certainly weren't. The cops around were starting to look uneasy now. The moment where the problem could conceivably have been shut down with a decisive moment of contained violence had gone, and now it was time to pass the situation up the chain of command.

'I'll admit to being undertrained for this situation,' said Drustan. 'One course in hostage negotiation, but that was really for drunk farmers with shotguns in remote longhouses. I might have to take this situation as more of a learning opportunity, if that's acceptable.'

Aedith sighed and holstered her weapon. 'Fine,' she said. 'But if they're not scraping us off the walls when this is done, we're talking serious cake debt. Officers! Let's put away our weapons and try not to scare our visitor. He seems on edge.' A subtle shake of the head to Agapos, half out of sight behind a pillar. *Not you, let's keep something on him.* Agapos nodded back. The rest of them looked at each other. No Saxon reeve ever fought to be the first to put away their weapon when faced with a nutter.

'Let's try this again,' said Aedith. 'Everyone look at the badge.'

She held up the warrant card. Three dozen pairs of eyes swivelled towards it.

'Now put your weapons away before I take them off you and ram them up your collective arses.'

Mass whispers of carbon fibre against plastic. The only weapon pointing at the man now was Agapos's and Drustan was fairly sure he was invisible from that angle. Not that the man seemed to care about much other than being seen by the camera.

Aedith put her card away and took a step towards the man, hands held up in supplication.

'Good afternoon, friend,' she said. 'I'm Captain Aedith Mercia and I'll be your designated negotiator for today. Do you mind if I ask what happened to your neck?'

The man seemed to see her for the first time. The mobile phone was still held high in the air, an old-fashioned model, Drustan could see now, plastic buttons rather than a touch screen. The man's thumb hovered over the central button. A second mobile, or the parts of one anyway, half-buried in the centre of the vest. Not the most efficient set-up, the signal having to be sent from the first phone to the local cell network to a satellite then back to the second to trigger the explosives that would kill them all.

'I am the Hook,' said the man. 'I called you before. Three times. I told you I was the Hook, but no one called me back.'

That last rather plaintive, as though he'd reported dog mess in the park, or a broken streetlamp.

'I'm afraid we've had a lot of calls today,' said Aedith, her tone patient, sympathetic. 'But I'm wondering if you're hurt. Your wound there looks pretty nasty. Perhaps we could get a doctor to look at it?'

'I killed,' said the man, swallowed and tried again. 'I killed Gorsedd Angwin and Eawynn Wettin. They were Fishers.'

'Apparently so,' said Aedith. She hadn't raised her voice once, as though she were chatting with a friend. 'I don't know much about the Fishers, although I did see the tattoos. I wonder if you could explain to me what they're about?'

'They hide their masks,' said the man. 'No, they hide their *faces*. Under a mask. Tell that reeve to step back.'

One enterprising cop was edging forward, hand creeping to his sidearm.

'Back up there, Constable,' said Aedith. 'Right now. If you want to be useful, you could go and get me a coffee. Maybe one for our guest here too. Do you like coffee? Maybe a herbal tea?'

The man ignored her, licking dry lips, mouthing wordlessly, running through something in his head. He's been primed, thought Drustan. Loaded up not just with a bomb vest, but a message too.

'Your neck,' said Aedith. 'What happened to you?'

Distracted, the man's eyes were wide with panic now. His free hand moved up to the bandage, touched it gingerly. 'I don't know,' he said. 'I mean, they didn't tell me.'

He winced. He was messing it up now and he knew it. Abruptly, the words came to him in a rush. '*I am the one they call the Hook I am the instrument of Woden on this earth and he will reward me in the afterlife for what I have done. I killed the Tash and the whore woman too and I will gut all the Fish traitors who want to let the races mix and turn the East into a nothing nation.*'

He looked pathetically pleased as he came to a finish. Whatever he'd come there to do, he'd done it.

'I am the Hook,' he said, and pressed the button.

THIRTY SIX

Drustan would remember that moment as much for the look of puzzlement on the big Saxon's face when nothing happened as for the absurdly useless step back taken by every cop in the building at the same moment. Even Agapos had flinched, Drustan using that moment to hurl himself between the sergeant and his target, closing the space across the foyer by the time Agapos had his weapon back up.

The man hadn't noticed, too busy holding the phone up, trying to get better reception. After a moment, the screen and exposed innards of the second phone beeped twice, but by that time Drustan had yanked it away from the bomb vest and thrown it across the floor.

The man moaned, a pitiful noise. Not the sound of someone who'd wanted to take as many cops with him as he could, but of someone who'd been given one job and had failed. He looked down at Drustan.

'Excellent work, DI Drustan,' said Tancred from somewhere behind him. He stepped forward, put the muzzle of his sidearm against the Saxon's head and pulled the trigger.

'Hook Killer Turns Bomb Nut, Taken Out by Special Ops Cop' was the headline on the biggest news site. The others went for something along similar lines. All found a rhyme in there somewhere. A few of them were distracted by an explosion in one of the trendier squares of the city, home to a cluster of buzzy cutting-edge media production companies, but early reports put it down to a faulty gas mains and no one seemed to know who, if anyone, had died anyway.

Back on the main story, the killer known as the Hook had been identified as one Stithulf Hatt. A security guard and part-time army reservist, he had recently been diagnosed with a tumour wrapped round the base of his brain where not even the best Pan-African surgeons would have been able to remove it, even if Stithulf had been able to crowdfund an operation, which seemed unlikely as he had the social-media footprint of a whelk.

He left behind an ex-wife and young daughter, to whom he was described as being 'devoted', although neighbours had described his recent behaviour as erratic, swinging from being withdrawn to ranting about conspiracy theories. He had quit his job two days before the body of Gorsedd Angwin had been found and hadn't been seen since. Mobile-phone evidence put him at the scene of both crimes, and a nail gun was found at the tiny flat to which he had decamped after the breakdown of his marriage, along with many publications of a conspiratorial nature and his seax, with a note saying he wanted it to be entrusted to his daughter, when she was old enough to claim it.

Acting Commander Tancred of Special Branch, the heroic reeve who had saved the lives of hundreds of brave men and women who had given their pledge to protect the public every day and whose work was often derided and ignored (not least by the many news sites containing the report), had put out a statement saying he wasn't looking for any more suspects for the murder of Angwin or Eawynn Wettin. He also stated that security for the Summit, which would formally begin the following day, would, as a formality, move up to high alert, with any employees suspected of belonging to the Fisher cult removed until certain investigations had made their conclusions. When a tame journalist asked if Tancred considered that the Hook might have done the authorities a favour in a way, now they knew these sinister 'Fishers' – at least one of whom had a terrorist past and a large cache of illegal weaponry, bent on who-knows-what un-Saxonish ends – were involved at all levels of the Summit, Acting Commander Tancred called an abrupt end to the press conference. But he didn't deny it.

'I haven't started on Hatt yet,' said Orva. Two bodies were laid out on trolleys in the morgue: Eawynn Wettin's covered from the neck down in a sheet, Stithulf Hatt's naked, Orva's surgical tools gleaming in a silver tray next to it, eager to be used. 'Wettin's tox screen came back. She was drugged, same as Angwin, but obviously the injuries are less severe.'

Drustan thought of Wettin's wide eyes back in the woods, staring into his, although he was sure it was the Fisher killer she was seeing. He'd held her up as long as he could, until the police, drawn by the sound of Wettin's screams, had arrived to help take her down. She had gone quiet, her eyes closed once more, by the time they finally got her stretcher into the ambulance, although her scream was still echoing around Drustan's head somewhere. He knew from experience that it wouldn't stop until the killer was found.

'We were told she died of a heart attack,' said Aedith.

'Likely from trauma, although there was serious blood loss, which damages the heart – can make it seize up, essentially.'

'I was at the scene,' said Drustan. 'There was surprisingly little blood.'

Orva shrugged. 'Not for me to say where it went. She would certainly have lost some from the wounds on wrists and ankles, although that's not what kills you. If the killer hadn't slashed Angwin's throat when he was nailed, he would eventually have died from asphyxiation anyway.'

Aedith frowned. 'I don't understand.'

'With the arms outstretched like that for a long period of time, the chest muscles get pulled out, the lungs can't contract properly, eventually you run out of oxygen. Horrendous way to die. The Romans were big on it.'

'So...' Drustan was thinking it through. 'Cutting the throat becomes, what, an act of mercy?'

'You'd need to ask a psychologist, but my view, for what it's worth, is that it was impatience. The killer wants his victims to suffer but isn't prepared to hang around for the long haul. He wants vengeance, but he's also practical. That's my unofficial opinion, obviously. Anyway, other than the obvious, Wettin was in good health. No signs of alcoholism, kept herself fit.'

Drustan thought of Angwin's past and the broken bodies of the other Fishers: Ethel Noakes, Ulf, more they'd never even know about.

'These people have something in their lives that makes them get that mark, become a Fisher. If it's not a physical addiction, it's something spiritual. The Fishers are offering them something these people can't get anywhere else.'

'Don't *all* religions offer things you can't get in real life?' said Aedith. Drustan couldn't help noticing the tattoos of Hel just visible on Orva's cropped scalp. Aedith followed his gaze and added, 'No offence, Orva.'

Orva shrugged. 'None taken. The gods don't care if you believe in them or not, they'll still be waiting for you, one way or another.'

Drustan said nothing.

'Your man Hatt, then,' said Orva. 'Had to wait for bomb squad to deal with the vest before he was passed to me. Some of it was genuine, in case you were wondering.'

Aedith frowned. 'Some of it?'

'Two bars out of the eight. The others were dummies, although you couldn't tell without chemical analysis. Enough to have blown up your man, and anyone else in the foyer, but not so much it would have taken out the entire building. Thoughtful, really.'

Drustan looked at the dressing, just visible on the back of the neck. 'Can we get this off?'

'Sure. You'll have to help me shift him, he's a big lad.'

Between them, Drustan and Aedith rolled Hatt onto his side. Orva pulled away the dressing with tweezers, looking at it doubtfully. 'Lot of skin coming away with this. You going to preserve it for evidence?'

Aedith nodded. 'Any way you can dry it out without losing fingerprints?'

'I'll do my best. You'll need to get him on his front if you want a good look at that wound. Just make sure you flip him back over before you go, the porters don't like me calling them in to move the dead ones around.'

It wasn't too hard to let Hatt's weight carry him over onto his front. The back of his neck was raw, skin peeled away in patches or missing entirely. Where the skin remained, it was blistered and bubbled.

'Looks like an acid burn,' said Orva. 'Two days old at the earliest.' She caught the look that passed between Aedith and Drustan. 'Is this significant?'

'Fuck, yes,' said Aedith. 'But it's also what senior management might describe as "unhelpful".'

A look passed between her and Drustan, not missed by Orva who, displaying a consummate professionalism that impressed Drustan still further, announced loudly: 'Time for my break. The vending machine down here broke, so I'll have to go to the one in reception. Takes about fifteen minutes.'

'So,' said Aedith after the door had closed behind Orva and she had pulled the power cable out of the room's one security camera. 'It wouldn't take the smartest officer in the world to conclude that Mister Hatt here and the suspect in the drone video are one and the same.'

'Indeed,' said Drustan. 'Same height and build, we didn't get a good look at his face in the video anyway, and this burn certainly matches the shape and size of the mark the suspect had on the back of his neck. Sparrow on the wrist too – it's not entirely the same as the one in the video, but you could justify that with night vision, compression artefacts and so on. Either way, I'm sure we'll find Mister Hatt spent his childhood bouncing around various care homes in the South-East.'

Aedith nodded. 'Let's put him back.'

Together they heaved Hatt over, sightless eyes gazing back up at the ceiling.

'So,' said Aedith. 'If you had a suspicion your investigating officers had got a glimpse of a suspect and you wanted to provide them with everything they needed to wrap the case up, why not dig up a six-foot-plus Saxon with a background in care – and the accompanying appropriate tattoo – a death sentence and dependants he desperately wants to provide for? Pour some acid on the back of his neck as though he'd tried to remove a tattoo, get him in a bomb harness and send him into the station to read a prepared statement on security camera and then blow himself up? I'm assuming a large number of pennies are going to drop into his family's account when all this has a chance to blow over.'

'It has a certain logic,' said Drustan. 'If you had the resources and the will. Our killer has the will, undoubtedly, but if he's a working-class Saxon on a police wage, there's no way he could arrange all this.'

'Agreed,' said Aedith sourly. 'Which puts a bigger hole in my lone-wolf theory than the one in Hatt's skull. So, who could? Who's backing him?'

'Good question,' said Drustan. 'And then there's the calls. Three from Hatt, working off his script, it looks like, and desperate to get the attention he's presumably been ordered to get, not realising there'll be the usual flood of false claims. But that first call, the other one that knew about the fish tattoo just a little too early.'

'The real killer.'

'I think so. But why would he call in himself? Why interfere with what seems like a well-established plan?'

Aedith looked at him. 'You think the killer doesn't play well with others, perhaps.'

'Perhaps,' said Drustan. 'Although whether he's going off-script or not, who's backing him?'

'According to my father,' said Aedith, '"Greater powers".'

'I can't say that's enormously helpful.'

Drustan watched as Aedith took a sheet, draped it over Hatt's naked body. It didn't seem a prudish gesture, more one of gentle pity, 'By Dad's standards,' she said, 'that's downright *explicit*.'

*

By the time Drustan and Aedith got back to the office, most of the team had gone home, a solitary Tribal cleaner working her way around the office, sweeping honeycake wrappers into binbags and gathering the half-empty coffee mugs while carefully leaving paperwork and grisly scene of crime photos untouched. Only Aedith, Drustan, Agapos and Naeku remained. Naeku opened her mouth, but Aedith shook her head before she could say anything, eyes flicking to the security camera high up in the corner of the office. 'Let's go to the meadhall.'

THIRTY SEVEN

Reeve bars were the same across the world, at least the ones Drustan had been in. The framed photos of uniformed officers, long dead now, might be different, the sports iconography varying from nation to nation, but the themes continued: a certain insularity, an insistence of order and tidiness that did little to disguise the chipped edges of the furniture, the sense of secrets being not so much kept as shoved under the floorboards. Half the drinkers here were Afro-Saxon, a third were women. The booze itself wasn't savoured, just poured down throats in a mechanical process that would continue until the throat-owner passed out or went home.

Above the bar was nailed an ancient woodcarving: a low relief rendition of Seaxnēat, little-loved son of Wodin, keeper of order with his stone sword. In the wall underneath, some drunken reeve had long ago scratched the crude outline of a police badge with the number '001' in the centre.

Aedith, aware the most important duty of a Saxon captain other than the generous distribution of overtime was to get the meads in first, was already at the bar, packed shoulder to shoulder with off-duty reeves.

'Unless you'd rather have a mineral water?' she asked. Drustan shook his head. He stood out like a lame calf as it was, although one or two of the officers who'd been in the building that day gave him curt nods of recognition, stopping short of actual pats on the back. The least he could do was flow with their cultural norms and sink a pint. Although one Saxon officer in particular was going to take more than a shared interest in honey beer to get over his day.

'I could have killed you,' grumbled Agapos, who'd been giving Drustan the stink-eye ever since Hatt's brains had been mopped off the floor. They'd found a table in the corner of the pub, the reeves who were there respectfully standing up to claim they were leaving anyway the moment Aedith approached. A little voice in the back of Drustan's head pointed out, without judgement, that despite the captain having nothing of the entitled Saxon princess to her manner, it seemed she usually got what she wanted anyway. 'How would that have looked for race relations in the capital?'

'I was hoping to keep the suspect alive,' said Drustan. 'Against everyone's instincts, including his own, supposedly.' He lowered his voice, unsure of just how free they were to talk. 'Where did Tancred come from, anyway?'

Aedith grinned at him. 'Talk as loud as you like. Sergeant' – here she nudged a nearby reeve, who by his flushed features was already on his seventh or eighth mead – 'what are your thoughts on the higher ranks?'

'Arseholes, every one, ma'am,' he mumbled through a cheerful belch. 'Present company not even slightly excepted.'

'Give my love to your wife, Cuthbert,' said Aedith. The sergeant touched his forehead respectfully and fell through the crowd to encouraging cheers.

'No bug here could pick up anything over the general shithousery,' Aedith continued, turning back to Drustan. 'And I'd like to see anyone from Special Branch try and get in the building, they'd get their dicks snapped off before they could order their first drink. So, you can consider this a free house in every sense of the word. And Tancred was my fault. He walked straight past me, cool as you like. I'll admit, for a moment, the appearance of our temporary Acting Commander made the bomb threat suddenly seem a bit less of an inconvenience. I was torn between letting him go forward and shooting him in the leg for his own safety. So, DI Drustan, let me be the first to cordially ask in the name of inter-force relations: what in the frozen hells were you thinking?'

Drustan took out the bagged-up deconstructed phone that he'd pulled from Hatt's vest, turning it over in his hand. He'd hung on to it ever since Tancred had taken out their one potential witness, and Special Branch hadn't asked for it yet. He'd have to put it with all the other evidence to be boxed up tomorrow, put down in stores once the case was officially declared closed.

'I was more interested in what Hatt was thinking. Clearly, he expected his phone to be the trigger for the bomb. The look on his face when it didn't go off told me that someone else was in control. Through this one.'

Aedith frowned. 'But it was going to go off?'

'Absolutely. The plan was almost certainly to use him pressing his phone as a visual trigger. Someone was watching through the security camera.'

Naeku looked up. 'Someone in the building?'

'I don't think so. Someone had a feed through to the camera. Given how often he looked up at it, I'm pretty sure Hatt had been instructed to face it when he made his little speech, to make sure it was recorded for posterity, and so whoever was watching would know when to trigger the device. Would have taken out a big chunk of the foyer, obviously, even if only a couple of those blocks were genuine, but the camera feed goes through a server in the basement then onto the cloud. The imagery, the message, that all would have got out fine, even if the entire building had been wiped out. When it didn't trigger immediately, I suspected some sort of delay before whoever was watching realised Hatt was ready to meet his gods. And I thought maybe it would be long enough to pull the second device out of his vest.'

Aedith looked at him levelly. 'Good job it wasn't rigged to go if it was disturbed, I guess.'

'I thought it was worth taking the chance, considering the alternative. Also, I have a suspicion Hatt was considered unreliable enough that no one wanted to risk the device detonating elsewhere if he changed his mind on the way in. Whoever it was, they wanted full control.'

Naeku was frowning. 'If someone's listening through the station security cameras, won't they hear everything? Is the whole investigation compromised? Was, I mean.'

Aedith shrugged. 'Maybe. Banba swept the server before she left today, said there were lots of live accounts still going which shouldn't be connected any more. Possibly one of those was being used to stream the relevant stuff before it got to the cloud. Anyone who wants to get back on will have to log in with five kinds of ID, fill out a tonne of online paperwork. My guess is, if they've bought off a bent reeve, or just duplicated an account or whatever, they're not going to risk going through all that. They've got what they want anyway: headlines across the web, now everyone's heard of the Fishers and half the public out there think the Hook did them a favour.'

Agapos drained his pint, gestured to the bar for more. 'Who's "they"?'

'Arsed if I know. My dad was trying to warn me of something earlier today, but not sure even he knew for sure. Important people who don't want the Summit to happen, or at least succeed. Either way, it's all well above our pay grade. Our target is the Hook. The real Hook. Get him, we can hopefully work back up the chain, and even if we can't, whoever's backing him will have to find another way to mess up the Summit. I can't imagine they've got endless religious fanatics in their back pockets, maybe they'll move to honest-to-goodness bribery. A proud Saxon tradition, after all.'

'So...' asked Naeku, still sipping from her first mead, 'What happens now?'

'I had a little chat with my current commanding officer about that,' said Aedith.

'How did the awards ceremony go, sir?' Aedith had asked cheerily, after knocking twice on the door and letting herself in, something she knew senior officers *hated*. Police Lieutenant Colonel Adamu's face had shown not a flicker of response. He was an Afro-Saxon cop of the old school: hard-nosed and gaunt, uninterested in scarification or uncovering his roots. Twenty years ago, he'd been running border-control operations in the North, breaking up protests he claimed were covers for mead smugglers and political agitators. He was probably right, but a lot of lawyers and kids were buried alongside those who'd foolishly taken up arms against the reeves.

Adamu slid a report across the table. 'Looks like your case got wrapped up quicker than anyone expected.'

'Does it, sir?' said Aedith, picking up the cardboard folder and leafing through it. 'Traditionally it's the investigating officer who writes the reports, of course, but this does look *very* thorough.' She had perfected a tone for this sort of encounter: interested and open to all possibilities and without a trace of subversion. Adamu didn't fall for it for a second.

'Our primary objective, Captain Mercia, is to keep the peace. I'm sure you would agree.'

'Without a doubt, sir.'

'The public have become somewhat invested in the ideas propagated by the killer calling himself the Hook. Acting Commander Tancred's prompt action draws what those above me would consider a convenient line under those theories. It seems best for all concerned the Hook is forgotten about as soon as possible.'

'I wonder, sir, if I could run an inconvenient, but hopefully plausible scenario past you?' Godsdammit, she was starting to sound like Drustan.

Adamu tapped a pen on the table for a considerable amount of time. 'Very well.'

'If – and this is just a theoretical scenario of course – if the man who threatened to blow up this station just a couple of hours ago was not in fact the Hook, but someone set up to take the blame, then the original killer is still out there. And I'd very much like to find him.'

Adamu laid the pen down, aligning it perfectly with the desk plaque commendation from the previous High King for services rendered.

'Then, Captain Mercia, I would encourage you to follow your heart in this matter.'

Despite herself, Aedith blinked. 'You would?'

'Of course. I have every faith in my senior officers' ability to know more about what's going on at ground level than I possibly could up here in the thin air of high command.'

'Very well, sir.' Aedith hated how uncertain she was sounding.

'Although might I ask one small favour before proceeding with your investigations? A case you might want to close first. Just for the look of the thing.'

Here it comes.

'Captain Ceolbert had been investigating a number of killings committed by the individual popularly known as the "Fengyr". This country has a ridiculous propensity for glamourising its killers with this sort of name, but we work with what we have. Ceolbert's moved on, case closed and so on, but there are concerns he might have left a few loose threads flapping about.'

Aedith frowned. 'You're re-opening the Fengyr file?'

'By no means. More that Ceolbert left it only half-closed and we'd like to see it shut a little more firmly. Double-check no stones were left unturned, that sort of thing. Take your time, wrap it all up for me with a full report on my desk, and then we'll talk.'

Aedith said nothing.

Adamu looked up. 'That's all, Captain Mercia.'

'Yes, sir,' said Aedith. She closed the door quietly behind her,

'I don't understand,' said Naeku, frowning into her mead. 'Now the Fengyr killings are important again?'

Drustan thought of the photos being taken down in the incident room on his arrival at Woden's Cross, photos of headless bodies in smart suits.

'He's trying to bury us,' said Aedith. 'Officially telling me to wrap up the Hook investigations would look bad, so he's telling me to clear the decks of the Fengyr's decapitated heads first, under the expectation by the time we've done that, the Hook's trail will have gone long cold.'

'Shit,' said Naeku.

Aedith waved a conciliatory hand. 'It's not all bad. We're out from under Tancred and I'm allowed a small team: Sergeant Agapos, you, tech support from Banba, although we'll have to share her with other departments. Technically, our association with our Tribal colleague here is at an end, but luckily he has an expert knowledge of ritual killings, so unofficially we'll be drawing on his skillset for as long as he's in the capital.'

Drustan frowned. 'I do?'

'I'll have to put something on the form to keep you on board. Any word from your top brass?'

'I don't really have top brass.'

Agapos and Naeku stared at him.

'You what?' managed Agapos finally.

'I can't honestly say I have a superior officer, not on this investigation, anyway. I work until the killer is caught, or I'm taken out of commission in the process.'

'Gods,' said Agapos, any resentment at being denied a kill now forgotten, 'is that how it works? We need to try that.'

'A reminder that DI Drustan has to work without a Forensics team, tech support, legal counsel, backup or a coffee machine to call his own,' said Aedith. 'So, let's not get misty-eyed over how they do things across the border just yet.'

'Perhaps worth adding,' said Drustan, his face entirely straight, 'that when I hand in my report, I have to do it in bardic verse.'

Aedith's turn to stare now. 'You've got to be kidding.'

Drustan shook his head. 'I file a report, obviously, but it's a sign of respect to the elders to give a secondary report in the form of… well, as I said. We're still not a literate culture, in the majority, so this way everyone gets to hear what went on.'

The others digested this. It was some time before Aedith spoke again. 'Erm, found anywhere to stay?'

'I have a lead to follow when we're done here,' said Drustan. 'Through a friend of a friend sort of arrangement. I'll text you when it's confirmed.'

He didn't add that the first friend specialised in stolen cars and the second was one of the biggest drug dealers in the South London area; why sour everyone's mead? He also didn't mention that accommodation was very much the second item on the agenda: he wasn't sure he even wanted to admit that to himself just yet. He discreetly pushed his glass to one side. Time to withdraw. If he knew Saxon reeves, this was just the beginning of a very long night.

'I don't understand.' Naeku was blinking owlishly into her mead. 'We can't pursue the investigation into the Hook – the *real* Hook – until we've cleared the Fengyr case?'

'Correct,' said Aedith.

'But... Ceolbert was working on that for months with a full squad and got nowhere. No one can prove the Fengyr even exists. What's changed?'

'What's changed, Constable Naeku,' said Aedith, draining her pint in time for her next glass to be brought to the table, 'is that now I've had a moment to read the invisible runes my father casually scattered before me last time we talked, I'm starting to think the High King himself might be on our side.'

There followed one of those moments where an entire building of people stopped talking at the same time. Coincidence, of course, but as the chatter started up again, Drustan saw Agapos reach into his shirt and hold his coin for a moment, murmuring something under his breath. Naeku just sat, frozen.

'Which,' continued Aedith as if nothing had happened, 'opens certain doors I had hitherto considered closed. I'll tell you the new plan now because I'll be too drunk to remember it later. Tomorrow, we box up all the evidence for Special Branch, everything by the numbers. But we let them come and pick it up, which if I'm right, they won't be bothered to do for weeks, which means it's available when we need it. We get all the Fengyr stuff back out of storage and pin it up all over the walls, so if Adamu or whoever walks past, it looks like that's the case we're focused on. Then when I clear the Fengyr case in a couple of days, we don't tell anyone, and we keep the stuff up as cover while we get back to investigating our Hook friend. The real one.'

Agapos and Naeku were staring at her now. Carefully, Aedith pulled open a packet of pork scratchings until it was flat and spread the contents out, ripe for the taking. 'Anyone?'

'Wait,' said Agapos. 'You're going to solve the Fengyr case *in a couple of days?*'

Aedith held up a translucent chunk of deep-fried pig fat and regarded it closely.

'The thing to remember,' she said, 'is that there are many gods, but above them all is Wyrd who men call Fate. And every now and then, you get an opportunity to make Fate your bitch.'

Aedith popped the pork scratching in her mouth and crunched.

'Awful,' she mumbled cheerily. 'See you tomorrow, Drustan.'

Drustan nodded, heading for a side-door. The others looked startled, hadn't even noticed him picking up his kitbag and slipping out. It was a skill he had. They shook their heads and went back to their drinks. It was as though he had never been there. Just the way he liked it.

On the way out he passed a framed photo hung proudly on the wall, black and white, thirty years old at least, a crew of grinning Saxon cops gathered around the body of a man wearing just a torn pair of jogging trousers and a torc, his bare chest revealing a prodigious number of Tribal markings. One of the cops was grinning, holding the man's head up by his spiked hair so the photographer could get a good shot of the face. The man's eyes were closed, a dark stain running from his nose into his drooping moustache. A similar dark stain sat over the man's heart. 'Warband 307 displays its 100th trophy' said the note under the photo.

Drustan let the door swing shut behind him.

THIRTY EIGHT

Aedith booked cars for them all to get home, taking some pleasure in charging it to the last of the investigation account before it was closed down for good. If she was going to continue the case under the auspices of solving the Fengyr killings, there'd be limited travel budget, no overtime, and while she'd have Banba, she'd have to share her with everyone else on that level. She stared out of the car window as the city lights slid by. Possibly she'd overhyped her ability to wrap up the boxful of missing heads, but wasn't that sometimes what a leader had to do? Make the impossible seem at least plausible?

Unbidden, her thumb started flicking through the photos on her phone. She'd never been sentimental about work gatherings but some part of her liked to record them when she could, knowing these combinations of people could be disbanded without warning, their unique combinations of skills never again aligned in that perfect combination that could crack a case wide open. Was that all leadership was, when it came down to it? Relentlessly assembling warbands over and over, breaking them down and building them back up again for new purposes each time, taking the credit when things went well, the blame when they went badly? The Pan-African management consultancies the top brass pulled in from time to time liked to stress how important it was to make decisions, to be active rather than reactive, always driving forward. Aedith had the sneaking suspicion that was just something leaders did to look busy; the rest of it was letting your team make a thousand tiny decisions while acting as a filter to shut out the more ludicrous ones. And poring over performance spreadsheets until the small hours, of course.

Hengist had been good at this stuff, keeping the shit off her back so she could do her job. She thumbed through to the previous year and here he was, looking faintly ridiculous at a spa day senior management had insisted they take, after a particularly pointless series of training sessions during which Aedith had only just managed to resist stabbing any of the hired efficiency gurus with their own whiteboard markers.

She remembered how hard it had been to persuade Hengist to remove the appalling African-print shirt he had insisted on wearing when the seminar was over. If he had known Aedith had her phone out, he probably would have taken it under the surface of the water with him. As it was, she had caught him a second before he plunged into the hot tub up to his neck, his bulk displacing enough water to create a tidal wave that threatened to wash all the others back into the larger cold pool.

Aedith swiped to the next picture, then stopped, went back. Using thumb and forefinger now, she expanded the picture instead: Hengist's torso filling the screen now. His body hair really was remarkable, reaching from the swim shorts up to his neck, rendering the tattoos across his torso almost unreadable. But not entirely.

Aedith rapped on the glass between her and the RoadWay driver, a fine-featured Tribal man with a cheap nickel-plated torc that was clearly causing some level of skin irritation, going by the redness under the ill-fitting collar. Lot of recent Tribal immigrants in the gig economy now, many tricked into pouring their meagre savings into buying a big four-door saloon, then the rates suddenly ratcheting up to the extent they'd never be able to pay them off. She'd have to remember to give the poor bastard a decent cash tip.

'Change of plan,' said Aedith, giving the driver Hengist's home address. Without complaint, he flicked his indicator, more of a token of good luck than for any clear purpose, and immediately swung off the main road, ignoring the aggrieved beeping behind him. They should get there in twenty minutes.

THIRTY NINE

Drustan hadn't been to the Western end of the city before. He hadn't even realised the Underground ran this far out, but enjoyed the quiet anonymity the rattling carriages provided, the closest anywhere in the city felt truly multicultural: Saxons returning home from work, groups of young Tribals, in threes and fours, heading out for a night's entertainment, the occasional Pan-African, a cultural attaché or junior diplomat bold enough to abandon the official car for an evening and explore the real London, which didn't necessarily mean sex and drugs, although statistically it probably did. An impressively tall Norse drag queen smirked over the heads of the elderly Saxon couple grumbling over their tabloids. No one ever quite made eye contact with anyone else, which was exactly how Drustan liked it.

Night had fallen by the time the train emerged into the overground, Drustan swiping his travelcard across the London Transport rune and climbing into the open air. The address the drug dealer had got from the chop-shop owner seemed incongruous: slap bang in the middle of an aspirational middle-class zone, where students from wealthy backgrounds pretended to slum it alongside older Saxons who hadn't quite accepted gentrification yet. But there it was, a discreet blue door up some stairs between a second-hand bookstore and a Nigerian spiced-beef chain restaurant.

Drustan knocked twice. After some time, a chain rattled back from its housing, the door opened a crack and a grey-eyed Tribal woman in her mid-thirties looked out. The markings on the left side of her face and the torc around her neck were traditional; the Moorish denim jeans and the t-shirt with a stylised depiction of an early Ethiopian emperor less so. Her dark hair was plaited and twisted with fine wire and coloured beads.

She met his shocked stare with amusement. 'They told you where to come, but not who'd be here, I'm guessing?' Her Tribal was just as Drustan remembered it: her accent not as far West as his, with the slight burr of the northern Dumnonians.

Eventually, Drustan managed to connect brain to mouth. 'I didn't mean to bother you. I can find somewhere else.'

'Don't be ridiculous,' said Conwenna. 'Come in, my husband.'

FORTY

Aedith had never been further than Hengist's doorstep before. Now she was sitting in his front room. Smaller than she had expected. Clearly, a Commander's salary didn't go that far these days.

Hengist entered, bearing a tray with two cups of herbal tea. Aedith had wondered if she was doing the right thing, going straight to his place from the meadhall, but the shock of what she'd seen had driven the last of the drink from her, evaporating almost into the air the second she had stepped out of the car. He had opened the door without even asking why she was there, just turned round and headed back inside, leaving the door open so she could follow him.

'It was that spa day, wasn't it?' he said. 'Thick as my pelt is, I knew someone would have seen the mark at some point. I'm glad it was you.'

Aedith couldn't help glancing up at the ceiling. Hengist smiled, shook his head. 'Willa's taken the kids to her mum's. We've been having a difficult time of it lately. I think we'll get through it, but these things take time.'

Aedith took out her phone, held the photo up to him. 'How long had you been a Fisher before you got Denby to do the mark?'

'No more than a year,' said Hengist.

Aedith hesitated before asking. It would have been over-personal anyway, even if Hengist hadn't been, until so recently, her commanding officer. But she asked anyway. 'Can I see it?'

Hengist grinned at her without mirth. He pulled up his t-shirt, emblazoned with the logo and tour dates of a particularly tragic folk-rap band and among the tattoos denoting sporting successes, first car, promotion, first case cracked, there it was: the simple outline of a fish.

'We thought people were getting cold feet, at first,' he said, letting the t-shirt fall back down. 'Some of the older members stopped turning up for meetings, but they were often the ones with the biggest problems, so when we started to hear about them taking their own lives or having accidents, it wasn't a huge surprise. I kept reassuring people, you know, telling them the first thing you learn as a reeve was that nine times out of ten, a tragic accident is just that. And I didn't know Angwin, so it didn't occur to me then that it could be connected. The way he was put up on that tree seemed like a bad joke, and everyone was so focused on the black hand, the fish wasn't in the first report at all. I knew Wettin, though; barely, but I did know her. When I found out she was dead, same method, I went back and looked at the coroner's report again. It was clear then that we were being targeted, someone was trying to scapegoat us as a way of undermining the Summit. That's when I knew I had to recuse myself from the case. Telling you why when I didn't know who was listening would have been throwing logs on the fire. The best I could give you was Denby's details; hope that would be enough.'

'He was useful,' said Aedith. An instinctive need to be honest with a senior officer she actually liked made her add: 'Sort of. But I have to ask. Well, I don't have to, but I'm going to. How did you end up joining the Fishers?'

Hengist sighed, sipped his herbal tea. The mug looked ridiculously small in his huge hands. 'Willa and I had been having problems for a while,' he said. 'All the late nights, the internal politics, just the stress of it all, you know? I was drinking too much, not sleeping, needed someone to talk to. I got chatting to another Commander on an away day. I knew he'd seen plenty of stuff in his career, but he had this aura of calm, like he'd put everything behind him. Thought he might be on medication, actually. I asked him how he was coping, he told me to come with him to a meeting.'

'So you... joined a cult?' asked Aedith. It wasn't meant to sound entirely disparaging: most officers joined a cult at one time or another. You joined one to help you climb the ranks, another to get tickets to the really sought-after sporting events, and some were thinly disguised drinking clubs that barely pretended to be anything different.

Hengist put down the mug with a pained clunk. 'It's not a cult. Not exactly. I'm not sure I know exactly what it is. We don't have any temples. We barely have a leader. Usually, it's just a group of us sitting on plastic chairs in a community hall someone booked under a false name, discussing passages from the book.'

'The red book.'

'It doesn't have to be red,' said Hengist mildly. He lifted a book from the table, held it up. This version was bigger, paperback, crumpled at the corners. It looked more like a manual than a religious text.

'I've got one, thanks.' Aedith remembered the last page she'd turned to at random: something about flame-covered wheels with eyes, turning beneath a throne. 'I can see how there'd be stuff to discuss.'

She barely managed to keep the disappointment out of her voice. It was like finding your teacher was secretly obsessed with one of those Afro-Futurist streaming shows, all spaceships and forcefields and CGI aliens that cost a fortune and somehow still moved like badly lit plasticine. You'd show the slightest glimmer of polite interest and suddenly all they wanted to talk about was some moment of trivia in series three that paid off in series eleven and showed that a particularly obscure fan theory on the internet had been right all along.

'Don't judge it by the first half,' said Hengist. 'We usually focus on the later parts, when the son of God turns up. It's really more about helping people around you, forgiveness, that sort of thing.'

'The son of which god?'

'Um,' said Hengist. 'It's sort of hard to explain.'

The stuff about flames and eyes and thrones had been more interesting, to be honest, but she tried not to show it.

Hengist flipped through the thin pages. 'Let me show you.' He held up a woodcut illustration, the man from the posters on the classroom walls, dressed in a loincloth, a crude crown on his head – were those thorns? The man's features could just about be made out as dark, swarthy. At first Aedith mistook him for a Tribal, then looked at the background: desert lands, hills, scrub vegetation. Add in ranks of solar panels, eight-lane highways, air-conditioned mega-malls and you could be in the Caliphate.

'And this is what happened to enemies of the Fishers?' guessed Aedith.

Hengist looked pained. 'This was *the* Fisher, the first one. The second half of the book is all about him. We strive to live up to his example.'

'And he came off the planks with new powers, is that it?'

It sounded like Baldur worship to Aedith. She hadn't really kept up with religion since her school days, but everyone knew about Woden hanging himself from Yggdrasil by his ankles – the proper way up – and gaining control of the runes that control the world, then passing the information on to his son. This was just a variation of the tale, a remix. Aedith thought of Coram's friend Sandon turning homelander propaganda into banging pop tunes.

Hengist rubbed his eyes, trying to conceal a wince and not doing it very well. 'That's not really how it works. That was the punishment meted out when he dared to suggest people find a new way of living. Put the old rituals aside, forget trying to keep a thousand competing gods happy, behave to others as you would have them behave to you, live a good life and find just reward upon your passing.'

'Huh,' said Aedith.

Hengist sighed. 'My wife had the same expression when I tried to talk to her about it.'

'Don't take this the wrong way,' said Aedith, 'but I don't see some psycho nailing up people just because they're into a book that basically just tells people to be a bit nicer to each other.'

'You'd be surprised,' said Hengist. 'Look, I'm sorry, I can't lay the whole thing out for you, I barely understand it myself. Most of what the Fishers do when we get together is try and work out what on earth the book is talking about.'

How did anyone have the energy for this stuff? 'Fine,' she said. 'At least tell me how your friends are mixed up in the Summit. Someone seems to have got pretty aerated about that. Religion and politics don't mix well, you know that.'

'Our involvement wasn't even supposed to be overtly political. Unofficially, we were just facilitators, getting people talking.'

'Except one of the most prominent Tribal diplomats was a Fisher. You're telling me you didn't know about that? It was just a coincidence?'

'You have to understand, I was just part of a small group. Angwin is – was – of the same faith but a different group, barely connected. He believed in the same things as us: forgiveness, charity, a better world after this one, but wanted to apply them more directly. I've just been nibbling around the edges of this thing. Angwin was one of those who lived it, wanted to take it out into the world. Fishers have been operating below the radar for centuries, not just here, across Pan-Africa too, but we've never had any real power, never really wanted it. Just small groups helping the poor, working in hospitals.'

And beating kids, and worse, in children's homes, thought Aedith, although she said nothing.

'The fear, always,' continued Hengist, 'was if we got too organised, came together in too large a number, we'd be pushed back down. It happened before, it could easily happen again, perhaps for good this time. The Summit was the most we'd stuck our heads above the parapet for a long time and look what's happened. Most of us have gone to ground now, hoping it will blow over.'

'It's not going to work,' said Aedith. 'Tancred seems to think that now he shot some poor stooge in the head he's free to go after your lot. He thinks you're the real danger.'

Hengist shook his great head, sat back wearily in a large armchair which creaked uneasily under his weight. 'We're not players in this.'

'Are you sure? If I find anything dodgy going on in Fisherworld, I have to follow up on it, you know that. I'm not going be doing favours.'

'That's exactly why, Captain Mercia, I felt I could recuse myself from the investigation and let you find your own path.'

Aedith grunted. The evening was catching up with her now.

'Do you want me to get you a ride home?'

'I'll do it myself. There any late-night takeaways round here?'

Hengist nodded. 'Venison bar at the end of the road.'

'Thanks.' She hauled herself off the sofa. 'I'll get something to soak up the mead and call a car. I'll keep you in the loop as far as I can.'

Hengist walked her to the door. 'What are you going to do now?' He stopped himself, put his hands up. 'Sorry, forgot I'm not actually overseeing the case any more.'

'It's fine. Next step isn't directly related to this case anyway.'

'It isn't?' Hengist's brow, a physical feature the poets would have described as 'mighty', was furrowed, either with concern or confusion, Aedith was too tired to decide which. 'Personal?'

'Not exactly. I'm going to see a man about a Fengyr.'

FORTY ONE

Conwenna had done well for herself since Drustan had seen her, what, eight, nine years ago? Her flat wasn't huge, but it was well-appointed: Moorish rugs over dark wood floors, walls hung with framed Tribal embroideries, even here and there some Saxon woodcuts. The faintest smell of some vanilla-like incense: benzoin?

'I've only just got in myself,' said Conwenna. 'A friend has opened a new gallery. He's got six now, I don't honestly think he needs my support, but it's a good way to meet new clients. Can I offer you a wine?'

Drustan shook his head. 'It's all right. Look, I'm sorry to bother you, I'll find somewhere else.'

Conwenna clucked her tongue at him gently in disapproval. He'd forgotten she did that. She was close enough now he could pick out her scent from the incense: jasmine and the faintest trace of woodsmoke. New regulations were clamping down on woodburners, but you may as well try and stop a Tribal from wearing a torc or giving up a grudge: they liked to burn things and that was the end of it.

'Don't be ridiculous,' she said, handing him a glass of something red and faintly oily. 'I always liked that we could be civil, even if our elders couldn't. You won't find anywhere to stay anyway, this time of night, and it's all in the job description. I offer my help and my knowledge to any of my tribe who needs it, at any time. That's the oath I took. Anyone else has to ask nicely and pay handsomely. Please, put your bag down and take off your coat, you're making me nervous.'

Drustan found himself obeying. He took a sip of the wine. It was faintly spiced, but not unpleasantly so. The glass was hand-crafted, like everything in the room, made of twisted strands, wrapped around a green crystal halfway up the stem.

'You're *noticing* things,' chided Conwenna. 'You need to take it down a notch.' Opening a drawer, she pulled out a case of tiny droplet bottles, laid them out on the low table between them. 'Lucky for you I already had the vape charging.'

Drustan watched as Conwenna's deft fingers flicked between bottles, selecting some, dismissing others, slowly adding a drop at a time to a small cylinder. Eventually some internal decree told her it was ready. She clicked the cylinder into the vape, slid it across the table. Drustan picked it up, looking at it doubtfully.

'I just go straight into it? I thought there'd be a little more ceremony involved.'

'Oh, sweetness.' Conwenna had genuine pity in her eyes. 'This is just to skip the whole "how are you, how am I?" thing. We'll do the vision quest in the morning.'

'Oh.'

'Would you sit down? I keep thinking you're going to arrest me.'

Technically, of course, Drustan would be within his rights. The ingredients of those little bottles were almost certainly non-certified, even if Conwenna's own credentials were framed and up on the wall. The exact legality of Conwenna's profession was ambiguous in the Saxon kingdom, although the Saxons themselves were superstitious enough not to want to go directly up against a group who might just have the power to, as they understood it, turn Fate itself against them. The end result was a blurred semi-legal state of being for people like Conwenna who had to put their profession down on tax forms as 'self-employed alternative therapist'. Still, to follow the path, sometimes you had to leave the path.

Drustan took a seat in something mid-century and Caliphate, picked up the vape and took a hit. The cold went to the back of his throat just a moment before the warmth spread through him, skin tingling, a loosening in his limbs. How had he not realised his shoulders were so *tight?*

Conwenna loaded a cylinder up for herself. 'I've got a spare room all made up.'

'Thank you.'

Her turn to draw on the vape. 'Don't get any ideas, by the way,' she said, her voice high and tight. She held the vapour in for a moment then breathed out a perfect ring which drifted across the front room with agonising slowness until it hit the wall and collapsed in on itself. 'I'm in a committed polyamorous relationship with a very nice Norse banking couple. They've asked me to move in with them. I'm probably going to say no, but it's very flattering. Although they keep offering to pay me in virtual ingots, which is setting off a number of internal alarm bells.'

Drustan took another hit and didn't hear anything after that.

FORTY TWO

The last thing Aedith wanted to do with her raging hangover the next morning was take it ten minutes down the road to a municipal sports ground amongst a host of yelling parents and emotionally and physically stressed teenagers. But it was Saturday, and Coram had claimed he wanted to be a professional wrestler one day, and Aedith had managed not to laugh, and now she was committed, apparently. At least he wasn't in front of a screen, remixing terrorist propaganda into pop tunes or whatever was cool with the youth these days.

The ground was so muddy, Aedith couldn't even be certain she was cheering on the right boy, but she persisted gamely until the last lad was hauled out of the mud, his arms aloft in triumph, and to her surprise, once he'd wiped enough sports field off his face that you could tell which way round he was facing, it was Coram.

'You must be so proud of your boy,' said the nearest mum, all leggings and fleece and gym achievement tattoos.

'I suppose so,' said Aedith, not realising how taken aback she'd sounded until the mum gave her a funny look and went off to join a cluster of women who, Aedith presumed, had actually given birth to their little sports stars.

'Good technique,' she told Coram, as he passed her on the way to the showers. Coram rolled his eyes, twisting his fingers to make the rune for 'sardonic mirth' and it was perhaps the best conversation they'd ever had.

While he was gone, Aedith took the opportunity to pull out her phone and arrange a meeting with someone who might be able to arrange another meeting with a man who, if he even existed, wore a mask with antlers and used an actual sword to cut peoples' heads off. Just as she was hanging up, the mum from before detached herself from her group and walked back over.

'I meant to ask, have we met before?' she asked. 'You look familiar.'

The other women were glancing their way but trying not to look as if they were.

'I'm a cop,' said Aedith. 'I'm do press conferences from time to time.'

The woman shook her head, blonde bob swaying. 'It's not that,' she said. 'Will Coram's father be coming along later?'

'Unlikely, I shot him six years ago. It was in all the papers. You might be thinking of that.'

'Ohhhhh,' said the woman, not even slightly abashed. 'That was it, I remember now. See you around.'

She walked back to her group with her gossip trophy, a blonde wolf having made a spectacular kill.

'Fuck's sake,' said Aedith to herself. She hated weekends.

FORTY THREE

Drustan woke moments before the dawn, a habit he'd got into a decade ago without quite knowing how. He took a shower and, finding some robes on the back of the door, put them on, once he'd assured himself that something made of towelling wasn't likely to be ceremonial.

'Morning, husband,' said Conwenna from the kitchen, holding down the lid of an electric grinder while she pulsed something dark and rattling into powder. 'Fresh coffee?'

'Please stop calling me that.' Drustan took a seat at the table, slightly gingerly. Whatever had been in the vape the previous night had been mild but persistent, the chemical equivalent of an osteopath crunching your neck so you felt liberated but also as though your head might topple off your spine at any moment. 'And yes please.'

'I'm sorry, I shouldn't tease.' Drustan knew full well Conwenna was physically incapable of looking contrite, but it was good of her to go through the motions on his behalf. She put the kettle on. 'I suppose eventually we should look into getting the thing annulled one day. Could do it in a Saxon court, even.'

Drustan didn't know what to say to that, so he said nothing. Conwenna slid the coffee across the table to him. 'Anyway, that's an adventure for another day. I've cleared the schedule, checked the supplies, and I'm pleased to tell you the ceremony you require is utterly within my ability to provide. Might just pop out and get a paper first, the first couple of hours drag a little from my point of view.'

'Do you have to be like this?' Drustan took a sip of the coffee. 'This is excellent, by the way.'

'Glad to hear it. I know how much importance policemen place on a properly ground bean.' She paused. 'Interesting. You're thinking of someone.'

Drustan was indeed thinking of Aedith and her Moorish coffee machine. He was already wondering how he'd explain his weekend to her. As minimally as possible, probably.

'I have a case to solve,' he said. 'And I'd very much appreciate your help.'

'Is it to do with your poor sod put up on the tree? I was reading about that. That nice Saxon woman too. The guy who wanted to blow himself up was a diversion, was he?'

'He was.'

'I thought as much. Finish your drink there and we'll make a start.'

'So,' said Conwenna, laying out three separate vapes on the table, one yellow, one green, one blue. 'What can I help you with? Forget for a moment we have a history and treat me as you would any practitioner of the medical and spiritual arts. What happens in this room is strictly confidential, any matter is up for discussion, this is a safe space and so on.'

'The Goddess has forsaken me,' said Drustan and sighed as it became immediately apparent Conwenna was this close to laughing out loud.

'I'm sorry,' she managed finally. 'It's just your face. I don't remember you ever looking so serious.'

'Possibly it's all the people who've died,' said Drustan. 'Or who might still die. I don't know, it might be that.' He hated how petulant he sounded when he talked to her.

Conwenna had centred herself now. Drustan was fairly sure she ought to be wearing some proper ceremonial garb but she hadn't even changed out of her pyjama trousers and outsized t-shirt. The sort of thing a romantic partner leaves behind, an irritating thought he wasn't quite able to ignore.

Conwenna patted his arm. 'I know it's not a laughing matter,' she said. 'And if I can help prevent more deaths, I'll do anything I can, I promise you. But the Goddess would never leave you. She's always there.'

Drustan shook his head. 'I've performed the ceremonies, lit the incense. I haven't seen her for four years.'

'Pffft, incense and ceremonies. You know things have moved on, right? You always were a traditionalist, under it all. We could be out in the woods, right now, covered in woad, crow feathers tied in our hair, it wouldn't do a thing if you weren't ready *here*.' She reached forward, tapped him lightly above the heart. 'Let me ask you this. Why do you even want to talk to the Goddess?'

To convince myself she's real, thought Drustan, but he couldn't bring himself to say it. Instead, he said: 'Because I can't do this alone.'

'Are you alone? I'm pretty sure you'd have talked to other cops by now or they wouldn't have let you past the special tape and into the crime scenes.'

'I mean...' One of the wall hangings behind Conwenna was distracting him, an abstract embroidery made up of faces turning into birds, or perhaps birds turning into faces. An odd strobing effect round the edges, reminding him of the Hook's online manifesto. 'You understand I can't go into the specifics of the case. It would be unethical and unprofessional.'

'Of course.'

'But the killer, who took the lives of Angwin and the Saxon woman Wettin. And many others, in all likelihood. He's very thorough. Leaves no trace. No, that's not right.' He was struggling to remember now. 'There are traces, but I think those are meant for us to find. I need to filter those out somehow, look deeper.'

Drustan wiped his forehead with the back of his hand. He wasn't hot, he felt cool, clammy if anything, yet the sweat was pouring off him. 'I'm sorry, I'm finding it hard to concentrate. Maybe we should do this another time.'

'Oh Drustan, my love.' He started then. Conwenna would never call him that, not even in mockery. He looked up at her, but it was another's face there, a woman he barely remembered, long dark hair pulled back from her forehead, old markings on the right side of her face, faded now, she'd been a teacher at his first school back in the West, the one the fundamentalists had burned down. She had helped the children get out but been trapped inside, turned round when she realised the beam that had collapsed across the doorway had blocked her only way out, smiled at them all, then walked back inside the building.

'Poor Drustan,' said Mrs Guinne. 'We started an hour ago, don't you remember?'

FORTY FOUR

The Pan-African Correspondents' Club was situated right in the heart of the city, a slingshot from the Folkmoot, another from the High King's Palace, the curved wooden roofs of which Aedith could just see from the staircase landing while she waited for the receptionist to find her name on the list.

'Sorry,' the young woman said, in a tone which didn't suggest apology at all, 'I'm sure you're on here somewhere.'

Aedith had left Lungpiercer in the car, but her warrant card burned a hole in her greatcoat pocket, begging her to pull it out and kick in a door, any door, in the name of the High King. In time, she told it. Good things come to those who wait.

Eventually the receptionist raised a blonde and immaculate eyebrow, dots above which had been drawn in to suggest Yoruba markings. Aedith would have been astonished to have learned the young woman had ever even left England.

'Mister Dryer is just through here,' she said. She led Aedith down a dark-panelled corridor lined with Kuba masks and virulently green ferns into a large room, which kept the general theme but added to it wide, black-framed windows with comprehensive views of London rooftops and an eclectic array of chairs filled by aged Pan-Africans of every tribe. Most of them were nodding off over day-old copies of the *Lagos Times*. Those who weren't watched Aedith with dull eyes as the receptionist stopped in front of a larger newspaper, one of the Moorish financials, which slowly lowered itself to reveal not a Pan-African at all, but a middle-aged Saxon, hair swept back from the forehead in a style that hadn't been fashionable in fifty years, let alone in the ten since Aedith had last seen it. His zebra-print shirt sleeves were rolled up to the elbows, revealing markings of a past in the armed forces, a move across to the civil service, a vow of undying servitude to the house of Mercia.

'Hello, Uncle,' said Aedith, removing her greatcoat and folding it over one arm before she started sweating any more than she already was. The Pan-Africans here, for entirely understandable reasons, liked the inclement northern European climate to stop as close to the front door as could be managed.

'I could never get you to stop calling me that,' said Dryer when the waiter had gone, leaving a freshly brewed coffee for Aedith and a tall extravagantly pink glass of something for him. 'You know I'm not a real uncle.'

'I always thought of it as an honorary title. Three not-real uncles on my father's side, two plus one not-real aunt, on my mother's.'

Dryer's expression didn't change at the mention of Sweterun, but his grip on the ridiculous drink tightened almost imperceptibly. Aedith had never known what had gone on there and, for one of the few times in her life, had decided not to ask any questions.

'Anyway,' she continued, 'I was wondering if you might be able to help me with a case I'm working.'

Dryer's eyes widened in mock alarm. 'You sure you don't want me to come down to the station? Should I give Edgar a call?'

Edgar was another Not-An-Uncle, a friend of Lod's from way back who ran a low-key but extremely expensive firm of lawyers able to get the well-connected out of any legal trouble ranging from speeding tickets to (for example) the unexpected discovery of a dead sex worker and a pile of illegal drugs in a boat house in Sussex. Aedith had met Not-An-Uncle Edgar on a number of family occasions and found him charming, funny and with an appealing subversive streak. She also looked forward very much to one day seeing him banged up for something very straightforward with CCTV and fingerprint evidence.

Not-An-Uncle Dryer moved in pretty much the same circles, but there had always been something more fundamentally solid about him; almost, but not quite, boring. He was connected to the government in some mysterious and informal way that often meant having quiet words in the ears of people who ought to know better and, post-conversation, realised they had been wrong about a number of things, often including the payment of tax, or where they'd been dumping chemicals in rivers. Unlike Not-An-Uncle Edgar, Dryer lived in a modest apartment, and his only vices appeared to be wearing awful shirts and spending as much time as possible in a private club where the heating was cranked up far too high for Saxon comfort.

'This is more in the way of a beloved almost-niece asking if an introduction could be made to someone I suppose is technically a government worker,' said Aedith, hoping she wasn't about to make a colossal idiot out of herself. 'They're a little hard to get hold of, and I felt an informal approach might be in everyone's interest.'

Dryer leaned forward, trying not to look intrigued. Aedith guessed this must be the sort of conversation her father had all the time: simultaneously perfectly within bounds but also hinting at wheels within wheels. And if just one of those wheels ever came off, the whole thing would collapse.

'Do proceed,' said Dryer. 'I can't guarantee I'll have their mobile number, but if I know a person who knows a person, I'm always happy to oblige.'

He was beaming at her now.

'I need to talk to the Fengyr,' said Aedith.

The smile vanished from Dryer's lips. He would have dropped the glass if Aedith hadn't quickly reached forward and taken it from him, setting it quietly down on the side table. She dreaded to think what protocol would have taken place if he'd dropped it, or worse, it had smashed. The whole building would probably have to be abandoned.

Dryer took a moment, the colour slowly returning his face. 'Do you have a clue what you're asking?' He wasn't whispering, but he was speaking low enough no one more than a table away would hear them.

'Holy shit,' said Aedith. 'He's real?'

'You walked in and asked me that and you didn't even know?'

'Up until thirty seconds ago,' said Aedith, 'I thought you were going to laugh me out of the room.'

'Believe me,' said Dryer. 'No one's laughing about this one.' He pressed the whitest of linen napkins to his forehead. In under a minute, Aedith had done what the oppressive heat of the Pan-African Correspondents' lounge could never do: make Not-An-Uncle Dryer break out into a sweat.

FORTY FIVE

'I guess you guys wear a lot of sunscreen up here?' asked the film star, loudly, pantomiming rubbing lotion on his own, more sun-resistant features.

At least, Drustan had been told he was a film star; he hadn't watched much Mughal cinema himself, back in those days. Of the few he'd seen he'd enjoyed the dance sequences, although he wasn't going to admit that to Bricius or Mochán, both of whom were legit special forces trained, unlike Drustan, who was skinny and had barely touched a weapon before they gave him a long rifle and told him to keep an eye on the hills.

The newer generation of Mughal films was grittier, about men who joined the army or fell into organised crime and found that although the comradeship and cash was attractive, ultimately both outfits expected loyalty to flow in only one direction and tended to be spiritually unfulfilling. Drustan had already worked this out for himself and found both the films, and his life as a low-level, barely trained military contractor, extremely dull, albeit punctuated by moments of high drama. The militias weren't too much bother out here, but you never knew when they'd sweep in with their pickups and flags, holding phones aloft in the hopes of a decent thirty seconds of footage to raise enough funds to upgrade those pickups, flags and phones.

Drustan frowned. The heat was bouncing off the rocks now and the film star hadn't even brought his own water. Technically, the film star was from this area, his parents raising him for his first few years in a village a hundred or so miles away, according to a film magazine Drustan had picked up back on the base, ignoring the mockery from his colleagues. A hundred miles was nothing, not out here, but Drustan already belonged more than the actor did. Or perhaps he just wanted to tell himself that. Perhaps he just wanted to belong somewhere.

'With your skin colour,' explained the film star, still talking over-loudly, as though to a child. 'I imagine you burn easily. Although probably not your colleagues so much, with their...' He drew a finger across his face in a crude spiral.

Bricius or Mochán barely had any visible skin of their original colour, the clan markings covering most of it, which made it all the more obvious when they rolled their eyes every time the film star said something. Drustan didn't think he was too bad, as it happened. The film star was barely older than Drustan himself, although when they had shaken hands, his skin was soft and pampered. He had a luxuriant moustache though. Drustan was thinking about going for a moustache himself one day, but not the drooping variety sported by his colleagues: something more modern, maybe a bit of a beard as well. Out here in the hills, you had time to think about that sort of thing.

Although officially employed by the Mughal state, Drustan, Bricius and Mochán were sometimes given tasks that felt a lot more like someone in the government doing someone in a big company a favour. Today was one of those days. The film star had a contract with a high-end luxury watch company, and the ad agency employed by the watch company wanted to get some dramatic shots of the film star squinting into the rocky hills, hand thoughtfully touching his chin, watch just catching the light. At least those were the shots Drustan assumed the ad agency wanted: those were the only poses film stars with watches ever seemed to take. Until now, he had assumed the backgrounds were green-screened in, and perhaps that was usually the case, but today, the ad agency had wanted to take the film star, a photographer, a make-up artist and the wardrobe assistant up into the hills, so they'd asked if the local governor would let them borrow some Tribal contractors, legendarily the most savage and fearsome of all mercenaries, to make sure they came back unscathed.

The film star was gazing with an unfamiliar affection at Drustan, who didn't entirely remember this bit.

'You look so young! I could never picture you without a beard, could never make it work.' It was the film star talking, but Conwenna's cadence. Of course.

'Why am I here, Conwenna?'

It wasn't Conwenna, though, it was the part of his mind that spoke in her voice, but the effect was much the same. The film star shrugged, went back to staring majestically, or at least squinting majestically (the wardrobe assistant hadn't picked the right sunglasses yet) into the foothills.

'I have no idea. Was it a big day? Were you shot at? Did you shoot someone? First kill, perhaps?'

Drustan shook his head. Nothing had happened here. They'd led the film star further up into the hills, he'd posed with the watch, taking turns with different sunglasses, they'd led him back down again. A long black car had picked him up and they'd returned to the airport, the crew following in a small white van.

Bricius had been shot a month later, by a Tsarist contractor in a dispute about a consignment of apple brandy. Mochán had taken to spending longer and longer off the base and had eventually disappeared altogether. Drustan had stayed in the province for another year, finally serving out his contract and returning West, working as a surfing instructor on the North Dumnonian coast while he studied for his exams. He could picture the instructor's beach shack now, where they smoked sacred herbs and watched the sun go down once the children of rich Saxons had gone back to their compounds for the evening. And there it was, just as he remembered it, the pile of abandoned flip-flops by the entrance, the cold-poured concrete floor, forever dusted with sand there was no point in sweeping away as it would just creep back in, apparently of its own accord.

Drustan looked down at the pile of tattered magazines left behind by tourists on a driftwood table. There, on the back page of the top magazine, was the film star, looking a little more handsome and a little more thoughtful than Drustan had remembered on the day. But the landscape he was gazing over wasn't the foothills they'd taken him up to see. They were jagged, paler, no trace of the small farms that had been clearly visible. The ad agency had taken the film star all that way, paid for transport, wardrobe, make-up, security – and digitally changed the background anyway.

It clearly hadn't mattered. The film star had gone on to make three separate franchises of exponentially increasing box-office returns, before his star waned with a tax scandal and a spell in rehab that resulted in a sober, wiser actor who would never work in the industry again.

Drustan had thought then, back in the real shack, looking at the magazine, of the colossal waste of money spent on that day.

Surely someone must have been fired from the agency, or the film studio? The investment wasted. But he was older now, and wiser, and knew that the money hadn't been wasted at all. The film star's image had been bolstered, everyone had been paid, including him, and the rewards over the next few movies had been far in advance of whatever had been spent getting the actor up a hill and back down again. The film studio had wanted their guy to look good, the watchmakers had wanted their product to be associated with an up-and-coming star and the middlemen had spent a lot of their money to make everyone happy.

'It's public relations,' said Drustan. 'Backdrops, focus groups, actors, everything. The Hook's real, but everything else is fake.'

'Ah,' said Conwenna's voice, but this time it wasn't Conwenna: it was something inside him, something older. 'There it is. A gift on a branch.'

A young woman walked past the window. She wore a faded grey denim jacket and a long skirt. Her feet were bare. She looked over her shoulder, half her face covered in swirling black markings, smiled briefly, and was gone.

Drustan awoke.

FORTY SIX

'The High King has always had a personal executioner,' said Dryer. They'd moved to a far corner of the lounge now, waiters summoned by a glance and knowing without being told to arrange folding wooden screens around them. The wood was dark and dense, carved with stylised depictions of charismatic megafauna. Wouldn't stop a determined eavesdropper of course, but the barrier was more psychological than physical. It would be a terrible breach of club rules to acknowledge anything beyond the screens even existed, let alone try to determine any details.

This was how, Aedith had always known, most of the world was run, but she'd always felt on the wrong side of the screen, even as a relatively high-ranking police officer. Being on this side was seductive, intoxicating. She needed to get out from behind them as soon as possible. But not just yet.

'The role has been mostly ceremonial, on and off,' continued Dryer. He had regained his poise now, waving away the replacement pink drink the waiter had tried to bring and ordering a large pot of herbal tea instead, although it wasn't any herb Aedith recognised. The waiter even placed a small jug of milk alongside the pot, which she initially thought had to be a mistake, but apparently not. Truly this club really was another part of the world, carefully excised and transplanted to Saxon London where everything could continue just as before. 'But sometimes it's applied more practically. It's really the dark side of the pardoning system. Towards the end of a High King's reign, he has the right to forgive those who committed certain criminal acts of their trespasses.'

'I'm familiar,' said Aedith. Whenever a High King took to their deathbed, reeves inevitably braced themselves for the sudden but inevitable collapse of certain cases centred on high-ranking officials who knew where too many bodies were buried. It wasn't as bad as it sounded: some crimes were beyond the pardoning system, and any crony of the King who was in deep enough to need pardoning usually had a few darker secrets buried away the reeves could get to eventually.

'I'm sure,' said Dryer. 'But you and the public see only the carrot. A High King must also have a stick. And some matters are beyond a pardon.'

'You're saying, just to be clear, all those heads were taken by someone acting on direct behalf of the High King?'

'I'm saying,' said Dryer, 'if you were looking into a select group of people who'd committed the gravest of crimes because they assumed their status would make them invulnerable and later turned up missing their heads, it was almost certainly the Fengyr enacting the punishment of the High King himself. And if that was the case, those killings weren't crimes at all.'

He poured the milk into the tea, swirling it around with a small silver spoon.

'Forgive me,' he said. 'I've been in a lot of meetings with the Mughals of late, got rather a taste for it.'

Milk in tea. Aedith tried not to recoil. She couldn't see it catching on.

'Eight people. All dead because the High King sees the sun going down on his reign and wants to settle some scores.'

'If he wanted to settle scores, it would count in the hundreds,' said Dryer. 'You must have uncovered in your investigation the sort of stuff these people were up to. The Kingdom is a better place without them.'

'They should have been charged,' said Aedith stubbornly. 'I know everyone in this room thinks this nation is a howling wilderness populated by drunk savages, but we have a process of law.'

'Agreed,' said Dryer, 'and the Fengyr is every much a part of that process as you are. Also, it's nine, by the information I have; you missed one. But you don't need to know about him.'

Aedith said nothing. Dryer sipped his revolting drink, placed the cup back on the table, leaned back in his chair. 'I can get word to people close to the High King. The Fengyr follows a process. There may even be paperwork. I can get you something to pass up to your senior officers. It will go no further than that, but it will be enough to see the case officially closed.'

'All this because my father is a friend?'

He smiled without mirth. 'All this because you asked. In the rules of the game, this is a perfectly legal move to make. If you were making it to advance your career, calling in a favour, I'd still be bound to honour it. Knowing you're making it just to do your job makes it easier for me to respond, I'm glad to say.'

He finished his tea. Clearly it was over now, as far as he was concerned, the matter dealt with. Aedith shook her head.

'No. I want to meet him. The Fengyr. I want to look him in the eyes.'

Dryer sighed. 'And what will you do then, arrest him?'

'Would I have grounds to do so?'

'If you tried, I'm sure you could find something. That's the beauty of the law. Whether you could make it stick, or live long enough to get the cuffs on, would be another matter entirely.'

Aedith crossed her arms, leaned back. She was going nowhere.

Dryer laughed, sounding genuinely amused. 'Very well, I'll set something up. Just don't do anything that leads to me having to write an apologetic letter to your father. He's very fond of you and almost certainly prefers you with your head on.'

He got up, gestured to a waiter who had been hovering across the room. Immediately more staff appeared, folding the screens, removing them as though the conversation had never taken place. The receptionist, unbidden, appeared with Aedith's coat.

Aedith made her wait a little longer. 'Uncle? Have you ever worked with anyone calling themselves a Fisher?'

He nodded, 'Here and there. A few in Ethiopia, a couple hidden away among the Norse.'

'What did you think of them?'

'They seemed like decent people. Although whether they were decent people because they were Fishers or were drawn to being Fishers because they were decent people, I couldn't tell you. Good luck with your case, Aedith.'

FORTY SEVEN

Once she was sure Drustan had returned safely, Conwenna had pressed a cup of herbal tea into his hands, arranged a blanket around his shoulders and left him to it. The shadows were beginning to lengthen. Drustan guessed he had been in the dream most of the day. Technically it took two hours to go in, another two hours to come out, but for a while you always wondered if you'd ever really emerged at all.

'I'm glad you're not one of those who lose total control while they're under,' called Conwenna from the kitchen, the sounds and smells of a stew drifting out into the living room. 'I'm low on towels and it's always embarrassing when it's someone you know.'

Drustan wondered when Conwenna had learned to cook. She'd lived on takeaways before, or traded favours for gifts from neighbours. Conwenna was always moving, making connections. If she'd been Norse, she'd have been a formidable hedge trader or maybe a journalist. A Celt living in London had fewer choices: criminality, performing arts (Conwenna had an excellent singing voice but her dancing left something to be desired), social media influencer or shaman-for-hire to the middle classes. All things considered, she had probably made the right choice.

'You sure you didn't know it was going to be me?' Conwenna emerged from the kitchen bearing two bowls of grey stew. Drustan sniffed his suspiciously when her back was turned. It didn't smell terrible, but it didn't smell enticing either.

Drustan shook his head. 'I asked for the address of a decent therapeutic shaman with a spare room.'

Conwenna pulled a face. 'Just "decent"?'

'Fine, I asked for the best.'

'And how did I do? Online ratings are very important, you know. You give me anything below three stars, my fees will start to drop.'

'I'll be sure to rate you very highly.'

Drustan took a spoonful of his stew. It wasn't bad. Conwenna sat cross-legged on the floor opposite him.

'Who was the girl? You talked about her while you were under.'

'In reality? Just someone I saw walking past a window when I was a young man.'

'Before you met me?'

'Around the same time. But then I saw her again. Or I thought I did. She led me to a crime scene. The second woman, the Saxon; Eawynn Wettin. And when I returned to the scene, I found a drone we'd lost in a raid. It had footage of the killer on it. Enough to identify him. Enough that whoever is behind him sent a decoy into the police station wearing a suicide vest.'

'Poor Drustan. You thought the Goddess had left you and she had been there by your side, all along.'

'Or the blast of the explosion sent me into shock. Subconsciously, I spotted something out of place in the distance and that led me to Wettin. When I returned later, in an attempt to reconcile what had happened, I realised the shockwave of the blast could have sent the drone in the same direction. And it was the constable with me who found it, not me.'

'One of the reasons I'm very fond of you,' said Conwenna, 'is you're the only person I know who could seek out a shaman to put you in a six-hour dream quest to help you understand an event, then emerge with an entirely rational explanation for the same thing. I'll never know whether it was becoming a policeman that made you like this, or if it was being like this that made you a policeman.'

'Is there any more stew?' asked Drustan. 'I can't say how impressed I am you've finally learned how to cook. Perhaps you'll let me return the favour next time.'

'You can stay one week, Detective Inspector Drustan. Beyond that, word might start to get around I have the *gwithyas* lodging here and what would that do to my online ratings?'

FORTY EIGHT

Things had picked up outside the Skeid. More broadcast vans had gathered, Pan-African and Caliphate journalists clutched microphones and talked into cameras with the frowning self-assigned gravitas common to every example of the species, whatever language they were using. The band of protesters had grown thicker too, wielding home-made signs on every topic from 'Keep the East Saxon' to 'Wi Fi won't take MY soul!' Some of them even seemed in direct contradiction, one middle-aged woman proclaiming 'Wecta is the ONE TRUE WAY!' happily sharing her Thermos of coffee with the bare-chested Tribal next to her who had decided that everyone should 'WORSHIP ONLY CERNUNNOS AND NO OTHER!'

In a previous age, Aedith might have taken this as an indication neither protestor was sincere, surely being paid to jeer and hold up whatever sign they'd been given; these days she wasn't so sure. Now, watching Tribal and Saxon mingling comfortably together, a small band of Orthodox Norse in black robes, tall men with long braided beards, statuesque women with ceremonial axes slung across their backs, moving politely through the crowd to hand out pamphlets requesting that people worship Odin rather than Woden, she was starting to think a degree of cognitive dissonance was no longer a drawback in such times. It might even be an evolutionary advantage.

Security had also been stepped up. Police in helmets and body armour, squat automatic weapons cradled across their chests, stood impassively at every entrance, not staring down the crowd, but not looking away either. Drones buzzed around the Skeid's aerials and satellite dishes like flies.

Distracted by the security theatre playing out before her, it was some time before Aedith's spirit animal fluttered its wings anxiously and she looked down to realise she had been discreetly flanked, dark, glossy shoes on either side of hers. Two security agents: one male, one female, both smart-suited with blond tied-back hair that did little to hide the flesh-coloured wires running up from the collars of their shirts and into the ear.

'Could you come this way, ma'am?' asked the male one, in little more than a murmur.

Aedith sighed. 'I'm police, you dicks.' She reached for her warrant card, but the female agent moved quickly, grasped her wrist.

'We know who you are, Detective Captain Mercia.' She was stronger than she looked. Aedith felt a moment of brief regret at leaving Lungpiercer in the car's glove compartment. Not that she could have pulled her hardware out and started waving it around in this of all places, but it was one less bargaining chip, and when Special Branch were about to take you to a secondary location, you needed all the bargaining power you could muster.

'Tell Tancred, if he wants to talk to me, he can do it without his handmaidens. He knows where I work.'

'Detective Captain, we're very much not with Special Branch. So as a special favour to the High King, would you consider not acting like a spoiled twat and just come with us?'

The female agent released her grip. Aedith pulled her hand back and looked around. Not a single person seemed to have noticed anything was amiss, perhaps distracted by a band of protesters who had turned up with a huge papier-mâché idol of the Hook got up to look like Woden himself, a hooded one-eyed killer with a seax in one hand and a gutted fish in the other. One protestor leaned forward with a taper and set it on fire, to a chorus of cheers.

Aedith put her warrant card away. 'You know, you could have just opened with that.'

They took her round the side of the building to a utility door that could easily have been overlooked if it wasn't for the armed men standing in front of it. They moved aside, never taking their eyes off the protesters in the distance, and Aedith was escorted down a long corridor, ending in a lift.

The female agent pressed the up button. 'Level six,' she told Aedith, and they both withdrew, leaving her alone.

An unearthly rumble and the doors slid aside, revealing an elderly man with an oxygen mask slumped in a wheelchair held by his youngish male nurse. Aedith stepped aside to let them leave, but the nurse waved her in.

'We're going up.'

Aedith nodded warily and stepped inside, the doors closing behind her. Was this some sort of general meeting? Out of habit, she glanced over at the nurse. She thought she might have underestimated his age, he had one of those faces that was hard to read. Not an ounce of fat on him, either. He wore a white long-sleeved scrub top over dark green scrub trousers. Holstered on his right hip was a firearm. Looked like a Norse-made automatic, highly accurate, low calibre. You didn't use one of those unless you were confident you knew where you were going to place every shot.

The doors opened.

'After you,' said the nurse. 'First door on the left.'

Wherever they were in the Skeid, this was far away from the Summit business. The background hum of negotiation and gossip had faded to nothing. The corridor was full of junk, boxes of pulled-out landlines, fax machines that must have been twenty years old and looked as though they'd never been used. Even if Aedith hadn't been told which door to go through, she could have guessed it was the one with a man with a suit standing in front of it. He murmured something into his sleeve, held it open for her. It was her father's paranoia that made her check behind the door as she passed through: he'd told her tales of government purges, only forty or so years gone. Floors covered in plastic sheeting, men waiting in the dark to put a bullet in the back of the head.

The carpet beneath her feet was beige. The room itself was little more than an extension of the corridor: trolleys overflowing with rolls of cable; ergonomically curved desks piled high with rolls of bubble wrap. The view from the windows was more impressive: in one direction the dark green of the royal park, in the other the stone roof of the Folkmoot. The Thames would be down there somewhere, older Tribals attempting to make their religious rites even as it slowly filled in with dumped weapons and stolen cars. An ancient reeve had told Aedith a story once, on her first probation. A gang had stolen a car to order, realised it was the wrong make and rolled it off a wharf, only for it to sit on the surface of the water, barely getting its tyres wet, such were the number of vehicles already abandoned.

'You'll need to keep back from the windows,' said the old man in the wheelchair from behind her. His accent was Northumbrian, same as Hilde's. 'More for my sake than yours.'

Aedith turned. He'd taken off his oxygen mask now, holding it idly, sitting up much straighter in his wheelchair. He looked, not younger now, but more vital. His eyes gleamed.

'Forgive me the theatrics,' said the High King. 'No one looks at some old bastard being wheeled around in his dotage. It's enormously handy when you need to get real work done, I highly recommend it.'

Aedith mouthed something wordless and, to her horror, found herself sinking onto one knee. The High King waved an irritable hand. 'Oh, don't start all that, we don't have time. You've got another thirty seconds to get it out of your system, then we have to talk properly.'

Aedith got back to her feet, brushed herself down for some reason that made sense to her at the time. 'Right,' she said. 'Yes. Sorry.'

'It's fine,' he said. 'Worse when I'm on the big chair, wrapped in a stinking old wolfskin cloak, the iron hat on. A few times a year they bring out some jumped-up alderman, raised a lot of money for charity, probably kept ten times that for himself, force him up the steps so he can kneel while I make him an honorary earl or some shit. The number of them that get overcome by the moment and piss themselves, right there. I cherish that moment, every time.'

He wheezed fondly until it turned into a hacking cough. Aedith expected the nurse behind him to fuss around him, offer a throat spray or something, but he did nothing. Technically, he was keeping Aedith in his view, but more like he was looking past her, or even around her. She'd seen that look before, when she'd combined operations with specialist firearms units: reeves who looked at nothing but saw everything, bringing their peripheral vision in as close as humanly possible so anything untoward could be reacted to by instinct and training before conscious thought kicked in. Aedith had little doubt that if she moved too quickly towards the High King or made any sudden moves towards a weapon she'd been dumb enough to conceal on her person, the nurse would put her down before the gesture was anywhere near done.

Eventually, the coughing subsided. 'The suicide bomber,' he said, as if nothing had happened. 'I assume he was a fake.'

Aedith swallowed, trying not to worry about how close the nurse's hand was to his weapon, but managed to nod. 'The vest was real, mostly. But yes, someone had gone to a lot of trouble to find a willing mark who could pass for the Hook. Same build, same background, same markings. Pretty sure he was supposed to blow himself up so we'd only have the security footage to go on.'

'And then Major Tancred shot him. Rather handily preventing him from being interrogated. Deliberate, you think?'

'I wish I knew,' said Aedith. 'I dislike Special Branch in general and Major Tancred in particular, but I feel like he's going with the flow rather than directing anything or following orders. I think as far as he's concerned, he was in the right place at the right time.'

'I'm in agreement with you there, Captain Mercia. If I had more time available to me, I'd consider clipping Special Branch's wings quite severely. They have their uses, but like all institutions, they've become more about protecting their own interests than serving the people they were sworn to protect.'

'Yes, sir,' said Aedith, and some suicidal part of her made her add: 'A bit like the monarchy, sir.'

The High King grinned at her. 'Gods, you're just like your father. Take that however you like. Anyway, enough sanctimonious bullshit from me, you wanted to meet the Fengyr.'

He clicked his fingers. The nurse reached into a pocket, and for a moment Aedith felt her heart slow, her spirit animal closing its eyes, accepting the inevitable, but instead he pulled out an envelope, marked with the High King's seal: the outline of a rose stamped into black wax, and held it out to her.

Aedith took the envelope with numb fingers. 'I'm sorry, sir. I don't understand.'

The High King jerked an irritable finger up at the nurse. 'Detective Captain Aedith of Mercia, meet the Fengyr. The Fengyr, meet Detective Captain Aedith of Mercia.'

The nurse nodded. Aedith was aware she must be gawping.

'You weren't expecting him to wear antlers and fatigues, were you? There's a ceremonial aspect of course: if you've pissed off the High King enough that he wants to settle scores on his way out, that's one way of letting you know who authorised your end before your flame is snuffed out. Usually, however, I like him to err on the side of discretion.'

The High King continued as though he had done nothing more remarkable than comment on the weather. 'It's unlikely you'll need to open it but if you do, you'll find inside documents from the High Table signing off some perfectly legal execution warrants. The case will then be officially closed, although of course a number of other questions will have been raised, and no one will want to answer them. My advice to you would be to let the existence of the envelope be enough. You'll be allowed to continue the search for the Hook, the real Hook, in a discreet manner, under cover of the fake investigation. If you do catch him, you will receive no commendations, no glory apart from a quiet mention in a report somewhere. As well as, of course, the grateful thanks of a High King who probably won't live long enough to do anything about it anyway. Also, when you're done, I suspect any killing of anyone anywhere with a fish mark will end up being quietly attributed to the Hook as a means of juking the stats: this is to be expected.'

A number was written on the back of the envelope in a close, precise hand. The High King followed her gaze. 'In case you need a government-sanctioned killer at some point. One use only, I must add; that number will be deleted the second the call's finished. That's about all the help I can offer, I'm afraid.'

The Fengyr took the handles of the wheelchair, the High King reaching for his oxygen mask. Aedith had just a moment to ask: 'Sir?'

He waved a hand at the Fengyr, looked up at her.

'The Unification Summit. You really think it can happen this time?'

'Will it be over and done with by the time my blackened heart finally stops beating? I doubt it. But it would be the closest thing I have to a legacy. Imagine it: no more car-bombs at the Wall, all the watchtowers between here and the West coming down. No wolfheads charging thousands of pennies to smuggle Tribal families East for a new start because they'll be able to walk across the border, work and live wherever they want. Three kingdoms, united. The rest of the world still thinks we're a bunch of primitives living in stone huts, throwing spears at drones, fighting over nothing. Let's show them we can be more of that.'

'How deeply is my father involved?' asked Aedith.

The High King grinned at her. It made him look like a much younger man.

'Enough to become a lot more powerful if it goes well and end up with his head on a spike, perhaps not just metaphorically, if it goes badly. He didn't want you involved at all, and you wouldn't have been, if someone hadn't set the Hook into motion. But this is bigger than him, and bigger than you. I'm not asking anything of you other than to do your job. Find the Hook. There are powerful forces ranged against you, but hopefully this meeting can balance things out a little.'

Aedith nodded, tucked the envelope into the inside pocket of her greatcoat.

'All right then,' said the High King. 'Wait here for ten minutes or so, would you? Then go out the way you came in.'

FORTY NINE

Drustan brushed dust from his sleeve where he'd had to squeeze between a desk and an empty filing cabinet. A dry-cleaners around the corner from Conwenna's flat had agreed to wash and press his suit overnight. They'd even dropped it on the doorstep in the morning and refused to take payment for it. Drustan had tried to press money into the woman's hand, not liking the idea she had perhaps been intimidated into giving her services for free, but Conwenna had made him put it away with a pitying look and started a conversation that was still ongoing when he got out of the shower and got dressed. It was Conwenna, not him, that the dry-cleaner wanted to repay in kind for some unknown service.

By the time Drustan left that morning, Conwenna had made social and informational exchanges with two other locals and a delivery driver. Lots of free gifts and coffee seemed to be involved. Drustan was starting to remember why he'd never enjoyed the brief time he'd spent as a beat cop, back in the West. As far as he was concerned, you had to keep bothering people and look grateful when they bothered you.

'Have a good day at work, dear,' Conwenna said to his departing back as Drustan headed for the Underground. 'Try not to oppress anyone.'

*

The new office, which was to say the very old office they had inherited, was spacious and high-ceilinged, too old to have a security camera, but with only half the amount of furniture they needed, even for just the four of them. Five, if they could find a way to justify giving Banba a permanent desk. What furniture it did have was chipped, scratched and covered in decades-old coffee stains.

Aedith's plan had been a good one: a whole day copying every piece of evidence connected to the Hook, every interview transcript, boxing it up and transferring it to the new office – leaving a clear paper trail, of course. Whatever Special Branch wanted they could have. Except Tancred had no real interest in following up the Hook killings now he had all the credit for taking him down and was going to be chasing Fishers around the city instead. Although with what Aedith had told them about Hengist's description of the Fishers as a loosely aligned group at best, with only the faintest possible whisper of a command structure, Drustan suspected the Fishers might not have too much to worry about. From that direction, at least.

'How's your new accommodation?' asked Aedith, only slightly dishevelled despite nearly a full day of box-heaving and furniture-shifting. Drustan tried to ignore the thin layer of dust already covering his cleaned suit. 'Slightly classier area of town, I noticed.'

'I don't know how long I'll be staying,' said Drustan. 'Better furnishings than the academy, but emotionally, it might prove a little wearing. The woman I'm staying with is technically my wife. Arranged marriage, when we were teens,' he added quickly. 'Political purposes only.'

Aedith smirked. Banba looked faintly embarrassed.

Agapos appeared in the doorway, dragging in a heavy wooden desk that probably hadn't been used since the days officers smoked inside the building and kept revolvers in a drawer with a clipboard you only filled in when you'd actually shot someone, and even then, you weren't expected to count the bullets.

'There's more going in Financial Crimes,' said Agapos. 'The High Table's been blocking them at every turn lately; their loss may as well be our gain.'

'Excellent scrounging, Sergeant,' said Aedith. 'This will be reflected in your performance review. Naeku, that's the last of it?'

'Four more to go, ma'am,' said the constable, hauling in the most recent in a succession of cardboard boxes. 'I'm afraid we've already used up the entire photocopying budget.'

'Something I'm realising about the Saxon system of policing,' said Drustan, helping Aedith pin a Fengyr crime scene photo up on the wall, stretching a length of red yarn from it to another, as far as he could tell, completely unconnected photo, 'is the possibility of using paperwork offensively. It's something that never occurred to me before.'

'I hate that it's something I have to do,' said Aedith, pulling a picture of a severed head from a box, grimacing at it and pinning it to the nearest board. 'But I hate more the fact that I'm really good at it.'

Finally, they were done. Drustan stepped back to the centre of the room. It looked more than good enough. If the Mughal film star had been starring in a feature about a small band of determined officers chasing a deranged serial killer, the director would have congratulated this level of set-design work. Gory black and white photos, reports cut out of tabloids with question marks drawn on them in permanent marker, discreetly taken observation shots of suspects (actually pulled out of cases closed, in some instances, a decade ago), many crossed out with bright red marker in a way that asked so many more questions than it answered.

Naeku had printed out prop documents from a board game she'd found online where you had to decrypt the confessions of an insane super-genius killer. She'd even gone as far as, in a moment of artistic genius unusual in a serving police officer, soaking the paper in herbal tea, and when it had dried, slightly burning the corners with a lit match. It now looked like a document dating back to the days when the industrial revolution had finally made it to the Kingdom's shore, centuries after everyone had got the hang of Caliphate looms and Pan-African steam power, dug up from the city's ancient records in a desperate attempt to solve an impossible case.

'Connection?!' Naeku had written on a post-it note stuck over the crabbed runes and deliberately indecipherable scrawls. *'Possible copycat?!!!'*

'Leads, then,' said Aedith. 'On the real case. Orva can't give us much more. If things were different, I'd look at the other dead Fishers, open the case files. The top brass wouldn't have been keen before, and with Tancred claiming he took out the Hook as he was about to blow up our station, they definitely won't be up for it now and we don't have the manpower anyway. Forensics have nothing significant. Small traces of Wettin's blood from the second site, nothing from the killer. What about Wettin's last movements?'

Naeku took out her tablet, scrolled through it. 'She was working late at the Skeid, went back to her car for something, wasn't seen again. Left her phone charging at her desk, so no chance of tracking her movements that way.'

'CCTV?'

Naeku tapped her slate, turned it round. Eawynn Wettin, walking down the deserted corridors of the Skeid.

'She's heading for the rear car park.'

A view from a different camera, then another. Wettin moving further from safety each time. Then nothing. Gone.

'The CCTV in the car park wasn't operational. No sign of her after that.'

'The camera's definitely not working? Not just missing footage? Forgive me if I'm starting to go a bit dark elves on this one.'

Naeku shook her head. 'They put in a repair order a week ago, seems genuine enough, repaired it, put it back in yesterday, which doesn't do us any good. There's another camera watching the road exit, but no vehicles left that evening. In fact, the only vehicle in the car park was Wettin's.'

'May I?' Drustan took the tablet, dragged his finger back and forth across the time bar, Wettin walking to her sad fate, being saved then pulled back to her death again over and over again. 'What about the drones? They're flying over the place day and night. Any way to see if any of them have anything useful?'

'Not without tipping our hand,' said Aedith. 'And it's not likely Diplomatic Protection would turn it over at the best of times. They don't like sharing their toys. What about…'

Aedith wiggled her fingers suggestively. Drustan frowned, bemused.

'Casting a spell?'

'Doing your little hacking trick. Can't ask Banba, it's instant dismissal, for both of us. And to be clear, I'm not requesting you hack into the DP servers, I'm just asking if it's possible.'

'It's not really hacking as Banba would understand it. More a few override passwords here and there. Anyway, it's possible, but again, we'd be tipping our hand. Also, bearing in mind I'm from an allied but foreign country, a likely diplomatic incident.'

'Well,' said Aedith. 'We wouldn't want that.'

Drustan handed the tablet back to Naeku. 'Angwin was called away from a bar late at night, Wettin almost certainly abducted from a secure venue at a similar hour. If the killer wasn't known to the victim, he seems to be able to call them away and get them to a secondary location with considerable ease.'

'Which a reeve could do,' said Aedith. 'Works late hours, trusted by members of the public.'

Saxon members of the public maybe, thought Drustan, but he didn't say anything.

Naeku was already scrolling through a database on the tablet. 'I could get a list of reeves who passed through or near the area Wettin went missing that night without setting off too many alarms.'

'Would Angwin have trusted a police officer though? Enough to go off with them late at night without leaving a note of where he was going? I can't see it.'

'Could it have been a date?' asked Agapos.

Aedith opened her mouth, closed it again. 'Hmm.'

'Didn't sound likely, from our source,' said Drustan. 'But not impossible. Certainly could explain why an already slightly drunk Tribal goes off with a big blond Saxon without asking too many questions.'

Aedith leaned warily on a table, as though expecting it to fly apart in a shower of sawdust and shards of laminate any moment. 'We don't have enough staff to go door to door asking Wettin's friends and neighbours if they saw anything. Banba will give us all the free time she has, but that amounts to shit-all of late. Although there's something I've been wondering. How was the Hook tracking down Fishers in the first place?'

'If he's a reeve,' said Agapos, 'maybe a beat cop, he'll meet a lot of people in the course of his duties. Keep a note of anyone with a fish mark, come back for them later.'

Aedith shook her head. 'It's only the kids from the home who had their marks put on where everyone could see them. The newer Fishers are more discreet.'

'Infiltration?' suggested Naeku. 'They're actively looking for new members, or they were, at least. Show an interest, join one group, take notes, move onto another.'

'Someone would have noticed, surely. Big blond guy starts sitting in on meetings, shortly afterwards Fishers go missing? Sounds like they were pretty paranoid before this all started. I think one of them would have contacted us by now or talked to Hengist at least.'

'That's how he got started. What if he's now finished?' said Drustan.

They turned to him. 'Do spree killers just stop?' asked Naeku.

'Usually only when they're killed or caught. But the Fishers have gone to ground, as best they can now they've been pulled out of the shadows. Special Branch consider them a domestic threat, they've brought all this attention to the Summit. What's to stop him fading away? The official word is the Hook was shot in the head in a police station foyer. He seems like a smart, patient guy, his DNA and fingerprints aren't on record, he could just lay low for a few years, maybe pick back up again when the dust has settled.'

'Thanks for that depressing thought,' said Aedith.

'…unless we tempt him out,' said Drustan.

They stared at him.

'You're suggesting, what? One of us get a Fisher mark, flash it around on social media?' asked Aedith.

'Interesting idea, although currently I think Special Branch might get to whoever did that before the Hook could. I was thinking instead of the public-relations firm he's been working with. If Banba's correct, I think their relationship might have soured recently. I think that may be a way in.'

Drustan stopped. The others were gaping at him. Aedith was the first to shake off the spell. 'Wait, he's been working with *what?*'

ᛘᛚᚨᛏᛉ

A knock on the door, which opened immediately, Banba silently letting herself in. She sat on a corner desk, holding a sticker-encrusted laptop close to her chest, looked at Drustan, who nodded in return.

Aedith was still reeling. 'A *public-relations firm*?'

Naeku and Agapos were saying nothing, a brief glance passing between them suggesting this was well above their pay grade.

'It makes sense. According to what your father said,' continued Drustan, 'there's a loose affiliation of powerful interests who don't want this Summit to succeed, correct? Interests who have more to gain through the three Kingdoms remaining divided. Let's say a loose conglomeration of billionaires and multinationals, a couple of tech giants who like things just as they are. Some Pan-African, some Mughal, but national borders mean very little at that scale, ironically enough.'

'That's more or less what he implied.'

'And that's how these forces operate on the earthly plane, isn't it? Through lawyers and thinktanks and, when you want to really influence popular opinion one way or another, public-relations firms.'

Aedith rubbed her eyes tiredly. 'Okay, look. What my dad said has been backed up since by… let's say sources I can't reveal. But so what? We can't take on those kinds of higher powers. We'd need an army of lawyers, a hundred reeves just to carry the paperwork, forensic accountants and we'd still never get near them. All we can achieve here on the mortal plane is to take down the Hook.'

'Perhaps,' said Drustan. 'But what if there was someone between that higher realm and a spree killer going around nailing up Fishers? Someone we've already brushed against throughout this whole case, but never quite knew what we had? Someone who might be within reach.'

Aedith sipped her tea, pulled a face.

'Go on.'

'That manifesto put out by the Hook was nonsense, wasn't it? Covered too many topics, had no logical through-line, but it got people's attention, didn't it? What did Banba say about the video? It was cheap, but whoever did the editing knew their stuff. Now it's possible that the Hook, as well as being able to lift up a victim with one hand and nail them to a tree, is also a talented media expert, but it seems unlikely. I think that stuff was put together by professionals. The sort of team you'd assemble to launch a new car or get a star athlete into the papers. Or keep him out of them.'

'The fake Hook, the bomber,' said Aedith. 'He'd been given a script, told to look for the camera. Are you saying someone focus-grouped his lines?'

'Maybe. Either way, we're not just looking for the Hook, we're looking for the professionals behind him. A team, who were asked to help disrupt the Summit and found themselves an enthusiastic killer to help them do it. And they had to be led by someone.'

'Wait,' said Naeku. 'My cousin interned for a public-relations firm for a month or so. They had her sending out press releases out to different journalists, posting positive comments whenever a client appeared on the gossip sites, that sort of thing. I don't think they ever killed anyone.'

She'd got more confident, Drustan thought, willing to cast doubt on his theory, and he couldn't blame her – it wasn't like he'd mentioned only putting two and two together via a drug-fuelled flashback.

But Aedith was shaking her head, her gaze still fixed on the laptop screen. 'I don't know,' she said. 'My family have worked with some of the big firms in the past. They're players, they can do some nasty shit, use the socials to swing a vote a few points in whichever direction you want, turn a war hero into a snivelling wretch or the other way around. This is definitely a move right off the board though.'

'Banba,' said Drustan. 'Show us what you found.'

She opened her laptop, spinning it around so they could all see the screen, currently occupied by an animated knot design, turning itself inside out over and over again, subtly changing form each time, from dolphin to hunting dog to hawk and back to dolphin again. The iconography was almost, but not quite, Tribal. The faint otherness of it was unsettling. Drustan had to look away after a while.

'My own,' said Banba, tapping the spacebar quickly, the animation vanishing, replaced by a series of overlapping spreadsheets. 'Not supposed to bring my personal tech in, but I'm with Property Crimes at the moment, and their stuff is riddled with malware. Someone in Novgorod really doesn't want them to know how much property in London is secretly owned by the Tsarist Conglomerate.'

'Not even going near that one,' said Aedith.

'Banba has managed to trace Ash and Stone,' said Drustan. 'Or whoever owns them.'

Aedith pulled a face. 'The party-supplies company? Thought they'd vanished?'

Banba's fingers flew across the keyboard. Spreadsheets started duplicating, nesting in infinite stacks. Drustan had to look away – it was even more discomforting than the knot animation.

'If they ever existed in the first place. They didn't have a real address, just a temporary location where items could be picked up and dropped off. Not quite a shell company, more of a disposable one. It's becoming more common with businesses that do a lot of different things, but don't want to get too tied down. You buy off-the-shelf corporate software that runs the invoicing, payments, all that.'

'So,' said Aedith, 'you found another party-supplies company run by the same people? I'm always happy to buy balloons and honeycakes, if that's the more legal end of their wares, but I'm not sure this gets us closer to the Hook.'

'What I went looking for,' said Banba, clearly trying not to sound as though she was being patient, 'was another company using the same combination of software packages, with the same serial number. The serial number isn't supposed to transfer across, but I thought if they'd been a bit slapdash before, using the wrong account to get that phone delivered all over town, they might do it again. I had run a brute-force comparison analysis—'

'Keep it simple,' said Aedith. 'We are but humble reeves here, unable to comprehend the higher dimensions in which you operate.'

'I found a bigger company,' said Banba. 'They had a licence for the software packages, the serial number matching exactly. Well, technically it's one higher because they refreshed it after Ash and Stone went down, but—'

'And that couldn't be a coincidence?' asked Aedith.

'I don't think so,' said Banba. 'Look at the address.'

She tapped a key. The spreadsheets fell away, replaced by a street map, showing a small office in what was normally a quietly prestigious part of the city, the sort of place where every property came with its own security guard, and anyone who couldn't tell the ad agencies from the art galleries clearly didn't belong there in the first place.

Aedith frowned. 'That's where they just had that gas explosion.'

'Moments before Hatt walked into our foyer,' said Banba. 'Which may not have been a coincidence.' She stalled, aware she might have just overstepped the mark.

'Please,' said Aedith. 'We're deep into the woods now, may as well keep pushing through.'

'The firm's called "Vargr",' said Banba. 'Or it was. What exactly they do is a little hazy, but as far as I can tell, it's brand management, crisis PR, stealth advertising. Links to all the major media sites, bot armies who'll spread rumours for you if you want a celebrity ruined – or defended. Run by Hildred Emor, the woman who set it up fifteen years ago. Mercian originally, divorced, no kids, holidays abroad a lot. Minimal social-media footprint, large property portfolio. She's wealthy, but doesn't show off about it, and no one's heard from her since the explosion, three days ago. The same day the fake Hook walked into our foyer.'

Aedith reached out to the laptop, finger hovering over the track pad. She looked at Banba. 'May I?'

Banba nodded. Aedith clicked on one of the news links. The explosion, according to one of the more reputable sites, had left at least five people dead, Emor thought to be among them, with significant damage to the adjoining buildings, including two more deceased on the opposite roof, having apparently chosen the worst possible time to head upstairs for a quiet smoke.

Banba closed the laptop before anyone else could start clicking around.

'All right,' said Aedith. 'But it's still circumstantial. We need a firm connection between that office and the killings.'

'Why?' asked Naeku. They turned to look at her. 'Do we even get to bring any of this up in front of a magistrate? Will any of this even go in a report?' Her voice was strained.

'We're operating in one hell of a grey area,' said Aedith. 'But yes, there'll be a report at the end of this, even if no one reads it.'

Naeku didn't look in the least bit convinced. Drustan held up a hand. 'I don't believe Banba is finished yet.'

'Phone records,' said the Pict. 'Calls made from within the office moments before the bodies of Gorsedd Angwin and Eawynn Wettin were found, to a mobile phone. None of the phones have been used since, almost certainly burners that have been dumped, but if Vargr weren't seriously involved with the Hook killings, that's a real run of coincidences.'

She closed the laptop and tucked it under her arm. 'I'd better go. Said I'd do a late shift on the financial stuff.'

The door closed quietly behind her.

Aedith sat back in her chair; exhaled. 'So. We have a public-relations firm, coordinating with the killer. They talked to him after the first murder, took Angwin's phone, arranged for it to be sent all over London by the courier, Fairgus Blaenu, to keep us busy. They talked to him after the second murder, which took place right next to Deedra's planned human sacrifice so the Kesair would be pulled into it, released a video and manifesto to undermine the Summit, then set up a fake Hook to walk into this station with the intention of taking the rap for both killings, then blowing himself up. Except DI Drustan here prevents that; but Tancred shoots him anyway, although I think because he's just that kind of guy, not because he's in on it. And then they blow up their own office, including the woman who runs the whole thing? That last bit sounds off to me.'

Agapos drummed his fingers on the desk. 'What if they wanted to get rid of the Hook? They don't need him any more, they've poisoned the public against the Summit – which looks like it was their real aim – and sent us a fake spree killer to cover their tracks. The real Hook becomes surplus to requirements.'

Aedith pulled a face. 'Blowing up their own office to get rid of a loose end? That brings a lot of attention, even if you can cover it up as a gas explosion.'

'My own theory?' said Drustan. 'They called in the Hook on some pretext so they could get rid of him, he saw what was coming and turned the tables on them.'

Aedith looked doubtful. 'The Hook knows how to make explosive devices? That's a whole new MO.'

'If it's Wulfstan, we don't know what he's been doing between leaving Rowan Berry House and now. That's twenty years to pick up all sort of useful information. I'm sure he could have gone around blowing up all the Fishers he wanted, but that's not how he operates. His Fisher kills are personal, symbolic, they have meaning for him. If he thought he was about to be backstabbed by the agency, I don't see him wasting time nailing anyone to the wall, he'd just want to take them out as quickly as possible. Hiding a bomb under a table or in a cupboard would do it. Maybe it really was a gas explosion, just not an accidental one.'

'Either way,' said Naeku. 'That doesn't leave us much of an agency to investigate.'

'The building? No,' said Aedith. 'But they'll have left an online footprint. Naeku, gather everything you can find on Vargr. Who worked there, who their clients were. Agapos, have a quiet word with the insurance people, see if it's still down as a gas explosion or if they're looking at something more deliberate. And I want to know if anyone found Emor's body. My hunch is, either she took the opportunity to get out of town and out of sight, or the Hook's got her nailed to a wall right now.'

'Seems unlikely she's a Fisher,' said Drustan. 'I think the Hook's quite particular with his methods.'

Aedith rolled her eyes. 'Chained up in a basement somewhere then,' she said. 'But if we can get to her before the Hook does, I think that's best for everybody.'

'What I'm wondering,' said Drustan, as the sergeant and the constable left the room, 'is whether this makes things better or worse.'

'PR firm loses control of their tame spree killer?' said Aedith. 'Yeah. If they take each other out, that might make our lives easier, although there's already been collateral damage. Or they both lick their wounds and withdraw. As you said, the Hook's patient, could just wait a few years then go back to hunting Fishers as soon as they start coming out of hiding. By which time we've lost momentum, and it's not like the top brass will be keen on admitting they got the wrong man first time round.'

Drustan said nothing, pulled a sheet of paper from the ancient printer. Aedith yawned. 'That's me done for the day. Want me to drop you off at your new lodgings?'

'You just want to meet the woman who is technically my wife, don't you?'

She grinned. 'I already checked out her website, but gods, yes. I want to know the domestic arrangements, who does the cooking, everything.'

'Sorry to disappoint you, but I've got Emor's home address. I thought I'd at least walk past on the way home, see if there's any lights on.' He glanced at the address, folded the paper up and slid it into his coat pocket.

'Hiding out in her own house?'

'She's not officially missing, let alone dead. Can't do any harm to take a look. I'll take a bus, it's only about twenty minutes north of here.'

Aedith nodded. 'If you see anything interesting, give me a call.'

FIFTY ONE

The bus took on more Celts as it went further north, and the houses grew larger and more expensive. Mostly domestic staff at the end of their shift or starting a new one. Tribals had a good reputation as bodyguards or tutors, fiercely loyal to their charges, working hard to send money home to their families in the West. Many played up to it, speaking in flowery aphorism that owed more to television stereotypes than reality. The young woman on the seat opposite was already wriggling out of her drab domestic uniform and into something short and glittery, wiping off the woad markings that positioned her as being from one of the more warlike clans and letting her hair out of its tightly wound braids. Off clubbing, no doubt. The high-born Saxon girl in Ghanaian-themed sportswear next to her glanced at Drustan and snaked her hand protectively across her girlfriend's thigh. Love across the barricades, thought Drustan, and inclined his head politely. Good for them.

Hildred Emor's house was large, three storeys high, and detached, next to the entrance to a gated community. As Drustan studied it from the bus shelter across the road, noting the shuttered windows and the glossy black four-wheel drive parked in the driveway, the mechanical gates closing off the rest of the road slid apart, a security van moving slowly out onto the public street. The driver and his partner peered suspiciously around them as though expecting the undeserving poor to storm the barricades any moment.

Drustan turned to study the electronic timetable running across down the bus stop's central panel. There was a strong likelihood the security guards would be Tribal: most were, and there was every chance that if he were stopped a simple reveal of his wrist mark would likely send them on their way, no questions asked. Or it might not. Either way, it didn't come to that. The driver glanced at him once and scowled, but the vehicle didn't stop. According to the timetable, the next bus was due in fifteen minutes. Drustan had a hunch if the vehicle returned after that time, and he was still there, the situation might develop.

The van disappeared round a corner, and a light went on in an upstairs room, a pale glow shining through a miniscule gap between the shutters. Drustan moved quickly, across the road then down a slim gap between a high hedge and the higher walls around the enclave. Across the narrow concrete path, a side door, the plastic mounting of a security light on the wall directly above, set up to blind him the second he stepped out from the hedge. On the other hand, the hedge was made up of tall flimsy shrubs, the sort that waved precariously in the slightest breeze, constantly setting off any motion detector in the vicinity to the extent most owners would eventually grow weary of the constant slow-motion strobing effect and disconnect them altogether.

Drustan took hold of a long branch, quietly pulling it over in full view of the security light. Nothing happened. Quickly, he moved across the path, trying the handle of the side door. It opened smoothly. Through the crack, a dark corridor lined with bookshelves was given the faintest illumination from somewhere above. Possibly the light in the room upstairs.

It was unlikely a Saxon reeve would have gone any further, without a signed warrant or a nod from a commanding officer at the very least. The glory of being a Tribal cop in the wrong country was that he had already vastly exceeded his authority the moment he had stepped onto private land, and in as far as he had commanding officers, very few of them had working phone numbers.

Although someone else did. Drustan brought up Aedith's contact details, sent her a text, then stepped inside, leaving the door ajar behind him. Important to get the details right.

FIFTY TWO

Hilde was fast asleep when Aedith got in, head on her folded arms on the kitchen table, snoring like a bear. It wasn't even that late. The television in the front room (twice the size she'd wanted, but Coram had persuaded her the bigger screen was necessary to get the nuance of various sporting events), was blaring out some sort of action movie, all gunshots and wailing sirens.

Aedith folded her greatcoat onto a chair. Her phone chimed: a text from Drustan. She'd get to it – but first, a brew. She edged her way around Hilde to reach for the tea canister. Maybe one day Aedith would tell her about meeting the High King. Hilde would like that. Northumbrians only got one of their own into the Palace every hundred years or so and fought each other to claim the closest kinship with the ruler every time. Hilde's family liked to announce themselves only five steps removed from the throne every time there was a royal proclamation, whether it was about foreign policy or traffic cones.

'Is this a hint I'm working you too hard?' asked Aedith. Hilde snuffled a little. Her own tea, half-drunk, was next to her. Aedith rolled her eyes. 'A pay rise for anyone who puts their hand up in the next eight seconds.'

Nothing. She patted Hilde on the back. 'Hey!' Still no response. She held her hand against Hilde's mug. Not just warm but still hot.

Hilde's mouth was open, her breathing unnaturally heavy, a thin line of drool running onto her sleeve.

Before she was even conscious of doing so, Aedith's hand was on Lungpiercer's grip, checking Hilde's pulse with one hand while quietly loosening the fastener on her holster with the other.

FIFTY THREE

The light was coming from upstairs, spilling out from a wide-open interior door. Keeping one ear cocked for anyone coming downstairs, Drustan moved quietly into the dark kitchen: the solid marble worktops worth more than most Tribal homes. A vast Moorish range cooker, glittering in the reflected light from the streetlamp outside; stainless-steel pans hung from the wall, unused, but a collection of takeaway containers were piled in the achingly well-designed bin that swung out from a central island unit. Drustan sniffed the top container. Jollof rice. Not warm but hadn't gone off either. Probably only a day old at most. The fridge's contents were exactly as one might expect from the owner of a discreetly very successful PR firm: empty apart from four bottles of sparkling Caliphate wine.

Only when Drustan had silently closed the fridge door did he notice what was stuck to it with a magnet: a child's small handprint in blue paint, the sort of thing done in primary school. But Emor didn't have any children, did she? Drustan removed the magnet, holding the paper up for a better look. It was yellowed with age, the corners of the cheap rice-paper crumbling. He put it back exactly as he had found it and turned towards the stairs.

FIFTY FOUR

The sounds of the television from the front room halted, just for a moment, then the sounds of shouting and gunfire and sirens began again. It was on a loop, Aedith realised now, although it wasn't just that which was unsettling her. Something felt familiar about the voices, the rhythm of it.

The relief, as she entered the front room to find Coram alone on the sofa, was so powerful she could taste it – at least until she realised the object he was cradling in his lap was a pistol. Hilde's pistol, to be precise. It was small, Saxon-made, not the sort of thing collectors went cross-eyed over, but accurate and reliable. Aedith had only seen it once before, on the day Hilde had been hired. It was normally kept locked away in the small safe in the kitchen, with a combination not even Aedith knew. Hilde took it out occasionally to clean it, or to take it to the range to test fire it, keep her stats up, but only when neither Aedith nor Coram were home. It was hardly necessary anyway; Hilde was perfectly able to take out any intruder or potential kidnapper with any domestic object close at hand, ranging from a ballpoint pen to a rolled-up magazine. It was one of the reasons Aedith had hired her – and as an added bonus it meant that Lod had stopped sending her links to home-security companies.

'Coram, I need you to put the weapon down on the table,' said Aedith quietly. You didn't try and immediately take the weapon from the subject: they could perceive it as an attack, panic and start shooting. Better to get them to place it down nearby where a second officer, the one who had been quietly moving in from the other side the whole time, could take it away and make it safe.

If only there was a second officer.

Coram didn't move, anyway. 'Have you seen this?' His gaze was fixed on the television screen. 'Obviously you were there, but I don't know if you would have watched it, afterwards.'

He was holding the handgun in his right hand, in a loose grip. Currently it was pointing away from Aedith. Maybe, if she took her hand from Lungpiercer, moved quickly enough, she might be able to take the weapon away from him before he could fire. It might even still have the safety on. Or it might not. Instead, she glanced at the television, and froze. The footage was from a bodycam, the owner moving through a block of flats behind a dozen officers all wearing body armour, weapons drawn. The woman behind the camera was clearly in charge, barking orders as reeves queued behind a door, waiting for the Afro-Saxon sergeant with a breaching ram. Aedith remembered the day perfectly. The bodycam had been hers.

'A memory stick came in the post,' said Coram. He could have been passing on some minor piece of news from school. 'I watched it on my laptop first, then I thought you ought to see it when you came in.'

'Coram,' said Aedith. 'I need to know what happened to Hilde.'

'She'll be fine.' An irritable shake of his head in the corner of her eye. 'I got some pills from someone at school, looked up how many I'd need to make her sleep for a bit.'

Aedith still hadn't taken her eyes from the screen. The sergeant – Agapos – was in position now, gently moving the ram head to touch the door, calculating the exact amount of force needed to burst it open.

'What about the safe combination? To get the gun?'

'I saw a thing online. You use sticky tape, put it over the pad, see which four numbers get used the most and then it's just trial and error. She was smart though. When I worked out the number it wasn't a birthday or anything. Hilde didn't do anything wrong. I don't want her to get into trouble.'

'You seem to have thought about this for quite a while.'

'You should sit down,' suggested Coram. For the first time, Aedith could hear a wobble in his voice. This was the point where you wanted nothing more than to lunge for the weapon, but it was the worst time to try.

'I'll stay here, thanks.'

On-screen, Agapos swung the ram at the door, smashing it off its hinges and stepping back. Aedith was first through the door, holding her firearm out in front of her exactly as she'd been trained in the academy: firm but not tight, bracing her right wrist with her left hand, keeping constant trigger pressure. The same weapon that was on her hip right now, although it hadn't been named by then.

'Do you know who sent this?'

Coram reached out for the controller, paused the footage. He stared at her, genuinely taken aback. 'Is that really what you want to ask me? Because I really don't care who sent it. I'm more thinking it's something I should have seen a long time ago.'

His hand, the one that was holding Hilde's weapon, was shaking now. There was a slim chance he wouldn't physically be able to pull the trigger, beyond the first level of pressure anyway.

It took more strength than people expected, otherwise the damn things would go off all the time.

'I'm going to put my weapon down now.' Aedith pushed the fastener back over Lungpiercer's handle, unbuttoned the holster entirely and placed it on the windowsill, backing up so it was out of reach of both of them.

Coram didn't look impressed. He didn't look anything.

'I'm going to sit down here.'

It was a long sofa, Aedith could sit herself on the far end of it and stay out of arm's reach of Coram; near enough they could talk quietly, far enough he wouldn't feel she was going to make a grab for the weapon any second.

Coram shrugged, thumbed the controller again. They were inside the flat now, a tall Saxon male with long dark hair screaming at the bodycam's owner. He wore a stolen tac vest over his bare chest, visible flesh scrawled with prison names and dates, tales of addiction and revenge, swinging round a shotgun he didn't even get to bring to bear on Aedith before she shot him, twice, in the head. Headshots weren't recommended at the academy: too small a target. Technically, she should have gone for the legs, but the shotgun complicated matters. The inquiry afterwards accepted she had made a difficult decision under heightened circumstances.

Coram didn't react as his father's body hit the floor, nor as the camera swung round to reveal a yelling woman, more clan markings than her partner, lank hair streaming round her face, spittle flying as she waved a heavily engraved seax with her left hand. Huddled in the corner of the room, a young boy, arms round his knees, wearing the cast-off clothes of an older child, eyes blank, staring at nothing. Aedith's weapon raising to the ceiling, yelling for the other officers to back off. The woman turning to the child, lifting the blade, Aedith shooting her, twice, in the back.

The video paused, glitched, went back to the beginning. Coram waved the controller and the image froze: Aedith pushing her way through armed and armoured reeves, into the room where she would kill Coram's parents over and over again.

'There was nothing about you shooting my mum in the report,' said Coram. 'I downloaded a copy years ago. It said she was the victim of an accidental discharge. No one at fault. That's what it said.'

'Your grandfather—'

'He's not my grandfather,' said Coram. His hands had stopped shaking now. He was looking down at Hilde's pistol as though seeing it for the first time.

Aedith nodded. 'My father had the report changed. The authorities wanted to put you into care. I'd seen the state of the care system at the time, so I applied to become your legal guardian. If it was on the record that I'd killed both your parents, that might have made things more complicated.'

'The authorities,' said Coram, face twisted with disgust. 'You *were* the authorities. And it wasn't just that though, was it? It's a blood feud, and you didn't want me to know about it.'

Saxon law was hazy on blood feuds. Technically, if an individual's family was wiped out by a second party, the victim had the right to claim a blood feud, take their revenge. It wasn't an open invitation to murder, but the courts were often sympathetic.

'Yes. Me killing your mum and dad allows you to declare a blood feud. Not supposed to happen until you're sixteen years old, but you could declare it right now, if you like. Bearing in mind I kept the information from you, I think many people would understand.'

Coram was fiddling with Hilde's pistol. He'd taken the safety catch off, Aedith could see that now. Probably a video he'd found on social media somewhere.

'Were you ever going to tell me?'

'I told myself I would when you were old enough. When the time was right. Maybe when you were sixteen. If you wanted to declare a blood feud then, we could have taken it to the courts, you'd have the right to independent counsel of course. Honestly, I don't know. Maybe it would have become eighteen, then twenty-one.'

'You shot her in the back.'

'I thought she was going to kill you.'

'She was just reaching for me. Or pointing at me. You don't know what she was going to do.'

'She'd threatened to kill you, before. Said that if she couldn't have you, no one would. That's why we turned up like we did.'

Coram moved fast, faster than she had expected. The pistol pointing at her face.

'I wish to avenge my mother and my father,' he whispered. 'I wish to take back the honour of my clan.'

His parents' clan weren't noted for their honour. They ran a low-level prostitution ring, dabbling in mead-smuggling and violent intimidation with a side-helping of racial supremacy, declaring war on rival Tribal clans across the postcode, although focusing mainly on the ones with competing business interests. It wouldn't help to say anything now, of course.

Aedith reached out a finger, laying it on the gun's barrel, pushing it down gently, moving it into line with her heart. 'I forfeit my right to defend myself and ask only that you make my death quick, to spare Sweterun and Lod any pain.'

Coram breathed short, rapid breaths, knuckles whitening as he gripped the pistol tightly, then jerking it suddenly back towards himself. Aedith was ready, pulling the gun from his hand and hurling it at the big soft armchair across the room, cushions swallowing it without complaint.

A sobbing noise, which didn't come from her, and then she pulled Coram in towards her, wrapping her arms around him as he buried his face in her shoulder.

'I'm sorry,' she whispered. 'I'm so sorry.'

Coram howled.

SIXTY FIVE

Drustan was halfway up the stairs when a voice called out.

'Would you like a drink, DI Drustan? I'm assuming it's you. I think your colleague Captain Mercia would have arrived rather more noisily.'

Impressive. He was sure he hadn't made a sound.

Hildred Emor was waiting for him in a long room running parallel to a high series of windows that would have looked out on the street below if the wooden shutters hadn't all been pulled shut. She sat in a sleek armchair in the far corner of the room, beneath an oversized standard lamp, the shade depicting northern temperate predators in silhouette: wolves, bears, a soaring eagle. She looked a little older than in the one photo Banba had managed to find of her online at some awards ceremony, a few more crow's feet, but no less elegant in a long grey shift dress, her ash-blonde hair pulled back in twin braids, the same style as Aedith.

On the table next to her were two glasses and a bottle of golden liquid. One of the glasses was half full. She held up the empty one.

Drustan shook his head.

'Ms Emor, I have reason to believe you are in grave danger. You need to come with me. I can have a police vehicle here in a few minutes, we can take you to the station.'

'Where you can ask me all sorts of interesting questions, I imagine.' Her accent still held traces of Mercian, although her file, such as it was, suggested she had left fifteen years ago and never returned. 'No, thank you, Detective Inspector. I think I'd rather take my chances here.'

'You don't understand. I know you had some kind of agreement with the killer known as the Hook. You broke that agreement when you tried to have him killed, and now he wants to take his revenge. I've seen his work up close, Ms Emor. I know there's every chance you've seen it, on a phone, or maybe a computer screen, but let me assure you, it's very different when it happens right in front of you.'

Emor took a sip of her drink. There was a scent of something woody in the air, smoky even, but something else underneath that. Harsher, more chemical.

She shook her head. 'You're making the entirely understandable mistake, Detective Inspector Drustan, of assuming that because I'm at the top of my profession, I have little or no knowledge of what goes on at the lower levels. I can assure you, I'm more than capable of getting my hands dirty when necessary.'

'I believe you.'

'Let me ask you something. You're a Celt – or is it a Tribal? It's so hard to know what terminology to use these days, what's considered offensive and what isn't.'

'Either's fine.'

'Do you have any interest in the Summit? Or the whole concept of Unification generally? I have piles of focus-grouped research, obviously, but there's something about getting a personal reaction.'

She took another sip from her glass. That scent again. Was she trying to delay him? Stalling him while she poisoned herself? If that was the case, she'd be able to down the rest of it before he could cross the room to knock the glass out of her hand.

'I try not to discuss politics while I'm on duty, I'm afraid.'

Emor nodded solemnly and put the glass down. Drustan took his phone from his coat pocket. She watched him interestedly.

'If it helps, you should know I'm really not in any immediate danger from our friend. You see, he came over earlier this evening. About an hour or so before you arrived.'

Drustan's thumb froze over the phone screen.

'I will say, one thing I've always prided myself on is being able to talk round someone with an opposing agenda. Not easy, obviously, particularly when they've come round specifically to dispose of you in, let's say, a direct and physical fashion. But it's astonishing how quickly you can find things in common with someone. And it turns out we have plenty in common.'

Drustan realised where he recognised the scent now. Not the whiskey, but the harsher, more abrasive smell, not coming from Emor at all, but from somewhere else in the room. It was the smell of hospitals.

'Ms Emor, I'm going to call my colleagues now.'

Emor nodded. 'You must do what you must do.'

Drustan brought up the contacts screen on his phone, scrolled to 'Detective Captain Mercia' and very nearly managed to begin the call before the killer stepped out from behind the door where he'd been standing the entire time. Drustan felt the sting of something small and sharp being pushed into his neck before he was hurled into the wooden shutters and through the window.

Fifty Six

Hilde put a hand to her mouth, lifted her head from the table and touched the damp patch on her sleeve. She looked at Aedith, confused.

'I've made you a strong coffee,' said Aedith. 'Get that down you before you start asking questions.'

She'd put the handgun on top of the kitchen cupboard for now, where she used to hide honey treats from Coram when he was little, she realised as she was reaching up. The ammunition had gone in an old biscuit tin, tucked behind the boiler in the utility room. She'd have to remember to get Hilde to change the safe combination. Assuming Hilde wouldn't want to hand in her notice.

Coram was asleep, after having taken, at Aedith's insistence, one of the tranquilisers he'd given Hilde. He'd sleep the rest of the night and there'd be a reckoning in the morning, but she felt like the storm she'd been trying to outrun for so long had finally passed. Whether the aftermath would be harder than the storm itself, only time would tell.

The memory stick, and the padded envelope it had arrived in, she'd wrapped in clingfilm, the closest thing in the house to an evidence bag. During the week, she'd quietly check it for fingerprints, see if her suspicions about who sent it were correct. Maybe Banba would be able to tell her where they'd got the footage from in the first place.

Only then did she remember the unread text from Drustan.

Captain Mercia. Was just passing the address registered to Hildred Emor, when I noticed a side door was open. I'm concerned someone may be taking advantage of the owner's absence to affect a burglary. Now going inside to see if I can gain any more intelligence.

The classic "a door was already open", friend to every police officer without a warrant or time to request one. She returned the call. It rang for some time before the voicemail came on.

Everything in Aedith's body was telling her to leave it, that there would be nothing going on at Hildred Emor's house. But if that was the case, wouldn't Drustan either have answered the phone, or turned it off entirely?

'Shit,' said Aedith. She scrolled through the contacts to another number and called it. 'Sergeant, are you anywhere near the address we have for Hildred Emor? I'd go myself, but I've got something of a domestic situation to resolve. I'll fill you in later.'

FIFTY SEVEN

It was the holly bush that saved Drustan's life, although his coat would never be the same. He was dimly aware of landing in something yielding, yet not exactly soft, then passing through it and being ejected, reborn, onto the pavement under a streetlight.

He could hear his phone ringing, feel it buzzing in his pocket, and he tried to reach it, but the fall had done something to his side, and there seemed to be pieces of glass sticking out of his clothes and, in some cases, him.

'It's all right,' a Saxon woman was assuring him, her phone in her hand. 'I've called for help. Someone's coming.' He blinked up at her. For a moment he thought it was Aedith, but it was a younger woman, in a smart business suit, the markings along her arms suggesting she worked for one of the larger telecommunications companies. She had a pink streak in her hair, which seemed to be a thing among the lower echelons of office workers these days for some reason. She was gripping Drustan's hand tightly. He wished she wouldn't: there was a piece of glass sticking in it, or perhaps that was just a cut from the holly.

'The ambulance is here. You'll be okay.'

Drustan could see the flashing lights from the vehicle already reversing up to the front of the house and was trying to explain why that was a bad idea, but the cold numb feeling from whatever the killer had injected into his neck was spreading out all across his body and the words wouldn't come. It wasn't a bad feeling really, washing away the sting of the cuts from the glass and the landing.

Drustan was aware a second person was standing over him now, and he wouldn't have minded if it had been a reeve, the worst kind of Saxon cop, the sort who posed with dead Tribals, lifting their faces up to the camera; but it was a paramedic instead, a large man with close-cropped blond hair, wearing dark overalls with the sign of the white apple on the chest pocket.

'You got here fast!' said the young woman, impressed.

'Lucky I was already in the area, miss,' said the paramedic, patting her reassuringly on the shoulder. 'It's all right, you've done well. I'll just get him in the ambulance and we'll be our way.'

The woman stood back as the paramedic reached down, scooping Drustan up with little apparent effort. 'Couldn't get the door for me, could you, love? Not supposed to attend jobs on our own, but my partner got taken ill.'

She opened the rear door of the ambulance and the paramedic carried Drustan inside, laying him tenderly on the gurney.

'He'll be all right, won't he? I don't know what happened, I was just passing and he came out of the window.'

'He'll be fine, miss.'

Straps were being pulled around Drustan, or he assumed they were; he could only hear the noise they made, couldn't feel very much of anything.

'There we go,' said the paramedic, reassuringly. 'Don't want you falling out now, do we?'

Drustan didn't hear anything after that.

FIFTY EIGHT

Agapos must have been at Emor's house for a quarter of an hour before Aedith got there. Hilde had emerged from her stupor and had the situation explained to her and seemed to grasp it without making any immediate noises about resignation. Although knowing Hilde, it might go better for Coram if she had. Aedith had got a neighbour round to keep an eye on the pair of them; an architect, or perhaps a graphic designer, something that required him to wear rimless glasses and ride an electric bike, anyway. Up till now, Aedith had never seen him without wanting to punch his stupid face, but after he had answered her request to keep an eye on Hilde and the sleeping Coram without hesitation, or even asking for more information, she was seriously considering him as dating material.

By the time she got to Hildred Emor's address, a squad car was already parked outside, blue light flashing excitedly as the reeves leaned on the bonnet, chatting amongst themselves. Across the road, a sour-faced older woman glared at Aedith from her upstairs window, scribbled something down on a pad and pulled her curtains firmly closed.

'Neighbours saw the DI exit the window on the first floor about half an hour ago,' said Agapos. From the amount of broken glass on the narrow lawn, and the wooden shutters hanging loose from a single hinge each, Aedith felt like he might be downplaying the situation somewhat. 'Ambulance took him away. Passer-by said he was only semi-conscious, lost some blood from the window, landed in that bush, which scratched him up pretty badly, but didn't seem like he was on death's door.'

'Anyone in the house?'

Agapos shook his head. 'I looked inside. Evidence of recent occupation, but whoever was there must have taken off after the DI... did whatever it was he did. Rear door was unlocked, there's a low wall at the back of the garden, could have been onto the back road and away in thirty seconds.'

'All right. Maybe DI Drustan can tell us more at the hospital. Where did they take him?'

Agapos pulled a face. 'That's an odd thing, ma'am. I rang around the local hospitals, no one reported anyone matching the DI's description. In fact, none of them reported any incoming at all. It's been a quiet night.'

'Might they have stopped on the road? Shit, if he went into cardiac arrest or something, they'd have pulled over. Put a notice out, would you? Any units in the area keep an eye out for a stationary ambulance in the vicinity. What the hells is this now?'

An ambulance was pulling in, a short plump paramedic leaping out onto the pavement even before the vehicle had come to a complete stop.

'We had a call someone fell out of a window? Sorry for the delay, we had a comms issue, just catching up now.'

'Good of you to turn up,' said Aedith, unamused. 'Although I don't think my colleague fell, so much as was pushed. But you're okay, someone's already picked him up. Maybe you could tell us where they took him.'

But the paramedic was frowning, scrolling through his tablet. 'Shouldn't have. We've all been stuck in a holding pattern for half an hour, waiting for the system to reboot.'

Agapos rolled his eyes. 'Glad we're not the only service at the mercy of the software spirits.'

Aedith ignored him. 'Wait,' she said to the paramedic. 'What do you mean, you're all been stuck in a holding system?'

'Happens every now and then,' he said, banging the side of the tablet with the heel of his hand. 'Can't go anywhere until the orders come through, and the orders can't come through until the server's clear, and that doesn't happen until someone in the IT department turns it on and off again, or whatever sorcery they can perform.'

'Shit,' said Aedith. 'Shit!'

The paramedic, startled, backed up to his vehicle. 'I'll, um, report this back to Dispatch, see what's happened.'

'You do that,' said Aedith.

Agapos was at her side now. 'Everything all right, ma'am?'

'We thought he was a reeve.'

'DI Drustan?'

'The killer! The Hook! He seemed to be able to go anywhere without question, move his victims around, get close enough to take them by surprise, like they just trusted him on sight. So we thought he was a reeve.'

'And now you don't think he is?'

Aedith stared at the paramedic in his dark overalls, glancing nervously back over his shoulder as he climbed back into his vehicle.

'He's a paramedic. He's got his own ambulance. And he's taken DI Drustan.'

FIFTY NINE

As part of his bardic training, Drustan had attended a number of musical-theory courses. Some of the lessons were at a local community college with plastic chairs and cracks in the walls and coffee made, quite literally, from ground acorns. Others were more arboreal, in yurts set up semi-permanently on clan grounds near the coast deep in western Dumnonia, where the instructors wore clothing they'd woven themselves, brooches and torcs that had been in their families for generations. None of that stopped them playing the fruit machines in the pub where they retreated to most evenings. Or having one mobile for friends and family and another to keep track of investments made on the proceeds of swiftly liquidated cargo containers, lured onto the rocks by hacked navigational software or GPS spoofing. They respected tradition, but they weren't *savages*.

It was in one of those pubs that a music lecturer slash day trader called Eseld explained to Drustan the concept of the Myrddin Tone: a sound consisting of the superimposition of sine waves separated by octaves. When Drustan, who was really more of a rhythm guy, and anyway wasn't sure whether Eseld was trying to seduce him or he was trying to seduce her, pulled a confused face over his apple brandy, Eseld called over to a table of old guys in the corner who were already on their third cider each and got them to demonstrate.

The elders (they weren't really elders, but Drustan knew well enough to treat any Tribal out of his clan over the age of forty as a source of infinite and well-tempered wisdom) had been singing ballads since the sun had gone down an hour ago and were happy to oblige. This time, instead of lachrymose ballads about Tribals who had died in glorious combat against the blond foot soldiers of the East, or puerile ditties about the legendarily loose women of the islands of Scilly, they lifted their voices together into something entirely more abstract. A stranger walking into the pub for the first time might have described it as a 'drone', shortly before being swiftly ejected, if they were lucky. But to Drustan, it was like a new dimension opening up before his ears: a sound constantly ascending yet somehow never getting any higher. He half-expected the slate roof of the pub to crack open at any moment, everyone inside rising up to meet the stars, pulled up by the voices of the gods themselves.

Eventually the song, if it even was a song, faded to a whisper. Silence fell across the pub like a veil, lifted when one of the old guys belched, wiped his mouth with the back of his hand and called for more cider.

'Good, isn't it?' said Eseld.

They would sleep together that night and in the morning, his musical education completed, Drustan would leave and never see her again.

Now, Drustan could hear that sound again, or something very like it. Much fainter and looser, the voices of many people further away, their chanting happening to come together in near harmony rather than deliberately calibrating vocals to achieve what was, after all, just an auditory illusion exploiting the human mind's constant need to predict patterns. But the effect was the same: a sound that threatened to explode into chaos at any moment but never quite did.

'Ah,' said the killer. 'You're awake. I thought for a moment I'd given you too much stuff.'

Drustan's whole body throbbed with pain. He took a deep breath, regretting it almost immediately when his entire left side turned to pure fire. A good chance he had cracked a rib at the very least, either going through the window or landing in the holly bush. He was sitting, slumped really, on a cheap plastic chair, the very sort used in those community colleges. He would have slid off some time ago, if his left arm weren't held above his head, attached to the wall by some means he couldn't work out right this minute.

He could smell damp and mould. The floor beneath his feet was rough, solid. Poured concrete. The only windows were narrow, horizontal, set high up in the wall. They were open, just an inch or so. Too narrow to crawl out of, even if Drustan could, by some divine event, get the twenty required feet up the wall. The ambulance was parked against the far wall, a ramp leading up out of sight. Was this a basement? It felt more light industrial, somewhere that had once been a workplace, now downgraded to a lockup.

The killer wore dark green overalls, the white apple on his breast pocket gleaming in the reflected fluorescent light. He was a big man, his hair blond and cut short. The dark patch on his neck could easily have mistaken for a birthmark.

'Wulfstan,' managed Drustan.

'Ah. Not these days. Was a while back. They gave me a fresh start after Rowan Berry, least they could have done really. I've had a few names since.' He sipped from a plastic cup, steam rising, the smell of mint and liquorice, the sparrow on his wrist briefly visible.

Drustan nodded, just trying to take in the details of his surroundings, something that might help. The sound was still there, the constantly rising murmur.

'Are we near the Skeid?'

Wulfstan looked impressed. 'Well done! The protests have ramped up a bit. All Hildred Emor's doing, that.'

His voice was soft, reassuring somehow. Not the voice from the video. Emor must have got an actor in. Done well to keep that quiet. Maybe given him a longer piece, cut the relevant pieces together.

'I thought...' Drustan was becoming aware of his arm now. He tried to free it with no result other than an arc of pain shooting down from his wrist, grounding itself in his shoulder. Was it tied, somehow?

'You thought I'd gone to confront her? Maybe get some payback for Vargr trying to get rid of me once I'd served my purpose? I'll be honest with you, that was my intention when I got there. But she's a remarkable woman. Very impressive. We talked for a while, found some matters in common.'

Drustan was turning his head, slowly, trying to keep the pain down to a manageable level, his gaze moving up the sleeve of his ruined coat. A steel nail fixed directly through his wrist, pinning it to the concrete barely covered by a layer of cracked plaster. There wasn't as much blood as you'd expect.

Wulfstan made a concerned noise, gestured to the nail gun leaning against the wall a few feet away. 'I wouldn't dwell on it. Only way I could think of to keep you still, I'm afraid. Apart from the obvious. Little mark of mutual respect to Emor before we go our separate ways. I've got a bit more work to do, then I have to go.'

'You understand,' said Drustan, 'that I'm not a Fisher.'

'Ah,' said Wulfstan, grinning, and lifted something that looked a bit like a nailgun, only much smaller, with a thin cable that stretched back through the open window of the ambulance. A tattoo pen. 'But you will be.'

SIXTY

Normally, Aedith enjoyed watched Agapos struggling to fit the stretchy plastic covers over his large boots before entering a crime scene, but right now the sight was just irritating. Forensics were making great play of dusting the ruins of the window frame for prints, but the whole thing was a waste of time. If Emor had been there, she was gone now, and the Hook wasn't even in the system. They were chasing wraiths.

Finally, Agapos was done. 'Sorry, ma'am.'

'So, can we track DI Drustan's phone?'

Agapos shook his head, holding up a clear evidence bag, shards of glass, plastic and electronic innards within. 'That's what I came up to tell you. One of the reeves just found this a hundred yards up the road. Whoever took the DI must have thrown it out of the window as he drove off.'

Aedith took a breath, peered at the scene below. More reeves arriving all the time, adding to those winding incident tape around Emor's front gate or asking neighbours if they'd seen anything. So far, not one of them had.

'All right, fine. We have to find another way. Naeku, any sign of the ambulance?'

Naeku shook her head. She'd come straight from the gym, greatcoat thrown over Lycra and sweats. Aedith hadn't seen her in anything other than business casual before. Annoyingly, she looked pretty good.

'Nothing, ma'am. Sounds like he's stripped out the trackers, comms unit, anything that would allow it to be tracked remotely. And if it's a standard ambulance, it allows him to go anywhere. I checked with the gated community along the road, they don't have CCTV pointing in this direction.'

'Of course they don't.' said Aedith. 'But someone was here. I can't see who it could have been other than Emor, hiding out after the Hook took out her office. Except I don't see her being strong enough to throw the DI through a window.'

Agapos grunted. 'I don't know. He's quite skinny.'

Aedith closed her eyes. 'I need everyone to shut up now.'

Drustan had entered the house, probably finding an unlocked door on the ground floor, although it would be described as 'ajar' in the report. He'd come upstairs, maybe through the kitchen. If he'd seen the painted handprint on the fridge door, he'd probably be wondering where that had come from too. Niece, nephew perhaps? But there were no family photos elsewhere in the house. Someone had drunk some fine spirits, maybe offered Drustan some, he would have refused, with irritatingly excessive politeness most likely. And then a fight.

Drustan was on the slim side, that much was true, but he could handle himself, Aedith could attest to that from experience. If it was Emor who had attacked him, there was nothing to say she couldn't have got the drop on him – it happened to the best of them – but unlikely in the extreme that she'd have managed to push him through the window.

The Hook had been here, or Wulfstan, whatever his name was. He had parked his vehicle nearby, come up to confront Emor, possibly to kill her – and she'd turned him around. She was a PR expert, after all. Your tame spree killer walking up your own stairs to add you to his tally meant nothing to someone operating on this level, adept at turning every problem into an opportunity, maybe proposing one last strategic alliance. This could have happened moments before Drustan turned up, which meant he'd walked straight into a trap.

Aedith couldn't imagine Emor's plan had involved defenestration of a detective inspector, even a Tribal one. Far too flashy a move. Too impulsive. Too much mess. So it had happened unplanned, and the Hook would have been encouraged to remove the wounded Drustan from the scene. Taking Emor with him? No, the passer-by had said the paramedic was alone, that he had even made an excuse for it. She would have noticed someone else sitting in the ambulance. Things were spiralling out of control, but Emor still had a plan.

Was she still intent on sabotaging the Summit? That felt too remote an ambition, too abstract. Emor had tried to dispatch the Hook originally, but he'd been pulled into her endgame. Whatever was driving her at this stage now was personal. You didn't go to these lengths just to fulfil a contract. Doubtful Vargr even existed as an entity at this stage. So what was her motivation?

Aedith opened her eyes. Agapos and Naeku were looking at her with anxious faces, but her gaze had fallen between them, on a signature wall, painted darker than the others, a series of outsized wooden frames, boxes really, displaying a carefully curated selection of objects. No photos in the house, but maybe something else could fill in the missing gap.

The objects, when Aedith had moved between Agapos and Naeku, were awards, in a variety of shapes, from glass masks to oversized coins, etched with her name or that of Vargr. Hildred Emor had apparently won a number of prestigious awards, although one of them was unlike the others. It was cheaper, made of brass, or perhaps even painted plastic.

Aedith took the trophy down from its frame and turned it over in her hands. 'To Cenhelm Reed,' read the small plaque. 'For Excellence in Debate.'

Cenhelm Reed. The name was never spoken in the Mercia household, in front of Aedith, at least. She was still living at home when Edric had gone to university, had been planning to follow in his footsteps and leave the year everything had gone wrong. Her mother, Sweterun, had fallen for the first time, in the garden. The doctor had said she was lucky she hadn't hit her head on the patio. And when Lod had returned to care for her, they'd all got the news together, from a nervous young Afro-Saxon reeve standing in the kitchen, helmet clutched in his hands so tight Aedith had stared, fascinated, thinking he was going to squash it flat, that Edric had been arrested.

'Constable Naeku,' said Aedith. 'You said Hildred Emor was divorced, didn't you?'

'Yes ma'am.'

'You don't happen to remember her name from her first marriage, do you?'

'Um.' Naeku screwed her eyes up, waved one hand in the air as though sorting through some invisible filing system. Perhaps she was. Everyone had their own method.

'Reed, ma'am,' she said finally. 'Hildred Reed.'

Aedith nodded, replaced the trophy in its frame. 'Sergeant, would you get word to my father that he's in danger?'

Agapos took out his phone, paused, confused. 'I'm not sure exactly what to tell him.'

'Tell him that the mother of the boy my brother killed fifteen years ago has been planning revenge against my family ever since. She tried to manipulate my adopted son into murdering me earlier this evening. She's probably tried to get to Edric too, but a psychiatric hospital might be a bit of a tall order to infiltrate, even for her. The real target is Earl Lod, and I suspect she's willing to burn down the entire Skeid just to get close to him.'

Agapos stared at her.

'Forget it, I'll call my father. You call Endmarsh, tell them there's a credible threat against my brother's life. Naeku, try and get to someone at the Skeid, send them the most recent photo we have of Hildred.'

Naeku took out her phone, paused. 'Captain, what about DI Drustan?'

It was a good question. There was one last die she could roll.

SIXTY ONE

Aedith held the doorbell for a full thirty seconds before the sour-faced woman stomped down the stairs and wrenched the door open, releasing a blast of stale air highly scented with lavender and mutton, almost certainly boiled, hopefully not together. Her look was of pure resentment, although it quickly changed to something more cautiously optimistic at seeing the warrant card held out before her.

'Good evening, madam,' said Aedith in her politest tone, the one reserved for senior officers and madmen waving their seaxes around in public. 'I wonder if I might ask you a few questions about the incident earlier?'

'Didn't see a thing,' said the woman, who had announced her name to be Elfreda. She had paused expectantly until Aedith, who knew when to take a cue, had carefully written it down in her notebook. The ice had been broken then and Elfreda had ushered her through into her front room, festooned with bunches of dried flowers, each quite possibly a decade old. A carving of Woden took centre stage above the fireplace, hanging by his heels, gazing poignantly to the east. The carver had given him large, soulful eyes and a floppy fringe. Aedith suspected the Woden posters up in her school library would have gone down very well with Elfreda.

'You didn't witness the incident?' Aedith knew full well Elfreda would have been the first on the pavement giving the reeves every detail if she had seen Drustan crashing out of a first-floor window, and that it wouldn't have helped much if she had. Aedith was after something else; but patience, as Agapos was fond of saying, was half of happiness.

Elfreda shook her head, her regret at not having seen Drustan shoved through a window palpable. She gestured at a tabloid newspaper. The headline read "Summit Rots From Head Down" with an illustration of a masked terrorist with a fish tattoo across his chest, then something about immigrants, by which they meant people from one area of London moving to another area of London.

'I was doing the puzzles,' she said. 'Then all the flashing lights and the noise and the police wandering around. Never hear when I call them, but as soon as one of your own is in trouble…' She paused then, her thread lost. Aedith had explained that it was a Tribal police officer who had fallen, and Elfreda clearly had difficulty reconciling the two concepts.

'That's all right,' said Aedith. 'What I was wondering was, might you have noticed any strange vehicles round this way earlier?'

'I notice strange vehicles all the time,' said Elfreda, a note of triumph in her voice. 'You'll have to be more specific.'

'This one would have been an ambulance. No flashing lights. Might have turned up any time from a couple of hours ago, perhaps.'

'Oh,' said Elfreda, a little crestfallen, who had clearly hoped to be asked something more difficult. 'That. Yes, of course I saw the ambulance. I wrote the registration down. Would you like me to get my notebooks?'

'I'd like that very much,' said Aedith.

SIXTY TWO

'You have to understand,' said Wulfstan, over his shoulder, 'that I have the greatest admiration for our officers of the law. From whichever Kingdom.'

He was rummaging around in the ambulance for something. Drustan tried not to care too much for what, as long as it kept him distracted for a few moments longer. He was a good six feet from anything remotely useful that could be picked up with his free hand. It was unlikely this was a coincidence. Wulfstan knew what he was doing. The chair itself had almost no weight. If Drustan even had enough strength to pick it up and throw it, he doubted the killer would even need to duck. It would be like throwing a wooden spoon at a tank. If Drustan could perhaps free his wrist from the nail, he might be able to stagger free, but he'd do a lot more damage to himself on the way and would almost certainly drop dead of blood loss in the following thirty seconds.

'I'm Detective Inspector Drustan, of the Dumnonian Tribal Police, currently attached to Woden's Cross Police Station.'

That was how you were supposed to talk to hostage takers: get them to see you as a human being, an individual in your own right, maybe someone you could eventually empathise with, start to think of as someone who could even be helpful to you. Drustan didn't really see it working in this case; he just wanted to keep

Wulfstan distracted so that he didn't notice that the plasterwork on the wall to which he'd nailed Drustan's wrist was nailed was cracked, flaking away in small pieces in some places, larger chunks in others. The force of the nail going in had caused a crack to run horizontally for six inches or so, intersecting with another crack running straight down. The piece of plaster threatening to come off the wall any second would be small enough that Drustan could just about conceal it in his free hand, but solid enough it could potentially be used as a weapon. Currently, however, it was very much attached.

Drustan sneaked his free hand up to the loose plaster, digging his nails into the crack, hoping the poor light would stop Wulfstan noticing the smears of blood on the wall. The plaster was starting to come loose – and the killer turned. Drustan pulled his hand back. Wulfstan was holding up a roll of duct tape.

'Got it,' he said. 'Don't take this the wrong way, but you look like you might be a biter.'

'Wait,' said Drustan quickly. 'I want to ask you about Father Oswin.'

Wulfstan froze.

'Ah,' he said. 'You went to the home. I was there myself, a couple of weeks ago.'

'Looking for the records,' said Drustan.

Wulfstan nodded. 'I didn't find them. I suspect the caretaker put them away for safekeeping. I would have hung around, sorted that out, but I was on a schedule.'

He crouched before Drustan, head tilted to one side. 'Are you trying to interrogate me?'

'I'm trying to understand you.'

'Oh,' said Wulfstan. 'That may be a Tribal thing. I don't think anyone's tried that before. Emor knew *what* I was doing, even how, but I don't think the "why" ever concerned her.'

His voice was still soft, not a trace of tension in his body. Drustan could see now, how Wulfstan could get so close to his victims. His uniform would put them at ease, certainly, but even beyond that, there was a gentleness to him that belied his size. If he hadn't nailed Drustan's wrist to the wall, would he be second-guessing whether he was the killer at all? Perhaps; perhaps not. Drustan had met killers in the past, even before becoming a police officer. They weren't a special breed, most of them just people who'd been in the wrong place and time and made a poor decision. Only a few got a taste for it.

'Father Oswin was your first, wasn't he? He became ill and you got the chance to finish what you started.'

Wulfstan nodded. 'As much as I lost my belief in a divine plan, that did make me wonder. I could have killed him that first time, right there in the classroom, but I lacked the will. When the reeves came, I prepared myself for my inevitable punishment, but then I found myself in just another building. Same meals, same grey walls, same cheap sheets. If it was punishment, it was no worse than before I'd even met Father Oswin. I kept my head down, tried to feel remorse. When I was out, they even helped me change my name, found me a training course where I could learn to be a paramedic – I wanted to help people, I really did.'

Drustan said nothing.

'If there's some sort of balance, and I still think there may be, I've probably saved as many lives as I've taken. But I'm getting ahead of myself. I was called back, you see. I'd been working for a year, was called to an open prison to pick up a man called Oswin, showing signs of heart trouble. I realised then it was a sign, the opportunity to finish what I'd started. Not given to me by the Gods, or any one God, but by the Fates themselves. I attended to him in the back of the ambulance while my partner drove. By the time we'd got to the hospital, I'm afraid poor Father Oswin had lost his struggle.'

'And Eawynn Wettin,' said Drustan slowly. 'She died in the back of your ambulance too, didn't she?'

'Two chances to finish every Fisher,' said Wulfstan. 'If I'm distracted at the scene, I come back later in my official capacity and do the job then. I couldn't give you a list, Detective Inspector, even if I wanted to. I've taken so many I doubt I could remember them all.'

'But why?' asked Drustan. His free hand was behind his back now, feeling behind the chair, nails trying for purchase on another crack in the plaster. 'Why the Fishers? You must know everything in that manifesto is false. They're not some secret society trying to undermine everything. They're nothing like Oswin; not the ones I've looked into.'

Wulfstan tore a length off the tape and paused.

'It's the hypocrisy, I suppose. They speak of love and forgiveness as though their God put them up on a pedestal. Do you know, in the back of that ambulance, Oswin tried to forgive me, for leading him astray all those years ago, for spoiling the purity of his soul just by existing? After I was done with him I tried to move on, to find something to fill that void within me, the human need to believe. I was spoiled for choice, of course. Wodenism, animism, ancestor worship, so many gods and spirits and finally I realised I didn't believe in any of it. I had been left with nothing. Do you know what it's like, Detective Inspector? To believe in nothing? To have everything you clung to taken away?'

'Perhaps,' said Drustan. His fingers were slippery with blood now and plasterwork wasn't coming away. 'Although I know one person who, as far as I can see, doesn't believe in any of it. And she might be the most contented person I've ever met.'

'She sounds wonderful,' said Wulfstan. There was a trace of wistfulness to his tone. 'I hope I get to meet her one day. But after Oswin I realised there was something left in me, and that was however rewarding it was to save a life, it's much more satisfying to take one. Not just the act itself, satisfying though that is, comforting even, but the process. The hunt, tracking down my prey. And hidden as they are, Fishers make the most rewarding prey.'

He reached over and pressed the tape across Drustan's mouth. Instinctively, Drustan tried to pull it off. Wulfstan wrapped his large hand around Drustan's smaller free wrist and pulled it away.

'I don't want to use that.' He nodded meaningfully at the nail gun on top of a nearby work bench. 'Just makes things more complicated later.'

Drustan stared into Wulfstan's eyes, just a few inches from his. The killer was right, Drustan would have used his teeth right now if it wasn't for the tape.

Wulfstan pulled Drustan's coat open and unbuttoned his shirt, lifting the tattoo pen with his other hand.

'If it's any consolation,' he said, 'I've never taken the life of anyone else who wasn't one of them. I promise you, I won't after this. I'm going to make it easy for them – to identify you as a Fisher, I mean. Ties it all up in a little bow, doesn't it, even if the mark's a little fresh. Can't see the reeves asking too many questions.'

Drustan, thinking of Tancred's gun pressed against Hatt's temple, couldn't disagree.

'It's nothing personal,' Wulfstan continued. 'You're just a means of concluding my deal with Emor. She thinks the discovery that the Tribal officer was a member of the very underground cult the Hook was valiantly trying to warn everyone about will be the final spark to begin the conflagration. After this, if there are any Fishers left alive, I'll be able to hunt them down at my leisure. I imagine when they're all gone, no work left to do, I'll take a quiet way out myself. And then I'll find out for myself just how big Oswin's lies were.'

He cocked an eye at Drustan's chest. 'Not much room, with all the other marking you've got going on. Perhaps here, just to the side.'

He clicked a button set into the pen, eliciting a low hum, and touched the point to Drustan's flesh. Drustan recoiled, tried to shout, but the tape stopped the noise in his throat. Wulfstan's grip kept his other hand immobile. All Drustan could move was his head. He slammed it backwards, against the wall.

'I won't be too long,' said Wulfstan, soothingly. 'I've practised this. It won't be as pretty as the other stuff you've got here, but I don't think you'll mind by then. But if it helps, go for it.'

Drustan jerked his head back again. Something came loose behind it.

'I'm going to start with the tail,' continued Wulfstan. 'The straight line is the hardest bit. Everything after that is just curves.'

Drustan took a deep breath, hit the back of his head against the wall for the last time. Darkness filled his vision, lights flaring behind his eyes and he screamed again, as best he could, but the flat piece of plaster behind him finally came free. His hand, slick with blood, slipped out of Wulfstan's grasp and he caught the sliver before it hit the floor.

'You can't—' began Wulfstan, and Drustan drove it into his throat.

Wulfstan coughed once, fell back and sat down heavily, both hands at his neck, bright crimson streams gushing from between his fingers. If Drustan had been able to free himself, he might have been able to save Wulfstan's life. A neatly folded-up towel had been placed on a small table a few feet away. Drustan would have held it to Wulfstan's neck to stem the bleeding, then used the mobile phone on the same table to call for help. It was procedure not to let anyone die in front of you if you could help it: they might have valuable intelligence, quite apart from the societal bonus of making them stand trial.

Gorsedd Angwin would have wanted that too. Drustan had read the Fishers' book – although the second half changed gear so clunkily from the first, it felt more like two books, pushed, not entirely convincingly, together. Where the first was concerned with natural disaster, pillars of fire, vengeance and begetting, the second changed focus to matters of forgiveness, salvation, promises of eternal life with a kind, benevolent Father, the one Oswin had claimed to represent.

Angwin had lived his life, and his death, according to the second book, and Drustan would have liked nothing more than to honour his memory. But Wulfstan had nailed Drustan's wrist to the wall, so the table might as well have been on the other side of the country. In time, the stream of blood from Wulfstan's throat turned into a trickle. His hands fell limply to his sides. His eyes stared into Drustan's until the light finally went out of them, his head drooping forward.

SIXTY THREE

According to Banba, the ambulance had tripped three separate traffic cameras in a straight line between Emor's house and the Skeid before turning off into an industrial estate.

'I know that place,' Banba had told Aedith over the phone. 'It's all lockups and underground garages. It's a maze.'

Aedith was there now, Naeku at her side. Agapos was already at the Skeid, only a few hundred yards away as the kestrel flew, but on the far side of a high concrete wall, the sound of the protesters' chanting rippling and flowing as the car moved further into the estate.

Naeku held Aedith's phone out for her.

'Sergeant, how are things at the Skeid?'

'There's a lot of people here, ma'am, more turning up all the time.' The tinny echo of those same protesters underneath Agapos's voice. 'Just milling around for now. Feels like they're waiting for something.'

'All right, find out who's in overall charge of security there. I need to get word to my father. Emor's going to try something, and it'll be sooner rather than later.'

'Yes, Captain.'

*

'Maze' was underselling it. There had to be dozens of separate units here, arranged in organic clumps of four or five at a time, some stacked on top of each other, accessible only by rickety stairways, others tucked away down dark alleys, closed off by steel shutters or locked double doors.

Naeku had her own phone out. 'Only one way in and out, by road anyway. Shall I call for backup, ma'am?'

'Do it, but tell them to keep sirens off, wait at the entrance until I call. Any sign of the ambulance?'

'Nothing yet. But there's no other turning between here and the next traffic camera. It has to be around here somewhere.'

It shouldn't be hard to spot if it was. No one was checking their storage units this time of night. The few vehicles scattered around were rusty, immobile, either abandoned or waiting to be stripped for parts.

'Banba, got anywhere with the ambulance owner? If it's Wulfstan, we can cross-check it with rental records.'

'Nothing so far, Captain. The ambulance was bought at auction, paid for with cash and the name's not coming up anywhere else so almost certainly false.'

'Keep on it.'

Aedith stopped the car behind something that had once been either a piece of agricultural equipment or an armoured personnel carrier, its tyres gone, half the bodywork pulled away for scrap. 'We'll proceed on foot. Don't want to let anyone know we're here.'

She was opening the boot before Naeku had closed her door, hauling out tac vests and a shotgun. 'Used one of these before, Constable?'

Naeku nodded, pulled her police armband over the sleeve of

her coat and took the shotgun. Aedith slid Lungpiercer from its holster, held it down by her side, pointing at the ground. No sense putting a hole in some poor sod who was working late and had stepped out for a piss.

'Great. Let's go find our DI.'

Drustan heard the car stop through the open window. Cautious footsteps, a boot opening and closing, someone muttering. It took almost all his remaining strength to pull the tape from his mouth.

'Here!' he shouted, but it came out as a hoarse whisper. He tried to pull the nail from the wall but it must have been inches deep into the concrete. He even tried to pull his wrist away, but the pain shot down his arm, connecting with his cracked rib, fresh blood flowing from the wound. Even if he was strong enough to rip his arm free, he'd be dead before anyone could help him. No conveniently placed object to throw at the window. The footsteps were fading away now. He was going to die here. They'd find him eventually, but it would be too late. He'd caught Angwin's killer, finally carried out the *geas*, but he'd never compose his final report to the elders, never shape the journey he'd made into a recital, never tell them of Aedith and Agapos, Rowan Berry House, the abortive sacrifice at Lamb & Sons. He thought of Conwenna, and for a moment he thought he could hear her, yelling at him from far away, but then he was finally alone. He was able to make his peace with it, briefly, before the blackness rose up around him.

It was only by chance that Aedith looked behind her at that moment. A slim shape, a woman, moving across the tarmac and behind Roadfucker.

Aedith tapped Naeku on the shoulder, pointed, but the woman was already gone. Shit.

Aedith signalled a pincer movement. Naeku nodded, took the long way around, keeping to the shadows. Aedith bent low, scurried around to the car's bonnet, waited until Naeku had caught up. Easing her warrant card out with one hand, she eased Lungpiercer's safety off. Catching Naeku's gaze, she held up three fingers, counting down; two, one.

'Captain Aedith Mercia! London Metropolitan Police!'

Aedith was pointing Lungpiercer at the empty night air. 'Godsdammit!'

Naeku backed up to the unit wall, scanning the area. 'Which direction did she go, Captain?'

'I haven't the faintest idea. You didn't see her?'

'Didn't see a thing, sorry, ma'am.'

Not a sound. Had she seen anything at all? They were all tired, stressed. Now, Aedith was jumping at shadows. She sighed, put Lungpiercer's safety back on, shoved it back in the holster, looked over at Naeku properly for the first time.

'Constable, I want you to move, very slowly, to your right.'

Naeku nodded, stepped aside, revealing the glimmer of light behind her trainers. Aedith had thought it was a streetlight at first, reflected off Roadfucker's flank, but it was a low, narrow window, slightly ajar, set into the bottom of the wall. A basement unit, illuminated. Someone working late, although Aedith couldn't hear any sound. She knelt by the edge of the window, peered down. An ambulance, parked at the bottom of a ramp that presumably emerged on the far side of the very unit next to which Aedith had parked. One man, large, in dark overalls, sprawled on the ground, a dark pool around him. A second, slighter figure in a dark coat, slumped on a chair shirt open to the chest, gunmetal torc gleaming in the neon light. One arm was held up, something glittering and metallic keeping it fixed to the wall.

Drustan's eyes were closed.

SIXTY FOUR

Aedith kicked the tattoo pen away from Wulfstan's hands where he had dropped it, took his pulse. Nothing.

'The DI's still alive, Captain.' Naeku had slung the shotgun over her shoulder, holding Drustan's wrist. 'We have to get him down, but there's going to be some bleeding.'

Sirens now, flashing lights visible in the high window.

'Go and show them the way in, would you? Otherwise they'll be milling about until sunrise. Any luck with an ambulance?'

Naeku shook her head, already halfway up the ramp. 'Traffic jam all around the Skeid, Captain.'

Luckily there was an ambulance right there. Wouldn't be great for the evidence logs but couldn't be helped.

'DI Drustan? Are you with me?' Not a sound. His breathing was faint. Needed to get him down from the damn wall. For years she'd kept a multitool in the car, but Coram had borrowed it two weekends ago, hadn't replaced it despite her nagging. Coram. She couldn't think about him now.

The ambulance was well stocked. Wulfstan must have hoarded supplies for years. Aedith grabbed a bottle of antiseptic wash and a handful of bandages, shoving them in her pockets. Useful, but she was skipping a step.

'Naeku, has anyone up there got pliers?'

'I already asked. Sorry, ma'am.'

Aedith cursed, kept going through the supplies. Oxygen tank, pregnancy kit, defibrillator – wait. She tore into the pregnancy kit, hurling aside plastic gloves, tubing, until she got to the forceps. Heavy, stainless steel. Could work.

The uniforms had arrived by the time she got back to Drustan, milling around the unit floor, gawping at the sitting body, at least trying not to touch anything.

'Tiw's bollocks, get out of my way!'

The forceps pressed down into Drustan's wrist but at least fitted neatly around the head of the nail. He stirred slightly as Aedith began to pull. By getting her other hand around the forceps' end, clamping it as tightly as she could and pulling, the nail began to slide out.

'Constable, take that bottle and the bandages from my pocket. When I get the nail free, you need to pour the stuff on his wound, wrap it up as quickly as you can.'

Naeku nodded. One last tug and the nail suddenly slid free from the wall, Aedith dropping the forceps and catching Drustan's wrist as it fell. Drustan's eyes flickered open, gazing uncomprehendingly at Aedith. Blood was already beginning to well between Aedith's fingers. By some miracle, the nail had missed an artery, but judging from the cuts across the rest of his face and body, Drustan didn't have that much blood left to spare.

'Detective Inspector? This is probably going to hurt.'

She held the wrist out for Naeku to splash purple liquid onto it. Drustan yelled, trying to pull his arm back, but Aedith held firm, Naeku winding the long bandage round his wrist, the first few layers soaking through with red, then gradually growing paler.

The last wind of the bandage was pristine white, the only thing on Drustan that was.

'Finish off with that tape.'

Drustan shuddered as Naeku ripped off a length of tape, wrapped it once around the bandage. Aedith patted him on the shoulder.

'You back with us?'

He nodded, feebly trying to button up his shirt.

'Here, I'll do that for you.'

Aedith paused halfway up. Drustan's face and hands were covered in scratches, most of which were already crusting over, but a mark on his side was surrounded with fresh red beads. A black line, just an inch or so. Aedith pressed a sterile dressing to it, feeling Drustan wince. She looked over at the body.

'Did he do that?'

Drustan nodded, tried to speak but it turned into a coughing fit. Naeku held a bottle of water to his lips and he drank thirstily for a long time. When he was done, he moved his free hand and tried to take over doing up his shirt. Aedith slapped it away, not unkindly.

'He was trying to convert you?'

'Trying to finish Emor's plan. Wanted to finish off the Summit. She's very committed to her clients; I'll say that for her.'

'She doesn't give a shit about her clients. She's using the Summit to get to my father. She may already be there.'

Drustan stared at her. Aedith finished buttoning his shirt, handed him the rest of the wipes. 'Here. Be careful around that side of your face, you've still got bits of glass sticking out of you. I need to see how things are going at the Skeid.'

SIXTY FIVE

The news wasn't good. More protesters arriving, thousands now, according to Agapos' latest text update. The roads were blocked, doors being locked, delegates pulled back by their security details to their inner sanctums. No one could get hold of Lod.

'But they're safe, right?' Naeku had been trying to raise someone on the inside now and had been on hold for twenty minutes. 'The Skeid's built to be impregnable. There are armed guards everywhere.'

Aedith scrolled through the latest pictures sent over by Agapos, who was somewhere in the crowd, brandishing a riot shield. 'I don't know, there's a lot of open-carry nuts here.'

At least a third of the protesters had seaxes, sheathed at their sides or slung across their backs. Flimsy, mass-produced tat for the most part probably, so heavily engraved with runes of protection and forum sub-thread allegiances that they'd crumple like cheap foil at the first swing, but that would be enough for the blood to flow. Or the protection details to start shooting. There'd be a massacre.

But that wasn't all. Scattered among the protesters was a different breed. Now Agapos knew what to look for, he was taking as many pictures of them as he could: militia types, professionals – bigger, broader, wearing military fatigues, army boots, tac vests dangling with zip ties, field dressings. Their seaxes were carried in quick-release scabbards. Masks worn under helmets displayed screaming faces, skulls, raven's beaks.

'Northumbrian militias,' said Drustan. His voice was shaky, his left arm strapped to his side, but he was standing unassisted now. Once it had been made clear Aedith's orders that he go to the nearest hospital were going to continue being politely but firmly rebuffed, she had told Agapos to deal with him while she assessed available intel. The sergeant had cleaned and dressed Drustan's wounds in a brisk, professional manner, but made it perfectly clear he wouldn't much mind if Drustan had passed out and left them to it.

Aedith nodded. More worrying that the militias weren't clumped together but spaced out amongst the crowd. 'They're waiting for something.'

'Agreed,' said Drustan. 'We have to get inside the Skeid, get through that crowd somehow.'

The sound grew louder, still unfocused, a sea of different – in some cases, *opposing* – war chants, but they were building.

'Waveforms,' said Drustan. Aedith and Naeku looked at him. 'Two outcomes to waveforms building up: either they start to cancel each other out and fall apart in confusion, or they reinforce each other and build exponentially from there. Glass shatters, walls crumble. That's what's happening here. Sort of. We have to get there, put a stop to it.'

'I don't know if you noticed,' said Aedith. 'But you're in no fit state to go anywhere, and it's not like the crowd are just going to let us through.'

'They might,' said Drustan. He pointed to the ambulance.

SIXTY SIX

'You didn't say how you found me.'

Drustan was pulling out one ambulance kit drawer after another, tossing the contents aside as Naeku steered the vehicle through the outskirts of the crowd. Aedith had flashed her warrant card at the perimeter police and they'd waved them through, if not entirely happily.

'I thought I saw a woman. Possibly Tribal. Acting weirdly, anyway, but she'd gone by the time Naeku and I got to the unit. But then we spotted the window and saw what you'd left of the Hook.'

Drustan stared at her. 'Tribal woman?'

Aedith shrugged. 'Didn't see her again. Asked the uniforms when they got there but no one had seen a thing. Like she'd vanished into thin air, although maybe she just turned sideways, she was a skinny little thing. Pretty, though. Long hair, little jacket and a long skirt. Anyone you know?'

Drustan froze, holding a small vial of something yellowish in one hand, syringe in the other. For a moment, Aedith thought he was going to laugh. Or pass out. But he shook his head and pulled up the sleeve of his coat, tearing the cuff of his shirt. He drew some of the fluid into the syringe, pausing as the ambulance lurched.

'Contractors used this,' he said, in answer to a question Aedith hadn't asked. 'Pushes you through the shock barrier, keeps you moving.' He tapped his forearm, looking for a vein. 'I don't make a habit of it. Increased chance every time that your heart'll just stop.'

'I wasn't judging,' said Aedith. Drustan aimed the needle and plunged it into his arm, gasping, eyes rolling back as he depressed the plunger.

Aedith moved up behind the driver's seat, looked over Naeku's shoulder. The Skeid was right in front of them, technically, although it was barely possible to see it past the field of protesters waving banners and cardboard signs. The sound outside had become deafening.

Naeku's hand hovered over a switch. 'Put the siren on, ma'am?'

'I don't know if that would help. Just keep moving at the same speed.' Aedith had the uncomfortable feeling they were somehow hovering just on the edge of the crowd's consciousness. The Hook had chosen his getaway vehicle well: the sight of the green apple triggered some atavistic sense in the protesters that they should step out of its way, but it wouldn't last for ever. She could already see militia members working their way through the crowd towards them, frowning as they conferred on mobile phones.

Aedith checked the safety on Lungpiercer, patted her greatcoat pocket. Two extra magazines, not that it mattered with this many civilians around. If things got bad enough that she had to start shooting, they'd already lost.

A clinking sound in the ambulance behind Aedith. Drustan had dropped the vial, grimacing as whatever he had taken worked through his system. He gasped for a moment, dropping the syringe into a cardboard dish, then pulled down his sleeve with a shaking hand.

'How we doing there, DI Drustan? If I'm going to be honest with you, I could do without incidents inside *and* out of the vehicle.'

Drustan nodded tautly. 'I'm good.'

'Great. Constable, don't lose momentum, we just need to get through the crowd. Someone's meeting us round the side of the Skeid, they can get us inside.' At least she hoped that he could.

Naeku nodded. The spell was beginning to break, hands banging at the side of the ambulance, placards bouncing off the windscreen, the vehicle slowing to a crawl now. It wouldn't take many protesters to stop it, only a few more to turn it over. 'I can't go much further, Captain.'

Aedith took Lungpiercer from her holster, holding it by the barrel. 'When we get out, bludgeon your way through if you have to. No shooting unless and until we are shot at ourselves.' She threw a spare armband to Drustan. 'Toss up if this helps or makes you a target, but at least the snipers on the roof can see who's who.'

Drustan used his teeth to pull the police band over his working arm. Naeku was already wearing hers. 'Ma'am, something's happening.'

The chanting had stopped, as had the banging against the sides of the vehicle. Silence. The protesters Aedith could see through the windscreen were looking down at their phones, placards drooping, a thousand faces bathed in the reflective glow of their screens.

'Don't stop. Every foot you can take us now is a load of skulls we don't have to crack later on.'

Protesters were absently stepping out of the way, barely looking up. They were within a stone's throw of the Skeid now, couldn't drive much further anyway, even if it weren't for the silent mass before them: low concrete barriers blocked access all across this side, armoured reeves behind them, gripping heavy shields in one hand, long clubs in the other.

Naeku stopped the ambulance, pulled on the handbrake. 'This is as close as I can take us, Captain.'

'The second we head out, we go left: there's another entrance, round the side,' said Aedith. She took out her mobile, fingers flicking out another text. Had the first even gone through? This lot did look like the sort who'd pull down any phone masts in the vicinity – recording it for internet likes while they did so, obviously. 'Any idea what they're all looking at?'

Drustan had his own phone out, working through open tabs. One went past glowing brighter than the others. He went back to it. No pictures, just a lurid scroll of text surely designed to look as amateurish as possible.

'It's the Hook's manifesto page. The latest one. They throw up a new one as soon as the last is taken down.'

A murmur ran through the crowd outside, turning to a roar. Placards fell to the floor, in some cases signs torn away from their supports to reveal steel poles, lengths of rebar, sticks the width of a Saxon wrist.

'It says, "The Fishers have taken over the Skeid",' shouted Drustan over the growing noise of the crowd. 'The High King has been murdered, Saxon England is to be carved up between the Tribals and the Norse.'

Naeku turned round, shocked. 'Is it true?'

'Of course it's not bloody true,' yelled Aedith. 'But these idiots will think it is. We have to get in there, now!'

She kicked the rear doors open. Protesters flowed around them, an elemental force now, floodwaters building inexorably against a dam that was going to burst any second. The reeves were breaking heads, clubs smashing down anyone who came within arm's reach, but for every protestor they beat down, two more took their place.

'There!' Aedith pointed at the side entrance she had taken earlier. No armed agents outside it now. She just had to hope that text had gone through.

They joined the flow, nudging leftwards when they could, letting the crowd carry them forwards when they had to. Aedith had lost sight of the militia members: her colleagues too, although when the crowd broke against a concrete barrier she saw Naeku slipping through them towards her, pulling Drustan in her wake by his good arm. The Celt's eyes were bright, whatever he'd put into his veins firing him up to get through this. Hopefully his heart could take the strain.

Aedith pointed to the side door, anonymous, grey, overlooked by the crowd bearing down on the reeves in what was now a frontal assault. Naeku and Drustan were catching up with her, ducking low to move through the crowd, but the militia were finding one another now, disparate men and women in mismatched uniforms and unit patches, flowing together: first in twos and threes, now six or seven of them, moving quickly, pointing out the cops to each other, mouthing words like 'traitors' over the roar of the crowd. Some of them were holding what Aedith took to be outsized pistols. For a moment she mistook them for airsoft weapons, oversized parodies of handguns, then realised with a chill they were nail guns. The Hook had inspired them in more ways than one.

Aedith reached the door first, hauled Naeku and Drustan towards her. She banged hard on the door with her fist. 'It's me! Open up.'

No response. Naeku's shotgun was held low, barrel pointed to the ground. The protesters fanned out, taking their time. Aedith released Lungpiercer's safety.

'I'm authorising lethal force. If you have to shoot, go for central mass unless they have body armour, in which case try for the legs.'

Only when she took Lungpiercer in both hands did she sense the door opening behind her, watch Naeku's head spin round, eyes widening in alarm. The figure on the other side of the door wore the same military garb as the militia members who were already freezing up in atavistic panic: black combat trousers, tactical vest, black fingerless gloves. Unlike them, though, he wore no indications of rank, however theoretical; no badges reading 'The East Will Rise' or 'Sons of Woden'. He wore a metal mask covering his entire face, ornate slanted eyeholes the only openings. The seax held in his left hand displayed no engravings, no maker's marks or threats or promises to honour any of the old gods. It was just a tool, designed purely for killing.

'You got my text, then,' said Aedith to the Fengyr.

SIXTY SEVEN

The Fengyr slammed the door shut behind them, sliding a heavy bolt across. The militia were already hurling themselves against it, kicking with their heavy boots. It wouldn't hold for ever. Aedith and Drustan moved with him to the lift, Naeku following after a moment's hesitation. There was no procedure for this.

'We moved the High King to safe ground half an hour ago,' said the Fengyr. He pressed a button, lights on the display moving with infuriating slowness as the lift descended. 'He granted me leave to stay. I'm at your disposal.'

'Excellent,' said Aedith. 'You see any of those arseholes with zip ties and nail guns in the building, feel free to take them out. Maybe don't cut any heads off unless you absolutely have to, though, eh?'

The Fengyr slid his seax back into its scabbard and swung a stubby automatic pistol round from a sling on his back. It was mostly black carbon fibre, the majority of the barrel set within the body of the weapon, just an inch or two of blackened metal poking out. Aedith couldn't even see where the magazine went in. The weapon had a hand-crafted look to it and at any other time Aedith would have gladly arrested the owner, the manufacturers and anyone even slightly involved in the design process for being into this stuff way too much.

'Do you know where my father is?'

'Earl Lod was transferred to the inner sanctum on the fourth level. I'll take you there now.'

A ping as the lift arrived, followed by a crunch as something heavy struck the other side of the door they'd come in through. Aedith stepped into the lift, hauling Naeku in after her. Drustan followed, peering interestedly down the corridor.

'Militias carry battering rams now?'

'They're not that hard to get hold of, if you know the right suppliers,' said the Fengyr. He pressed the button for level four, keeping his weapon trained on the doorway as the bolt gave up its struggle, the door collapsing inwards, militia members urging each other in with seaxes drawn, faces strained with anger and, Aedith could see plainly now, exhilaration. These people had been primed for this moment for years, psyching themselves up with online conspiracies, social media confirming every dark thought they'd ever had, telling them they were victims – which they were, but not in the ways they believed. Emor hadn't needed the full force of a marketing campaign to turn these people to violence: they'd been driven mad years ago. All she'd had to do was throw a lit match onto the oily rags.

The Fengyr kept his weapon trained on the nearest figure until the lift doors closed with only inches to spare, then dropped the weapon to his side and reached up to tap the side of his mask.

'Confirmed breach in the southeast quadrant,' he said, and Aedith realised there must be a radio built into it. What else? Night vision, a respirator? 'Multiple armed threats, advise containment if possible, elimination otherwise. I'm escorting guests to level four.'

Naeku, crammed into the lift right next to the Fengyr, was trying not to look directly at him, her body language tense, her shotgun gripped tightly with both hands. Aedith thought of the boxes they'd all seen in the investigation room, the photos of headless bodies, and reached across, gently pushed the barrel towards the ground.

'Try and relax,' she told her. 'He's on our side.'

Naeku nodded tightly. For a moment, the only sound was the tinny pipe music coming through the lift's speakers and their ragged breathing, the Fengyr's amplified by his mask into an echoing rasp, until the lift jerked to a sudden halt. Aedith glanced at the display panel. The lights were blinking out one at a time. They'd only got to the third level.

'Control have shut down the lifts,' said the Fengyr. 'Probably multiple breaches. They're trying to contain them to the lower levels. We'll have to work our way up on foot.'

Drustan pressed the button to open the doors, with no result. The Fengyr eased him politely to one side, inserted his seax into the gap between the door and twisted, opening up a tiny space.

'A little help?'

Naeku swung her shotgun over her shoulder, and pulled one door back while the Fengyr took the other. The lift, it became clear, had stopped between floors, the ground just below eye level. The corridor ahead of them was clear, quiet.

'I'll go first,' said Aedith, holstering Lungpiercer. The Fengyr nodded, stepping back as she hauled herself up, slithering out of the lift onto the ground. Chanting, from a couple of floors below, maybe. They didn't have much time. She reached back, pulled Naeku out after her.

'This may not work,' said Drustan, looking down at his strapped-up arm. His tone was mild, conversational. Without a word, the Fengyr crouched in front of him. Drustan stood on his back, getting one hand up to Aedith, who hauled him up, the

Fengyr following him out, barely getting both feet on the floor before the first protestor, a middle-aged woman in a smart coat, her face painted to resemble a skull, fire extinguisher in one hand, rounded the corner.

The Fengyr reached for his seax.

'They're unarmed,' snapped Aedith. 'I'm not saying they aren't dangerous; I'm saying minimum force.'

He nodded, but to Aedith's horror, swung up his machine pistol instead. Before she could stop him, he fired a single shot, the extinguisher exploding in a white cloud, the skull-woman collapsing, the protesters behind her reeling in shock.

'One more flight,' said the Fengyr, pointing to a nearby stairwell. 'I'll hold them back as long as I can.'

The protesters were recovering now, picking themselves up. The Fengyr reached to one side, casually smashing the glass case around a fire axe. He pulled the weapon off the wall and spun it, swinging it once to test the weight, then weighed in, wielding it butt first.

Naeku was already up the stairs, Drustan close behind her. Aedith looked back once, to see the Fengyr vanish almost instantly under the protesters.

'Fuck it, then,' she said, and followed them.

SIXTY EIGHT

Tancred's men were waiting for them at the top of the stairs, the barrels of half a dozen automatic weapons pointing at them. The sight of Drustan, limping and tattered, practically glowing from within from whatever he'd taken, might have done for them all, but Aedith managed to sprint up the last few steps ahead of him and Naeku, wielding her warrant card like a shield.

'Detective Captain Mercia,' she snapped.

Tancred nodded at his men. 'Let them through. Anyone behind you?'

'One more of ours and a dozen or so protesters so far,' she said. 'Only improvised weapons. There are other guys with nail guns and zip ties, but I think they're round the other side.'

'Improvised weapons are still weapons,' said Tancred. He was grey-faced, sweating, out of his depth. 'I have orders to hold the line.'

'You'll be killing civilians,' said Naeku. 'Angry ones, who probably want to kill us, but still.'

'I have orders,' repeated Tancred. His men were stressing out now, casting sideways glances at each other, radios crackling with reports of breaches all over the Skeid. The balance of power was shifting. Special Branch were used to stepping over lines with impunity, not holding them. Always quick to use lethal force, they were the wrong people at the wrong time. 'We need to assert control. If a few get sent to Woden's hall before their time, so be it.'

A commotion from the bottom of the stairs, out of sight. Glass smashing, yells of pain. Tancred's men braced their weapons, those at the back loosening their seaxes in their scabbards.

Tancred pushed between Aedith and Naeku. 'I don't have time for this.' Drustan stumbled then, falling towards Tancred. The Major might have shot him, if the Celt wasn't so abjectly pathetic a figure, crumpling forwards, clutching at Tancred's leg for support. Only Aedith saw the flicker of a syringe in his hand, the swift dart of the needle between the armour plates on Tancred's thigh, his thumb depressing the plunger.

Tancred gasped and staggered back, mouthing words that wouldn't come, pawing at a wall for support.

Aedith moved swiftly, catching Tancred as he slid slowly down the wall. 'Officer down!' Tancred's men turned in confusion, only the front line seeing the Fengyr rounding the corner, limping up the stairs towards them, cuts across his arms. One of the horns of his mask was sticking out at an odd angle. If he'd been armed, that might have been the end of him, but the fire axe had been lost along the way, machine pistol slung behind his back, seax still at his side. He held some form of warrant card out in front of him. Aedith had heard rumours it bore an ancient sigil, one hard-coded into security camera software that wiped any trace of his passing when displayed. Disappointingly, it looked instead to just be a governmental seal of some kind.

'I am the hand of the High King,' said the Fengyr. He said it lightly, as Aedith might when announcing herself at an interdepartmental meeting. 'I am the instrument of his will and answer not to the High Table. When I pass, there will be another. When the High King passes, another will be chosen. What happened to him?'

He nodded at Tancred, now slumped in a corner, eyes closed, breathing heavily.

'Major Tancred appears to have been overcome by events,' said Aedith crisply. She carefully didn't look at Drustan, already back on his feet. No sign of the syringe, although Aedith made a mental note to check behind the base of the large pot plant next to the now-snoring Tancred at some point, if they got out of this. Wouldn't do to leave that sort of thing lying around.

The Fengyr made a gesture at Tancred's awestruck men, dividing them up with a gesture. 'Two groups,' he said. 'You, hold these stairs, no shooting unless you see non-improvised weapons. The rest of you follow me to back up the Norse delegation. They're barricaded in the upper cafeteria; they'll be glad to see us.'

A moment's hesitation, until Aedith fired a shot from Lungpiercer into the ceiling. It was against protocol, and she'd probably need to fill in a number of reports after this, but it got their attention. 'It's not a suggestion. Do what he says and maybe I won't have you all strung up for actively plotting to murder civilian protesters. Go, now!'

They broke then, just glad someone seemed to know what they were doing. The Fengyr paused before Aedith, touched a finger to the eye-ridge of his mask – a salute, she supposed – before pulling a fire escape map off the wall and handing it her. He pointed to an octagonal room down the corridor from the stairwell they were currently occupying.

'Your father's security detail should be along that corridor, holed up in the boardroom.'

Aedith gazed at him levelly. How many enemies of the High King had the Fengyr killed, she found herself wondering? Not just the ones whose photos were tucked away in a box back at the office. There must have been others. More than the Hook? Did he take pleasure in his work? She couldn't exactly imagine him going home at the end of the day to his Fengyr wife and little Fengyr children.

The Fengyr nodded at her, turned and walked away, a half-dozen of Tancred's men following. Aedith didn't watch them go. She wasn't sure she cared what happened to any of them. She turned to Naeku.

'Constable, I need you to stay here. Keep an eye on the rest of this lot, make sure they don't pull any shit when they think no one's looking. Also,' she added, somewhat reluctantly, 'if things get out of hand, I suppose someone ought to make sure Major Tancred gets taken to safety.'

SIXTY NINE

'Out of interest,' said Aedith, as she and Drustan moved down the corridor. 'What was that you stuck in Tancred?'

'Something I found in the ambulance. Should knock him out for a couple of hours without too many side-effects.'

'Got any more of those?'

Drustan shook his head. 'Out of tricks.'

She snorted. 'I doubt that.' She put a finger to her lips. One of the doors along the corridor was ajar, a light inside flickering. She motioned to Drustan, who pushed it open with his free hand as Aedith stepped out, Lungpiercer in hand, to cover what was now revealed to be an empty storeroom. She turned off the light, pulled the door shut. They carried on towards the board room.

'You know,' she continued quietly, 'I did wonder if Tancred might be on the take. From Vargr, or Emor in one of her many forms. Braced and ready to let the protesters in. Although I suppose a massacre might suit her just as well.'

'I suspect Major Tancred is indeed on the take,' said Drustan. 'But not from Emor. A lot of your senior officers have consulting contracts with the big media sites, feed them good stuff once a month or so, look the other way when their more ambitious scoops go awry.'

Aedith stared at him. 'You couldn't have told me this before?'

'My apologies, I assumed you knew.'

'Clearly I never got the invites to the right cult meetings.' Female officers never did, not to the ones that taught you the finger runes for 'let this guy go, he's a fully paid-up member of my longhouse' anyway.

Aedith pointed to a set of double doors at the end of the corridor, interior windows on either side, blinds down. Lowering her voice, she said: 'That's the boardroom. If my father's in there, we join up with the security detail, get him to the east side of the building: there's a tunnel out to the car park, other side of the protest, should be able to arrange a pickup.'

Drustan knelt by the door, put his ear to the panel.

'Anything?'

He shook his head.

'Okay,' said Aedith. 'Same arrangement: you give the door a push, I'll cover you.'

Drustan took a deep breath and shoved.

A huge room, another door at the far end, chairs arranged around a long table scattered with papers and abandoned laptops. Two bodies slumped against the wall, agents wearing tactical vests over dark suits, one male, one female. Drustan bent down to investigate the bodies.

'Both shot in the head. Didn't even have time to draw their weapons. He straightened up. 'If Emor was here, she didn't take your father out the way we came in. Must have gone out of the other door.' He turned the handle, quietly pushed it open. A short corridor, another set of stairs. 'Where do they go?'

Aedith moved over to the window, took the map out of her pocket, unfolded it. 'Up.'

SEVENTY

Drustan gasped as the cool evening air hit him full in the face. They were high above the protesters now, the chanting from those that were still outside now broken up by shouts of pain or ragged threats. Hundreds more reeves had poured out of riot vans, marching steadily to the beat of baton against riot shield, likely either breaking the rioters up into smaller, easily punishable groups or penning them into one big throng, to be processed at leisure. Drustan hadn't noticed many Celts among the rioters, making the latter more likely. He couldn't hear any gunfire, which boded well.

The injection he'd taken was starting to wear off. The ache in his ribs was becoming less dull by the second, fighting for attention with the fire that had been lit in his strapped-up arm, running from wrist to shoulder.

The section of roof they were standing on was slightly lower than the others, blocked off by air-conditioning ducts and rows of solar panels. Drustan had counted at least four snipers on top of the Skeid last time he had checked, but their attention would be on what was happening below. Even if they did realise what was going on under their noses – and they had to soon with drones and police helicopters hovering overhead, crows to the battlefield feast – the angles were all wrong. The Skeid's architects had envisioned an attack from below, but not from up here.

Stumbling out from behind a ventilation housing, Lod looked dazed. At least, Drustan assumed the big, bearded man in the dark suit, hands ornate with rings and tattoos, was Aedith's father. A trickle of blood was already drying on the side of his face, presumably from where Emor had used the butt of her handgun to get him moving. She was pressed behind him like a lover, her seax held close against Lod's throat.

Emor wore the jumpsuit and hard plastic plates of a street reeve in full crowd-control armour: not the military wannabe stuff the militias sourced from online stores, but the real deal. The gun was holstered, no longer needed. Her hair had come unravelled from its braids, floating, ghostlike in the wash kicked up by the circling helicopters.

'Hildred Emor,' said Aedith, raising her voice to be heard. 'I am arresting you for consorting with foreign powers to subvert the rule of law, for aiding and abetting the killer Wulfstan, also known as the Hook, and for abducting a free citizen of the land through force. Put your weapon down and I guarantee you will go unharmed.'

One of the helicopters came closer, a reeve inside holding a long rifle. Aedith waved angrily at it with one hand, Lungpiercer pointing unwaveringly at Emor in the other. No chance they could get a shot without taking out Lod at the same time.

'I planned to kill your brother at the trial, Captain Mercia,' said Emor. 'That was my first intention. I even found a way to smuggle Cenhelm's seax through the metal detectors – you'll forgive me if I don't give away the details – but when I saw your family gathered around your dear brother, I realised that wouldn't be enough. I wanted your whole line burned out of existence.'

'Put the weapon down,' said Aedith. 'I won't tell you a third time.' She was edging forward as Emor moved backwards, closer and closer to the roof's parapet.

The helicopter was backing away now. Emor barely had to raise her voice. 'And then my dear weak husband died and I either had to turn my attention to taking over the business or drown in debt. Luckily, I turned out to be rather good at lie-smithing, and after a few years I took on some new clients, with some interesting ideas about the future of all the kingdoms on this island, and to my surprise, your father was intricately bound up in them.'

Lod was shaking his head now, trying to say something, but the words weren't coming. Even if he was starting to shake off the effects of the pistol-whipping, Emor had moved them both far too close to the edge now.

'Hush, dear,' said Emor. 'I see our Detective Inspector has also come along for the ride. Poor Wulfstan bit off more than he could chew, I assume?'

Drustan said nothing.

'With three kingdoms bound together as one, your father's noble house could expand, become a major player. But he knew he'd need a piece on the board. Your brother would never do, but what if there was another? A cleanskin, someone who'd never been involved in politics, a fresh face on the arena.'

Aedith wavered then. Not her weapon, which remained locked on Emor, but inside, Drustan could see it. Her eyes flickering to Lod, whose face had dropped. He looked tired. Defeated.

'You don't get my son,' said Aedith. Drustan realised after a moment she was talking not to Emor, but to Lod. 'He's been through enough. He deserves his own life.'

Emor smiled, pressing her cheek against Lod's face. Too close for a head shot.

'Poor Lod,' said Emor. 'Always the bridesmaid to power, opportunities shrinking away as age takes its toll. But I'm not talking about the boy you stole after killing his father. Doubtless he'll grow up to become another Mercian monster, although perhaps the footage I sent him will give him the chance to break free.'

Emor had stopped, right at the edge of the roof now. She only had to let herself fall backwards and she would take Lod with her. Aedith hadn't moved.

'No, you fucking idiot,' continued Emor tiredly. 'I'm talking about you, Captain Mercia. Years of public service, your father there to pull strings behind the scenes; what's to stop you going all the way to the top?'

'Dad,' said Aedith. 'Tell me she's wrong.'

Lod raised his great head, met her gaze. He said nothing. Emor moved her seax from his throat, just a fraction of an inch.

'Oh, fuck this,' said Aedith, and fired.

SEVENTY ONE

'This stupid bloody island,' said Emor.

She lay on her back at the edge of the roof, staring up at the night sky, left arm shattered and useless. Aedith's shot had grazed Lod's side and destroyed Emor's humerus, knocking her sideways, Lod just able to drop to his knees rather than roll back right off the building.

Drustan had picked up her seax – her son Cenhelm's, going by the inscriptions – and thrown it behind him. The injection was starting to wear off, lights flickering at the edge of his vision. He was starting to wonder if he really should have stayed in the ambulance.

Lod, now sitting up against a low wall, was breathing more steadily, Aedith helping him hold a wad of torn-off coat sleeve against the wound in his side, sidearm trained on Emor. Indeed, it had never left her. The helicopter had backed off, seeing the immediate crisis was over, and seemed more interested now in covering the mopping-up operation below, scores of disgruntled protesters lined up and pushed into waiting vans.

'If you have anything to say,' said Aedith, 'save it for your lawyer.'

Emor ignored her. 'My father was Norse; did you have that in your files? Mother was Mercian, father was a lawyer from

Edinburgh. Son of a minor Jarl but that was really all there was to him. She left him when I was six. Pulled towards weak men, the women of my family, but we free ourselves eventually.'

With her good arm, she dragged herself up into a sitting position, her face tight with pain. The roof ledge was behind her, a straight drop of seven storeys to the ground.

Aedith took a long look at her. 'What's your point?'

'The Summit will fail,' said Emor. 'We hate each other too much. This shitty little island, never quite one thing or another, just a plaything for greater powers. I should have taken Cenhelm abroad. One of the great Moorish universities would have suited him, I think.'

'Perhaps,' said Aedith. 'I never met him. But I believe in the rule of law. Come with us in peace, make your claim before a court. I'll back up your statement.'

She holstered Lungpiercer, rose to her feet. For the first time since Drustan had met her, she looked weary. Crossing the roof to Emor, she crouched before her, reached out a hand.

Emor looked up at her and smiled. 'I wish your piece of shit fake son had killed you,' she said and pushed herself backwards off the roof. Drustan didn't see what happened after that, the blackness rising up to claim him.

SEVENTY TWO

'I brought you an apple,' said Aedith. 'But then I ate it. It's very boring, waiting around for someone to wake up.'

Drustan lay still for a moment, blinking at the lights above him until the pain flooded back in from all across his body. Muted though; bearable if he didn't breathe too deeply. The hospital room was a good one, spacious, without that singed-flesh smell, just cleaning fluid and the sharp, musky scent from a bunch of small white flowers next to the bed. Wood anemones. Conwenna's favourite.

'Yes, your wife stopped by,' said Aedith. 'She seems nice. Well-dressed Norse couple with her. Not sure what's going on there.'

Drustan ignored her, his eyes following the drip disappearing beneath the fresh bandages over his left arm and wrist, right up to the fingers. Someone had dressed him in a hospital robe, short sleeves revealing multiple cuts on his other arm, smeared with yellow ointment.

'How's the Earl?'

Aedith rolled her eyes. 'Bitching like an old woman in his private hospital. Bullet went near the liver but not through it. I asked him if he'd rather I'd gone for the headshot and he went quiet after that.'

'And Emor?'

'Dead. Case closed, although of course the case was already considered closed, but I tied it all up with a little ribbon on the top, wrote a full report with details of our friend Wulfstan and your part in his demise. Even dropped a mention of our friend in the mask, although I imagine that'll be cut out before the rest of it gets buried somewhere. Officially, of course, the whole thing ended the moment Tancred shot the guy in the foyer.'

'And unofficially?'

'The people who need to read it still can. Top brass know Wulfstan was the Hook, working with Emor's company to undermine the Unification Summit. Constable Naeku will be over later to get a statement from you, add it to the files, although I doubt anyone will ever read it. I think she's wondering if you'll be sticking around.'

Drustan shook his head. 'I'll be out of here once I'm healed.'

Aedith nodded, took a large crunch of the apple. 'That's what I said. I imagine the Tribal crime rate back West has skyrocketed in your absence. Mass oxen theft, outbreaks of unlicensed poetry, kohl shortages, that sort of thing.'

Drustan laughed then, despite himself. 'Captain Mercia. You're *such* a dick.'

Aedith grinned. 'Guilty as charged. Anyway, I'll be taking some time off myself. Need to work through some family issues, maybe throw a ball around the garden with my son a few times until he feels he can trust me again.' Her expression didn't change, but she went quiet for a moment. 'Maybe even book some spirit-counselling, who knows?'

She sat silent for a moment, then said: 'It didn't work, by the way.'

Drustan still felt woozy. It was hard to keep up. 'What didn't?'

Aedith held up a newspaper, one of the heavier broadsheets, and dropped it on his chest. Drustan winced but picked it up anyway. The headline read: 'Summit Makes Tentative First Steps to Unification'.

'Unexpected.'

Aedith shrugged. 'Protests lit a fire under their arses, I think. While the main delegates were all holed up in the panic room, three storeys underground, they started to realise there was more uniting them than dividing them. According to Agapos, anyway. He got pulled into the protection detail. So, who knows? You come East again, twenty or thirty years' time, maybe you won't even need papers.'

A sudden movement outside the open door, figures in green scrubs dashing past, a couple of reeves behind them.

Aedith's phone pinged, echoed by call alerts outside. Drustan's too, although it was on the other side of the room, unreachable. Ignoring his body's shrieked complaints, Drustan pulled himself up on one elbow, craning to see out of the door. A cluster of medical stuff crammed into a corner of the ward, staring up at something just out of sight. A television? Patriotic music playing under the low sombre tones of the newsreaders. Something had happened.

Aedith hadn't looked up from her phone.

'What's going on?'

'A bomb. A big one. Centre of London. No one's taken responsibility yet.'

'Many dead?'

Aedith put the phone back in her pocket, her face grey. 'Dozens so far. Only one name confirmed.'

Drustan let himself fall back on the bed. He could feel whispers in his mind, but not just from the Goddess. She had returned to him all right, but she had brought others, and they all had something to say. 'Who?' he asked. The voices were telling him already, but he may as well get it confirmed.

'The King,' said Aedith. 'The High King is dead.'

Here's a sneak preview of the second instalment of Pagans, coming soon...

LONDON, PRESENT DAY

The runes spraypainted on the shuttered front of what had once been a family butchers read 'Fuck The Reeves,' and although Constable Wynflaed Haldane had only been in uniform for a month, she was already inclined to agree with the general sentiment.

Six months after the old High King had been turned into a pink mist on a four-way traffic intersection, there was still overtime available for anyone who fancied raiding the homes of Tribal protesters, patrolling the streets in riot gear and looking fierce, or just hanging around public spaces shoving anyone who wasn't walking fast enough. And yet here Wynflaed was, alone, walking the silent streets of West London at two in the morning, in something that wasn't quite rain but was definitely wet, all because someone had seen a man asleep on a roundabout and it wasn't quite far enough away to justify taking a patrol car, what with the fuel budgets having been cut and everything.

Wynflaed was quite up for the 'walking the streets' element of the job. Her uncle Garulf had been a reeve and, judging by his stories, the job had been as much gossip as crime prevention – although it was possible the two overlapped. His beat had been the high street of the London borough where he and Wynflaed's family had lived for generations, and his method was to spend the day walking from one end of it to the other, popping into every shop, tavern and minor temple to say his hellos, catch up on rumours and find out what the three or four actual Bad Lads in the area were up to at any given time. He hadn't once drawn his seax from its scabbard and had died, on the job, from a massive heart attack, ceasing to be instantly and in the manner he would have wanted: flirting gently with the owner of the only Frankish pastry shop in a two-mile radius. The local people had come out in their hundreds to pay tribute and had a whip-round to pay for brass symbols of the Haldane family's spirit animal, a puzzled-looking stoat, to be laid into the pavement every hundred metres or so.

Wynflaed wondered what historians of the area would make of those in a couple of centuries, when Garulf had been forgotten. Probably five years would do it, she thought gloomily. It didn't help that her stab vest didn't fit properly and was starting to chafe.

Turning the corner that marked the boundary between a street of family businesses that had closed down and a row of Caliphate-development-funded light industrial workshops that no-one had chosen to take up, Wynflaed could now see the roundabout, the streetlights illuminating the prone figure the helpful member of the public had called in an hour or so ago. Or to be strictly accurate: posted a photo of on Tumult and tagged the reeves in underneath in a 'Why hasn't anyone done anything about this?!!!?!' sort of way. It had fallen to Wynflaed to strap on her seax and go out into the drizzle to see if the guy was still there.

In the centre of the roundabout was a big rock that Wynflaed knew (because she took an interest in local history) had once been a shrine to a minor Saxon victory over the local Tribals a few centuries after the Romans had buggered off for good. It had been carved with figures whom centuries of weather had smeared down to a sort of blur of arms and legs and things that might have been horses. Currently lying next to it on the patchy wet grass was a man, staring up at the grey sky. He looked to be somewhere in his mid-forties, wearing a smart, high-collared suit that looked vaguely foreign-ish (Wynflaed wasn't one for fashion).

As Wynflaed drew closer, she could see he had a shaved head with markings denoting a long service with one of the city's bigger delivery companies. This didn't entirely tally with the expensive suit, and as Wynflaed carefully looked both ways before crossing the road (she hadn't seen any traffic for twenty minutes, but you never knew), she also took in that the man's face was jowly and florid, despite the rest of him tending towards the slender.

'Evening, sir!' called Wynflaed in a bright, cheery tone, trying to tread the difficult path between waking the man up, but not shocking him so much he leaped up and ran into the road, where you could guarantee a bread van or something would immediately appear and mow him down, which wouldn't look good for her first month on the job. Also, it was always nice to go home from a day's policing *without* being directly responsible for someone's demise.

The man didn't respond. Wynflaed couldn't see any obvious chest movement either. Mead stupor? Some of the home brews people were trying out these days, you could put yourself into quite an efficient coma within twenty minutes or so.

Wynflaed tried again. 'Sir? Not the best place to sleep it off, I'll be honest with you.'

Still nothing. She was standing next to the man now, looking down at him and took the opportunity to nudge him gently with her regulation boot. No response. He looked pale and must have been there a while: the drizzle still hadn't turned into proper London rain, but the suit fabric was soaked through.

'Made visual confirmation and contact,' said Wynflaed into her collar radio. 'No response, so I'm taking a pulse.'

She lifted his arm and tried the wrist. His arm was limp, and the skin was cold. Which didn't mean a thing, it had been drummed into her at training college your job wasn't to go about declaring people dead until you'd exhausted all the possible avenues.

'Not finding anything,' said Wynflaed into her radio. No-one was interested enough to reply, or maybe this was one of those negative zones which soaked up radio waves like a sponge. Wynflaed found herself shivering a little and muttered a quick prayer to Erce the Earth Mother, although she was careful to turn the radio away for that one, because reeves were only supposed to invoke the tougher gods of the street, like Vegdeg or Tiw. You could go straight to Woden if you wanted, but it was generally considered overkill.

Right, she thought. *One more check before we go mouth to mouth.* Pushing two fingers deep into the man's collar, she felt around under the jaw for the carotid, but instead slid inside something cold and wet and sticky. Wynflaed quickly snatched her hand back, wiping it on her trousers. She had already been thinking that matters might be past the point artificial ventilation could have helped, but her suspicions were decisively confirmed when the head separated from the body entirely and rolled into the road.

Later, it was commented upon approvingly by Wynflaed's colleagues that she'd had the presence of mind to not only step on to the road and retrieve the head – which was surprisingly heavy, by the way – putting it neatly to one side of the body, but also call in the incident on her radio (and this time got a reply, as the station's communication officer was back from the toilet). She'd gone a bit quiet after that, and when the van full of colleagues appeared a few minutes later, sirens blaring and tooled up for war, none of them thought badly of her for going up the road a bit and being sick down a drain so as not to spoil a perfectly good crime scene.

PRE-ORDER NOW   SCAN ME

GLOSSARY

Aunt Nancy: (Pan-African, slang) Term for trickster, troublemaker. Usually a tabloid columnist or talk-radio host, in recent times more likely to appear on social media or streaming news sites.

Caliphate: Islamic Caliphate of Southern Europe. Includes France, Spain, Germany, Italy, politically tied to Islamic Caliphates of North Africa and Middle East but generally considered socially more liberal.

Dumnonia: Tribal lands covering much of South-west Britain.

Fomóir: Banned Tribal paramilitary organisation, last active over one decade previous to events.

Franks (Saxon): Mildly derogatory term for the French region of the Islamic Caliphate, often thought (by East British Saxons) to be Islamic in name only, especially regarding a relaxed attitude to alcohol, and secretly yearning to return, or be returned, to Saxon ways.

Gwithyas (Tribal, slang): Police.

High King: Head of Saxon state of East Britain, elected (or re-elected) every seven years by a council of earls from the major Saxon regions (Mercia, Northumberland, East Anglia, Essex, Kent, Sussex and Wessex).

High Table: Council of high-ranking Saxon state officials, appointed by and responsible to the High King.

Hnefltafl: Boardgame thought to be of Norse origin, popular across Britain. Play is asymmetric, where one player attempts to use their twelve soldier pieces to escort a 'king' figure to safety (one of the four corners of the board) while the other player attempts to use their twenty-four soldiers to stop them. Play ends when the king escapes or is captured.

Indij (Saxon, slang): Derogatory term for indigenous Celtic people, now mostly pushed West into Tribal Lands.

Kesair: Notoriously violent and troublesome Tribal group based, unusually, within Saxon borders.

Longship (Saxon, police, slang): Police van, usually armoured with metal grille over windscreen, plastic skirts on sides to prevent petrol bombs, etc.

'Lungpiercer': Captain Aedith Mercia's personal sidearm. A Byrhtnoth P224, 19mm automatic, subcompact variant of the military issue P228 – standard Saxon issue police firearm.

Masai: Pan-African people from the Kenyan and Tanzanian regions, famous for their stubborn independence from the Pan-African state and great wealth from their many cattle grounds, mineral rights and advanced solar-power industries.

The Meadow: Luxury London hotel, briefly infamous a decade prior as the site of a number of tabloid stings on celebrity clients. Now under new management.

Moors: Saxon term for Islamic Caliphate of Southern Europe.

Morrigun: Tribal deity associated with war and fate. Thought to appear in the form of a crow but can also take the form of female individuals known to the worshipper. Although other female Tribal deities exist, only Morrigun insists on the title 'Goddess'.

Picts: The last remaining Tribal people of the generally Norse Democratic Republic of Scotland.

Pan-Africa: Federation of African independent states. Often regarded jealously by the rest of the world for its concentration of natural and intellectual wealth. Home, in the previous century, of the Industrial Revolution, which saw the federation pull ahead in terms of economic growth, rivalled only recently by the Islamic Caliphates and the Mughal Empire of India.

Reeve (Saxon, slang): Police, usually, but not exclusively, street level, uniformed.

Seax: Traditional Saxon weapon, single-bladed long knife/short sword. Traditionally of great cultural importance to Saxons, given to children on significant birthdays, etc., although becoming less popular in modern times after the release of a government public-information film, *Edmaer Stubhands*, which focused on the dangers of leaving swords around unattended young children.

'Roadfucker': The personal vehicle of Captain Aedith Mercia. A Norse-made Hrafn, a two-door rear-engined, high-performance sports vehicle.

Skeid: The largest conference centre in central London, regularly used to hold the Unification Summits. Named by its Pan-African designer after the traditional Norse longboat, leading to accusations of cultural insensitivity.

Tash (Saxon, slang): Derogatory term for indigenous Celtic people, more directly insulting than Indij, referring to the drooping moustaches of Tribal elders.

Torc: Metal ring, usually made from twisted wire, worn around the neck by many Celtic tribes.

Tribals: Blanket term covering the various Celtic peoples of Britain, now mostly displaced to the Western Tribal Lands.

The Wall: Heavily defended border between Saxon England and the Democratic Republic of Scotland.

Wayland the Smith: Heroic smith of Saxon legend, often worshipped as spirit ancestor by those in electronic industries.

Woden: Chief god of Saxon pantheon. Legendarily hung upside-down by heels from Yggdrasil tree for three days and three nights to gain wisdom.

Wolfheads: Tribal people smugglers, specialising in transporting people across the Channel into the more prosperous Caliphate, although some groups, mainly Pictish, operate in the even more dangerous area of the Wall between Saxon Britain and the heavily defended Democratic Republic of Scotland.

ACKNOWLEDGEMENTS

Many thanks to Fiona for pushing through her horror at the whole 'It's history but also I'm making it up' thing, and for general Celtic and Pictish info (perks of a wife who's also a Medieval historian), my agent James Spackman for not letting Pagans go when it was too crime-y for the fantasy publishers and too fantasy-y for the crime publishers, my brilliant editor Emma Waring for picking it up with ferocious enthusiasm, Jack Jewers and Christi Daugherty at Moonflower for being supportive and amazing, and Dr Kate Wiles for working out the Old English for 'radio' (amongst other things), and being on call for annoying questions.

Thanks also to Jasmine Aurora for interior design/maps, Jack Smyth for cover design, Tory Lyne-Pirkis and Liv Houghton for PR, Louise Voss for proofreading, Katherine Rhodes and Martin Palmer for sales and Nessa Urquhart and Bea Carvalho for huge amounts of enthusiasm and support.

Finally, thank you to my children Eliza and William for being generally wonderful through lockdown but also giving me the precious gift of silence, at least in the mornings, and being bribable with ice creams thereafter.

BIBLIOGRAPHY

John Fletcher, *The Western Kingdom: The Birth of Cornwall*
(The History Press, 2022)

Adrián Maldonado, *Crucible of Nations: Scotland from Viking Age to Medieval Kingdom*
(National Museums Scotland, 2021)

Marc Morris, *The Anglo-Saxons: A History of the Beginnings of England*
(Penguin, 2021)

Cat Jarman, *River Kings: The Vikings from Scandinavia to the Silk Roads*
(William Collins, 2021)

Thomas Williams, *Lost Realms: Histories of Britain from the Romans to the Vikings*
(William Collins, 2022)

Michael Wood, *In Search of the Dark Ages: A History of the Origins of Britain*, expanded and updated 40th anniversary edition
(Penguin, 2023)

Kari Maund, *The Welsh Kings: Warriors, Warlords and Princes* (The History Press, 2006)

Nicholas Evans and Gordon Noble, *Picts: Scourge of Rome, Rulers of the North* (Birlinn, 2022)

FURTHER READING

Alternative history fiction has its own appropriately long and convoluted back story with many standout texts, but these are some of the novels (and one graphic novel series) that I couldn't have written *Pagans* without.

Kim Newman, *Anno Dracula* (1992)
Kim Newman and Eugene Byrne, *Back In the USSA* (1997)
Matt Ruff, *The Mirage* (2012)
Alan Moore and Kevin O'Neill, *The League of Extraordinary Gentlemen* (1999-2019)
Keith Roberts, *Pavane* (1968)
Michael Moorcock, *Gloriana* (1978)
Naomi Novik, *Temeraire* series (2006-2016)
William Gibson and Bruce Sterling, *The Difference Engine* (1990)
Kim Stanley Robinson, *The Years of Rice and Salt* (2002)
Michael Chabon, *The Yiddish Policemen's Union* (2007)
Jo Walton, *My Real Children* (2014)

Seething Lane

Jack Jewers

SCAN ME TO FIND OUT MORE

January 1670. London is enduring its worst winter in decades. But for Samuel Pepys, the darkest days are yet to come.

Investigating the brutal murder of a libertine aristocrat takes him from the backstreets of London to the glamorous world of the theatre, where nothing is quite as it seems. But whatever the dangers, he may find that the deadliest threat lies closer to home…

Reimagining one of Britain's greatest historical figures through a 21st century lens, Seething Lane is a thrilling new mystery from the author of *Sunday Times* historical fiction of the year pick *The Lost Diary Of Samuel Pepys*.

About the author

Jack Jewers is a filmmaker and writer. His 2022 debut, *The Lost Diary of Samuel Pepys*, was named one of the historical fiction books of the year by the *Sunday Times*, and a book of the month by the *Independent* and the *FT*. Jack's passion for history has led him to many unexpected places, from uncovering hidden love stories in 3000-year-old poetry, to sending a portrait of Shakespeare into space. He has also served on Parliamentary committees for the arts and been nominated for a BAFTA.

"A page-turning crime thriller." **SUNDAY INDEPENDENT**

"Gorgeously written… a brilliant jewel of a book."
EMMA HAUGHTON, AUTHOR OF *THE DARK*

"A splendid adventure." **THE FINANCIAL TIMES**

Piece Of My Heart

Penelope Tree

SCAN ME TO
FIND OUT MORE

Fame. Money. Beauty. Sex. Love. Ari wants them all. And when she becomes the face of the 1960s, it seems like they're hers for the taking. Overnight, her life is transformed into a dizzying whirlwind of drugs, photoshoots, and parties, all with notorious bad boy photographer Bill Ramsey by her side.

But in the fickle world of fashion, nothing lasts forever – and addiction, Ari's eating disorder and increasingly dysfunctional relationship with Ramsey send her life spinning out of control.

How much more of herself must Ari lose to keep the things she always thought she wanted?

About the author

Model, writer and activist, Penelope Tree was the ultimate Sixties It girl. Discovered at the age of 13 by the photographer Diane Arbus, Penelope became David Bailey's muse, appearing on the cover of Vogue and travelling the world. Now a practising Buddhist and charitable ambassador, Penelope has two adult children and splits her time between Sussex and London.

"Totally gripping." **THE SUNDAY TIMES**

"I loved it." **KATE MOSS**

"Beautifully written, wise, funny and all so true."
ESTHER FREUD

MOONFLOWER

The Fortunes of Olivia Richmond

Louise Davidson

SCAN ME TO
FIND OUT MORE

After a terrible tragedy, governess Julia Pearlie finds herself with no job, home, or references. When she's offered a position as companion to Miss Olivia Richmond, she's relieved. But Mistcoate House is full of secrets. And Julia has more than a few of her own.

As the danger grows, and the winter chill wraps around the dark woods surrounding Mistcoate, Julia will have to fight to uncover the truth, escape her past – and save herself.

Original and engrossing, this Victorian Gothic thriller is an outstanding piece of storytelling from an exciting new talent. Perfect for fans of Stacy Halls and Michelle Paver.

About the author

Louise Davidson was born in Belfast. Growing up in Northern Ireland backgrounded by the Troubles led her to develop a fascination with history, and this combined with her love of all things gothic inspired her to write her first book, a dark Victorian thriller set in a neglected and isolated mansion. Louise lives in London with her husband and step-son.

"A darkly gothic historical mystery in all the best traditions of the genre – a standout." **HELEN FIELDS, SUNDAY TIMES BESTSELLING AUTHOR**

"Magnificent. Gothic writing of the most compelling kind."
MY WEEKLY

"Absorbing and twisty." **HEAT MAGAZINE**

The Coming Darkness

Greg Mosse

SCAN ME TO
FIND OUT MORE

Paris, 2037. With a double threat of rising temperatures and new diseases jeopardising public health, the world has never been more dangerous.

French special agent Alexandre Lamarque notices signs of a new terror group and connects it with an ominous sequence of events: a theft from a Norwegian genetics lab; a string of gory child murders; a chaotic coup in a breakaway North African republic, and the extraction under fire of its charismatic leader. And as the one man able to see through the web of lies, Alex may be the world's only hope.

About the author

Greg is a director, writer and writing teacher. He has lived and worked as a translator in Paris, New York, Los Angeles and Madrid. He now lives in Sussex with his wife, the novelist Kate Mosse.

"Superb. Greg Mosse writes like John Le Carré's hip grandson."
LEE CHILD

"Admirable audacity. One of the best thrillers of 2022."
THE SUNDAY TIMES

"A clever, fast-paced thriller." **INDEPENDENT**

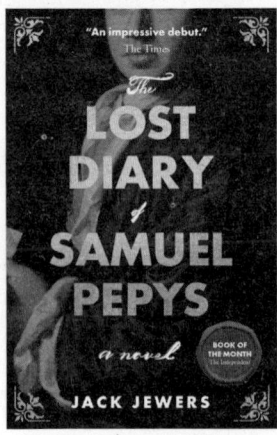

The Lost Diary of Samuel Pepys

Jack Jewers

SCAN ME TO
FIND OUT MORE

The diaries of Samuel Pepys have enthralled readers for centuries with their audacious wit, gripping detail, and racy assignations. Pepys stopped writing at the age of 36. Or did he?

This action-packed historical thriller picks up where Pepys left off as he is sent from the pleasures of his familiar London to the grimy taverns and shipyards of Portsmouth. An investigator sent by the King to look into corruption at the Royal Navy has been brutally murdered, and it's down to Pepys to find out why. But what awaits him is more dangerous than he could have imagined.

About the author

Jack Jewers is a filmmaker and writer. His 2022 debut, *The Lost Diary of Samuel Pepys*, was named one of the historical fiction books of the year by the *Sunday Times*, and a book of the month by the *Independent* and the *FT*. Jack's passion for history has led him to many unexpected places, from uncovering hidden love stories in 3000-year-old poetry, to sending a portrait of Shakespeare into space. He has also served on Parliamentary committees for the arts and been nominated for a BAFTA.

"Book of the month... A zestful imagining" **INDEPENDENT**

"One of the best historical fiction books of the year." **THE TIMES**

"Swashbuckling action-packed drama." **WOMAN AND HOME**

Blue Running

Lori Ann Stephens

SCAN ME TO
FIND OUT MORE

In the new Republic of Texas, guns are compulsory and nothing is forgiven.

Fourteen-year-old Bluebonnet Andrews is on the run across the Republic of Texas. An accident with a gun killed her best friend but everyone in the town of Blessing thinks it was murder. Even her father – the town's drunken deputy – believes she did it. Now, she has no choice but to run. Because in Texas, murder is punishable by death.

About the author

Lori Ann Stephens is an award-winning author whose novels for children and adults include Novalee and the Spider Secret, Some Act of Vision, and Song of the Orange Moons. She teaches creative writing and critical reasoning at Southern Methodist University in Dallas, Texas.

"Book of the Month" **INDEPENDENT & THE FINANCIAL TIMES**

"If there's one teen novel this year that readers will never forget, it's this one..." **BOOKS FOR KEEPS**

"Brilliant." **HEAT MAGAZINE**

"Gripping." **THE GUARDIAN**

MOONFLOWER

About Moonflower Books

The Independent Publishers Guild's Newcomer of the Year 2023, Moonflower is a young, UK-based, independent publisher. Our award-winning books are the kind that make you sit up in your seat. Books that break the mould. That are hard to categorise. In short, the kind of books that deserve your attention.

moonflowerbooks.co.uk

MOONFLOWER